STRANGE NEW VARIATIONS ON LIFE

The Pystead Group: Escape from Planet Earth

Science Fiction Adventure in a Dystopian Era

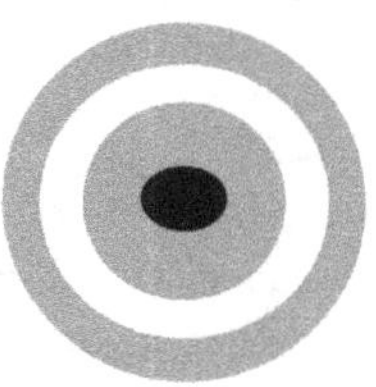

James Pryor

THE TECHNER GROUP, LLC

*For Diane
my wife and muse*

ACKNOWLEDGEMENTS

I am thankful for readers Diane Willen and Mark Willen whose advice influenced content and style leading to a better written story. Final decisions were the author's alone.

TABLE OF CONTENTS

1

FIRST ALERT

Still groggy, Philip opened his eyes with the thought, *This place is weird…strange, feels like a tin box instead of an apartment. I have not adapted to being aboard ship.* The bedroom door was half open, the side panels on their canopy bed were pulled back, the faint smell of coffee reassured him that some normality had slipped aboard with them into their new shipboard world. He heard a cabinet door close in the kitchen. *Ice is first awake just as on Campus.*

Philip was soon up and surprised to find Ice in her mermaid Amanda role—wearing her cranberry-red, sheer-lace lingerie. She smiled, and he kissed her good morning. "I don't yet feel normal aboard ship, Amanda, and much as I'm fond of you I need to talk to Ice this morning."

"Don't let the bacon burn, Poseidon." Mermaid Amanda swam away.

Ice soon appeared in her aqua pantsuit. "I'm pleased that you want your fiancée. Did you have a bad first-night dream?"

Philip smiled at her. She was wearing her crepe silk pantsuit, revealing her mermaid's figure without showing the skin. He was glad that Ice's pretend persona had survived from Campus days although his unease persisted. *Can our daily life be fulfilling with no outdoors?* "Ice, does this apartment seem as strange to you as it does to me?"

"More a nuisance than strange. The utensils and pans are hiding from me. I will say that the aroma of the bacon settled me, and I decided to be mermaid Amanda. I thought the eye-candy would be a good first morning."

"Amanda is fun, but surreal like these walls."

Ice stepped over to the frying pan and grasped its handle, not actually checking on the bacon. "Having a relapse to land-lubber days?"

"No, no. I'm just as real-world as I was last evening. I suppose the difference this morning is that the new-found me is feeling his regeneration acutely. Being a player in the physical domain is quite a change from being a sheltered professor. It's like jumping from a metaverse fight into a fist fight."

Ice gave Philip a quick smile and turned the bacon. "Please remain real-world, lover, I need your reassurance. Please start toast. We should begin with comfort food in our cozy apartment. I'll do hash-browns and eggs."

"I suppose the bacon will not last long once we set sail?"

"Too true, still be optimistic! Lois assures me the abiotic-grown bacon is good, even if it will be available only a day or so every week."

"A small price to pay if we can escape this dystopian world. After all, since being fired without cause and later abused by police in the States, I was shot at by somebody's goon on Nevis!"

Ice sighed. "Joan told me we are no longer allowed to take aboard personnel without approval and monitoring by the United Nations. When you arrived on Nevis only seventeen days ago, the U.N. merely suspected our advanced technologies. Now that they know for sure we will not be allowed to exist. The one-world powers do not tolerate over-mighty subjects. We either escape the Earth or become poor, dead-end workers in unsafe cities, should we be lucky enough to escape execution."

"More oppressive every day. And I thought the West Indies would be safe."

"Phil, we are vulnerable anywhere until we escape the U.N. Still, let's be positive about Amanda and this surreal ship." Ice closed her eyes, *Is his subconscious still having trouble with our situation? Will he think our undiscovered future lives as tenuous as our past lives—and again not want children?*

Philip nodded and asked, "Have you checked our in-processing time?"

"This afternoon from two until four o'clock."

✳ ✳ ✳

Whoo oo oh! Whoo oo oh! Their apartment's public address speakers sounded two shrill, warbling whoops. The tones repeated twice more followed by an announcement. "This a Red-Two Alert. This is not a drill. Each person with a jumpsuit is to put it on with boots and gloves. All persons must listen to announcements and follow instructions. This is a real alert and not a practice. Adults, be prepared to be seated in a high-backed chair with a seatbelt. All chairs and other furniture have been latched to the floor before you boarded. Notice that many chairbacks can be raised, and high-counter stool legs can be lowered and their backs raised. Stay near any children and the elderly, and secure each with a net or seatbelt according to your training."

"What training?" asked Philip.

"I'm trained. Everybody allowed to board early has a trained crewmember in quarters. Our seats are ready, and we have jumpsuits to put on. Let's get them."

"Ice, could that rouge U.N. Admiral possibly damage this ship?"

"Granddad just sent me a kom message that he'd like to come by. He didn't sound worried. We need to suit up in case we are needed to help somebody."

"Sounds good in theory."

"Move faster, love. As I recall on Nevis, a half-Halo shirt saved you from a bullet in the shoulder. We can have breakfast once you're dressed. Why not wear your jumpsuit with the blue top?"

"You have never told me about your grandfather's gemstones. Did he find gemstones that he used to fund Pystead in the beginning?"

"Not at all. From the beginning in nineteen ninety-four, he sought investors from around the world. We have seventy. All but a few were billionaires who already feared for their lives or for the future of their children. Pystead has spent ninety thousand million kicu on our Nevis campus and our nine ships."

Hearing knocks on their front door, Philip donned his white medical facemask. Opening the door he found himself face-to-face with Ice's grandfather wearing a beige facemask, an ivory island shirt, Bermuda shorts, and his gem-studded golden sash. "Comte, come in."

"Hello, Philip. Commander Joan asked me to inquire if you and Ice would like to observe operations on the flight deck as an informal start of your cross training for Reserved Line."

"Are you sure I'm invited, Granddad?"

"Most certainly, Ice. No introductions, and no questions except whispered among ourselves. This is not a social call."

"I'll get my medical mask and our wrist koms."

"Philip, you should know that I do not always set a good example with personal issues. Our current peril falls short of getting me into a jumpsuit."

The party of three set out for the flight deck. After a few changes of direction in the ship's corridors, Comte held his wrist kom to the wall and a door opened at his command. The upward acceleration of their elevator was startling. Within a few seconds they stopped and were soon standing in an entry alcove facing a round-cornered door. Ice was close to the wall and held up her wrist kom for entry. "Comte and Ice Germaine with Philip Russell, invited by Commander Joan, request entry."

Ceiling speakers instructed, "Look at the white lights for facial recognition." When the lights went out, a slight mechanical sound caused Philip to look back and see a wall section slide into place sealing them off from the main corridor. The speakers told them, "You are approved for entry. Stand clear of the door swing."

Philip mused, *O Cosmos, tight security even aboard ship. And I'd say not just anybody can use that elevator.*

⚹　⚹　⚹

The flight deck was not as large as Philip had imagined. *Feels crowded.* At front were three high-backed, swivel chairs, set about two meters before a round window port that looked outside. *Think twice! Ah, yes, the viewport has enough depth and shows end-of-hull lines. Four ends! The ship has three pressure hulls, so this flight deck must have an additional pressure hull.*

A man in a gray jumpsuit with white epaulets stood at the far side bridge chair. He was wearing an oxygen mask with its ribbed supply line leading down. Comte led his group left to a rear-side position. A gray floor mat could be seen in front of the three bridge station chairs. Around the sides and back of the room were instrument panels divided into five stations with two seats each, all sections separated by short partitions, and separated from the central floor area by a handrail. Annunciation lights illuminated the instrument panels at each station and above the large front viewport.

Behind the ten seated crewmembers at instrument stations walked three crewmembers in full Halo suits with hard helmets and oxygen tanks on their backs. The walkers were looking over shoulders at the instrument panels. Philip noticed they wore boots and gloves. *Ready for smoke, loss of pressure and oxygen, loss of a crewmember. Seems Pystead is onto real-world issues. Why risk operations to a central oxygen system if you don't have to? The ships, personnel, procedures...must be relatively untried. Does seem impressive this complex space of dull metallic silvers, off-whites, and colorful little lights. Reminds of that secret, mysterious, flying, egg-shaped craft that Ice used on automatic on Nevis.*

After a few more seconds of looking around, Comte motioned them to a set of four seats on top of a floor console. The area was the widest of all the perimeter sections. Comte remained standing with his facemask on; Philip and Ice followed his lead. Before

Philip had time for a second look around, a bell-tone sounded a quick four rings and the room's speakers announced that Admiral Joan was on the flight deck.

Philip turned his head just in time to glimpse Joan's face as she stepped by in a white Halo suit, her helmet not deployed, her light brown hair up in its small bun on the back of her head. Her expression was stern, more intent than he had ever seen his new friend when on Campus. *Same cool-red lipstick. I'm sure her red necklace is missing.* He checked from his side position. *Same red wrist kom. Belt is red; boots are red. Necklace or not, the Red Queen has arrived.*

Comte whispered to Philip that an individual ship would be called a key by the flight-deck crew. He said that of Pystead's nine ships, the seven that yesterday morning served as pontoons for the superstructure of their floating fish farm were now liberated to serve as the spaceships they were designed to be. The fish-farm superstructure was at the bottom of the ocean, except for its useful materials and equipment now stowed aboard ships and in the tank building on Campus. When mated together the seven ships would form one disk-shaped ship called the Wheel, although it would be an incomplete disk until their two remaining ships in the Pacific Ocean joined them.

✳   ✳   ✳

The flight deck and operations were familiar to Ice, herself a crew-member holding Pystead's highest rank of Commander, although she served in a staff and not a line position. Line Commander Joan, acting as an Admiral, made decisions unilaterally because there was no time for discussion. Alice was pleased that her fiancé was engaged with events. *After this experience the ship should seem real to him!*

Joan stood at the front and center bridge chair. A male voice from the rear called, "This is Captain Asif speaking from Key Bury. Admiral Joan will direct defensive operations."

"Joan here, I have the bridge on Key Bury. My deputy, Admiral Andrew, is assisting."

"Andrew here, on Key Bury."

Joan announced, "Should this bridge station fail, command passes to Admiral Ethan on E Key."

The accounting for personnel on *E Key* called each officer for a response. Joan, watching the indicator lights, was satisfied. She said on speaker, "Key Bury's Captain Asif is standing by."

"Aye, Asif here to fly the seven-of-nine Wheel."

Joan explained that the Federation Council had voted to abandon Nevis once surveillance had revealed the U.N.'s plans to capture their Campus by force. Manager Robbie would make a Wheel-wide announcement later in the day.

As Joan sat down and deployed her Halo suit's helmet, Ice nudged Philip to watch. Clear strips rose from her suit's thin backpack and then pushed forward, guided around the slot in her suit's thick, oval collar. White strips followed to make the sides and back of the helmet. Once her head was surrounded, the strips bent over her head and sealed together. Joan plugged in her oxygen line.

Two minutes later Joan stood, saying on speaker, "All keys, confirm that your hull doors are sealed, locked, and guarded." After confirmation she ordered Flight Operations to set a plan to have the seven keys present form the Wheel.

She next called for a status report on Operation Ferryboat. The flight deck's speakers responded, "Our two ferryboats will be in view within five minutes. As anticipated, fighter jets have scrambled from Florida and Cuba, and have been visually identified by our waiting foo fighters. In addition, we have strong radar blips on three aircraft approaching fast from the south—unexpected."

"Let's identify them, stat."

"Roger."

Joan called, "Sound General Quarters on the ferryboats. Keep them briefed."

Ice asked Comte, "Why send ferryboats before general loading on Campus?"

"Joan is testing her intelligence on that United Nations' Admiral Telaobade."

"Granddad, those ferryboats could be sunk! Who's aboard?"

He whispered, "Crew bringing light equipment from Campus. Philip, the ferryboats' deck houses and hulls are tough, armored— the same liquid-metal as our outer hull. Their windows the same as our structural glass viewports, stronger than most steels. If necessary our fighters will protect the boats." Comte nodded before adding, "Our foo fighters are radar stealthy and procryptic enough to be unseen by the eye. The U.N. jets don't know they are being followed."

The flight deck's speakers continued, "The American and Cuban jets are manned, but not armed with missiles. As to the jets from the south, we will have a look at them in four minutes."

"Fine," Joan replied.

"This is so risky," Ice said to Comte.

Comte nodded. "As was our lot on Campus, now still a life-and-death venture! The U.N. and its major powers will kill to prevent self-determination by any group, especially by a technologically advanced group that they now know us to be."

"I feel safer aboard ship than I would on Campus," said Philip.

The three visitors to the flight deck sat in silence, observing a momentary stillness in the room, except for the present creeping pace of the three suited walkers. Finally, the speakers, "The jets to the south are Chinese Arrowheads, autonomous stealth fighters. They are paired one atop another for six fighters returning three strong radar blips. They will separate for any attack to take advantage of their stealth design and numbers."

"Copy. Keep me posted."

"Will do. Out."

Again Joan spoke on speakers, "Ferryboat Captains, Larry, and Leon, expect a strafing attack. If it's across the bow, return to Campus. If not across the bow, our fighters will take them out at first shots."

"That would be appreciated."

Philip noticed blinking pink lights above the viewport that went off. *Voice, lights, walkers double-checking, even inexperienced we should avoid mistakes.*

The incoming jets from the north flew directly for the ferryboats as though not aware of Pystead's stealthy fighters close behind. The two Cuban jets shot across the bow, and the two ferryboats promptly came about for Nevis. The three Arrowhead pairs lingered to follow the ferryboats but did not separate.

A woman's voice was heard on speakers, "Admiral, we have maneuvering details for forming the seven-of-nine Wheel."

"Issue the plans."

✳ ✳ ✳

Ice and Philip returned to their apartment. "Quite an introduction to your training for the Line, my man in full."

Philip observed, "Well before noon, leaving us time for Amanda."

They felt the ship move, a sign that the seven ships were joining together.

"Ice, what holds the ships together?"

"Do you remember the row down each side of our ship that looks like large, dark portholes?"

"Yes."

"Those are electromagnetic ports to hold ships together with as much or as little force as needed. At sea or in space they can hold a ship with no propulsion power during highest acceleration."

"Can you check your secret Blue channel and find out why we are joining up?"

She found the answer. "That U.N. Admiral Telaobade's battleship is approaching to stop us from sailing even if he has to sink us. Joan wants to make that seem easy for him. She doesn't want him searching for a ship that escaped."

"Cosmos, are all ships to pretend to sink?"

Ice read on. "Joan says Admiral Telaobade knows about our guards' protective Halo suits. He knows we have unseen, armed drones. He is already looking for our procryptic craft that fly over Nevis. Since he fears our toys, he must either have them or destroy them. Because our stealth surveillance pods follow his battleship, Joan knows his plans. We've had a week to prepare for his shooting at us. As a last resort, we simply fly away."

A few minutes later Ice reported that the Admiral had conducted a live-fire exercise at sea using his battleship's big turret guns, the World War II guns. "After that, he came about and is headed towards us at flank speed. Joan says he plans to sink us!"

"O cosmos!"

"Phil, Joan has told me we will never take a hit because our technology is advanced an order of magnitude beyond the U.N.'s."

"I'd say I have another training session coming up? Perhaps I'll soon get to some of Pystead's secret technologies."

"All in due time. Yet this morning, my man in full, you have another matter needing attention." Ice pursed her lips and took his hand.

2

ALICE

At two p.m. Ice changed into her aqua pantsuit. They put on their white, medical facemasks and headed to sign the crew manifest. The sign at each processing station read PASSPORTS.

Philip grinned. "Shouldn't that sign read outward bound only, Ice? The U.N. certainly will not honor them, but perhaps the Martians will?"

"Philip Russell, I know there are no Martians!"

"How would we, the public, know? We are merely misinformed subjects these days."

"We are now informed citizens of The Pystead Group. Let's get our passports."

* * *

When the video lights came on for Ice's photograph, men turned to look. She was gorgeous in her aqua pantsuit with her short, vanilla-blonde hair glowing in the lights.

Quite a picture, my fiancée.

"Hello, Philip."

He turned to face Rathy, Lois and Dusan. Lois, a tall, attractive woman with black hair falling below her shoulders generally seemed somber to Philip. Dusan, her male compliment in bearing, had soft black hair cut short like most men aboard, a caramel-brown complexion, and a Roman nose. Now Lois's lips twisted slightly to one corner, looking intent. She was Ice's friend and Director of Administration, and Philip wanted to tease her. "Lois, don't you think one-way passports would be a more apt description?"

Without a smile she said, "I want to impress upon our new crewmembers the circumstances, yet not unduly worry them. We will be nearby another week with chances to get off before departure."

Philip asked, "Could my friends from California and my cousin in Baltimore be brought aboard before departure?"

"Sadly not. Late pick-ups will not begin until after this Wheel ship has sailed."

"Your time to sign, Philip," said Rathy. "Smile for us women, we want to see your ash-blonde hair and blue jumper in the lights."

When Philip returned, Rathy told him, "Harinil got off last night after our farewell dinner."

She looks sad although wearing a bright orange and purple dress showing her figure, slightly beyond slim, probably in her early fifties. Last night at our farewell dinner she was also sad, anxious. "Rathy, he's staying on Earth?"

"Yes! Said his paintings were selling too well to abandon his career. His scenes range from pornographic to naked, to veiled naked and abstract naked. 'Art for all,' he claims."

"Are you staying aboard?"

"I'm staying and changing my name from Rathy to Revathy. Close, but different. I have no future with my husband. He paints naked women and sleeps with the models—probably doesn't pay extra. Like you, he's handsome and tall."

Philip frowned. "I'm pleased that you're rid of him." He turned to look for Ice.

Revathy asked if he would still attend the Eastern Philosophy Club with her. She advised he begin first classes without her, and she would call him when ready to socialize.

Ice was back. "Rathy, this may be only the second or third time I've seen you not wearing a sari. One would make a great passport picture."

"I'm changing my life. Changing my name and leaving my husband. Lois will tell you. My number is up for the passport."

"I too have changed my name, now I'm Alice."

"I've heard that about one-half percent of spouses decided not to stay aboard, both men and women. We can form a support group." Revathy went for processing.

Alice and Philip both frowned.

Lois said, "Alice, let me drop by for a drink, say four o'clock?"

"Alright."

Lois turned to Philip. "Why don't you and Dusan have a drink together in a lounge somewhere at four o'clock, and not with Revathy."

"Fine."

"Now, Phil, we should return to quarters and make room for others."

Lois gave Philip a beige-masked kiss on his cheek. "You are a dear."

Alice waved goodbye, and the couple donned their facemasks and headed for home.

I'm a dear, just put out and not under the leaves of the green O. Dusan and I will do for an evening. Perhaps our last evening without rationing of drinks?

3

BRIEFING ALICE

Philip and Dusan arrived early at a large lounge on the perimeter of the ship, distant from their tip-end neighborhood on *Key Bury Saint Germaine*. To their surprise the bar stools were full, so they took one of the three remaining tables. Philip noticed Melita entering the lounge and waved to her.

Dusan said, "Being married to Lois you would think I'd know how you met Ice, well Alice, but Lois said it would be best for me to learn that socially. Is it a secret?"

Philip shook his head. "I happened to buy a painting that she painted, at the Co-op. We met and I asked her to dinner. She accepted."

"That's abnormal for a Pystead Commander to accept a date with an unvetted person!"

"Your administrative maven took care of that. She read my vetting report, checked with Melita, and called Ice to tell her about me even before I had thought about buying a painting!"

Dusan asked in almost a whisper, "Has Ice told you about the Joan-and-Melita duality?"

"A few days ago, Joan told me about her alter personality as Melita and their different crew duties and voices!"

⚹　⚹　⚹

Two women caught their attention and paused at their table. The brunette said, "I'm surprised your wives let you out for happy hour." Philip held up his left hand showing no wedding ring. "So handsome, and unmarried in your thirties?"

"I'm engaged."

Dusan waved to Melita.

"Wonderful. May we join you two for a few minutes to chat about our tiny community? We want a mature male's perspective."

The brunette turned to see Melita approaching. "You know the counselor?"

"A friend from Campus days."

Melita said, "Lois told Joan, and Joan told me where to find you two."

The brunette said, "We'd like to chat another time soon." She smiled, and the two women stepped away.

"Protecting Revathy?" Philip asked Melita.

She took a seat. "Revathy needs protection only from loneliness."

"Why were we asked to avoid her this evening?"

"She is grieving Philip, not from the loss of Harinil, but for much of her life that should have been better lived. She needs time to be alone. The women will call and visit her. Revathy will call you, Philip, when she's ready to attend that Eastern philosophy club. She hopes you begin without her. For anything else you should know, I'll call."

Melita stood and smiled. "Dusan, Lois or I will keep in touch with you until Revathy is ready to socialize. You and Philip are her closest male friends. She will need you when she reappears. Now friends, I'll be right back with my own wine. Please save a few sips to drink with me."

Dusan mentioned to Philip that Lois had said he was pursuing cross training for Reserved Line officer.

"Not yet formally, but Joan will accept me when I apply. With virtually all recruits now known, her prospects for Security Branch standby officers are limited."

"That's tough training."

"Surely neuroscience and your surgery are tops on toughness?"

"I suppose, but at Pystead medical residency is a normal life, unlike the overworked and underpaid medical residencies in the world at large. Training for the Line is somewhat hazardous Dusan thought he should explain. "Our small flying craft are shaped like eggs and hence called Eggs."

"I know because I've flown in them."

"Lois could have shared a bit more before sending us off for drinks."

The two men glanced up at a cute young woman passing their table.

After a few sips, Philip told Dusan, "Joan will let me keep my crew duty and my research project, and proceed at a slow pace for Reserved Line training. After all, there's no foreseeable need for supporting the active-duty Line."

"I heard that," said the approaching Melita. She scolded them, "Joan needs trainees in the Line's pipeline, and she needs them flowing quietly."

"Who asks a medical doctor about Line trainees?"

Melita proposed, "A toast to The Pystead Singularity."

"And to Joan's pipeline," said Dusan.

"I can drink to Joan's unknown pipeline." The men smiled.

Philip wondered. *I'll have to ask my friend the Red Queen about secrecy in her pipeline.*

Melita spoke quietly, "Women on Earth are weary and fearful of on-Net personal introductions that do nothing to eliminate the dominators, liars, and psychopaths. Here, the women know that Pystead's functional-brain-scan vetting has rejected those undesirables, both men and women. Unmarried women here are excited about a crew of decent men and a future of safe dating experiences." Melita smiled for her audience of two. "Safe and happy, although in a small and fixed community. Women wanting first choice among the eligible men realize that meeting men as soon as possible is to their advantage. Even a married man may know a single man. Even here, a married man can be an enticing prospect for a woman not wanting a steady." Melita looked around. "Many women from nineteen up, I'd say, are trying assertiveness in lieu of waiting to be approached." Melita looked at Philip, then at Dusan. "You two must be pleasant, even chatty, while letting a woman know that you are not available. You should not discourage the psychology of agency that women are feeling. I know because they talk to me as ship's counselor."

Philip sighed. "Melita, if you hadn't walked in when you did, we would have chatted with the two women who stopped at our table. What if another friend had seen us chatting? Would heshe have interpreted the chat in terms of a new cultural norm? Would Lois or Alice or my cousin?"

Melita nodded. "Impressions today would vary. I'm sure Alice would not be concerned, nor Lois or Revathy. We established crew women expect that Pystead's circumscribed community will transform social customs, as has always happened with the emergence of liberating circumstances in an era of personal freedom."

Dusan asked why men and women didn't register on the computer dating algorithm.

Melita smiled. "The dating system will not be used until all have had an opportunity to meet, shall we say, organically. That will take several months because of the rotation of duty shifts to begin on Mars. Until then and afterwards, officers and extroverted individuals will be supported with refreshments to give small parties for friends and neighbors. Duty groups will host mixers to welcome new members and those cross-training. Dusan, you must help Lois with her administration's gatherings. Philip will help Alice with her art galleries staff, and Alice will attend Philip's welcoming mixers. Prince and Joan will help with each other's events. As a ship's Counselor, I will attend mixers and encourage the men to introduce themselves to women and chat, as I continue to mingle as a hostess."

"I'm surprised Prince will allow you such socializing even as Melita!" Philip said softly.

"He tolerates socializing for Melita. As his wife, my alter Joan may mingle formally. He disapproves even of her social kisses."

Joan kissed me socially when on Campus, mused Philip. *She must not share all her personal life with Melita!*

Melita waved her finger at the men. "You must allow your woman to flirt in passing to promote socializing among the crew. We are a small community, and each of us should get to know as many people as possible. We ought to be cordial or friendly with everyone because they will be our only friends and neighbors for the rest of our lives!"

Philip asked how many would be aboard the Wheel.

"Each ship will sail with two hundred sixty to two hundred eighty-five people, including children. With our relatively low percentage of children, we will average about ninety adult singles of all ages per ship. For the entire Wheel, over eight hundred adult singles. I must say with more men than women unless Lois's late pick-ups go as planned."

Dusan noted, "Even with an equal number of men and women, surely some will have to marry older or younger than their ideal."

"That's true, the mitigating factors being that everybody is healthy, attractive enough, educated, and equally employed."

Having taken only a few sips of wine, Melita stood. "Philip, Comte is briefing Alice. Joan asked me to invite you for cross training on Key Bury's flight deck in forty minutes—full jumpsuit." She turned to Dusan, "Go home for a top alert, not a drill. The U.N.'s battleship is almost within range."

Cosmos! Drinking with Dusan was a pretext to get me out of the apartment. "Melita, why wait round for a battleship that wants to shoot at us?" Philip wanted to know.

"As Counselor Melita, let me say not to worry about the battleship nor women seeking your company in public. I must go because Joan is due on the flight deck!"

✳ ✳ ✳

Before opening his apartment door, Philip reminded himself of his promise to Alice made after dinner last evening, not to inquire about her duties as a secret Cobalt Blue, as she would tell him all she could. As he entered, Comte stood and waved for him to join them just as the public address speakers sounded a shrill, rising whoop of middle to high tones; after a pause the tone was repeated, and after another pause, repeated a third time. The speakers announced loudly, "This is a White-One alert. This is not a drill. Each person with a jumpsuit put it on with boots and gloves. Line's defensive and damage control crews report to duty stations. All other personnel remain in quarters ready to strap in."

"Phil, your jumpsuit is on the bed."

Philip looked again and caught his breath. *Comte in a jumpsuit! And how can any duty of Alice's be involved, secret Blue or otherwise? She's a Staff Commander, an artist, yet Comte briefs her alone for this top-level alert? Why Comte? Leading the Federation Council is a management position, and I'm sure he's old enough to be retired once or twice. Of course, as founding principal not seeming to age, he's still involved with everything—surely the strangest person aboard.*

Alice urged, "Please hurry into your jumpsuit, Phil. No daydreaming during General Quarters!"

A bell rang three times. Manager Robbie was about to speak. His voice was calm but serious. "Good evening, ladies and gentlemen of The Pystead Singularity. I want to make it clear. Each of us is a decent human being, and as a group we are a bona fide singularity of humanity. We are not the anticipated computer wisdom nor cyborg beings of so much speculation. We are, however, a true singularity of such importance that those intent on being the only arbiters of world influence and power cannot tolerate us, even though they know little about us. That is why the U.N.'s battleship is approaching and intends to sink us! Do not worry! Our secret surveillance pods always track the battleship, and we have known about Admiral Telaobade's plans for over a week. We are ready for the attack and intend to deceive the Admiral into thinking he has destroyed us. We want to remain in hiding for another week before departure, and we do not want the U.N. looking for us. We will submerge and proceed into deep water as a submarine. Do not play loud music, do not bang on anything as the sounds we make can be detected in the water. Even our electrical transformers have been designed to minimize the natural sixty-cycle and four-hundred cycle hums they induce into our structure. We can run silent if each of you refrains from making loud noises! Now please listen for announcements, and you must be quiet in your quarters."

WHITE-ONE

Commander Joan and her deputy were seated at the front bridge chairs. Each person on the flight deck wore a Halo suit or jumpsuit with helmet not deployed and an oxygen mask, except for the three seated in full Halo suits with hard helmets and oxygen tanks on their backs—the three soon to walk and watch the instrument panels as double checkers and replacement crew.

Comte led his group to the side. The viewport was open, making directly visible the lower two-thirds of their ship's deck. A small view of the upper deck level was displayed on video just above the viewport.

Silence pervades this waiting flight deck. We visitors wear medical facemasks, the crew is safe on oxygen. Is this life-and-death on the line? After all, this top alert is for circumstances understood stochastically, implying that our responses may go beyond established procedures. O Cosmos!

Joan calmly stood up to survey the flight deck, before turning back to study the annunciation lights set around the viewport. She spoke to the officer standing at her side, and they both peered out.

Joan nodded, saying, "We need visual. Ian, give all keys video on those approaching helicopters. Captain Asif, rotate the Wheel to maintain Key Bury facing those copters. If they begin to land, move the Wheel to have them land on our lower deck. Now, Ian, I need visual on the battleship, from our point of view. Use side panel details, our line-of-sight perspective." An aye, aye came from somewhere and Joan was silent. Within seconds the helicopters and the battleship were seen on screen. Joan said off speakers, "All battle stations, keep a visual double check on my annunciation lights. Also, double-check the gun turrets on the battleship. Only one turret of three big guns will be allowed aimed our way. Also, watch the small turrets and the missile launcher."

Philip noticed that most of the illuminated lights over the main portal were steady green. He reasoned that the large, top center panel illuminated white and showing a large, red number two, indicated the present alert status on the flight deck. The room's speakers came alive, and each of the seven flight decks of the assembled Wheel reported in turn that all their systems were a-okay. Joan was called "Admiral," and told that her annunciation lights were showing correctly.

No time for discussion, Security Branch Commander Joan, normally a Manager, is now an Admiral giving orders.

Joan spoke, "That leaves the Campus. Need a linear display of the Campus's back lawn and view out to sea. Also need a view from our main gate out." The requested views appeared on a wall to the left of the portal window that now served as a screen. Showing to the right was video of the helicopters. "All stations, be sure to give me voice as well as a blinking light for any shipboard fault or bogey." Joan continued on speakers, "Now, for peace of mind, Wheel's propulsion drives, laser cannons, pod intercept group, and then Campus security, each report status."

"Key Bury's eight mains are on-line, rated for red-line performance." Soon a combined report for the seven ships said a-okay to red-line for all fifty-six main engines and propulsion drives.

A male voice informed the flight deck, "Our pod defenses against incoming shells have passed computer gaming simulations and physical intercept exercises. Twelve intercept pods are ready on deck. The Wheel's seventeen laser cannons with line-of-sight are a-okay and ready."

Campus security reported, "Campus robots are armed and active."

Joan asked, "Clair, what is your assessment on defending the Campus?"

"Our surveillance pods have found twenty flying gun drones, plus seven heavily armored, small tanks having a projectile or laser cannon. We'll need smoke-and-mirrors to hold the perimeter if they send all those in one wave. Their troop transports are positioning marines for a second wave invasion. A definite smoke-and-mirrors need there."

"All smoke and mirrors are unbound."

"We copy for unbound, Joan."

Comte whispered to Philip, "Beam weapons have been ruled illegal by the U.N. Evidently, they give the Western powers too much opportunity to separate combatants from civilians used as human shields. The reasoning must be that civilian casualties and the subsequent demonizing of any country protecting itself from terrorists are still desirable to much of the world at large."

"So, we must kill them?" Philip took Alice's gloved hand in his.

"We will beam them first. Their shielded troops, the elites, we will have to hit with something more substantial—trying not to kill. Their military robots are more a problem because we can only estimate those capabilities. Fortunately, our robots are technologically more advanced. Our concern is to avoid being overwhelmed by sheer numbers! The good news is that the Wheel can be quite fast if we need to fly."

Joan called, "Attention all keys and Campus, the use of smoke and mirrors is authorized. Repeating: unleash smoke and mirrors! Campus, if LSTs are launched, immediately sink any carrying heavy weapons."

"Aye, aye, to sink upon launch LSTs with heavy equipment."

"Per standard procedure minimize casualties." There were several ayes. "Key Bury engine crew?"

"Here, Joan."

"Make six Admin Tank engine-drives set to deploy."

"Roger for six Tank drives set to fly."

"Campus, what is your loading status?"

"Each approved recruit will be instructed this evening on readiness and departure. We will have all awake and ready to board by four-thirty in the morning. The back lawn is clear and secure. Both docks are prepped for general boarding and protected. We are expecting three ships with a ramp down at zero-four-thirty hours, Campus time."

"Roger that. And final evacuation of Campus?"

"Final recruits and processing scans, critical equipment,

supplies, and documents have been moved to the Admin Tank. The Tank is prepared to fly carrying last crew and robots. Backup evacuation is by armored train to each dock for a rescue ship."

"Fine, Joan out. Can you hear me, Marianas Key? New Ionia Key?"

"Aye for Marianas. We are ready for the world to come."

"New Ionia is following."

"Geri, Sam, we need derring-do on a few pickups per contingency plans."

"We have received details on a few dozen pickups. Marianas will execute with Ionia covering. All systems are go. We have received eight additional foo fighters and ten top pods. The plan is to meet you on the backside."

"Roger for the late pick-ups. Negative on the backside rendezvous. We will most likely meet on Pluto. Option details are almost complete—expect transmission within minutes."

"Aye to skip the Moon and prepare for rendezvous on far away Pluto."

"Right, Geri. We do hope to wait for you beyond the Moon before proceeding."

"Roger, to look for you, but we made it to Mars and back, and we can find the dwarf."

"We'll drop a communications pod if the Moon Base runs us off too far. If necessary, we'll drop something on the Moon Base. One high-speed, frozen chicken should take out that flimsy missile dome."

"I'd prefer a turkey!"

"A-okay for a turkey."

⚔ ⚔ ⚔

Joan spoke with her deputy and then asked on speaker, "Special-Ops, Valkyrie, are you listening?"

"Aye, Joan."

"Linda, do we have a willing herbalist?"

"We do. Evidently, he will gain status in the tribe if he can point the Admiral for killing that mask maker."

"Is our palm-reader double ready?"

"She is ready. The only dicey part seems to be getting the herbalist into an Egg. He was reluctant at the loading trial."

"Pay a girl to get in first. He will be shamed in. Put the girl out."

"Sounds good, we will have a fearless female standing by."

"Linda, that herbalist absolutely must have his pointing bone! If he has lost it, make him a new one."

"Roger to bring a pointing bone."

"That's all."

"Aye, Joan. Valkyrie will be ready to fly."

After a moment Joan spoke again, "The U.N.'s helicopters are now in view. Confirm that all hull doors are sealed and locked on each key."

A report on speakers confirmed that all hull doors were secured, and scans were negative for weapons aboard the helicopters, although they surely brought mini drones for spying. A dozen Serval robots were ready on deck to catch and kill spy drones.

Three helicopters approached the low hull level of their ship, and Pilot Asif continued moving the Wheel to keep *Key Bury's* deck below the helicopters. The flight deck's three suited walkers stood and began their rounds. A voice announced, "Copters feathering rotors to hover…they are landing." The helicopters' doors opened as their wheels touched the deck, and people emerged with children among them.

Comte leaned over and spoke to Philip. "I recognize them, the K.L.J.H. group of human cyborgs led by their Dr. Osgood. They were a constant problem on Campus."

Alice whispered to Philip, "The adults don't know who fathers a particular child. A baby is taken from its mother at three months old and raised in the domestic group by the retired adults, grandparents who don't know their own grandchildren. Mothers visit the children after six months and can't recognize their own child. They visit infrequently and never know their own child."

Alice was briefed for what role? He replied, "We knew on Campus that Dr. Osgood was a heartless enabler for whoever controls this group of spying cyborgs. And now he brings them to the top of a sloping and slippery ship's deck to be shot at!"

✵   ✵   ✵

After a status report that the helicopters were closing their doors and rotor speeds increasing, Joan called distinctly, "Operation Sub, it's time to sink both mini subs under that battleship. Try to flood their aft compartments, especially the engine and battery rooms. Let's see if the extra weight will rip them off their docking grips. Try to conceal your presence." After an exchange, Joan confirmed, "Yes, sink both mini subs immediately!"

Philip asked Comte, "That U.N. Admiral cannot shoot his nuclear warhead at us?"

Comte shook his head. "We know that the big gun bores all measure sixteen inches, and the nuclear warhead was built for a

31

missile tip at twenty inches in diameter, over four inches too large for the big guns. We got a surveillance rod inside the battleship when the warhead was loaded, but the rod couldn't get out until the technicians were loaded a week later. To go air nuclear the Admiral must use the rocket launcher, and its down and locked. The nuclear warhead has not been brought topside. It's still shielded and stowed. The radiation count is steady at one place below decks. Our indicator light for that is steady green." Comte nodded. "The Admiral has good reason to believe his sixteen-inch shells can put an end to us."

In a medical facemask, Comte's nodding at merely the Admiral's opinion of our destruction is disturbing.

Joan asked on speaker, "Does the U.N. have eyes on us?"

"Yes. Three hovering drones, one video scope in each chopper, and four gyro-stabilized telescopes on the approaching battleship."

"Asif, hoist the Jolly Roger. Pick a weight that will fly."

"Aye. Expect to be under the Black Flag in one minute."

Comte told Philip and Alice, "The U.N. has forced Kitts-Nevis to revoke our ship's charter. Without that charter we are considered pirates whether we fly the black flag or not. As palm-reader and psychic on Nevis, Melita told the Admiral he would sink a large ship under the black flag. We are setting the scene Melita described."

A minute later Joan stood. "How many on our topside?"

"Forty-seven, including about a dozen children. Six of them estimated under sixteen, and a couple must be under four. All are wearing magnetized shoes, steady as they stand, cool in the breeze, with several children crying."

"Standby a moment." Joan rose from her chair but stumbled. She put her hands out with her knees bent, as if trying to steady herself on the floor. Her deputy got to his feet.

From Comte Saint Germaine came a loud "Aaagh, huumpht," as if clearing his throat. The deputy, Andrew, looked over. He seemed to blink. Then Philip saw that Saint Germaine was holding his left hand, the hand beside the wall, at waist level and shaking it sideways from the wrist. The deputy turned his attention back to the status lights and did not speak.

"Granddad, Is Joan sick?"

"I think not," he whispered. "Probably surprised. She told me earlier today that she was well trained in everything except an actual killing. Evidently Telaobade is willing to sacrifice his K.L.J.H. group to keep us a fixed target. They die if we fly or if we are hit. If we fly, the U.N. will surely take video of us killing them!"

The three visitors watched as Joan rose to her feet and gave a slow wave to the five control stations. She asked, "Can we get immediate A-B-C-D scans in situ?"

"Yes, Admiral. The equipment is ready in the isolation room at entry fourteen."

✳   ✳   ✳

Joan stepped away from her chair and was soon facing Alice. "I don't have time to reach your mother. You are next in line and briefed, you must speak for her."

"Surely not."

Comte whispered, "Alice, you are the keeper of the diadem and next."

"I'm not yet thirty-five years old, Granddad."

"Melita assures me, Alice, that you are mature at thirty-two."

I thought only sailors considered Melita a psychic? Does my fiancée also have mysterious dreams like Melita?

Joan persisted, "I am bound to have a second opinion! In this moment, Alice, you are first among equals and must speak for your mother."

"I agree," said Comte.

Alice looked at Joan and seemed to set her shoulders, but she closed her eyes. "I'd save the children and save the grandparents for the sake of the children."

My real-world fiancée will risk endogenous issues for the sake of the children. Is this part of her secret Cobalt Blue role, akin to Melita's intuition and mysterious dreams? Yet, Cosmos, saving them will keep us immobile for at least a few minutes—an easy target. Covered in her briefing? She would know anyway! Could Alice also be a Reserved Line Commander?

✳ ✳ ✳

Joan returned to her chair, bent over, and took off her red boots and white socks. She stood on her floor mat in bare feet and ordered, "Okay, kill their drones. Then put a crew out for A-B-C-D scans of the people. Use two crews if you have them." Joan and her deputy Andrew sat down. Joan asked, "Have we confirmed identification of who the forty-seven might be?"

"Roger, they are that K.L.J.H. Organism from Campus, who claimed a right to be hired as a group. They are standing in two subgroups. The subgroup of twenty-six has the children. They must have a working subgroup and a domestic subgroup."

Joan called, "Security, scan the group with children."

"Aye. We are beginning to scan the children's group using two crews. We have chocolates for them."

"I need status on that battleship and its mini subs."

"Admiral, the battleship dropped both subs before even one docking grip began to strain. Taking no chance on jamming, I'd say."

"Battleship course and speed?"

"Still coming at us flank speed. At that rate it reaches our red line in twenty minutes. The white light is set to blink ten minutes before that fight-or-flight mark."

Comte stood. "I want to follow commands."

Philip looked around. One of the three walkers was standing still, watching a control panel. *The time is near for K.L.J.H. especially. I'll bet not one of them has any idea what's happening. Model U.N. subjects—so-called 'citizens of the world' on deck to keep us from flying!*

Joan said resolutely, "Lois?"

"Yes, Joan?"

"Prepare to receive the twenty-six people now being scanned." Joan hesitated. "Battleship technical?"

"Aye, Admiral?"

"Who is speaking?"

"Jon."

"Jon, do we have confirmation for Attack Option A?"

"Negative. We know nothing about the sixteen-inch shells except they test negative for nuclear material and were delivered unshielded."

"Is the Commander ready to execute Attack A?"

"Roger that. Meister Merkle is ready for A, B, and C."

"Jon, execute Option A. Use those new rods to plug the two outside barrels on the turret."

"Aye, to plug the two outside barrels."

"Security, let's stop those the A-B-C-D scans. Get those twenty-six into isolation. After all are in, seal the hull and corridor doors.

Be good, be quick. Secure them for inversion. Purge corridor fourteen and keep it isolated. Complete the scans. Also, we do not want any of the group or Dr. Osgood knowing what happens now or when we depart. Turn off your public address speakers. Within about five minutes, sedate Dr. Osgood so that he has no memory of motions or time."

A woman's voice responded, "Aye to move the group with children inside pronto and clean and secure the access corridor. We'll complete A-B-C-D inside. We will keep them from experiencing announcements and maneuvers until further instructed. Will sedate Osgood."

"Be aware, they carry mini spy drones as small as a honeybee—possibly smaller. Check the soles of their shoes, in the hair, everywhere!"

"I hear you. We will be thorough."

※ ※ ※

Joan's voice was calm as she directed, "All stations, all stations, make ready pods to deflect incoming explosive projectiles, or if necessary use lasers to destroy them." She then asked, "Anybody, did I forget anything?"

A woman's voice called, "There will be twenty-one adults remaining topside."

"Yes, the working adults who aren't allowed to know their own children! Are nets out?"

"Aye, nets are rigged for the low rim."

"Rescue, can you get floats and vests to people once they are in the nets or water?"

"We can."

"Ready them for that group of twenty-one adults; also have two large rubber boats ready for them."

"Aye."

"Seems to me, if we demagnetize the hull and tip them toward the water they should land in the nets? Anyone disagree?"

Rescue's voice replied, "They would catch the net unless rolling fast or pushing off when they go over the side."

"Give them public address instructions on sliding. After that they take their chances. Once they are in, fly those nets down and dump them into a boat, asap. Thereafter, use pods to save the drowning and assist the badly injured. Bring aboard anyone incapacitated, in too much pain, or hysterical. We don't want survivors noticed tonight. You might toss in some lines and whatever will help to fish out those overboard. No boat radio, lights, or kom, and no flares—no flares! No white-light flashlights. Kill any drones."

"Roger, Joan, we will get the lucky souls into a dark boat without flares."

"Turn off the boat's panel lights. Can you get them small, red-light flashlights?"

"Aye."

"Once in the boats, tell them how to motor to shore and that they must run for their lives before the police get to them."

"Roger."

Philip relaxed and took Alice's hand. *There's no Red Queen at Pystead, but what's with the Valkyrie?*

Alice whispered, "The unlucky souls we bring aboard tonight will be the lucky ones tomorrow."

Joan and her deputy sat down. The status lights over the portal window were now a mix of colors—a yellow and two white lights were blinking.

"Let's raise our seatbacks, and fasten seatbelts," Comte said quietly.

Joan called, "Captain Asif, time to take the helm."

Asif came from the rear and spoke briefly with Joan, who then turned and walked toward Comte. Joan's deputy remained, watching the annunciation lights and video.

Alice held Philip's arm. "I'm worried."

"Let's not worry until Comte is worried."

✼　✼　✼

Captain Asif had all keys use maximum hold on their docking magnets. Then he began flooding tanks to submerge to the Wheel's high-water mark. Asif explained that if Pystead was to have an easy next week the U.N.'s Admiral must believe he had sunk all seven ships.

Joan again approached the three observers. "I believe we are well positioned. Do you find any problem, Comte?"

Comte stood, saying, "No."

"Let me check on the fog pots and the faux fires. I really want Telaobade to visit our palm reader double on Nevis tonight." Joan's voice lowered, "Comte, those adults remaining topside are in for a terrifying amusement park ride at best. I surely killed sailors sinking those mini subs. The first I have killed, but I had to act. Admiral Telaobade I kill unforced. I'm a Valkyrie! My training is complete."

"Joan, you did as much for the K.L.J.H. group as reason allows."

Joan sighed. "Loss of the battleship's mini submarines will

never be known. But if we sink slowly one L.S.T. the media will report a merciless attack on a U.N. inspection team. Today's investigative reporters are highly paid to travel, party, and relay official bulletins as if they were personally confirming events."

"Be consoled, your plan to deal with the battleship is magnificent. The battleship will surely fire on us. Two barrels will be split into strips like a banana peel. We will create our own news ziff videos. If the U.N. wants to discredit our video, they will have to keep the battleship at sea and fix it with plastic barrels. If they do that soon enough, we will video the repairs!"

"Fine, Comte. I'll double-check preparations."

Captain Asif remained commanding the ship, his copilot and Joan's deputy at his sides. Most indicator lights on the viewport panel were green, with only a few still blinking, yet the alert level number panel above the viewport that had been a red number two was now blinking white without showing a number.

Comte whispered to Alice and Philip. "Joan has managed to orchestrate all our objectives. Even that the battleship should leave this sea arena promptly in order that Admiral Telaobade can visit our Melita Rose double tonight."

Philip asked how the Admiral would be able to visit the double. Comte said Telaobade had helicopters and his men had already cleared everybody off the beach nearest Melita's house. The Admiral was sure to want Melita, and he would be eager for her psychic reading now that his pirating subs were underwater for keeps. He would want reassurance of his promotion to four stars and easy riches as Governor of the Oceania Protectorate.

Philip glanced around. The walkers were walking. The annunciation panel above the viewport was still flashing white, but at a faster rate than before. *This rapid flashing must mean a number soon. And number one will mean that we stay and fight!*

Joan remained seated. The flashing panel went steady white, showing a large black 1. *The die is cast—we fight. Next up, the binary beings. O Cosmos! If I'm to train for the Line, I must trust our binary beings. Mano-a-mano is done! Computers and robots are the weapons of today.*

Comte sat down. "Time for helmets." Alice tugged at Philip's arm, opened a suit flap, and pointed to his hood. He flinched as the slats of his hood popped up behind his head. They pushed around his head, guided by the track inside the thick collar of his jumpsuit. Comte pulled a packet from the wall and donned a soft hood with an oxygen line. Alice deployed her helmet.

A speaker in Philip's helmet came to life. Comte told them, "Sit with your feet lightly on the floor mat, and rest only on the upholstery of your seat. A close hit could send a severe shock wave through anything rigid to structure."

Aah. Hence the shock mounted frames in the art galleries and buffet lines, and the cushy walking strips in corridors, and the floor mats at all chairs here. Ship's features never envisioned solely for a peaceful life of fish farming and seasteading! And in space, a meteor hit could produce an incredible, shocking structural event. This ship was surely designed for space travel from the get-go.

※　※　※

Before Philip could rethink the situation, the speakers sounded a series of whooping tones heard both in his helmet and through it. *My helmet's ports are open, I'm not on oxygen.*

Asif's voice followed. "Attention, all ships, all crew—this is not a drill, not a drill. Everybody, give me your full attention. This alert is not a drill." He paused, then continued, "I am Captain Asif speaking. Now hear this: Key Bury will dump our remaining topside intruders into the sea while all keys begin making smoke. We will create a fog so dense the lifeboats cannot see our ship as more than a shadow. After the battleship attacks, we will appear to sink by diving in place under cover of our own smoke. Our suction produced will not pull the lifeboats under, but they will feel it.

"We will proceed underwater to beyond the horizon and into deep water where we will remain submerged in hiding. Everybody must remain quiet in quarters! No loud music, no banging on pans or walls. No screaming children. Use a gray pill to sedate a child if necessary. Read the instructions. This is a matter of life-and-death!"

Asif called to the flight deck, "Have all keys sound the White-One alert."

After the shrill alert tones were heard, he explained, "All persons, any moment now we expect an incoming forty-centimeter explosive shell." After a momentary pause he added, "We are prepared to stop a salvo of nine shells, but we will not allow more than three big gun barrels aimed our way. We expect only one barrel to send a shell our way. We have posted pods in between us and the battleship, and our lasers are ready as backup intercepts before we move the Wheel out of the line of fire. Their shells will take a few seconds to arrive after guns are fired. In other words, the shells are big and slow. Our risk is less than you might imagine because a single hit would not breach our second hull, and we are not about to get hit. A pod will get under any shell on target and nudge its trajectory up to overshoot us. Our smoke and faux fires will mask its explosion in the water behind us. Maybe their video analysts will find it in a few days—too late! We will make smoke and fake explosions. We will blow chaff to simulate fragmentation."

Then in quick cadence Asif commanded, "All stations be set to execute. Expect an incoming shell any moment. We dive in place only after faked explosions and much smoke making. Our faux fog will thin in fifteen minutes; we'll be under in ten! Fog crews, keep those lifeboats obscured from us and from the battleship. Get set standby laser and primary pod defenses for incoming shells. First topside faux fire must erupt only at the very moment their shell should hit the ship—timing to the millisecond needed."

Asif took his seat and raised a small control console from the floor. He said aloud, "As discussed, we will provide help for the unfortunates now on deck. Ready now crews for their public address, safety nets, and two rubber boats."

Ayes were heard and three lights blinking yellow went steady.

Asif ordered, "Demagnetize our hull."

"Hull is neutral."

People on the hull were slipping and falling. Asif pushed a few keys on his control panel and their flight deck tilted forward. "The Wheel is tilted forward by thirty degrees." Their viewport and video showed some people sliding feet first down the tilted hull with legs wide apart and heels pressed to the hull as advised by the topside public address. Other screaming adults, however, slid or rolled in all positions. Wails faded as people went over the side. Asif pulled the ship's outer edge up and the remaining sliders came almost to a halt before going over.

Joan's voice was heard. "Give us maximum blow on those fog pots."

Philip checked Alice's seatbelt. Asif's voice returned, "We are putting several meters distance between this ship and the two lifeboats in dense fog. We don't need up-close witnesses tonight or ever. Our fake explosions will provide only flashes of illumination. I hope our chaff doesn't hit anybody, but it's a must for authenticity. The battleship's radar will pick it up."

Joan spoke, "Check on survivors using pods and bring aboard those in need of immediate assistance."

✼　✼　✼

The video display revealed several people in the dark water. Philip watched a man being tossed back and forth but ignored by those already in a boat, and he felt a lightness in his own stomach. It was due to the slight movement of the ship, a sensation reminding of his horrible train ride from Wheaton to Savannah while in police custody. Still, he watched video of the outside fog swirling and rising, veiling faces and then whole lifeboats in darkness.

A view of the Wheel disk from above was shown. The speakers sounded one quiet but shrill note just before a bright explosion colored the scene of their video. The almost obscured disk of the ship peaked at its center, at what Philip knew to be the flight decks, spouted red-orange flames and multiple, deep toned, prolonged, stomach wrenching growls. Within moments more orange and red flashes leaped skyward from adjacent key ships. Then a huge fireball of orange and black smoke erupted. Philip squeezed Alice's hand. *We're not all-knowing and powerful, as Alice often reminds me.*

A report explained, "We are not damaged. We are not yet clear of the battleship." Whooping tones followed in a lower and slower pattern than Philip had ever before heard. An unfamiliar voice said,

"We are submerging. Water to the flight deck in eight minutes. We don't believe they can see more than quick and changing views of small areas of the hull. We're burbling smoke and flames from dozens of heated places—impossible to fake on short notice. Thanks to our stealth surveillance pods, we have had several days' warning to prepare! To anybody watching we are burning and sinking."

Two minutes later rather mellow tones sounded, announced as a Yellow-Five alert level, intended to maintain furniture and drawers secured, with normal clothing and activity in quarters. Relief crews for damage control and combat stations were told to remain suited.

Comte stood. "Alice, have you wine to spare?"

Alice sensed cheerfulness in his voice. "Oh yes, Granddad."

"Let's raise a glass to our world to come."

✳   ✳   ✳

Philip and Alice walked with Comte. Philip remarked that Telaobade could not afford K.L.J.H. survivors telling how they came to be atop a pirate ship.

"I'm afraid not. If we could influence the world, or escape the world while remaining in it, we would not need to leave…alas, we are vastly outnumbered and considered an illegal community."

"That's another forty-seven missing persons not missed by the world. All those poor wretches known collectively as the K.L.J.H. Organism. Who's even to ask their names?"

Comte added, "While on Nevis, we investigated the group and Dr. Osgood, but could find no mention of surnames. Their second generation had no outside acquaintances other than the manufacturer's representatives who called on them and provided their design expertise in exchange for procurement specifications. They used the European design approach in America, also taking credit for the manufacturer's designs while denying sole-source equipment specifications."

"What kind of existence is that?"

"They lived without visits from their unknown, extended family members. Their vacations were group excursions to theme parks."

Philip recalled the group's administrative and political leader on Campus, proudly introducing himself to an assembly as Dr. Orlando Murphy Taws Osgood. He had arrogantly dismissed Pystead's policy of hiring only individuals, insisting that his group sanctioned by the U.N., called the K.L.J.H. Organism, must be hired in accordance with the world's commercial laws. A group of forty-seven including children that Pystead must accept unvetted to fill twenty advertised engineering positions. Cyborgs with implants, including in the brain, having their own computer system and showboards. They had little to no engineering education. Their work was to push a few keyboard tabs to download a manufacturer's design files, to push the design computation tab, and upon completion to save and print the final design documents. The group had refused to study Pystead's engineering manuals or to demonstrate any competency using Pystead's computer. Once individuals, but now dominated by their artificially intelligent showboard and Dr. Osgood, they were more biological robots than humanity.

Philip felt both regret and unease. *Are they unconcerned about their origins, their children, their personal expertise, their group's product, their tomorrow? Ever wonder about their sustaining manna? Can they think introspectively? Do they inquire about the protocols of their world? Ever wonder if knowing how to push a small set of tabs for one computer is knowing enough about a profession?* Philip concluded aloud, "Osgood must have provided whatever outside worldview they needed. What a heartless facilitator."

Comte nodded. "We hired Dr. Osgood as an ethicist, one of two. He arrived as leader of the Organism!"

Philip pondered the situation. *Which is worse: a cultural idealist, a religious fundamentalist, or an innate sociopath? Perhaps all the same if one wants a live-and-let-live world? Pystead's selection process has certainly done its best to avoid those types.*

❉ ❉ ❉

As they entered the apartment, Alice motioned for Philip and Comte to sit down. Philip remained preoccupied, *With no friends, no resources, no habit of thinking for themselves, no experience in the world, not even a change of clothing, the Organism's survivors must be doomed. Anyone who gets off the beach will be reported for suspicious activity! O Cosmos, we must hope that saving them at sea saves a few on land. Comte must believe our Pystead Group is viable. I know from Campus that Lois is apprehensive, yet still crew. No better option like the rest of us? I wonder if Magnus Osgood saw the writing on his wall? In any case, the K.L.J.H. Organism will be resurrected—far too useful to do without. And nobody to inquire about the newly disappeared among the two million missing persons worldwide.*

Comte at the couch removed his medical mask. At his gesturing, Alice and Philip took off theirs. Philip's head was swirling. *I was ready for our farewell dinner aboard ship last night. Seems it will prove not my last dinner on Earth since we are going into hiding. Perhaps my last dinner above sea level? Of those aboard, how many of us know enough to realistically assume we will be happy here…wherever?*

Comte and Philip sat quietly as Alice poured and handed out flutes of Ste Wolls champagne. "Here with us, Phil?" she whispered. "If not, please daydream later."

Comte lifted his glass. "Lois has long sought a sign of our rebirth. Let's be optimistic for her and toast, our world to come."

"Our world to come," said the three.

They sat quietly in their moment of entangled joy and sadness. Philip recalled Osgood's complaint about their group's Poseidon statues. *One may not have Hestia before Poseidon, except in the mind of an idealist like Osgood. Our statues on Campus reflected the real world, not Osgood's view of authoritarians as philosopher kings. Cognitive science would profit from scanning Osgood's brain for intentionality and empathy. Sociopathic from birth, or lacuna in his cultural wiring? He constructed his ethics to allow, even require, sacrifice for his intended common good. Of course, in Osgood's case, the sacrifice always falls to someone else! His a case of cultural menticide or of simple ego gratification with promised rewards for loyalty extending into his retirement—the American model.*

If the Osgood types could contain their wiring unto themselves and their friends, there would be little need for the rebirth of Poseidon. Comte's world, our world, is of bone and blood. Ours a ceaseless struggle waged in the physical domain against disorder, doctrine, greed, and malicious envy. Success entangling joy and sadness must be a moment of Poseidon's nirvana! The bittersweet fate of Saint Germaine and Pystead?

✳   ✳   ✳

At twenty hundred hours an announcement informed all ships that Commander Robbie Markwaters, General Manager of The Pystead

Group, would speak in ten minutes. His information and perspective would be both urgent and critical for anybody not already an established member of the crew. Alice turned on her big-screen kom and was ready when Robbie rang his bell.

"Good evening, everybody, we are resting on an outcrop of the continental shelf at great depth." Robbie raised a hand. "We are undetectable to routine surveillance practices as long as we rest silently and do not let the U.N. follow one of our Egg craft. We have pods above and below sea level watching for any deep-water surveillance rovers." Robbie shifted his gaze to look directly at a video camera. "Everyone, no pounding on your room walls, cooking pots and pans, toy drums, and no loud music, no screaming child or barking dog!"

Robbie frowned. "I do not know of anybody who in their country of origin was not struggling to maintain their position and integrity as a professional, trade specialist, or corporate officer. Our founder, Comte Saint Germaine, believes that the arc of world society has been changed for the foreseeable future. Times are dystopian in the Caribbean and in all the world. The middle classes in the Western countries are being reduced to the status of those in countries run by an autocrat or single political party. The wages of professionals and skilled tradespeople are shrinking, and neither the skilled nor their families or friends are safe from abuse to set an example! Master tradespeople are as oppressed as medical doctors. One should have little difficulty understanding that Comte was able to recruit qualified crewmembers initially from Europe, especially from the Low Countries with rising sea waters. Lois Hensson, our Commandant of Administration, recruited when eighteen years old, became Comte's first permanent crewmember not a financial principal."

Robbie shifted his stance and even seemed to rock side to side. His voice deepened, "Although you know why you are here, I ask that you reexamine your decision within the next day or two. We have learned that our immediate future is more dangerous than thought just weeks ago. The U.N. tried to sink the entire Wheel ship to be rid of us. They will try to stop our final evacuation from Campus. If they can find us with all the radars around the world now conveniently dedicated to tracking nonexistent E.T.s, they will try to shoot us down as we depart the Earth. The same danger awaits us on the Moon when we pick up pre-positioned supplies. Although we are confident in our capability of defending the ship, we are not all powerful. We can surely intercept their missiles, but we have no defense from the gamma rays of an atomic blast that happen to be columnar and focused in our direction. A strong gamma beam could hit large portions of the ship or produce narrow beams that hit only one or more individuals. Gamma rays can kill or incapacitate in the moment or have unknown consequences in the future: damaged eggs in females, damaged cells that lead to cancer and other diseases in anyone."

Robbie squinted his eyes and looked aside, but quickly returned to face the camera. "To put it bluntly, pilgrims, we will have to fight our way out of Earth! We are confident the ship will survive intact, but we cannot guarantee that any given individual will survive now or be undamaged for the future.

"We possess new science and technology and the ideas of decency and progress. We plan to escape from Earth and boldly go into the unknown. We expect a new enlightenment of intellectual and cultural reforms. Many of the resulting new variations on life anticipated by much of the crew will be voluntary. Simply by going you choose the first and perhaps most significant variation on life that you will face. Overnight you become part of a hunted, intentional community that is feared for its science and technology! Later, you will need to accept cultural changes that will surely arise from living in close quarters and sharing equally with everyone. Our significant good fortune is that we are not taking the world's problems with us into spacetime!

"I ask each of you to reassess your decision to go! The meek of heart or mind must not go into spacetime with us! We will deliver those wanting to depart to a country that will honor their nation's passport and their right to exist. We will provide funds to restart lives. This opportunity is available for two or three days and thereafter is problematic."

Manager Robbie smiled. "I'm staying!" He paused several moments before saying, "May your mysterious spirit bless you and keep you."

After Robbie said goodnight, Philip and Alice sat in silence, holding hands. Several minutes later Alice stood and said, "I'll have to stop banging on the frying pan to wake you up, Phil."

"A new variation on life already!"

GUT REACTION

The three sat and sipped champagne. "Philip is lost in thought, Granddad, daydreaming. I know the look."

Philip lifted his head.

Comte said quietly, "I should mention something to both of you."

Alice moved to Philip's chair.

Comte leaned forward. "Philip, your cousin in New England and your friends in California have been approved on our end."

"I was worried."

"Each has been told to keep their kom on their person."

After single glasses of champagne, Philip and Alice followed Comte's lead and put on their facemasks. Comte assured Alice that her parents were fine, but communications limited. He would keep her informed. He said goodnight, suggesting they follow Alice's Blue kom channel that would stream Operation Valkyrie.

Philip pressurized the unfinished bottle of champagne. Instead of relaxing, he worried. *I never received a reply from Rhonda and Earl.*

When he asked Alice's opinion, she pointed him to the site for late pick-ups where he found his invitation. He confirmed that Rhonda was listed as a chef-in-training, and her father as a recently retired barbecue cook and small-scale farmer.

He messaged Rhonda saying she and her father should meet with him in Jupiter, Florida, to discuss terms for a small restaurant in Jupiter. *Seems plausible. Even during my Utrecht University days, Jupiter was prosperous with enzyme and other biotech businesses. Rhonda wants a city restaurant. Given the miserable circumstances I experienced just passing through Middle Georgia she and Earl should be ready to relocate! Rhonda liked me and we swapped kom addresses.*

Alice checked her secret Blue channel and learned that the battleship had departed west without searching for survivors. Joan still expected Admiral Telaobade to visit Melita Rose's residence on Nevis well before midnight. Alice set a flag for the event, and they sat quietly with her black cat for company.

Alice broke the silence, "We are submerged at three hundred thirty meters, being one hundred eighty fathoms. Oh Phi, I would be lost without you."

"I feel the same. Now that we have this new beginning, I'm apprehensive about the future and sad about old dreams vanishing. You are my grasp on reality because even our walls seem surreal, tin-box solid yet lacking. I worry that our journey will produce a void as well as a beginning."

She took his hand. "My feelings too are mixed up."

"I know life should become whole, but the wholeness I have sought for you, myself, and friends seems merely a nebulous potential in a gossamer somewhere."

"That must be how Lois has felt for years as her daughter was growing up in the poor and unsafe world Lois was working to escape." Alice frowned. "Cezanne remarked that it's so fine, and yet so terrible, to stand in front of a blank canvas."

The couple sat in their alert chairs, confronting their blank canvas. To the human mind, a real and tangible thing, even Cezanne's blank canvas, is more comforting than a gossamer somewhere in spacetime, an unknown niche of the cosmos. They rested holding hands, experiencing a mingled sadness and joy.

Perhaps I should have tossed in a coin at Trevi Fountain so long ago? Alice would have.

Alice's lips were slightly parted as if a smile had just faded. *My divine Philip longs for his lost academic life, yet knows this starship world is our only hope for a safe and full life. The lineage of Saint Germaine shall continue with our children! Pystead's League of Saint Germaine must awhile endure, for the sake of all our children. Now that I am speaking for Mother, I must be more observant, more aware of circulating memes of mind.*

✳ ✳ ✳

They were dozing when Philip's kom sounded. The message was from Rhonda in Middle Georgia. WE ARE IN TROUBLE. POLICE ARRESTED MY FATHER AND TORE UP THE WALLS OF OUR RESTAURANT AND OUR HOUSE LOOKING FOR AN OLD CANNON OR SOMETHING LIKE THAT. THEY HELD EARL FOR A WEEK WITHOUT LETTING ANYBODY SEE HIM OR EVEN SPEAK TO HIM. HOW CAN THAT HAPPEN? HE CAME BACK WITH A CRACKED WRIST THEY REFUSE TO TREAT. A MEAN FEMALE COP TOLD ME WHEN SHE GOT ANOTHER LEAD SHE WOULD BE BACK. BOTH HOUSE

AND RESTAURANT NEED EXTENSIVE REPAIRS, DAD NEEDS SURGERY. THE WHEATON POLICE SEARCHED OUR GREENHOUSE AND DUMPED SEEDS FOR PURE MEANNESS.

Philip waved for Alice to take a look. She asked, "How long were you there?"

"Less than an hour in Earl's Barbecue restaurant for supper. The old man's daughter, Rhonda, was a waitress." Philip glared at the message. "Wheaton gothics! My few days in jail there were hellish, merely held as a witness. They failed to crack my wrist, but not for lack of trying." Philip looked at the base of his thumbs, still scarred from the rips inflicted by being jerked around in handcuffs. He made a fist. "It's easy to understand why corrupt officials and their goons cannot allow even one niche of decent, high-tech people. Avenging Valkyries cannot be allowed."

"That's in your past."

"The same police in Wheaton who trumped up my detention as a witness and then mistreated me are now after Rhonda's father, Earl, a frail old man who should be long retired. The old cannon mentioned by Rhonda refers to my boxes of old books, which the Wheaton police system dubbed the old canon. Evidently their officer Burk, a mean one, thought 'old canon' meant a large gun. I'm the reason Earl is in trouble!"

Alice said, "I'll message Lois about their plight. We need crew, especially women. Is Rhonda single?"

"I'd guess so."

"She may be interested in you!"

"I'm taken. There are lots of single men aboard."

As Alice sent the message to Lois, her big-screen kom emitted a series of tones. The Melita Rose event was beginning, uncensored.

"Phil, you must have an honorary Level-Five clearance."

"Perhaps Joan doesn't plan to let me off the ship?"

"She is my best friend, after all."

"What about me?"

"You are right, love, you are my best friend, and Melita is my best female friend—not her alter Joan."

"Already I feel better in the void."

"You have retained your good nature. Let's watch operation Valkyrie. I'm dying to know what you put Joan up to with that herbalist-and-bone chat after dinner last night."

✳   ✳   ✳

By nine o'clock they were sitting, watching video of the Admiral and seven bodyguards approach Melita's house on Nevis from the direction of the beach, looking ghoulish in the red and blueish images of merged infrared and starlight videos. All eight wore baseball caps with visors tilted down to their eyes. They wore island clothing with a bulge of shirttail hiding a pistol. Three of the guards carried bulky briefcases, and one big man carried a long bag holding a few fishing rods. "Alice, I'll bet there's a rocket launcher in that long bag of fishing rods."

"Oh my, they come heavily armed to visit a palm reader—well, our double for the palm reader. No palm reading for the real Melita when her alter needs to be Commander Joan."

Admiral Telaobade and five guards stopped beside a tree across the street from Melita's backdoor, and the other two continued around front. The three guards with briefcases crossed the street to Melita's. Philip could envision Pystead's procryptic, flying, surveillance pods producing the video. The speaker at Melita's backdoor asked, "Who is there?"

The female guard punched in the Admiral's entry code: 5-2-0-1-1-2-3-7. Melita's double said, "The door is unlocked, come in." The guard took off her sports cap and exchanged it for the hat she held in her hand. She entered holding her briefcase and sports cap. The two male guards remained at the backdoor.

The kom's audio-visual feed switched to an inside view of the living room, showing the double for Melita Rose seated at a narrow table in the living room, adjacent to a very curved wall. Behind her, a string curtain of lavender and violet beads decorated the scene. The view switched to show the Admiral's guard.

Alice pointed. "That low table is from Melita's abandoned palm reading tent. The guard is the Admiral's nurse."

The nurse said nothing and pointed to the hat she was wearing—a military hat. The double for Melita remained seated and spoke, "I can fathom the seas, I can reach the stars, and I know the Admiral's hat."

"If you have the gift, tell me my name."

"The gift is generally not so specific. The gift speaks on events for which I am given information to tune my insight."

The nurse seemed satisfied, so Melita's double said, "On a guess, I'll call you Trilby."

The nurse, about to speak, visibly froze. She recovered and told the palm reader, "Your blood tests were negative. Have you bragged to your girlfriends about your new client?"

"Psychics share neither their clients nor their readings."

"That is good. If you gossip, you will compromise the Admiral's reputation and your security. Stay clean and stay quiet." The nurse bent and opened her case, taking out a scroll-like item. Melita's double stood, holding her red-lace cloak together at the waist. The nurse said, "Only weapon and identity scans are necessary if you have followed my instructions?"

"To the letter."

"If the Admiral is to take a reading here, I must have his men search the house."

"Expected."

The nurse spoke to her wrist kom. "Enter." The two guards at the backdoor entered with their cases. Without a word they went to the kitchen and began their work. Said the nurse, "I am curious, Melita Rose, why were you not at your tent the day after the Admiral's visit?"

Melita tossed her head. "I wasn't in the mood to work."

"Why have you reduced your hours since then?"

"I enjoyed my day off so much I reduced my hours for the season."

"You may have a prosperous life, but you cannot continue to live like a princess with only a few clients. You must maintain appearances. You must work until an inheritance is found."

"I still work almost as much as the other palm readers even though my fee more than doubles theirs. Before, I was working far more, and I have a much nicer, stormproof house."

"That's good to know. Is this framed painting secure enough to support my screen?"

"Yes."

The nurse hung the top of the scroll on the frame and unrolled it to floor length. The Melita double knew the procedure from a previous encounter in Melita's tent. She stood in front of the screen for scans. After they were completed, the nurse took a bottle of sweet bourbon cocktail from her briefcase. "You may give this to the Admiral, unopened."

"Thank you."

"Now take your seat until he enters. I will leave a video monitor on the doorknob. The Admiral will turn it off. My search team will install a unit watching and securing your front door. Do not try to open it."

"I have no need to go out."

Alice told Philip, "Her guard pods' lasers can cut the door's lock in a few seconds."

The nurse leaned close to Melita and whispered, "As a safety precaution with the Admiral, do not speak on any sensitive topic except in a whisper. If he asks you to read, whisper in his ear. This will give you an opportunity to be close." The nurse looked around and called, "Done yet?"

The two men soon appeared from Melita's bedroom. "The place is clean," said one. He demanded of Melita, "Why the curved walls?"

"The curves remind of my oval tent, they help with images. I don't know why."

The nurse warned, "Whisper the reading my dear palm reader. The Admiral is as agitated as I've ever known him. He will seek a reading today if nothing else. I know how disappointing that can be." She and the two men departed out the backdoor.

"The double is good," observed Philip.

"Oh yes. She has been doubling for years, because Melita often needed to be Joan on Campus or at the fish farm. Also, Melita kept long hours if customers were waiting. She would take a short break, and the double would return for her. Tonight, Melita's double has four guard pods and our Halo-suited guards hiding behind the bushes. She will come directly to the Wheel ship in a foo fighter

Egg before it returns the herbalist to his tribe. Melita's house will be purged of its Egg hangar within an hour thereafter, as was done for my apartment on Nevis."

"Is her tent still up?"

"No. A self-proclaimed psychic already has the location."

"Look!" Philip pointed.

The Admiral was across the street speaking with his nurse, rubbing her stomach. He soon headed for Melita's backdoor and went in without knocking. Their video switched to look over the double's shoulder.

The Melita double stood, holding her lace cloak together at the waist. She said warmly, "I can fathom the seas, I can reach the stars, and I know how the round ship died."

"That is not public knowledge, Missy. Tell me more."

The double stepped over to the Admiral no longer holding her cloak together. "I have been advised to whisper."

He ogled her and grinned. "Walls can have ears."

"Surely not mine."

"Take no chances."

The streaming video shifted up. The Melita double slipped her arms out of her red-lace robe. She stepped forward, kicking off her shoes. The Admiral grinned. He reached out a huge hand, obviously fondling her breasts. The double raised her left hand and took the Admiral's big right hand. She leaned in and whispered, "I see movement in your stars. Let's lie down and whisper and do what we want. There's a sofa here and a bed in my room." The Admiral led the naked woman toward her bedroom.

"Our double has to endure so much for us. Phil, how far will this go?"

He found Alice's hand and squeezed it. "According to plan, not beyond the bedroom door for the double. Joan found his tribe's medicine man, likes to be called an herbalist, and he needs to point this killer, Telaobade."

The Admiral threw open the bedroom door and stepped in, pulling the woman by her hand. The video shifted to view over his shoulder. He took only another step from momentum. Waiting at the foot of the bed, before a very curved wall, was a thin aborigine man in an animal-skin loincloth. He was bare chested, painted with bold white stripes. He wore long white feathers in his curly black hair. The video panned down to a clutch of short feathers at each knee, and then on down to focus on leather shoe pads with netting that held a thick layer of small feathers for the soles.

"The herbalist," said Philip, "walks on feathers without making a sound."

The thin man stood erect, hands at his side, eyes wide open, glaring. The Admiral jerked his right hand free from the woman, reaching for his pistol. The thin man slid silently forward raising his pointing bone. The short, pointed bone had feathers and a few strands of black hair tied to its back end. The hair would never be noticed by most, but the guilty look for a sign. The Admiral froze. The sharp bone was jabbed at him, never touching him, and his right hand—his gun hand—grasped his stomach. He stumbled backwards, bumping into the shoulder of the naked woman, which yielded little, the woman having turned sideways and braced herself. As the Admiral paused, the thin man jabbed twice more with his feathered bone, not touching Telaobade, uttering nothing. The Admiral's eyes rolled up as he inhaled sharply and clutched at his stomach. He groaned and spun around prepared to move the woman, but she was not there, having fled to her front door.

*   *   *

Outside her door, pulling together a Halo bathrobe, wearing a towel wrapped around her head to conceal her Halo helmet, the Melita double saw the Admiral's two waiting guards raise their pistols. Dense red beams struck their hands. They screamed as their pistols dropped. The double reentered her front door.

The video returned to the Admiral who was now across the back street with his nurse and guards. His nurse tried to stroke his cheek and kept asking what was wrong. Holding his stomach with his left hand and saying nothing, Admiral Telaobade ran his group back toward the beach and his waiting helicopter.

Pystead's video feed ended, not following the helicopter. For a long minute Philip and Alice sat quietly before he said, "I believe it's working."

"What's working?"

"The Admiral was grasping his stomach. I would say he's sick."

"Sick from what?"

"Nobody knows, Alice, nobody knows. If we could get functional M.R.I. brain scans until he dies, science would benefit."

"Dies?"

"Yes, within hours to a few days of an unknown cause."

"We have killed him?"

"His own tribe's medicine man killed him, although Joan made it possible."

"I'd say you made it possible."

"I simply mentioned the possibility to Melita and talked to Joan."

Alice looked up, shaking her head. "After watching the Admiral threaten to put Melita in jail to be raped by his guards, and then undress and grope her in her tent, I have no sympathy for him."

"Under Western law, the herbalist committed no crime as I understand the matter. Still, the situation leaves me feeling less than satisfied. I felt no charm for the medicine man, nor do I feel remorse for my role in the killing. The Admiral abuses anybody at his pleasure for sex or money. And it's clear his mind is wired into his physiology in ways ours are not."

Alice broadened the conversation, realizing anew how fortunate she was to have a fiancée interested in ideas. "More than one of my art professors held that the tribal cultures are on a path to modern aesthetic and analytic maturity and are not behind in terms of evolutionary time periods."

"What law of nature implies that evolution should reach similar wirings of mind from different nurtures and environments? Including perhaps random mutations!"

"True, even from the same cultural wiring, the Admiral was wired bad and the herbalist good."

"And both knew who was bad. I'll say an example of humanity's innate instinct of justice."

For both artist and professor, primary process surely juggled signifiers and symbols difficult to assimilate. Only time reveals the synthesis. And the time of the cosmos is, like most things, relative.

Alice blinked her eyes and ruffled her shaggy hair, kissed Philip and pushed back to lie down. "Our entire Pystead crew, even my parents in Florida, all are still targets. The U.N. will not forget about us!"

"True, I'm sure."

"Joan feels certain that K.L.J.H. Organism is—well, was—a

U.N. group because the spy drones they dropped on Campus were identical to the U.N.'s mini drones. She said that without U.N. support they could not have gotten aboard our topside at sea."

"Put aboard to keep our ship from fleeing so their battleship could shoot at a fixed target. Attempting to use our morality against us! My terrible experiences from Compton to Wheaton, U.S.A., then on Nevis have surely been backed by the U.N.'s dark money."

"Joan believes the U.N. keeps small nuclear bombs orbiting Mars. She will find and destroy any before our ships land there."

Philip stroked Alice's cheek. She looked beautiful, but also fragile. "Even on Mars we will not have escaped the Earthlings!"

"Because the U.N. attacked our ship, we will destroy any offensive weapons on Mars before landing. We can easily stop any attempt to rearm. We will be the vastly dominate power on Mars during our stay."

6

JUPITER LOOMING

Philip and Alice slept with inversion straps at the ready. They slept soundly, arm in arm. Philip woke early, wondering if he had dreamed. Then he remembered Alice's carry bag with champagne for their friends. "O Cosmos!"

Alice stirred. "Phil, what's wrong?"

"Merely thinking."

"Want to tell me your thoughts?"

"About our engagement party, perhaps too, pondering how in a void, a gap, one's morning musings may be spent in the clouds or in the pit, regardless of the anticipated day. Alice, I am concerned about our limited supply of champagne."

"Nectar of the gods, these days."

"Perhaps such nectar should be reserved until more of our friends are in a better mood to enjoy it?"

"Specifics?"

"Isaac in the hospital with a broken leg, Samantha's husband not yet rescued, your parents not yet aboard, the Wheel hiding in hostile waters, and ships Marianas and New Ionia with derring-do scheduled."

"Yes! Comte, Joan, Lois, Sasha, and many others must be in less than a festive mood with late pick-ups needed." Alice paused. "Are you suggesting we postpone the engagement party?"

"No, I'm wondering if we should save the champagne for the wedding—not serve it at the engagement party."

Alice sat up and put her arm around Philip. "You say some of my favorite things in bed."

❉ ❉ ❉

When Alice checked her Blue channel, she found bleak news. "My friend Sophie on Nevis was stripped and slapped around by three goons trying to find me. The U.N. has linked me with Charleston's art gallery. Sophie has asked to go with us. Sophie and Samantha's Albert will be rescued today or tomorrow. Isaac won't be off crutches for two months. Melita's brother, his horse, and his twin girlfriends are in an entry quarantine neighborhood for new arrivals, expected out in another twenty days." Then Alice gasped. "Oh, no! My parents' schedule has slipped again!" She said quietly, "I'm worried about them and you."

"Why about me?"

"Joan told me you will need to help rescue Rhonda because she knows only you."

"Ah, Alice, I'm at a loss to say why I should, or why I shouldn't, except I feel that each of us should do as much of our own work as feasible."

"Just thinking about a rescue is frightening. If Joan worried about you using your old kom on Nevis, why not worry about you going near the police again?"

"Jupiter isn't near Wheaton nor in Georgia. Jupiter is a moderately sized town in Florida—no big-city police department. Joan will use smoke and mirrors if needed. It's an ocean-front town, which is to our advantage for access."

"Promise me you will not take chances. You owe me that much."

"I do promise, wonderful Alice."

"I'm asking Joan to watch you closely because you have no experience."

"I helped rescue the boy, Norman, and Isaac!"

"Yes, the unexpected outing that got both of you shot, and Isaac almost killed."

"As you say Alice, we aren't all powerful, but we are dominant in limited encounters. I was hit wearing a half-Halo shirt and only bruised. I'll not take chances. I'll ask Joan if I should have a makeover to avoid facial recognition on the street."

⁂ ⁂ ⁂

Mid-morning the public address instructed each household to provision their quarters with food, water, and space sickness pills for a future three-day, isolated stay, and to remain in their neighborhood. "That was unexpected," said Alice. She looked and discovered their quarters were pre-provisioned for several weeks in isolation. They could relax, reading and listening to music.

The morning and the afternoon passed without news until Comte called on kom. A surveillance pod had delivered paid receipts to Rhonda and Earl for their train ride to Jupiter, Florida, with instructions to stand on Channel Street at six o'clock in front of Legal Drugs. There, Philip would meet them for dinner. Comte said the mission was rated at a low echelon for mortal danger and for a high probability of success.

Alice was shocked. "Granddad, no! What's the echelon for getting almost killed? Philip's not trained."

"He will be prepared. Joan is personally handling the rescue. He will be half-Halo and protected by guard pods, but not armed. His role is to be recognized by Rhonda, and to identify her and Earl."

"Granddad, we can't anticipate everything the police might do!"

"Joan is sending top pods, Halo guards, and backup foo fighters. Also, we have local resources such as tow-truck pods in the unexplored, underwater caves of Mexico's Yucatan Peninsula. Smoke and mirrors will be active."

Alice took Philip's hand. "Promise you will be careful."

"Of course I will, I promise." *We must get to Jupiter and back promptly!*

⁂ ⁂ ⁂

After an early dinner at their neighborhood galley, Alice proposed a visit to Isaac and Brian. "We should also visit Samantha because she and I are becoming friends."

"Oh?"

"She is interesting with tales to tell."

"No doubt."

"You might like to know that we have assigned roles for you?"

"How so?"

"I am your lover and best friend; she is your special platonic girlfriend."

"Sounds right. Should we visit Isaac first?" *Love those big blue eyes.*

"Let's try, and we ought to see the boy, Norman. He and Isaac ask about you. Without your help Isaac would have been killed, and the boy still a desperate orphan."

"I stumbled into helping them."

"And then you went out of your way, my man in full. Even the twelve-year-old knows that. At least in Jupiter you will have ready backup."

✳ ✳ ✳

That evening what seemed like any time of any day or night, Philip and Alice relaxed in their family room, pleased with the day's visits. Isaac was no longer in pain and would recover good use of his leg although physical therapy would last months. Samantha had cried at the thought of her husband, who had been found but not yet rescued. Philip and Alice had managed a quick visit to Melita's brother and his two girlfriends in another quarantine neighborhood. Alice observed that Frank reminded her of Isaac, a macho male with more than one girl.

"Oh?" was all Philip could think to say.

Alice squinted, looking away. *I shouldn't have mentioned Isaac. Phil must at least suspect.*

Alice turned to face Philip and took his hand. "I want to tell you about me and Isaac. Samantha told me about your dinner date with her at Lamancha House when you saw us together."

"That was before our time."

"I said goodbye to Isaac as a lover. I was already smitten with you."

"How did he respond?"

"We knew from the start we were only friends-plus, which has allowed us to remain friends. He always had two or three girls. He was kind to me, helped personally when I needed assistance, like the day you met him at the Co-op. Will you mind if we keep up with him socially?"

"It would be a loss if we didn't. Friends are not easy to find."

Alice kissed Phil sweetly. They rested in quarters, dividing their attention between reading and keeping an eye on Fednet postings. News that once would have churned the stomach now evoked only sympathy for the Earthlings. The U.N.'s Oceania Protectorate had declared all in-house business Networks to be dark sites and mandated their immediate closure. In-house Networks and secret societies of all types were forbidden. Even a chess club of over six members was required to register with the Protectorate, pay fees, announce all meetings, publish a list of attendance for each meeting and event, and report the names of all officers and event coordinators. Secret voting was not allowed. All money or benefits received had to be promptly reported. Harsh fines were listed for the merest technical infraction of a regulation.

We are getting out just in time. How did I get so last-minute lucky?

7

SEVEN COME ELEVEN

Joan returned Alice's call and reassured her that the mission would have backup forces, and that assets would be available from their secret cave base off Mexico. She promised half-Halo civilian clothes and a soft-pack helmet in Philip's shopping bag. Alice was placated although still concerned.

Philip sensed the rescue would be more dangerous than he had envisioned. *Still, Joan is not sending me to roll even a seven in the real world.*

Joan invited Alice to observe Philip's facial transformation. She sat and watched him receive a new nose and chin, both connected by a thin cord resembling a facial wrinkle concealed in makeup, ending in a finger grip under his shirt collar. One tug and Rhonda would see the face she expected. Alice accompanied Philip to the ready room and stayed for his final briefing on where to land and go to watch for Rhonda and Earl. Video of the street and restaurant were shown, as taken by surveillance pods since before Rhonda had known about the meeting. The location was on a peaceful commercial street. The plan was for Philip to leave a nearby hotel room rented by a friend and take a bus to the surf shop across the street from Legal Drugs where Rhonda and Earl were to stand. They would all walk a few city blocks to Peter's Steak House. Their pickup location was behind a row of tall shrubs bordering the walkway entry to Peter's.

The interior video of the steak house was enticing, and Philip said he would like to use their reservations and have dinner. Joan smiled and told him that would not be possible because the police already controlled the restaurant. She had wanted the police to discover his reservations for three, and they had. As they approached the restaurant, the three would slip through a gap in the hedges and disappear, picked up by a foo fighter Egg. Joan then called in the mission's pilot, Brad, and next the two support pilots and six Halo guards. Alice said she hoped they would not be needed. She kissed Philip and departed. Her grandfather was waiting for her.

⚹ ⚹ ⚹

Joan waved the pilots and the guards away and locked the door.

Not a good sign?

"Listen carefully, Philip. We have here your insurance policies covering a host of risks both known and unknown. Try this earpiece and let's get communications down. You have an open line to me with specialists listening." Joan's voice tensed, "We have seen Wheaton police on the street with facial recognition systems. The U.N. must think they are more reliable than Jupiter's police."

"When I went through Middle Georgia, the Wheaton police were working for that local and unidentified U.N. facility."

Joan agreed. Within the hour she briefed Philip for a third time and had him dressed half-Halo without gloves and with a straw sun hat. A collapsible half-Halo helmet and gloves were in his shopping bag. Joan gave him a second kom and went over a few hand and foot signs for good measure. Then she ran him physically through a few evasions and takedowns built on his kung fu lessons from long ago in California. She cautioned that both men and women could be very quick and strong. She said Brad would call for him and left the room.

Philip felt a surge of exhilaration lasting a few seconds before realizing he would be entering the States illegally. He sat thinking about the drone scanner Joan had mentioned being in Jupiter, although up the street at the restaurant. *The U.N. is involved because they were the source of the drone scanner on Nevis. Why not bring it here? Why not bring two or three?*

He stood, scratched his head, and tried his concealed microphone. "Joan?"

Joan answered and agreed the U.N. would bring in more gun carts at the last minute. She was confident that Philip was not vulnerable because Pystead was prepared for multiple drone scanners and gun carts. She explained that four top pods would cover the street for him. If a gun cart appeared it would be hit the moment its gun door moved.

"Okay."

"Otherwise, we want to avoid the use of lasers, especially from our flying security pods. Let's keep those a secret for our local rescues tomorrow."

"Fine. Assure Alice I will be careful."

✻　✻　✻

After a slow ride with lunch in a foo fighter, Brad dropped Philip behind shrubs near the water and he easily found his hotel room and bus schedule. An hour later he got off the bus near the Surf Atlantic shop on Channel Street. He felt surprisingly at ease, having heard so many good things about Jupiter during his Utrecht University days from fellow student Judy Hyatt, who had worked for an enzymes and bio-molecules research company with an office in Jupiter. *What can go awry? Surveillance pods have watched the area for days. The police are set to grab us inside the restaurant.*

During a quick visit to the surf shop, which was as much gift shop, Philip spotted a clear glass ornament larger than a navel orange, having an impressive array of interior bubbles. He counted seven large bubbles and eleven small bubbles. He bought it as a present for Alice and took it out in his shopping bag. *Hello Channel Street, hope this visit is short and sweet.*

Across the street in front of Legal Drugs no one was waiting. Philip glanced up and down the way. A few vehicles passed by and a few shoppers were out, but no one who could be Rhonda. *Window-shop,* he remembered his cover. Although not the best street for window shopping, Philip soon thought he had perfected the pattern of a casual male shopper who didn't miss the opportunity to ogle a passing woman. Finally, from a nearby door emerged a tall brunette wearing a loose white blouse and black slacks. *Rhonda?* He didn't move. *The right height, the right long hair, the right clothes and curves appropriately veiled. What's wrong? Where is Earl?* Philip remembered Joan's warning that anybody who looked like Rhonda or Earl, but of whom he was uncertain, was probably part of a trap.

Cosmos, she's too much a dinosaur! Rhonda's a giraffe. If a trap, they already have Rhonda and Earl.

He adjusted his straw hat. *Why did our surveillance pods not see this woman brought in? Ah, because the police were able to work around us using their own drone scanners! Must not forget that our pods are merely advanced drones. The U.N. surprised us on Nevis and destroyed two pods even though we ultimately prevailed. Lots of effort and unknowns here on both sides. Dumb luck could decide the day. O Cosmos, she's on the wrong side of the street. Rhonda was told precisely where to stand—clever of Joan!*

Philip paused to look in a display window at The Game Deck, advertising "Team with an expert." *No word from Brad on facial recognition. Surely we know the real Rhonda received the tickets? This one's hat brim shadows her face.* Philip thought of moving in her direction. *Can simply walk past.* His mind took a step, but his foot didn't follow. *No word yet on electromagnetic shielding, or weapons, or whether human or robot. Of course, Brad can't get a good scan if their drone scanner is covering me. I should walk away as if I have not recognized her. If their scanner follows me, Brad can get a clean scan. What if they have more than one scanner? It's probably up the street towards Peter's. Should know soon!* Philip walked slowly away, watching windows. Then it occurred to him that Rhonda should be watching for him as much as he was watching for her. The woman, however, was making herself seen, but not watching for anybody. He pushed his legs to the walkway, checking his fitness to sprint. *Cosmos! Rhonda and I exchanged kom addresses that evening I stopped at Earl's for supper. That kom link marked me. Rhonda is the bait. I'm the fish!* Philip moved past two stores before again pretending to window shop. He took another look around.

Almost across the street from the faux Rhonda, now stood another Rhonda, dressed in a modest yellow blouse and white slacks. *A giraffe! Don't look closely at either one.* A tightening gripped his stomach. *Two of them and no indication either has seen me. Are they both traps? The one across the street surely could be Rhonda, but they could have a gun on her. No, they have Earl.* Philip moved to the next shop window, showing swimsuits. *So I want a present for my girlfriend? That should be perfectly normal.* He stepped into the shop and stopped behind a rack of beachwear, covered his mouth, and whispered, "Jupiter Jack."

"Jackie here," answered Joan's voice.

"This must be a trap. The woman in front of our shop, wearing yellow and white, could be the real Rhonda, in trouble because Earl is not with her. The woman on my side in black and white is a lure or coincidence."

"We found only one drone scanner staying with you. Brad will send a pod to check the back end of the shop for Rhonda's handlers and Earl. We will confirm her facial scan as the woman who received the tickets. If she's the same person, we may have to shoot the woman on your side of the street who just scanned having a pistol. She should get a signal to shoot you, probably in the leg to take you alive. In your half-Halo a square hit could crack a bone. Stay alert. We should have an advantage because the police presence is focused on surprising us inside Peter's, confirmed by a surveillance rod we got in with a delivery. Let's concentrate on handling the faux Rhonda on your side. We'll try for tactics not using a pod's laser."

Philip clinched his teeth and turned for the faux Rhonda. His earpiece told him, "Check your kom and confirm if the man is Earl."

Philip gulped. "Looks like Earl."

"He's cuffed in the back end of our rendezvous shop, guarded by three Wheaton policemen. We may as well do the pickup behind there. If you can carry Earl that's the best way out."

After a few more steps, Joan's voice spoke, "When you are ready and near the woman in black and white, Brad will take out the police guarding Earl. They all scanned unshielded. Expect the faux Rhonda to draw. Your guard pod will hit her using a stun beam, but if that fails you should take her down. Let's keep pod lasers a secret. Don't turn your back on her until you have the purse."

Philip caught a breath, recalling the unexpected rescue at Lamancha House when he had been physically overpowered by his attacker and saved only at the last moment by a pod's laser. *She could be a female velociraptor!* "Joan, let's go with pod laser at the ready."

"On a hair trigger! Brad's scan was negative on beam shielding, and she isn't a robot, but she is carrying far too much steel in that purse. Be sure she doesn't fake a beam hit. If she shoots she's not going to miss. Take her purse."

Philip turned his head but watched intently. "Beside her in steps, hit them!" Four steps later, the faux Rhonda's right hand went for her purse. Philip pressed the tab that dropped a face-net beam shield from his sunhat. The woman jerked and crumpled straight down onto the street. He bent over. Her legs were quivering, muscles useless. *Can't fake that trembling.* He grabbed her purse and ran for Legal Drugs.

Philip approached the yellow Rhonda. "Follow me, Rhonda!"

"Who are you?"

"Face screen up and nose off," called Joan's rising voice in his earpiece.

Philip stopped on his left foot converting forward motion into a wild spin. He pulled off his hat and found the tab that ripped off his false chin and nose. He saw recognition in her expression. He held the shop door an extra moment just in case a guard pod was following.

They ran through the drug store making a mess, sending customers rushing for cover. At the door to the rear, Philip stopped with alarm and took a good look at Rhonda. *It is her!* In the back room, three policemen were lying on the floor. Earl was leaning against the rear wall. "Rhonda, you and Earl must do as I say and come with me before more police arrive. You will both have to stay with my company. Let's get Earl out of here." The old man was cuffed hand and foot. Philip held the captured purse and his shopping bag out to Rhonda. "Bring these."

"Avoid Dad's left wrist, it's cracked." Philip lifted Earl, who groaned.

"Rhonda, I'm taking you in an egg-shaped craft. Through the back door now. Get in and sit on the rear floor—move quick to let us follow. Listen for instructions from the air. Don't try to help unless asked."

"Okay."

"Be careful with that purse, there's a loaded pistol in it." Rhonda looked out the back door. Philip picked up Earl.

As Philip turned around, one of the policemen shifted, and Philip's face flashed and twitched, his head drooped with eyelids and lips trembling. Joan said in his earpiece, "We got him again, but he hit you in the face with a stun blast. If you can hold Earl, Rhonda can lead you out and we'll avoid using backup."

Philip never heard his pod's instructions to Rhonda, but as

she entered the room, a policeman got to his feet. He grabbed her bodice and jerked her forward. She screamed. Philip could not lift his head nor speak to be heard. There was a long pause in which nothing happened. Then came a terrible blast. Through twitching eyelids he saw that Rhonda was standing. He tried again to call his guard pod but could not utter a word.

"Philip, follow her," Joan called in his ear. Philip's hanging head soon found the policeman on the floor. Joan said, "Rhonda shot him."

Philip staggered, his head drooping with little control. Rhonda took his arm and tugged. "This way."

Joan's voice said confidently in Philip's earpiece, "Slow and easy will get you out on your own."

He got through the store's backdoor and glimpsed the Egg's door closing. The Egg craft moved as Joan's voice called loudly in his ear, "Drop to the ground—gun cart!"

Earl screamed when they hit the ground. A gun cart turned the corner a few stores away but blasted into the air and not at them. Philip tensed. A pod's air-voice told him, "Lift Earl into the Egg!"

Rhonda pulled with him. "Lift Dad…up, up, now this way."

Joan was in his earpiece, "Police are on the run from Peter's."

Cosmos, use our backup! Head drooping, Philip took a few steps carrying Earl, following Rhonda's pull.

"Push Dad through the door."

Philip pushed and Earl groaned horribly. Rhonda followed him in. Philip got one of his own legs through the foo's door. He pulled, but his head rolled, and he stopped for fear of twisting his neck.

Brad called from the pilot's seat, "Philip, need help?"

"I've got him," said Rhonda. She steadied his head and pulled him by the belt. With her assistance he got through the doorway.

The foo moved before Philip's left foot was in. Rhonda pulled again and he was all in.

✻ ✻ ✻

Philip held his neck with one hand. The craft's acceleration rolled him against the cabin wall. Earl groaned. A burst of ear-splitting pops ran across the hull. *We're hit.*

"Hold his head steady!" he heard Brad say.

We're flying.

Rhonda shifted on the floor to better cradle Philip's head and followed with a kiss to his forehead. She said, "You saved us. We love all of you! Don't bump Dad's left wrist."

Haven't any idea where. Rhonda steadied his head. At the next turn of the craft, his head swayed and she shifted to cradle it firmly between her breasts.

"Philip's neck is hurt," he heard Rhonda say loudly.

"Keep it from twisting," Brad told her.

Rhonda said firmly, "Philip, do not move!"

I'm moving?

In his earpiece Joan said, "You should begin recovery."

His eyelids were responding, and he realized he was drooling.

Brad told them, "We're away, no pursuit. Shouldn't have to toss you around again."

Philip let his eyes close. *Now more tingling than numb.* He focused all efforts on his neck.

Rhonda's hand steadied his head. "Don't try to move."

Getting better…no need to move. Soft my cushion. Philip tried to speak. "Joaaa?"

"I can hear you, Philip. You are sounding better."

"Tell Ali."

"Just did."

Philip felt that he might speak again. He swallowed hard and whispered, "Av pres ent."

"A seven-come-eleven whatnot."

"Oou hav tha gif."

"I have good video too. Now, we have learned from this adventure, but let's not share too much."

"Fin."

"Your voice is returning nicely. You might like to know that Comte has kept Alice company and mostly away from her kom." Then Joan asked, "Brad, any problems?"

"None for Ops. We need two medics on arrival."

"We'll be in the hangar. Philip, you should let me speak with Rhonda."

He managed weakly, "Stel cus."

"Copy. Rest and let Rhonda talk." Joan's cabin voice was speaking to Rhonda, but Philip rested without following the conversation. A minute later he realized his head was cradled between Rhonda's breasts.

"Jon!"

"Yes?"

"The vid o!"

"What video?"

"Gud."

"What are friends for?"

A touch of kindness.

PEACHES AND PEAHENS

Joan, Alice, and Samantha, all wearing medical facemasks, were waiting in the deployment hangar. Loudspeakers announced the arrival of Jupiter Jack. Crew in the vicinity put on their medical masks. With a pop of air pressure the end of the nearest launch tube swung open. A spray of water preceded the dull-silver, egg-shaped craft that seemed to fall out and catch itself before hitting the floor. Joan held Alice's arm to keep her in place. The craft floated over a few meters and came to rest on a shape-matched landing pad. Half a dozen suited crew were immediately at its door.

Philip backed out feet first under his own power with one hand steadying his head. Alice breathed a sigh of relief. Joan told her, "His neck is still weak. Help him keep it steady." She ran to him and, carefully, they embraced. A thin, old man was soon slid out the Egg's doorway onto a stretcher. Joan arrived beside Philip, and Alice moved to get a better view. One of the hangar crew had her hand out to help as a long leg in white slacks extended through the doorway. The woman slid herself out slowly and stood, holding her ripped, yellow blouse together. She was tall and gorgeous! A nurse helped her into a gray poncho and handed her a white medical mask. Rhonda kissed her father before a bubble canopy was closed over him, and he was carried away.

Rhonda said to all, "Thank you, everybody, for saving our lives."

Alice asked Joan, "How can such an elderly man have such a young daughter?"

"She was adopted at age seven."

My man in full didn't know why he should or shouldn't help rescue her!

Rhonda and Philip were shown a decontamination pad to step on, and the floor was sprayed where they had stepped exiting the Egg. Both were given eye masks and medical facemasks and sprayed all around. Once ready to travel, Rhonda looked around in disbelief. Philip and Samantha were also taking the opportunity to observe the crowded hangar space. Egg-shaped craft were stacked two-high in working docks with a panel of lights mounted at each station. Some craft were separated by clear wall shields. Flying pods and autonomous carts carried tools and personnel in white jumpsuits. The silver, white, and gray scene was ordered, busy, and eerie, taking Philip several seconds to identify its strangeness. *Too quiet for so much mechanical and human motion!* When a power wrench rattled nearby, both Philip and Samantha turned to look.

Philip had to catch his neck with a hand and told Joan, "My neck is still weak."

She called for a neck brace, then introduced herself to Rhonda and explained that since she and Earl had been in the custody of hostile police, they would have to be carefully screened before joining the crew. Philip assured Rhonda that was standard procedure, and the medical care top quality. Joan explained that after blood tests Rhonda would be able to have visitors from her quarantine neighborhood in her quarters, but when others visited, they would have to meet in a divided room for the next two weeks for screening to find any germs coming aboard ship.

Another medic arrived, and Philip was soon wearing a neck support collar. Joan, impressive in her white jumpsuit and red accessories, led Brad, copilot Mark, Philip, Alice, Samantha, and Rhonda to a small room for decontamination. Joan seated the men facing away from the women and brought out oxygen-eye masks and ear plugs. She got Rhonda's poncho off and all opened their tops and all zippers. A nurse arrived and closed the door. After three abrupt and drastic sucking changes of air pressure, the room filled with a disinfectant spray. They sat and stood for five minutes of pressure surges accompanied by soothing cello music before the spray was purged and oxygen masks removed. The medics had each person exhale strongly and blow their nose into a special mask. After closing their eyes for a final spray in the face, all refastened zippers and buttons and put on new medical masks.

Joan asked about Rhonda's torn blouse and sent her for evaluation. Rhonda called out a muffled, "We love you all." Joan told Brad and Philip their debriefing could wait.

Philip quietly asked Joan, "How did Rhonda shoot that cop through his vest?"

"She jammed the pistol under his belt."

"Ouch."

Joan reassured Philip, "We were only two seconds from using a pod's laser."

"How did the police get off shots at us while we were escaping?"

"Brad was two seconds from using the foo's laser. Rhonda pulled in your foot just in time."

"He let them shoot at us?"

"Not really, a half-second burst at best to hit."

"They did hit us!"

"One twelve-point-seven won't penetrate."

"So they get two in the same spot?"

"No way under the circumstances."

Philip grimaced.

"Brad was spinning the Egg."

Alice wiped her eyes. "This was more dangerous than I imagined."

"We were never in trouble," Philip assured her. "Neither the pod's lasers nor the backup guards were needed."

"Maybe they should have been!" *How do you call a neck brace no trouble? How do you call Rhonda a cook? She has a figure like that woman whom Sven dumped me for on Nevis.*

Alice took Philip's hand to go. Joan motioned to the remaining group. "Let's take a brief tour and hope for quick lab results on Earl and Rhonda." Brad offered to show all of them around. Alice stayed, and they all looked at an Egg with an entire end removed. Brad explained that it was being fitted with a projectile cannon and would lose its cargo space behind the pilot's seats. He added that most deployment hangars were located at an outer hull wall for short launch tubes. They stopped and two at the time sat inside an Egg for a good look at its instrument panel.

Joan checked her kom and exclaimed, "We've learned why our shielding scans were inaccurate for those three policemen guarding Earl. Rhonda had lotion on her chest from the hand of that policeman who jerked her by the blouse. It's like sunblock lotion, except for beam-gun frequencies. The police were only partially incapacitated, as was Philip with his own face and neck treated with a frequency block lotion."

✼　✼　✼

Once alone, Philip told his distraught fiancée that their guard pod's lasers were not used and remained a secret that would make next rescues safer, especially for Albert who was always guarded. Alice agreed that waiting to use the lasers was justified. Still, she was angry with Joan for sending Philip untrained, and upset with him for going. She was convinced that kom video at the proper times would have been sufficient for recognition. Philip did not contest the point. On the way to their apartment, Alice became moody, finding no pleasure in the concourse parks and rejecting dinner with friends even though the alert level was at its lowest, Green-Seven. Philip's suggestion that they find an old movie to watch only irritated her further.

"Phil, I love you dearly, but I need a nap. Would you be content to rest quietly, or would you rather explore the concourse?"

✼　✼　✼

Too hyper to rest, Philip walked to the little park where he had proposed to Alice the night before they boarded the ship, and where she had accepted for the second time. *At least I did it right the second time. Now she's unhappy?*

He walked on and came to the portal doors connecting the next ship, *Shandong-Nevis*. To his surprise just before the portal was a security station with two Halo-suited guards. They wore four chevrons on each sleeve, like sergeant's stripes of silver, blue, green, and gold. Philip looked again at the ceiling trim, five narrow stripes of gold. *There are four ships with fully trained crews, with one in the Pacific. Each chevron color must represent a Federation ship. Ours is gold.*

The portal crossing was consistent with his visit to the ship on the demonstration flight for recruits. He took three long steps to cross into the next ship. *With three hulls for each ship, our passage between ships has real length.* The new ship had a security station; the ceiling trim was one stripe of yellow and one of red. *Shouldn't get lost after learning the ceiling trims.* His curiosity led him to the security station. "May I ask why so much security at this lowest alert level?"

"We monitor the portal's status and can take emergency action to seal or open our hull door. We watch for anybody who might have left quarantine. That's all unless a robot or somebody goes berserk."

"Glad to know. Thanks."

✳ ✳ ✳

Philip stopped at the next small park and sat down. He thought a woman in the concourse looked familiar. She came over. "I'm surprised to meet you here, Philip. Is Alice visiting someone?"

"She's at home, Revathy, sad and resting."

"Melita is listed as Counselor for your ship. Her shipboard duty, when not needed. . . ."

Philip couldn't help a smile. "I know she can't be in two places at once."

"Most do not know. Who told you?"

"Joan."

"I thought Joan was fond of you! Opinions spread fast in our close social circle."

"I believe Alice is upset with Joan—please keep it quiet—for letting me go to Florida and help pick up an acquaintance."

"Philip, do we know each other well enough for confidences?"

"I'd say so."

"Alice feels that her first boyfriend on Nevis misled her and dropped her for a sexier woman. With the emergence of that Georgia peach you brought aboard, Alice could be a bit jealous—envious."

"Alice is as sexy as anybody!"

"A woman can easily feel outshone."

"I'd have never imagined that could be an issue."

"Just my guess. Lois is a good friend, and I happened to see her a few minutes ago. To change the topic, Philip, you didn't recognize me until I spoke, did you?"

"I wasn't sure. My facial recognition seems to be slipping. Too, I've only seen you a few times briefly without the facemask. Sitting beside you at our farewell dinner hardly counted as actually seeing to recognize you!"

"Do you like my sari?"

"Charming."

"It's one long piece of cloth, you know. I'm showing my tummy because I'm an older woman, now unmarried, and want to show that I'm in good shape."

Philip nodded.

"I'm not mourning the loss of Harinil, rather I'm celebrating in my favorite peacock decorated sari. Don't tell a soul, but Harinil hadn't touched me in over three months before he left."

"Count on me not to know."

"I've kept in shape, trying to compete with those models of his—did no good."

"You're a beautiful woman, Revathy."

She leaned close and whispered, "I want you to take me to the Eastern Philosophy Club next month. I need something more than teaching Indian and Asian history. I'll wear a risqué sari wrap for you."

"You could get me in trouble."

"Every now and then will get neither of us in trouble." She winked. "When we're retired you can unwrap me."

"What?"

"Alice hasn't told you! Well…it's not a sure thing."

"What?"

"We retire at age fifty-six if a qualified replacement is available from the younger generation."

"And?"

"And, your future grandfather-in-law has an idea that retired life should be quietly spiced up to maintain the energy and participation of the retired crew. By then, many may be unmarried like me. Close friends will be allowed intimate secrets, and those secrets will tend to keep them close."

"Well before then you should be happily married."

"Should old friends be forgot, and never unwrapped?" Revathy laughed. "Eastern Philosophy next month, please. Next month, Poseidon, I'll be more alluring and I'd like to see a smile on that handsome face." She waved goodbye with her fingers.

Alice told me spacetime would bring strange new variations on life! Already we have the mysterious grandfather Comte ever looking merely in his forties and wearing a king's ransom in gemstones. We have the alter personalities and duties of Joan-Melita. The extroverted Joan smothered by her overly possessive husband. The single Melita Rose, a palm reader believed to be a psychic. Samantha and Albert with a sometimes-open marriage. The reserved Lois, who I hardly know, except that on Campus she worried about Pystead having a future. Flirtatious artist Barbe with a figure like the third mermaid in Alice's painting—lots of sail for such a slim ship! And unexpected, my very own Alice who shared a casual lover with one or two other women during two of her three years on Nevis. According to her own worry and Melita's opinion, Alice has one or more unknown demons lurking in her subconscious process! Her ex-lover, Isaac, still a close friend and unexpectedly aboard ship! Revathy, a new personality now involving me. My very own, very small social circle has come aboard bearing a few variations on life!

As Revathy passed from view, Philip realized that his social circle must be as primed as any for strange new variations. *I don't want anybody unwrapping Alice!*

Philip sat for a few minutes before heading home, having given Alice an hour of solitude. If he did not intuitively ponder strange new variations of life one would be surprised, knowing of the unrelenting machinations of the mind's primary process. *Not only strange these future variations, but unknowable now according to theory in cognitive science. The human response in a future moment is not known until primary process decides its truth at that very moment. Could Comte's exceptionally long and varied life of experiences have revealed a truth about instinctive humanity? What of our little group of friends? Well, we must I suppose as Melita Rose often says, 'Wait and see!'*

DAYDREAMS

I asked him to give me an hour and never slept. Alice went to the pantry and looked through their food. *My friend Lois did this for us, our favorite vanilla-bean muffins from Nevis.* Alice took a bite and savored the taste. She looked again. *All the same flavor.*

Granddad says that after greenhouse crops we will again have some variety. Perhaps I'd like a chocolate chip, my former passion. What else would Phil choose? Oh my! Do I want him to have a raspberry, a…a…. what's wrong with me? A sweet peach! Would I love him enough? Could I love him more? Could he love me more? Would he love me enough? What is love?

Alice fled to the family room and sat on the sofa with a second muffin. *Come home to me, Phil. I need you. Oh Phil, I will stop being jealous, envious, beset with woe when all is well. I will not complain because you have become the real-world person we both wanted.*

Alice went to the countertop and checked her big-screen kom.

Her request returned: NO OVERVIEW VIDEO FOR OPS JUPITER JACK. "What?"

"Kom, call Commander Joan Windsor at her quarters."

Alice reached Joan, who asked if she was feeling better.

"I was, until I discovered the no-video for Jupiter Jack!"

"I'm sure Philip didn't want video of his drooling mouth and twitching eyelids. Rhonda didn't want video of her in a ripped blouse. There is video of Philip pretending to window-shop. You can find video of the beam-gun hits to the police and to Philip. Video of Philip carrying Earl. You will find video tabs in all sections of the report."

"I'm sorry for being angry. I suppose I'm not as real world as I'd like to think."

"Dear Alice, stay an artist. Keep yourself and Philip on the conceptual side of the real world."

"You would drop his Reserved-Line training?"

"Yes."

"Oh, Joan, I really can't ask that. He wants the Line as his cross training."

"I wouldn't accept him if he didn't."

"I know! When we became engaged for sure, he promised not to worry about my secret Cobalt Blue duties. I have faith in you and Phil, I'll do my best not to worry about his Reserved-Line training."

"He will experience what you did in training. Becoming an Egg pilot is the same for Line and Staff Commanders. He will become a more proficient foo fighter pilot. He will learn capabilities of the ship's systems and repair shops, and our exercise and maintenance schedules. Finally, our course on defensive strategy and tactics."

"Joan, I haven't mentioned potential retirement variations to Phil. Please stop flirting with him."

"Alice, you know Melita and I adore him, but we don't truly flirt. I want him to avoid Melita and socialize with me."

"I was upset about the rescue mission. Ignore my mood if it happens again."

"Dear Alice, Melita told me about the disappointment with your first boyfriend on Nevis. She said your insecurity was undue."

"I never confided even to Melita about my mistaken approach to boyfriends."

"Which could possibly be?"

"After three duplicitous boyfriends in graduate school, I have always chosen and seduced my boyfriend, especially Isaac."

"Your mistake?"

"Men you seduce don't give you confidence, or the thrill of being seduced."

Joan replied, "Good psychology, I'm sure."

"Even with Philip, I was insecure and set the scene, was easy for him. I will say that we had hours of perfect conversation before, and I knew of his vetting approval by Lois and Melita. I've been lucky with both Isaac and Philip."

"Alice, Philip asked for the full fidelity scans during in-processing on Campus, even though he was exempt because of your crew status and his brief relationship with you. Even so, he scanned committed to you in all dimensions of mind."

Alice smiled. "Joan, do you realize this is our first woman's chat in the three years we've know each other?"

"I do! Melita was always your best girlfriend. I never knew why."

"Subjective on my part. Melita is more…say, more a Shake-speare's 'hey, nonny-nonny' type."

"Alice, I grew up on a family farm in Romania. Only after Comte sent me to college in England did I see a few of Shake-speare's plays. The Tempest was my favorite."

"I suppose Melita offered an escape from my complexes, which I seem too have without naming them."

"I understand."

"Like you Joan, Philip is quite nitty-gritty and real-world even if he doesn't yet know it."

"I agree. And I'm pleased that you talked with me. Let's chat more often."

Alice's apartment door opened. "Must go, Phil's back, bye." *Now, hey, let me be that former fiancée, revived to sweet nonny-nonny.*

10
REALITY BITES

After a day of rest without intrusions from their outside world, Alice answered a kom call. Joan hesitated before telling her that Philip had impressed his duty Commander when he had assisted the Imaging Center on Campus.

"Oh, no!"

"For the sake of our children, we are double-checking security scans on a group of recruits. As much as I hate to say it, being Romanian, we cannot afford people who pass. We will live on the margins and do not need discontent driven by sociopaths as on Earth. Time is of the essence, Alice! We have two sick analysts and Commander Snyder requests Philip's assistance." Alice did not respond. Joan repeated, "Alice, for the sake of our children!"

"Please keep close tabs on him. I know protesters are being imported from Kitts, and your last report said the U.N. is staging military robots a mile beyond our west gate."

"All true, but no troops are deployed. Our intelligence is that they intend to block entrance or exit at Campus, not invade."

"I know we need the recruits. We also need a promising lineage of Saint Germaine!"

"A developing possibility for additional recruits, mostly women, and with needed talents is emerging. Help from friends at Technion Rehovot in Eilat should allow us to overcome the losses caused by obstruction in the United States. Still, the recruits already on Campus will be significant if they pass their vetting scans."

"For the sake of our children, I cannot refuse."

"I know your primary role, Alice, is to continue the lineage of Saint Germaine. Too, however, Pystead must succeed long-term."

"I'll get Philip."

⚹ ⚹ ⚹

Philip was impressed by the underground water tunnel that allowed arrival of his foo-Egg inside a Campus building without having ever taken to the air. His pilot explained that the U.N. was watching from sea level up. Pystead had realized when building the campus that the secret passage could become important. A one-car tram took Philip to the Admin Tank, the four-story, metal building standing on ten tall columns. It was an oval shape in profile, resembling a fat flying saucer. Philip descended the rather steep steps leading down to concourse level and the base of the tank's supporting columns. Comte met him at the large central column, and they took the stairs up, with Philip wondering why they had not used one the elevators in a perimeter column.

By midnight he needed a break and decided on a breath of fresh air. Joan caught him at the elevator and asked him to stay on the concourse level, wear a mask, and keep his kom set to his special

95

channel from his days on Charlestown's streets.

"Ah, nine-four-six. Why so cautious? What could realistically happen here?"

Joan was serious. "We don't know. We do know the U.N. is aggressively seeking details of our Plan B."

"How could anybody get this far on Campus?"

"We are not all powerful, Philip, and we have moved many defensive assets to our ships at sea. The K.LJ.H. Organism dropped mini-probes that were active for a time before we found them. We could have missed a few. Recall that we learned the hard way about compact drone scanners and gun toting ice cream carts. The world certainly has weapons unknown to us. Perhaps the U.N. has secret military robots?

"I'll remain alert."

"Do me a favor and stay under the tank. You can sit on the base of the Poseidon statue at the central column."

"Fine."

"I'm sending one of my surveillance rods to stay near you. You can talk directly to security and me on your nine-four-six kom channel, or via the rod."

"Alice asked that you personally watch me?" Joan nodded. "I'll stay alert and be quick."

"We need you with a clear head, don't rush."

⁂ ⁂ ⁂

Philip rested with eyes closed until his kom buzzed and announced unidentified activity outside the west gate. A moment later he tensed at the sound of sharp footsteps. A woman not wearing a facemask was headed for the steps up to campus level. *Not on Joan's watch list.* She disappeared over the top into a burst of red flashes and sharp metallic clashes. Philip was on his feet as his unseen rod announced hostile mini probes on the concourse. He stood, looking at the center column in front of him. His wrist kom's small screen flashed and he had a view of the west gate. Dark flying blurs filled the air above Pystead's fence. *Military robots!* Laser beam flashes hit and missed their targets. Philip sat down and watched Pystead's flying Serval robots dart about his concourse level, evidently biting and crushing hostile mini drones.

Then a large form appear from behind the center column. Philip moved, seeking cover behind the Poseidon statue, but a metal tentacle uncoiled in a flash and wrapped around his left leg. Instinctively he called, "Joan!"

Her voice reeled off, "Take the trident; it's a terrible swift sword." The tentacle pulled tight as Philip grasped the staff of the trident—he was being pulled, torn, forward.

The entire front of the robot's form opened. *A robot box for taking me…will pull me in or pull me apart.* The tentacle tightened. Philip lifted the trident, throwing his right arm forward to lower its blades. He was pulled slowly forward and went without resisting to maintain his balance. He could not avoid the monster's open belly, but he got the trident in first, catching the hinged side of the door. Sparks flew.

He pulled back on the staff as Joan said, "Strike the arm. Hit it." He swung the trident's blades against the tentacle and sparks flew with sharp pops. He pushed and cut deeply. The tentacle fell limp. "Keep the trident clear to your side and run for an elevator." He ran for a side column elevator escorted by two of their Serval robots.

As Philip rose to Admin level, he observed one Serval holding onto the big-box robot that had attacked him, and others circling, darting to bite something a few times before dropping it. *Those mini probes must be target-finders for the big one.* With a quick rocket blast the big-box robot began to roll. A second Serval took a bite of metal and held on. The robot's rockets fired again, but it was brought to a halt just before exploding into pieces. One piece of debris on the concourse looked familiar, and on second glance proved to be the body of a Serval—less its head.

Philip was tense, clenching the trident's staff. Joan's voice called, "Philip? Philip? Do you feel off balance, dizzy?"

"No."

"When the elevator door opens, place the end of the trident's staff into the sleeve on the cart. Be sure it is seated."

"Okay."

✳ ✳ ✳

Philip reassured Joan he was ready to return to work. She pointed to his leg. "My jumpsuit, even unenergized, cushioned the tentacle's grip. I'm okay. I'd like to know what happened to the woman who went up the steps."

"She was annoyed by small robots making noise and shooting red light beams. She was frightened, but never in danger. We stopped five of them at the fence. They were heavily armored and fast. Evidently their sole purpose is penetration and distraction. Lightweight without fuel for a return trip, without weapons or a self-destruct charge. Three got through to the Admin Tank. We have one undamaged. We had hoped to capture the big robot that attacked you, but it self-destructed. More lessons learned about the U.N."

Philip wanted to know how such a large robot had evaded their defenses. Joan explained that it had hopped the fence with the rush and appeared to be down ten seconds later when a guard pod arrived. It had, however, dropped its outer shell as a decoy and moved away resembling a one-car tram. Joan assumed that its look, its routing, and its apparent preferred target area were provided by spy drones released by the K.L.J.H. group. Disguised as a tram, the big robot passed two automated security checks before being spotted by a human analyst for using similarly textured balloons for both packages and a rider. The big robot had knocked down the first two Servals intercepting it.

"Was Alice watching?"

"Not continuously. Comte has been distracting her."

"On second thought, Joan, I'd like to sit for another minute before returning."

"Please have that leg checked."

Again, Philip sat on the base of the Poseidon statue, nervous, keeping eyes open. *Once near that box, you are taken or dead. I'm okay physically, may never again be of same mind. Guess I've learned the secret behind those impossible disappearances of decent politicians: they really happened. Learned that the hard way! Best get back upstairs because I don't have a handy leister. If the U.N. has video of that trident in action, they will surely put it on their must-have list. Of Pystead's smoke and mirrors that I've seen, it's the most unbelievable.*

11
OUT OF NEVIS

The ship's horns sounded a medium alert at four-fifteen in the morning. Philip sat up. He had slept less than two hours. Alice hopped out of bed saying, "Grey-Four alert." Her big screen kom posted a personal message from Joan that Comte was on Campus speaking with her parents. The public speakers announced ten minutes to strap in and secure children before their flight to Campus to evacuate crew and equipment.

Philip got up looking for his house slippers. Alice's Blue channel revealed that their ship and *Logos Key,* both Federation ships, and *Key Shandong-Nevis* were now separated from the Wheel and each other, submerged off the Atlantic side of Nevis, positioned for an early morning Campus evacuation. Trouble was not expected because police at the Campus gates were there to isolate the Campus and had neither the weapons nor numbers for an assault. No armored vehicles or big guns were within range of the Campus unless the battleship sent sixteen-inch shells rocketing across

Nevis. The alert was intended to avoid any surprise with most aboard still asleep.

Ship's motion became apparent. The big screen showed a view of the ocean from above, until it became a spot of rippling water in the moonlight. On video the three gray wedges breached the surface with water flowing across their top decks and off their sides. Key Bury surfaced first.

Seconds later the three ships rose and turned to the same direction. They felt acceleration lasting about five seconds. The video showed them just above the surface. Within a few minutes land and trees were seen ahead. In another five minutes deceleration pulled them forward into their seatbelts and the ship rose abruptly to clear the island's trees. A sharp deceleration and drop took their breath. A slight shudder of the entire ship brought them to a stop.

An announcement informed them their ship was on the back Campus lawn, and the other two ships would load at the sea docks. They were to remain seated with seatbelts fastened. Departure was expected within twenty minutes.

Philip asked Alice, "Could we get our friends in this group?"

"Your friends holding in Savannah will be late pick-ups, not done until after our Wheel ship departs from the Moon. Only those rescued locally, like Samantha's husband and artist Sophie, will be aboard the Admin Tank when it abandons Campus to join us."

"Why not all now?"

Alice's big eyes tensed. "Once we are back at sea, the Admin Tank will join us and be carried under the Wheel, but not now. Joan says that when we move the Tank or make distant rescues the U.N. will intervene."

"Maybe the Tank can't submerge?"

"Phil, there's no word on Blue about that terrible Admiral Telaobade dying."

"He must be dead or dying, but the U.N. will not announce his death, or even his illness, during a deployment. The use of Kitt's police to isolate our Campus, instead of U.N. troops, probably means the Admiral is not involved. His marines are evidently left floating offshore while the Security Council debates a course of action."

The public address announced, "We have surprised the U.N. and have no opposition to boarding. Please remain seated for departure in fifteen minutes." Alice and Philip waited quietly.

Kom video showed their huge ship from above, reaching within a few meters of fence to fence on the back campus lawn. Three cargo-bay doors were down. People walking quickly emerged from the back campus trees. Watching the flow was captivating. There followed two bulldozers, ditch diggers, dump trucks, and a tractor-mounted crane. Then a dozen or so boxes were loaded. The cargo-bay doors rose from the ground and closed.

"Our cargo will be secured for travel within five minutes. Remain seated for departure."

✷　✷　✷

The return flight was not dramatic. Within ten minutes a flood of water over the ship ended their video. *Back to the safety of the deep.*

Alice was apprehensive. "Granddad hasn't called about my parents!" She waited silently, close to tears until Comte called with the news that Joanne and Jeffrey were not aboard. Due to a quarantine imposed on all tourists entering Kitts-Nevis, their travel plans had been cancelled. They would await pick up in Kissimmee, Florida.

A subsequent announcement to all ships explained that three ships had recovered Campus personnel and equipment, and the seven ships from the old fish farm would rejoin as the Wheel and remain submerged in the Atlantic Ocean off Nevis at a depth of three hundred thirty meters, maintaining communications silence, with no loud noise made in quarters.

Philip thought out loud, "We are surely living in a gap of space-time, but not as bad as waiting to be brought aboard."

Alice nodded, tears in her eyes. *My parents have endured so many delayed and cancelled moves over the years—now this!* "Are you worried, Phil?"

"I'm glad to be escaping my time served on Earth. More annoyed by the alerts and announcements than worried."

"Consider them part of the training you missed on Campus."

"You're right. Much that's said is surely on-the-job training."

The ship's speakers gave further instructions. "All personnel, you have eight minutes to move about in quarters, but be seated again by five-twenty to receive aboard our final arrivals from Campus."

✳ ✳ ✳

Their video soon displayed a view of the administration building on Campus, the Tank, and then panned around for the view out to sea. As they watched, five spherical objects glowing on their bottoms were approaching the island, flying only a few meters above the water. Within seconds they spread around the tank structure, each hovering near a different support column. "Alice, I suppose the glowing circles are propulsion drives like our ship's main engine-drives?" She nodded. One of the elevator support columns fell away to the outside, and a glowing orb slipped into place under the tank just as the large clear column took a bounce off the surrounding berm and landed on top of the red stairwell cover. The end of that column was still sliding down the walkway cover when a second column fell. Before either column ceased motion, two more columns dropped. The engine-drives slipped into positions and the tank building rose. The fifth and last glowing orb moved into the center-position. Without hesitation the fat tank shot away over the ocean.

The video feed turned back to show the ocean from above where a dark patch of water was clarifying itself to delineated edges. Water flowed over those edges as a disk breached the surface and moved up: all seven of their local ships were assembled. Audio announced, "Our Wheel ship is five meters above surface swells. All is proceeding according to plan. The Campus administration building, the Tank, is arriving to abandon Campus. We will hold position and extend a cargo ramp to transfer personnel and light equipment from the tank. Please be seated for the transfer and for our departure from Earth to follow."

"We are leaving my parents for a very late pick-up!" Alice shook her head.

A flashing message in red appeared at the top of their video: THREE FIGHTER JETS ARE INTERCEPTING THE FLIGHT OF THE ADMIN TANK.

"Oh no!" shrieked Alice.

Philip tried to assure her that the Tank was defended. *Of course she knows that.*

She gasped. "The Tank doesn't have an armored hull like our ships. Just one missile hit could kill people even if the Tank would survive. With Comte, Lois, Rao, and so many recruits aboard."

Another line of red posted: U.N. FIGHTER JETS HAVE LOCKED TARGETING RADAR ON THE TANK.

Alice looked away. Philip tried to calm her. "Joan told me we could win small battles to escape from Earth." He put his arm around her. "I'm sure the Tank is well defended."

"Phil, you should read about robots attacking the Campus last night. Some got all the way to outside Admin."

Philip kept a straight face. "That means we will be on high alert today." He pointed to their kom screen. "Look at the post. Our foo fighters are escorting the Tank." Philip was himself reassured because only the three hostile jets could be seen on video. "Joan once told me that the U.N. has old, slow, fighter bombers." He looked again and tensed at the jets: stealth fighters, but not Arrowheads. "Those jets aren't old fighter bombers."

The three jets turned in different directions and red laser beams shot past them. Suddenly, two foo fighters uncloaked. The attacking jets could only fly by them and shoot their rockets at the Tank.

Alice covered her eyes, and Philip's stomach knotted even as lasers fired from the foos. The attacking jets twisted into turns, but they were not the targets. The red beams methodically picked off the attacking rockets, which were small and fast but not taking evasive action. Then the foos turned to intercept the jets as they were coming around for another pass. This time the jet's rockets were shot at the visible foo fighters. Red laser beams from the foos missed the rockets and hit the jets. Philip remained tense. The foo fighters, however, simply slipped out of harm's way and again matched the sky in color, seen vaguely as sky-blue blurs on video if you knew what to look for. The attacking jets turned away and soon one parachute was seen.

"Oh no!" cried Alice. Two attacking rockets were on course for the Tank. Alice opened her eyes just as laser beams from the Tank hit them.

"It's over," concluded Philip.

Alice struck the countertop with her palm. "The U.N.'s suspicions about us have been confirmed with our lasers used against their pirates at sea, against their gun cart and passenger drones on Nevis, against Admiral Telaobade's guards at Melita's house and their robots attacking Campus. As well as our beam weapons used in Jupiter. Now, after losing at least one fighter, the U.N. might pretend their rogue admiral is still alive and find a way for him to get his hands on a nuclear missile."

Philip reminded her, "We don't know that Telaobade is alive."

"Long ago Joan told me that our surveillance pods spotted a double in uniform for Admiral Telaobade. They can attack our ship with a nuclear weapon and claim a rogue admiral did it out of concern for humanity. Then they can demonstrate their virtue to the world by trying him for the crime and executing his double."

"If the Admiral be dead, the execution would simply be faked and his body shown."

* * *

A public address urged everyone to fasten seatbelts as sensations of movement became apparent. Their video showed the hovering Tank tremble and begin to fall, but only pieces of a bottom shell dropped. Next, a cargo ramp began extending out from the Wheel and the Tank moved slowly toward its end. As the tank ship almost touched the ramp, a cargo door slid open and the ramp entered the opening. The two ships held steady with the Wheel's cargo ramp sloping up to the Tank. People and equipment flowed out and down the ramp.

What technology holds these massive structures stable? I must talk to Vanderhought for more details on our aether energy of spacetime, and field-resonance drives for propulsion.

Their video view changed every minute or so, but the two ships held positions until the flow of humanity and material seemed routine. In ten minutes the loading ceased as abruptly as it had begun.

Their video moved to a side view of the huge Wheel ship, which rose higher above the water with its motion almost imperceptible to Alice and Philip. The Tank slipped beneath the Wheel and soon looked steady in an off-center location. Philip asked, "Why carried off center?"

"It shouldn't block our center opening. I don't know why."

The scene froze. Text and audio explained that pods providing the video were recalled to the ship along with foo fighters patrolling the perimeter. Good news followed: the Tank was secure under the Wheel. Although it obstructed main engines, its five smaller engines significantly compensated.

"It will take a while of Line training for me to learn as much as you already know, Alice. There's so much to learn about this ship even without the highly technical details."

Alice was pleased to explain, "We are under powered but still fast because our water tanks are not full."

⚹ ⚹ ⚹

The alert horns sounded one long, shrill, rising whoop, waited, repeated, and waited before the third and last piercing tone. The expected calm voice declared a top alert, a White-One that was not a drill. There followed reassurance that the alert status was a prophylactic measure due to potentially hostile armed forces. The voice instructed everybody to remain in quarters. The big concourse and rim doors between ships were being closed. Soon, neighborhoods, lifts and stairwells between decks would be sealed. Everybody not assigned to a duty station was to remain seated with restraints fastened and listen for further directions.

A soprano-register carillon ring was followed by a serious female voice warning all persons that their seats must-must-must be turned to face the wall having the two stripes of ceiling trim, and seats must be locked in that position. The speaker emphasized that these were must-do instructions, not advisory. She said that anybody in a bed must be secured under its net with the back of their head toward the two ceiling lines. An adult should be seated near each small child. Once properly oriented, she said that seat-belts and bed nets were to be kept fastened as their angle of flight would rise to seventy degrees.

"My goodness," Alice exclaimed.

The announcement continued with another voice explaining that the ship would fly east over the Atlantic for fifteen minutes, flying low to avoid radar and flying slow because the Wheel was not aerodynamically streamlined without all nine keys assembled, and the grips holding the Tank were not designed for supersonic flight. Should more speed become necessary, the Wheel and the unmanned Tank would disconnect and fly separately—an unlikely scenario.

The couple relaxed. Philip observed, "This venture has become a true adventure!"

"The worst is yet to come. We must prepare for zero gravity with no training. My stomach does okay, Phil, but don't be surprised if yours doesn't."

"Do you have a pill for me?"

"No. I think we need to know who gets sick and how sick."

"Wonderful, I've always been a fan of the experimental method."

"If the sickness is terrible, the medics will give you a shot."

"Why not a pill?"

"Oh Phil, once the stomach gets sick it shuts down and a pill does no good."

"Thanks for the warning." *Being sick as a dog should complete my Earthly experiences as a despised canine.*

Through the next announcement, they learned that the Wheel would be launching in opposition to Earth's rotation over the open ocean from a low latitude. This for the first time for Pystead or any other launch, as all before had gone with the Earth's rotation to gain that little extra momentum. By using this unexpected flight pattern, Pystead hoped to avoid a continuous radar track, since the tracking station that should expect them last would be first. "In any case, with our technology," said a casual voice, "we have the propulsion power and fuel to launch however we please. We will fly into space as a plane flies to altitude instead of being sent up like a rocket on a ballistic path. We can change direction and speed at will. Even if Earth sees us, the authorities may not believe their own radar. Even if they believe it, we do not know of any missile capable of catching us at altitude. If it could, we would shoot it down. You should rest easy, and if wearing your seatbelt facing the correct wall, or away from it in bed, you will enjoy the ride out on your back and not on your head. That is all."

That's why the beds can rotate ninety degrees! "Alice, if we are going to steep angles, do you think Char Cat will be able to hang on?"

"Oh no!" Alice was up and calling Char. She admitted, "I never completed the course on cat care aboard ship. I'm so ashamed. I must finish it tomorrow."

They pushed a reluctant Char Cat into his pet pod. Philip took Alice's hand and pulled for her to come back to the alert chair. "All's well. This living aboard ship will require effort. We must learn and remind each other of new ways until they become routine."

"Granddad believes you will do well in space."

"Good. Did you secure the two latches on your side of the beast box?"

"Yes. Please speak kindly about Char. He loves you too. Did he scratch you just now?"

"No, he is nice to me. My old indifference to pets has waned. I'm fond of Char."

"Good, we'll keep you!" Alice smiled, pushed her eyes wide open, and arched her back. *This pose always melts him. My strange attractor pose, I believe he would say.*

Alice's kom rang. She called, "Granddad, are my parents here?"

"No, Jeffrey and Joanne are still in Kissimmee. During the day, like typical vacationers, they are lost among thousands at one of the local theme parks. Do not worry, Marianas Key will pick them up even if they must add an alien-invasion event."

"I hoped they would be a local pickup, but I feel better with them lost in crowds."

"Philip, your cousin and your invited friends from Compton are all holding in Savannah. Foo fighter Eggs will collect them for New Ionia Key now submerged off the coast of Georgia."

"Thanks, Comte."

✳ ✳ ✳

Philip and Alice almost relaxed sitting in the presence of their night-and-day, split-faced, old twenty-four-hour analog clock. After what seemed like a long wait, the Wheel reversed direction and flew from east to west, increasing altitude and speed. An announcement pointed out that they would not circle the Earth for a last look because of potential hostile actions using hypersonic missiles, given recent preparations for the arrival of E.T.s to meet with the United Nations.

Philip thought aloud, "Must be an indirect way of saying the U.N. is onto our ability for orbiting and is using the pretext of E.T.s as cover to try and hit us with a satellite killer missile. Our complete departure from Earth should come as a surprise?"

"We hope so."

"We have employed far too much martial capability to be allowed liberty. We could attract followers and expand as an unknown and hidden entity. We might even think of ourselves as avenging angels."

Alice nodded. *He's real world enough for the Line.* "I'll get treats for us and Char."

"You have five minutes before seat belts."

"Almost nine."

"Let's save contingency time. I'll watch the clock."

Alice sighed. *Why anxious in this flight of hope? Careful thought must inform the heart on journeys through life. In many and various transits the heart may find peace, surely aboard our magnificent spaceship of vetted and self-selecting humanity.*

✶ ✶ ✶

Really, what isn't mysterious? Pystead learned to use the aether energy that pervades spacetime, learned to convert that energy into a resonance field that can push or pull against the fabric of space itself. Still, Pystead cannot explain what is happening in mathematical or physical terms. Even the well-known magnetic fields are mysterious. Do they take up space; do they have weight? If not, how are they material things? If crossed magnetic fields do not break through each other is that an indication of something being physically present—somewhere? What is any field besides spooky action at a distance? Why does the movement of electrons here create a magnetic field over there? How can a magnetic field exert force on certain elements, moving them if not restrained, in a way that increases the density of the field? Pystead's scientists believe an analogy may hold for different densities of aether energy flow occurring throughout spacetime as a function of the distribution of mass in spacetime.

Philip shut his eyes. *Vanderhought thinks the intersecting volumes of space density around masses result in a force of attraction entraining the masses along with their spheroids of aether-energy density that is the fabric of spacetime. He believes that a dense spacetime creates shorter physical distances than a less dense spacetime, changing the wavelength of light in different densities of spacetime. Who's to say?*

How little I know. What is light, energy, mass? How does energy curl up and become mass? How can mass exist and vibrate in magnetic, electric, and temperature fields without having to consume energy to do work to stay curled up and stable? Well, Vanderhought did say an aether energy field pervades the cosmos, structures the cosmos, is spacetime, and is absorbed by mass to power its quantum agitations. Might not the pervasive neutrinos result from imperfect absorption as well as unstable quanta? He thinks that directional adsorption of aether energy creates a directional force on mass, producing local gravity in the direction of the local flow of the aether field. Regardless, aether energy explains our ship's unlimited supply of energy!

Philip checked the time. "Alice, two minutes until seated, please."

Cosmos, what explains Poseidon's trident? Pystead's advanced technology is worth killing to have. The U.N. doesn't want us to work for them. They want our secrets and us dead. They would torture to the death anybody who might be able to reveal a Pystead secret. Tesla was lucky, dead without being tortured. Somebody knew he kept his scientific papers in his apartment, and that was enough in those bygone days.

⁂ ⁂ ⁂

"Phil, we need to check on our inexperienced friends. A duty of the established crew. Granddad has drilled me on procedures and policy for years. We should do a group chat on kom."

Philip agreed and Alice made the call. Samantha said she had thought the talk about living on Mars was an exaggeration. Her husband, Albert, just rescued, replied, "Had you been kidnapped because of your services to a predatory monopoly and enemy of the people's happiness, you might think of Mars as being too close for comfort." Isaac and Brian agreed, with Brian saying that by merely being a security guard at a hotel he had become a target of the U.N. Philip asked about Norman. Isaac assured him that the boy had friends his age, including the boy, Bau-Tu, coerced into being a Cupid and rescued on Nevis along with his mother.

Isaac added, "I want to adopt Norman once I've recovered."

Alice smiled to herself, leaning back in her seat. *I didn't make a mistake with Isaac as a lover or as a decent human being.*

Earl was heard in a weak voice, "Must be the same folks that got me."

Rhonda spoke up, "I'm a single woman. What am I going to do, marry a Martian?"

Alice called out that there was a balance of men and women aboard ship, and she would not have to accept the first man who asked her out. The vetting process selected attractive and healthy people to facilitate matchmaking and procreation for all among their small and unchanging group of pilgrims—one of the world's problems left behind.

Alice's artist friends from Nevis raised no questions.

Alice reminded the group, "For now, everybody, we must fasten seatbelts and keep seats locked facing the ceiling trim as announced, and those in beds facing opposite. Is anybody not facing in the correct direction?"

❊ ❊ ❊

Alice wiped away a tear. "Phil, we just must have a final view of beautiful Earth. Also I want to see it as that pale-blue-dot I've heard so much about."

"We will have to do our homework on distances out for viewing. The view at marble size is enchanting. The pale blue dot is vanishingly tiny and doesn't resemble the Earth. In any case, we could have great views of the Earth and Moon. Surely the Council will have planned for that?"

"Let's have a looking-back party! We'll need a poem to go with our last, close-up view of Earth. We'll need the enchanting scene and fond thoughts to warm our hearts for a lasting memory."

Philip nodded.

"Oh Phil, there are dangers to crewmembers still on Earth. Joan told me a year ago that the U.N.'s intelligence agency was improving rapidly and investigating suspected business relationships and families of a suspected crewmember. The U.N. could still identify and arrest crew not yet onboard, like my parents! How could anybody survive emotionally with a family member left behind. I know our two ships in the Pacific Ocean will pick up stragglers and rescue others. My parents have guard pods. Pystead used pods at Lamancha House, but the U.N. found and destroyed two of them! A pod could lead the U.N. to its owner!"

"Joan learned about the U.N.'s very compact pod scanners. And our technology has great advantages, like modern fighter jets against the propeller fighters of World War II. Don't worry."

"If I were in Kissimmee, would you worry about me?"

"Okay, don't over worry. I'm sure pods no longer follow close enough to be associated with a crewmember. *Cosmos, this world of Earthlings deserves a good leaving alone. Too few decent types in positions of power, and populations not abstract thinking enough to distinguish boldface lies from reality. And the decent types are being reduced to marginal existences of hard work without meaningful voting rights. Applications engineers, truck drivers, medical doctors, accountants— most replaced by computer algorithms. Managers and lawyers replaced by alien artificial intelligences for maintaining without progress. We must escape the Earthlings as a whole! Truly, we are the elect.*

✴ ✴ ✴

At five minutes after six in the morning of the tenth of June, a Monday in the year twenty fifty-two, a chime sounded, and the floor began rotating. The ship surged forward and upward until their inner ears felt they were going straight up. "We shall never pass this way again. Phil, I'm so sad." A long arc of the sky blue and cloud white sphere could be seen on video.

The alert horns played a melodious carillon song ending on a wavering, mellow note. Subsequently, a female voice said, "Our ship's calendar begins today, our Day One out of Earth. Please remain in quarters and resume normal activity, but do be careful in our one-fourth gravity."

"What now is normal?" mused Philip.

Before they were out of their seats, the General Manager's familiar bell rang and he exclaimed, "We are in space! We are pilgrims! Now we begin our own way of life. May we be strong and help each other. May our way bring us peace and prosperity."

Philip stood slowly. He bent over and kissed Alice on top of her head. "I have resumed normal activities."

"You're sweet."
"We can let Char Cat out of his box. Where are my house slippers?"
"You are a natural-born spaceman."
"Every man has his niche."

12

THE FLIP

Alice smiled sweetly before reminding Philip that the floor latch on each furniture leg needed to be checked. He said, "All latches were set before we came aboard. Doesn't that display on kom?"

"Yes, but please double-check them while I prepare breakfast. The kom's opinion will be of no consolation if the sofa lands on top of us when we flip about."

"You remind me of an announcement."

"We must put all loose items in the drawers and latch them. Let's strap down the champagne. It already has foam separators around each bottle."

"Aye, aye." Upon finishing his appointed tasks, Philip discovered that Alice had hung a painting in the loo, Vermeer's *Girl with a Pearl Earring*. He told her it was exotic, especially in the loo.

"Good, it should spice up our small parties. Note the tantalizing reflections of light on her lips and the shine on her earring. Not to mention her alluring glance, don't you think? In its day not recognized as a great work, but it was expensive to paint with the head scarf's rich blue pigment of lapis lazuli, and the red lips' pigment from an insect. Vermeer thought it worthy expensive paints. We have another copy of *Earring* in Pystead's art collection. I'll try to find the name of the South American insect for the art gallery's plaque."

"Yes, that source of red pigment is best not shared with our guests if we want a party atmosphere!"

⚵ ⚵ ⚵

Pystead had devised a new calendar. Day one began at midnight before departure, preserving the evening and the morning as the first day. Days out were to be counted without the use of weeks or months until reaching Mars. Once on Mars, maintaining sixty seconds to the hour would not be practical because the day would be longer. On Mars, 98.96 seconds would be added to each hour, with Mars seconds lengthened as Mars flicks rather than seconds. Also significant, alternative duty shifts of other than eight hours were proposed by many. On Mars, time keeping could be debated and alternative duty shifts tried by individual ships.

Robbie's bell sounded. A familiar but less-than-mellow voice said, "Hello pilgrims, this is Manager Robbie Markwaters speaking. Please give me your attention."

He's no longer just plain Robbie now that the newest crewmembers and their families are aboard.

"We will stop on the Moon to recover pre-positioned supplies of lead, electrical cables, and fiberglass pipes. We will use these and other materials to build a radiation shield until our water tanks are filled. Too, we want to linger until Marianas and New Ionia keys have completed their pick-up missions and departed the Earth. On Pluto we will fill our outer shell tanks with a half-meter of water for increased radiation shielding all around. We now have all our water in the hull sections between us and the Sun. After leaving the Moon we will install electromagnetic shields to protect the entire ship en route. Also, on the Moon we will pick up a few more decoy packs; each pack opens to visually resemble our ship and to replicate our radar signature. We have not anticipated specific needs for these decoys, but we do feel better having them."

Again, Robbie rang his bell. "Everybody, your close attention is required to prepare for our upcoming orbiting of the Moon about six o'clock this evening. You must remain in quarters and be prepared to strap in at the appointed time. Furniture latches must be secured to floor or wall. Utensils, loose items, and pet pods must remain secured. Precautions are necessary because we must cease acceleration and rotate the ship top to bottom so that we can decelerate for landing while maintaining gravity through the floor. Your floor and ceiling will change positions—so must you. The problem is that you will be weightless for up to thirty minutes. Also, when announced, each person and pet should take the appropriate pill for space-sickness."

Again, Alice knew more. "It's unfortunate that this first rotation of the ship, this first flip, must be taken slowly. As one assembled structure, we have no experience with the maneuver. The trained crew outside the flight deck have many things to accomplish: covering or draining watering troughs and ponds that the livestock use, securing each animal for inversion, securing the hanging gardens, stopping the leak irrigation of the farms and parks, The ship's kitchens, laboratories, recycling facilities, and hospitals all have low gravity and inversion issues. Our kitchen and home appliances have low gravity problems which you must read about for us. Now that we have used cups and dishes, even though light plastic, we need to put them inside the cabinets. Imagine our quarters upside down with loose things floating all about, especially liquids. We must prepare!

Robbie's voice returned and talked about the issues Alice had mentioned., with the usual precautions on timing and requesting assistance. Then he added, "After rotation of the ship is completed, listen carefully for instructions pertaining to orbiting and landing. That's all for now."

Philip was pleased that preparing for the rotation was almost like preparing for departure. Alice said the Manager had decided to wait until all were better trained before withholding sickness pills, and then from only one ship at the time, allowing help personnel from all ships to be available. She suggested that Philip eat and drink little in hopes of minimizing any sickness. She wanted him to rest and compose a poem for their looking-back party, which should provide both a visual and a poetic memory.

A new voice on the speakers, without any preceding tone, interrupted their thoughts. *Key Bury's* Manager Asif spoke, advising everybody to study the alert levels and their restrictions. This was of particular importance for families with young children because one could get stranded on the wrong side of a sealed pressure door during an alert. Asif pointed out that as the alert level became more critical, indicated by smaller numbers and higher tones, the ship would be sealed into smaller and smaller environmental zones. The physical zones of the ship, he said, were important for services such as food, water, medical care, and seatbelts. He asked that each person learn the fundamental structure of shipboard life as soon as possible. Reading while strapped in would be a good use of one's time.

Next up was ship's rotation, the flip, which would occur half-way to the Moon. Since trained personnel were limited, everybody was asked not to call for physical assistance until absolutely neces-sary. Their orbits of the Moon would feel gravity free and sickness pills should be taken at the announced time because the pills did not help once sick.

Alice added, "We have several hours of normalcy before Char goes back in for the flip at about six hours since leaving Earth."

✼   ✼   ✼

The alert horns sounded at noon. Manager Asif was solemn in telling the pilgrims to take their space-sickness pills immediately, remembering their pets. He said that during the zero-gravity period the ship would rotate, interchanging ceiling and floor positions. Heads would then be positioned away from the Moon. At that point they would still be moving fast and would begin deceleration producing low gravity, and finally circle the Moon in microgravity too weak to notice. During and after landing, low gravity would return, and everybody could move about in quarters for an hour while the pre-positioned supplies were loaded aboard.

In minutes Asif returned, loudly, "Now hear this! Deceleration begins in ten minutes. Find your places and strap in!"

As a group we are already living a new variation on life by liv-ing through the constant training we were cut short of on Earth. Not counting that we are now hunted rather than simply oppressed. Alice and long-time crew have lived with this highly disciplined and risky variation on life for years, many for decades. Confined in circumscribed communities on a small campus or aboard a large ship. What of us new crewmembers?

Without alert tones a Grey-Four alert level was announced with no explanation or further instructions. Alice explained that Grey-Four suspended normal public activities, and doctor's offices were closed except for the emergency clinics. Under Grey-Four, pressure doors were closed to the sector level, meaning that the two or three ships with door's open to each other were environmentally isolated from the other ships. Families should stay together and place pets in their pet pods when the family was out of quarters. Alice said there were no horns or instructions because the alert was for trained crew only.

Philip double-checked the cat's pet pod and their kitchen and bathroom appliances. Alice checked their chairs and told Philip that all their chairbacks could be raised to serve as alert chairs, although most apartments had only three extra alert chairs. Philip responded, "Good to know." *I'd say that random choice of apartments we were told about was from a subset of special apartments. We must be configured and supplied to assist others and to host Alice's meetings for her art-gallery staff.*

The alert horn sounded a mellow note, apparently declaring the beginning of deceleration. Within seconds Philip felt the returning gravity. "I'm not likely to get sick orbiting. I did alright on the demonstration flight off Campus," he told Alice.

"That lasted a few minutes. This will be longer now, and hours when orbiting the Moon. We will not let the Moon Base see our aircraft like flight capability nor our normal acceleration. We are showing only one-quarter power on this flight to the Moon."

They sat and waited, thinking it strange to exchange head and foot positions without sensing the change. Philip's stomach was feeling a bit unsettled before the flip was completed with floors oriented toward the Moon. Deceleration began, bringing a return of varying gravity for acquisition of a high orbit. Thereafter followed no gravity in high and low orbits. Those feeling completely well, their speaker's voice suggested, should try floating about.

"My stomach is still good, Phil. I'll try a float in the hall."

"I'll go with you and hope for the best. Then I'll use the last five hours of orbiting to sleep. Don't think I can concentrate to read about the ship."

"Alice tenderly caressed his back. "Oh my, you were working on Campus almost all of last night."

13

LOOKING BACK

Mellow carillon music played as the Wheel landed on the Moon near pre-positioned supplies, out of sight of the U.N.'s Moon Base and on the cusp of illumination. Philip regretted that neither his cousin nor friends from Compton were aboard. He asked Alice if she could invite Rhonda's father and Samantha's husband to the looking-back party. "Earl is frail and in the hospital for his wrist. Albert has extended medical observation because he was held captive by the U.N. The five artists and their two men are still in quarantine, but can attend in jumpsuits since all passed the blood and other tests. They with Samantha and Rhonda will make the party." Alice felt the warmth of Philip's expression and turned away for a sly smile. *I get credit for including the Georgia peach, in a bulky jumpsuit.*

The couple ate a one a.m. snack. Alice opened a kom line to her invited friends who were soon buzzing with questions about the three days of rations they were to pack for the party. Alice was the expert. She explained that the food was for an emergency in which they might be in a space sealed off from sources of food and water. After all, the ship was very much still in the vicinity of hostile Earthlings. All agreed on bringing a sandwich for day one. Alice suggested a can of irradiated meat for day two, plus one of the flat packets of shriveled-up, hard, twisted-looking, freeze-dried spinach—for which she had run processing machines at their campus on Nevis. Alice said to take a hot water injection bottle in case their observation lounge had not been serviced. She recommended the freeze-dried chicken and rice for day three, with perhaps a freeze-dried lemon pudding and another injection bottle. For a snack or dessert, freeze-dried strawberries could be eaten directly out of the pouch and were delicious. She was taking four pouches of drinking water per person, plus a packet of juice. She cautioned that a pill for space sickness should be taken now, and three extra pills packed. Then the artists raised questions about the jumpsuit. Even as new arrivals, each had received a full jumpsuit, sticky soles, and a portable cooler. Alice explained that the sticky soles would hold lightly to the soft walking strips in the corridors and allow easy walking in low or no gravity. She would talk about the jumpsuits as they walked.

The apparent privilege enjoyed by the partygoers concerned Philip until he recalled Joan saying that somebody had to be first even among equals. *Why not have good purpose a selection factor? We are learning from Alice on this excursion. And I'm learning that life in space is not the picnic most imagine—even in this ship advanced well beyond Earth's little rocket ships. At least there's no worry of rats or lice, of polluted water or tainted food. What is our worry, my worry? The unknown! The loss of our natural life support, agoraphobia? Life with a missing dimension, different for each of us. I'll beat two apparent psychological issues, cabin fever and claustrophobia. Yet, is my sense of this surreal ship and the void beyond a fear of being lost in vastness, kenophobia or astrophobia? Perhaps cognitive science has taught me too many phobias? Is it likely that some or most of us will develop some complex psychic disorder? O Cosmos! Both cognitive science and Melita Rose agree that we must wait and see on the personal as well as the group level. The realities of this new life are slowly dawning on me, and I suppose on each new crewmember. I've never had longer working hours and less sleep! A variation on life that should end once the Earthlings are left behind.*

Ship's Manager and Pilot, Asif, announced on speakers that everyone must remain in quarters and be prepared to strap in for departure within forty minutes. He notified Alice by kom that the art galleries were to remain closed regardless of alert level until reliably normal conditions returned. She was glad to have the official word and relayed the message to her staff. She posted a notice on the Networks with links to virtual tours. Then she and Philip rested with Char Cat. At one-thirty Alice told the partygoers to meet in ten minutes at door A connecting their Neighborhood 1 with number 2, wearing full jumpsuits, unenergized.

This is life in a new city, not knowing your way around even in your neighborhood. Philip took Alice's hand. *Alice is not privileged in having this party. She and most of the trained crew have lived eviscerated and dangerous lives for years or decades to make possible our chance for a new beginning. She earned the right to this party.*

They met the others and headed for the viewport lounge. Alice told the three single artists that Issac, a kind and interesting man, was getting out of the hospital in a few weeks, about the time they would be out of quarantine. It became apparent to Philip that none of the artists suspected that Isaac and Alice had been long-time lovers on Nevis. Samantha, who had once seen Alice with Isaac at Lamancha House, said not a word.

We know as little about each other as about our neighborhood and ship.

Alice used the map on her kom to lead the partygoers down the empty corridors and lifts. She explained the features of the half-Halo jumpsuit and how to access the tabs that energized the suit and those that deployed the helmet. Critically, how to pressurize the suit to avoid the bends if caught in a decompression situation. She stressed that the jumpsuit was an indoor spacesuit because it did not have layers of radiation shielding as did a Halo suit. Within a few minutes they reached the bottom deck. Alice soon found their destination, the Wally Schirra viewport—for their final up-close look at their planet of birth. A single large round port, now closed, was set in the center of the space. Two rows of segmented handrails ringed the port. Alice was pleased to see a large kom screen on two of the walls, although she knew the plan was to have a viewport look at the Earth and Moon.

From his demonstration flight as a recruit, Philip knew the handrails were to assist those standing for the best view. High-backed chairs were latched to the raised platform around the perimeter wall of the room. A few other people were already seated.

Alice asked Philip to sit or stand at the end of their little group to see everyone when reciting his poem. *I'll sit at his side and buffer him from the sweet Peach.* Two families and one more adult joined the small assembly. Alice told her group to keep their koms ready to take video, and they went to stand at the handrails for a close-up view of the luna surface when the viewport cover opened.

"I must warn you," Alice said quietly to her friends, "we will have a serious alert if the Moon Base begins unpacking its outside pod containing a nuclear warhead. Our surveillance pods are watching it."

After a moment's thought, Sophie asked, "If they shoot a missile at us when we leave, wouldn't we be safer in our quarters with more shielding from radiation beneath us?"

A crewmember with another group answered, "We wouldn't know where the warhead might explode, and a few more decks of shielding are little help. One of our remote-controlled Eggs will get in front of any missile and create a magnetic field to mimic proximity to our ship, hopefully allowing any missile to signal Moon Base of an impact detonation, which would probably destroy the entire Wheel."

While her friends fidgeted at the handrails, Alice remained calm. She told them, "I have to look back at beautiful Earth. My granddad says any missile shot at us will be too small to see until it explodes, and that if we see the explosion the ship will survive. If any explosion or the sun would be too bright for direct observation, our viewport covers will close and we will have video. We should concentrate on our last close look at our magnificent, glowing, blue-and-white orb."

Philip added, "Surely, we would be remiss as human beings not to look back. Haven't we all bonded with the beauty of our Earthly sphere, the O."

⁂ ⁂ ⁂

The two wall screens showed outside crew in white Halo suits with golden helmet visors pulling camouflage coverings off boxes and bundles of long, gray pipe. The flying tank from Campus, formerly their administration building, had separated from the Wheel and landed beside them. The crew loaded supplies into both the Wheel and the Tank. The gray pipe and large, thin sheets of lead in plastic frames were flown up by pod power and secured on top of the Wheel.

Their video panned up to show drones overhead. The public address identified them as surveillance drones from the Moon Base and said that Pystead would not interfere with them. Alice's little group returned to their seats.

By two twenty-five, later than scheduled, all the pre-positioned supplies were loaded, and their video ended. They would fly across the illuminated surface of the Moon before positioning the Wheel for a look back at the illuminated Earth. Nothing remained for their *Marianas* and *New Ionia* ships to retrieve. The U.N. was intended to believe they had seen the last of The Pystead Group. Until, of course, *Key Marianas* backed up by *New Ionia* began their blitz of final pick-up operations on Earth.

Once flying, the viewport cover retracted, and all the viewport guests went to the handrails. To Alice and Philip, the gray terrain slipping below was surreal—sometimes smooth, mostly rough. Each moment both different and the same, with each prominent surface feature followed across the viewport by turning heads.

"Of what we are seeing, any frame could be a modern painting," Alice mused aloud.

"Yes, I've seen the single-color canvases called fine art," said Philip.

"An orbit of the Moon could be shown as an installation run on a continuous loop, but what else to add?"

"Well, Alice, we don't make sound passing over."

"Perhaps an installation video would show supply packages rising?"

"A fine scene. The most surreal thing here is the unseen thing—us."

"Yes, silently above in a titanic ship. The fascination of the scene is in our head, not in its images. Truly like too much of our contemporary art."

"Our minds can replay the same construct of meaning with each new pass."

"Oh, yes, look at the continuity of form and color, paralleling culture. With the scene now and then adding an unexpected feature, the modernist would ask how more brilliantly could an installation portray an event, progress, or a problem."

"I understand the construct but cannot feel it."

Their small group returned to the seats. Alice said quietly to her friends, "Philip has a poem."

I'm not a poet yet have this command performance. He stood. "Now see, the orb glows brightly white and blue. / Remember season's changing leaves and glow. / And feel the trod of foot on earth and snow. / Recount the wonders winds and rains can do. / Did hear your pets and songbirds singing true? / Did smell far surf on morning airs that blow. / Did taste fine fancy cakes with milk and joe. / In mind and body Earthly things are you."

Alice said, "We must hold in our hearts this joy and our positive stories from Earth."

Philip continued, "So hide awhile the deserts, ghosts, and fears. / Let scenes and loves recalled full warm thy heart. / Sense still the power of mighty Earth—when near. / Yet know the power brought that you impart. / Your blood, the magnum opus of that sphere. /

Your charge, a sacred trust to reach the stars!" He breathed deeply.

They sat thinking back through time, wiping moist eyes. Philip took his fiancée's hand. He gazed into her eyes. *Her orbs are Earthly white and blue, my children I do hope for you.* He wiped his own eyes. *For the children we certainly do have a sacred duty to reach a suitable star system and planet.*

⁂ ⁂ ⁂

The room's speakers intruded. "Pilgrims, we are departing the Moon. Video is available on all Networks—our last direct and close-up view of the Earth and Moon."

All the guests returned to the viewport. Alice told her group to hold the railing with both hands and stand with feet apart and knees slightly bent. She lamented, "My granddad told me that we go for ourselves never to return. Surely, our distant descendants will want to visit." Philip covered Alice's hand with his, and she placed a hand on Barbe's hand; the link spread with the motion of the liftoff.

Again via the room's speakers, "There is no activity at the U.N.'s Moon Base. We will pause above the surface and secure the Tank while we have a good last view of the illuminated Earth."

The view was grand and for ten minutes they smiled and wiped their eyes. Then the ship moved and they were soon above the dark surface with the Moon's horizon in sunlight. Within seconds the dark side of the Moon became a shadowed, blank form with its horizon seen against the stars. The viewport's cover closed.

A crewmember from another group called, "We should take a seat and fasten our seatbelts."

"Thanks," replied Alice.

* * *

Within a few minutes their chatting was cut short by a soft, but shrill rising whoop pervading the room, followed by a voice declaring a White-One alert. "We are being tracked by radar from the dark side of the Moon."

Alice had everyone put on gloves and helmets and energize their jumpsuits, but not pressurize them. The room's three pressure doors clanked shut with motors whining softly as they sealed airtight. They all sat uneasily, locked in.

Then came a report, "A missile has been fired at us from the dark side of the Moon. Remain calm!"

Philip squeezed Alice's hand and felt a heaviness in his stomach. No one spoke or moved, but heads shook and most breathed deeply. Alice's wrist kom rang and she put it on speaker. Comte asked if everybody had three days of rations. "Be calm," he said. "We have deployed a decoy pack that we are now outdistancing in line with the Moon's radar beam. Moon Base is now tracking the decoy and not our ship. We are capable of twelve times the acceleration they have ever seen us have!"

Ship's acceleration was immediately felt. Their video showed a close-up of the approaching missile having three large, solid-state booster rockets almost obscuring the center warhead. Flying nearby were three of Pystead's large pods and two Egg craft. Speakers noted that the Wheel was accelerating with its topside in the direction of travel and could release the Tank between the Wheel and the incoming missile if necessary.

Before anybody spoke, the alert horns sounded shrill staccato tones and acceleration jolted them, reminding Philip of his very first ride to Alice's apartment in her foo fighter Egg. Their video display blinked and continued. In the next moment a bright blue dot flashed inside a yellow dot, both vanishing in the instant. A surge of acceleration pushed them against seatbacks. The ship rotated as if thrown to one side and the acceleration continued even as the public speakers sounded mellow tones and said damage reports would be received within seconds.

Philip whispered to Alice, "This is my kind of adventure. Disconcerting, tense, but not horrifying, not like having toughs surround you and your family." *Speed is courage, especially when one's chance of being hit is miniscule.*

"Phil, this is real life and death, not a metaverse adventure."

The viewport cover slid open and they all peered into the starry cosmos, brighter than seen from Earth. Ship's acceleration changed and began nudging them sideways in their seats. The speakers announced that a five-megaton atomic bomb from a dark-side missile base had been fired at them, but was detonated at a safe distance. The Wheel had managed to get clear of the Moon Base's radar beam, and probably had escaped optical observation as well. Even if they were still optically tracked, Earth should believe that Pystead's personnel were fatally dosed with radiation and the ship out of control. Some of the lead panels that had been carried topside from the Moon had been released and scattered using still attached lifting pods, to be interpreted as debris from the ship. And a few lead panels were being sent directly at the radar's source to interfere with tracking if not end it. Earth's orbiting research telescope was not in position to search for them, and they were for a while shielded from Earth's asteroid tracking telescopes by the Moon itself.

The public address voice changed the topic, announcing that pressure doors were opening and any sick person should be reported. The ship was now spiraling away from the Moon at constant speed as if uncontrolled. There would be no gravity until they set course for Pluto. Anyone unsure how their stomach would react should take a space-sickness pill every twenty-four hours. Philip shook his head. "Pretending to be dead is certainly a new variation on life. I'm afraid our stay on Mars will not be peaceful."

Alice stood, deenergized her suit, and removed her gloves. She pulled Philip aside to look at her secret kom channel. The Moon Base had used a never disclosed missile site on the dark side of the Moon, which Pystead's infrared scans had not detected. The missile had closed at high speed because it used three asteroid interceptor rockets. Pystead had lost one decoy wheel, four guard pods, and two autonomous Eggs. The danger to their ship and crew at the distance detonated came from the x-ray and gamma ray bursts, and measurements revealed only acceptable levels of radiation received at any one Geiger counter location. The blast had been well over forty kilometers away, and its radiated heat-flash had not damaged the hull. Alice's Blue channel promised updates.

✻ ✻ ✻

Alice told her friends, "We must get back to quarters. Don't forget your coolers and gloves." A buzzer at the viewport sounded. They turned to see Sun beams glaring through, obscuring Earth and stars.

"Let's go, we have manuals to read." Alice led the little group. The single artists, Sophie, Barbe, and Colette walked arm-in-arm. Alice whispered to Philip that she was concerned about her parents and Philip's cousin and friends not yet aboard.

Philip agreed conditions were not ideal. "Marianas has another ship assisting. If we are waiting for Marianas and consort, shouldn't be more than a few days before all is known?" *And Cosmos help us if the news is bad.*

Rhonda suddenly gasped and scream, "They're going to kill us! They're already on Mars waiting to shoot again. They can use their super-fast artificial intelligence talked about so much to outthink us! Our escape from Earth was not enough. How can we survive?" Alice rushed over to hug Rhonda and reassure her that Pystead would be much more powerful on Mars than the U.N. That Pystead had artificial intelligence as powerful and fast as anybody's. Alice assured her little party that Pystead had the resources for their defense and future comfortable lives. Before reaching their neighborhood, Rhonda was calm, walking with Philip, while Alice walked with Samantha.

14

DRIFTING

Alice and Philip slept until noon and went for an early dinner. The public address sounded a melodic chime, followed by three rings of the familiar bell. "Hello pilgrims, we have a preliminary damage report. All seven ships of the Wheel and their critical systems have passed physical inspections and testing algorithms. Any equipment problems found later will be minor. As for personnel, no sickness has been reported. We will have a final report within a few days; thereafter only any D-N-A damage should remain unknown."

After a long moment of silence, Robbie said, "Although our destination is Mars, we are taking a roundabout route by way of far-off Pluto. We intend to avoid being found until just before reaching Mars. We want to begin monitoring the U.N.'s Mars Station with probes before they know of our arrival. We hope to intercept communications that will give us a hint of the U.N.'s intentions and capabilities on Mars.

"Another thing to know! The Wheel is not under power and is

continuing at its constant, low speed, hence without gravity, and not in the direction of Pluto or Mars. We have turned our narrow side, our sheer, to the Moon, and we detect no radar. Even if a telescope has found us, the U.N. should conclude that we are adrift and irreparably damaged, not proceeding in any expected direction of travel. Also, we must install radiation shielding for the Wheel. That work is best done at constant velocity and in sunlight. The ship is designed so that our hull thickness and linings plus almost full tanks of water provide protection against the high radiation that pervades all of space. Our stores of water surround us in two perimeter hull tanks that are created between our three enclosing pressure hulls. On Earth we were protected by a combination of the Earth's magnetic field and its atmosphere, especially by Earth's atmospheric ozone layer. Until we reach Pluto and fill our water tanks, we will need to install a strong magnetic field around the ship to compensate for having too little water. We will also install thin lead panels under the magnetic field at critical locations to catch radiation that penetrates the magnetic shield. Secondary emissions from the lead will not be as strong as the incident radiation. Video of the outside work will be broadcast." He paused before adding, "This evening, pilgrims, I hope each of you can appreciate and celebrate your escape from the vast majority of the Earth's military might."

The next day after breakfast, Robbie asked everyone to think of drifting as a time to relax and learn the neighborhoods and ships, a first step towards returning to a familiar way of life. Once powered flight resumed, the flips that allowed them to produce the effect of gravity would return. Schedules would then resume with five days of work and school and two days of rest. New crewmembers would begin on-the-job training.

Philip asked Alice if she had set a date for their engagement party.

"I need to ask our event consultant about possibilities."

✱ ✱ ✱

Two days passed before Alice and Philip donned their jumpsuits to visit friends in quarantine. Alice imagined she would be met with a range of emotions from them. Philip was reminded again of her personal dedication to the wellbeing of the new pilgrims.

"Alice, did you ever have a seminal intuition or dream? After all, you have already spoken for your mother on a decision of major importance."

"No, but the morning after the battleship's attack I felt quite positive lounging around, almost like one of your lapses into daydreaming."

"This is a bittersweet moment for me—cheered at having won the fight, yet bitter over the attack and the inevitable hardships of remaining prepared to fight again another day. Too, the problems of living healthy in low gravity are unresolved."

"Phil, please be positive about prospects. Our scientists are working on a technology of local gravity to replace the need of continuously accelerating, flipping, and then decelerating." She kissed his cheek. "Let's visit our quarantined friends."

Because Philip and Alice were wearing jumpsuits and on oxygen they were allowed in their friends' quarantined quarters. Their helmets were designed to allow speaking, and Philip spoke to everyone, trying to accept moods and keep the moments simple. He avoided Samantha and Rhonda, except to become better acquainted with Samantha's husband, Albert, and Rhonda's father,

Earl. Each man seemed to be recovering both physically and emotionally from his abuse at the hands of police. Philip empathized, as he was still recovering from his own fears inflicted by Wheaton's police in Middle Georgia. The three men agreed they had left Earth none too soon.

The women were apprehensive, already concerned about living and having children in a low gravity and high radiation environment. Recognizing their worries as warranted, Alice urged confidence that Pystead's scientists would find a practical remedy. *I'm sure there is One Above who cares for Pystead. Needed dreams will continue! Are not Comte's huge gemstones and the diadem signs given?* She reminded her friends that quarantine would end in about two weeks, and the single women could decide if they wanted to continue living together or each have her own efficiency unit. Alice felt the visit had relieved anxieties when friends thanked her and Philip with handshakes and hugs for their visit beyond the quarantine screen.

The couple headed for decontamination to clean their jumpsuits. *Okay, okay, what is decontamination chasing?* Philip kept the thought to himself, deciding he didn't know enough to question a medical policy.

❉ ❉ ❉

On the way home Alice wanted to have lunch at an unfamiliar galley. They found savory entrées not available in their local galleys. "Variety is the spice of life," she said. The tables were crowded, and conversations overheard, revealing worries about settling on Mars now that the U.N. had demonstrated its hatred of Pystead even beyond the Earth.

Walking back to their apartment, Philip expressed surprise that he had not overheard anyone mention the practical problems of living on Mars, such as loss of bone mass resulting from a long stay in low gravity. Alice agreed, turning to her own preoccupation. "Every aspect of having a child on Mars is a serious problem because of low gravity. The male's sperm is affected, men produce too many male babies. Babies carried in low gravity do not develop properly. Children raised in low gravity do not develop properly. Our only solution at present is flying forever in our ships with three flips per day, allowing us to have full gravity at what is considered a safe top speed."

Philip raised his eyebrows. "I have assumed from what Vanderhought told me about our aether-energy engines producing a measurable amount of local gravity, that Pystead had a practical solution for producing artificial gravity other than continuously accelerating or decelerating about a median speed."

"Oh Phil, our scientists do have ideas based on those engine-drive findings, but no equipment design nor manufacturing process. They are working on a gravity mat as our top technological priority."

"Perhaps we continuously fly and flip around the red planet, keeping watch on farming domes below?"

"I'm confident that one of our scientists will have an idea leading to a gravity mat. Why should our helpful dreams get us here to lead debilitating lives? I'm sure One Above who cares is still immanent in our lives."

✻　✻　✻

The couple rested arm-in-arm and fell asleep. When Philip woke, he lay pondering their situation. Alice was already up and decided,

"Phil, I want us to visit the three art galleries in this key. Do you know that our neighborhood is the one located at the tip of the ship? We have the Wheel's primary flight deck at top."

"I thought so, deduced from my two trips up."

"Ours is the only neighborhood from the tip out. There are four amid-ship neighborhoods, each half width of the ship. Then come three adjacent neighborhoods around the outer rim. There is only one deck level at the very outer rim, outer perimeter. It's as high as it is wide. It's high outer wall can serve as a full gravity floor if we must ever spin for gravity in an emergency. Evidently, our present drifting will not last long enough for the trouble required to move hospitals, kitchens, and such to the rim, and to reconfigure living quarters from their floors to walls."

"I have assumed that the hull areas of the neighborhoods vary because the number of decks decreases towards the outer rim."

"Yes, the neighborhoods all have about the same number of apartments and people. Each neighborhood has one of the ship's main engines and its own environmental systems and emergency facilities for food, water, and medical care."

"I do like knowing about the ship. I'm probably a good fit for Reserved Line."

"I agree, and Joan agrees." *Though I'm a bit concerned about the extracurricular treats her training might cover. Oh my! If Joan's husband weren't so possessive, she would flirt less. Phil loves me. Why be overly possessive? What is married love freed from present cultural norms? I certainly want all his children and only his children! And all his time and help while raising our children. Yet have we instincts to help friends in need? All seems right for a retirement culture of sweet nonny-nonny in the sweet bye-and-bye.*

Alice spoke to her wrist kom. "List directions to the three art galleries in this ship." She smiled for Philip. "After our work in the two antiquarian galleries, we can see the modern art before returning home."

"Perhaps mermaid Amanda can teach me Poseidon's secrets for no gravity?"

"Probably."

⚥   ⚥   ⚥

Next morning their video showed the work beginning on the hull to install the radiation shield for the ship. Crew in bulky Halo suits that were also outside spacesuits, were exiting via the personnel doors in the two abrupt rises of the hull. Each crewmember was tethered by a line and wearing a Zoom Pack for use in the event he or she became separated from the ship and needed powered flight to return. Security cables had already been installed across the hull to work locations. The crew moved their tethers along the cable until reaching the bundles of fiberglass pipe that had been picked up on the Moon. A pod was secured to each end of a pipe and it was flown to a crewmember waiting at a pole location. Looking closely, Philip could see a port in the hull that slid back to create a holding slot for the bottom of the tall pipe. From the port the crewmember pulled up an electrical receptacle and pushed it into a recessed plug inside the pole—electrical power was connected. With over two hundred poles remaining to be set, Philip and Alice headed to their nearest galley for a hot breakfast.

Their daily routine became established: eating, tending Char Cat, changing art gallery displays, watching video of the outside work, reading appliance manuals, chatting with friends via kom or during a meal, and calling Amanda. Her techniques for low gravity proved a spice added to lovemaking, and the couple went to bed early to get enough sleep.

⚹ ⚹ ⚹

They watched video to catch each phase of the work. A half-man high, bee-hive shaped coil of cable was plugged in and secured atop each pole. But there was more. The large, thin sheets of lead in plastic frames were attached half-way up many of the poles, and a magnetic tipped plastic brace swung down to hold to the hull.

Two days later, Alice and Philip were talking by kom with Rhonda and Earl during the final installation of lead panels. Earl said they must be in the ugliest spaceship ever built because it looked like a junkyard.

Alice told Rhonda, "Quarantine ends soon. You will met people and have parties! We will have chamber music and stage plays."

The couple and their new friends joined a kom chat to witness the energizing of the Wheel's new electro-magnetic shield. After the last crewmember reentered the ship, a switch would be thrown in each of the fifty-six neighborhoods of the seven-of-nine Wheel, providing power to all hull areas of the shield. Red lights glowed atop the energized poles, and within a second or two all were glowing. An unidentified voice announced that a red light indicated that a pole's magnetic field was detected. Alice reassured her friends they were fully protected from radiation and a normal social life would return within a couple of weeks. "We want each of you to visit our apartment for a dinner party with wine."

She gave Philip a kiss. "Socials with our old friends will be limited for a while. As established crew, we must host small socials to introduce neighbors and promote entertainment venues. We will include the children." She stood and went to their bedroom. "We will have another day or so of no gravity and your wife would like them with a man in full."

15

OUTWARD BOUND

On day seven out of Earth the Wheel accelerated at one g-force on a course for distant Pluto. Lois Hensson introduced herself as Commandant of Administration and began her briefing. On-the-job training would begin for new crewmembers according to schedules sent by kom. Orientation meetings with tours of the ship would be provided separately for family members. Lois asked each individual to acknowledge receipt of the schedule and ask any relevant questions.

"It's becoming apparent this is no cruise ship," Philip told Alice.

"Oh, it is a cruise ship!"

"How so?"

"We have the amenities of a cruise ship bound for some exotic destination!"

"That much is almost true."

Alice smiled and ran her fingers through his hair. "The difference, Poseidon, is that we are the staff and not the paying guests, but let's keep that thought to ourselves."

After six days of powered flight with the added inconvenience of unscheduled flips timed to provide full gravity for a medical procedure or some manufacturing activity, and with no signs of an alien presence, including Earthlings, Commandant Lois declared a Wheel-wide extra day of rest. The next morning Ship *Bury's* pilot and manager, Commander Asif, announced that the Wheel's daily flips would be executed more quickly since the crews of all ships were experienced. The flips, as Asif called them, would occur every twelve hours until they reached the orbit of Mars. The flips would allow good gravity to be maintained through the floor as the ship accelerated and decelerated above and below their median speed.

Asif added for those interested that the Wheel would arrive at the orbit of Mars with no forward speed to allow time to prepare for transit across the asteroid belt between Mars and Jupiter. They would send two probes ahead to lead the way, one at twenty-four hours lead, and the other at eight hours. Then the Wheel would rise above the solar plane of the asteroids and follow the two probes. Going around the asteroids would be much safer than going through them. Their transit above the asteroid belt would take thirty days. The final leg from Jupiter's orbit would bring them to Pluto by day sixty-five out of Earth, assuming their anticipated median speed of two-and-a-half percent sol included a brief period of sustained five percent sol, as a trial for their future interstellar flight.

"As planned," said Asif, "we have released communications pods to provide directionally misleading communicating links to our ships Marianas and New Ionia—they know to ignore them. A satellite was left orbiting our Moon as a distraction and will surely be found and destroyed. Another communications satellite, small, smooth, and nonreflecting, will be difficult to find. It's following the Earth at L-5. We will continue on to Pluto upon receiving word that Marianas and New Ionia are out of Earth, beyond the Moon, undamaged, and en route following us. Both ships have completed their pick-up missions, but delayed departure. They are making their way as submarines to the Antarctic Ocean and will depart Earth near the south pole. We believe they can avoid being tracked from there as most of the early-warning military radars watch the northern polar region."

Alice was anxious about the delayed departures, even as she accepted Philip's opinion that the two ships would leave Earth and bypass the Moon before the U.N. could respond. At least Pystead had completed all pick-ups, including her parents and a few needed specialists. Plus, the pick-ups had almost balanced the spectrum of men and women in the crew. "More women mean fewer endogenous issues," Alice explained. "No need for some women to have two husbands!" She smiled playfully for Phil.

✻ ✻ ✻

The list of cross-training categories was extensive. For ship's maintenance: structural, main engines, standby power systems, electrical generation, electrical distribution, lighting, propulsion drives, robotics, radar, telescopes, environmental systems, farms, ranches, recycling, water purification, repair shops, adhesives, venue maintenance, kom and public address Networks, jumpsuits, Halo suits, and ship's various weapons. For care of personnel, the list was also long, covering medical facilities, instruments, prescription drugs, canopy beds, appliances, furniture, supplies, clothing, toys, parks, playgrounds, pets, and cosmetics.

Philip mentioned that he could find nothing on cross training for Line officer, medical doctor, orbital mechanics, ship's guard, chef, musician, actor, artist, brain scanning technician, counselor, or college teacher. Alice knew that those and other specialties were by invitation only unless somebody took the initiative to ask about one. She suggested that he look for entertainment venues because their present daily routine would becoming boring.

Within minutes Philip proposed tennis. Alice agreed to give it a try, though not immediately. She said she would be too busy as trained crew with mentoring roles and with socials to host and attend. She suggested dancing lessons would require less time, expose them to music, and would be of practical value when expanding their social circle.

He nodded for okay. *No wonder social circles are small—simply not time enough for many close friends. Already I'm on for neighborhood socials, mentoring new friends, the Eastern Philosophy Club, and now dancing lessons.*

⚹ ⚹ ⚹

Life was normal except that everything was ajar! Philip's routine of crew training and socials was made no more exciting by their importance. After another week he felt that the Wheel's flips structured life more than the lighting levels that passed for night and day. And he and Alice had not yet begun attending entertainment venues, increasing his yearning for bygone days.

Then Asif announced two days of zero gravity as they rested at the orbit of Mars, interrupting daily routines. He asked everybody in *Key Bury* to avoid using space sickness pills. Those who experienced severe or prolonged sickness could receive an injection. Asif explained that stomachs adapted to weightlessness once the mind began to rely on visual cues for balance instead of the inner ear. He expected that before reaching Pluto everybody who tried could adapt and cope without a pill. Philip and Alice counted themselves fortunate, having experienced good space stomachs. Making homelife easier, Char Cat also did well when weightless. Now with little to do, Philip felt both bored and stranded in limbo. Alice urged him to read something interesting and daydream. Nobody had said being a pilgrim in space would be an exciting vacation excursion, she reminded him.

Alice's Blue channel informed her that ships *Marianas* and *New Ionia* were two days behind, flying faster and would reach Pluto before the Wheel. She felt relief with the news that her parents were arriving on schedule for a change. Lois had told her that both *Marianas* and *New Ionia* had accomplished derring-do in complete surprise and gone into hiding, delaying departure to avoid the Earth on high alert. Operations had succeeded without fatalities on either side. Alice's parents were aboard. Most of the invited recruits had showed. A few strays got aboard in San Diego, with some kept, but most expelled in Central Park, New York. From the park, three cargo Eggs had crossed the border into Canada and picked up a dozen vetted European royals ostensibly out riding horses, but seeking normal lives as thinking human beings. Lois' post said that *Key Marianas* was able to complete a stop considered uncertain, making a pick-up in Eilat, Israel after flying below radar in rift valleys. Some of the crew had contacts in Rehovot who had assisted Pystead in recruiting scientific types such as biologists. Plus, as a most helpful social bonus, the pick-up provided a seven-to-one ratio of women, helping balance genders on the Wheel.

After the two days of no gravity, Manager Asif informed the pilgrims that the Wheel would begin powered flight above the Asteroid Belt under Yellow-Five alert conditions. He explained that Pystead's four Federation ships had long established crews. Their three-deep redundancy in critical positions allowed them to provide skeleton crews for the five ships with mostly new crewmembers. On Pluto, each non-Federation ship would be paired with a Federation ship as a sector for the journey to Mars.

Later in the day, Asif addressed the pilgrims with operational details he thought were interesting. When crossing the Asteroid Belt, the magnetic fields holding the seven ships together would be weakened to help absorb the shock of any asteroid hitting a ship. He told the pilgrims that the U.N. had radar stations on both Pluto and its moon Charon. Rather than destroy those radars, the Federation Council would continue beyond Pluto to pretend to investigate space at termination shock, where the solar wind of the cosmos begins deflecting and slowing the Sun's solar-wind particles, thereby reducing its pressure. At some farther distance out, our Sun's wind pressure merely equals that of the cosmos and our solar system ends—called heliopause. Once beyond the U.N.'s radar, however, if the quantum bottles in Pystead's probes proved operational, the Wheel would release three probes to continue to heliopause and beyond into deep space. The Wheel would then return to Mars.

✳ ✳ ✳

To further test their stomachs, during a flip Philip and Alice floated out to their nearby galley for a full lunch. All the food came in a tube! The tastes were fine, and they initially endured eating the gastropod fare in silence. As a distraction, Philip asked Alice about hazards to those working on the hull. She took a peek at her kom. The practical problems would likely be a malfunctioning spacesuit, or a large solar flare, now less an issue as they would have sufficient warning time to allow outside crew to return inside.

Philip again was troubled. *In the future, risky jobs should be done by older or retired crewmembers when neither physical strength nor the stamina of youth are necessary. The retired have lived most of their lives. Give our young a better chance.*

"Alice, have you eaten this tube food before?"

"Yes, although I'm surprised we are having it as the entire meal on first appearance."

"It's disgusting."

"It's not bad for recycled…whatever!"

Recycled whatever? "O Cosmos, my stomach may not rise to pilgrim status."

"Phil, you should eat a full meal to test your stomach."

"Closing my eyes doesn't help." *Surely I'll adapt?*

According to Alice, the psychologists felt that being a pilgrim would prove challenging for each individual in some way. She kissed Philip on the cheek. *An ideal time for a vanilla-bean muffin for my divine fiancé.* "Love, we need to recover a life with events we can enjoy together. Listening for details about our journey is not so important. Let's go home for a pastry and coffee."

Philip took her hand. "We can check for events, activities. I hear that chamber music concerts begin within several days. We have viewports for star gazing."

"I want us to spend more time together, Phil. We need not let training consume our lives. The new things we need to know and experience are many and important, but need not be learned in just a few weeks."

He nodded. "I have been compulsive learning about the ship! We should have a richer life, and I should make time to find my sponsor, Arthur Vanderhought, and a few others I met as a recruit on Campus."

"Those distant people can wait until Mars. We need to promote socializing in our own neighborhood. We must not remain strangers passing in the halls."

⚹　⚹　⚹

Alice decided to go ahead with their engagement party since her parents would not be aboard until all ships were joined on Pluto. She and Philip decided to hold the party on day thirty-two out.

The next day the list of persons picked up by *Marianas* and *New Ionia* was to be transmitted. Philip lapsed into daydreaming. *Can't imagine how I'd recover from a child left behind and I don't even have a child. Soon we may have grieving individuals who regret coming. And what's to become of those twenty-six K.L.J.H. people, cyborgs, essentially forced upon us? O Cosmos, some endogenous problems are easy to imagine. Still, if we can avoid the Earthlings on Mars our prospects must be fine. As predicted by Joan, our ship is performing perfectly. As a group we can devote our attention to living better lives.*

"Phil, you are too quiet. Anything troubling you?"

"Nothing in particular, everything in general." He hastened to add, "I'm happy that we have a date for the engagement party."

Perhaps life is ajar, although he's coping. "Phil, since we have good gravity let's walk about and see if others are returning to normal." Alice led the way to the main concourse and pointed to several children. "I hoped children would be out of apartments and playing." She turned off the concourse and soon they had to move over for a bicycle peddled by a boy looking to be in his early tweens. After a look around the local playground, Alice approached a woman sitting on the edge of a sandbox that held four small children playing with little shovels and pails. "Hello, my name is Alice. I'm pleased to see life beginning to look normal again." After a brief chat Alice returned to Philip, smiling. "That woman is a new pilgrim, and all the parents she knows on her hallway are getting their children out to parks and playgrounds." Back in the concourse, they saw a group of children lined up at a kiosk for ice cream and donuts.

"Alice, do you think I'm too old for an ice cream?"

"Not if you take a small cone."

Philip stood in line and took a small, vanilla-chocolate swirl. He tasted the treat and said, "Alice, this custard is very much like tube food. I think it's helping me adapt to the texture of gastropod fare!" They returned to the playground, and before Philip finished eating his ice-cream custard he had pointed a few mothers to the source.

❊　❊　❊

As they passed a concourse park in *Key Burry,* Alice spotted Revathy sitting on a bench—crying. "We must talk to her, Phil."

Alice waited until Revathy had seen her and then walked over. Revathy spoke first, "I was coming to see you."

"What's wrong?"

"RAM Key is the primarily American key, and few are sympathetic to my belief that I led a past life as a Catalan woman in

French Catalonia. I told one neighbor and a day later everyone seemed to know."

Philip asked, "When did you realize you'd lead a past life?"

"A decade ago I visited Barcelona and was drawn to Perpigan in French Catalonia. While walking the narrow, winding road up to the castle, I was overcome by resonances of a past life there. I don't know the period. Several words in Catalan came to me spontaneously."

"This bother's others?"

"Besides finding no sympathy in RAM, a young woman whose parents died the day after coming aboard is creating disturbances in my neighborhood and making me the butt of taunts for my crazy Eastern ways. She says that in the Western tradition I'm considered clinically mad. I'm afraid I'll be shunned and perhaps sent for therapy."

"Move to Key Bury with us, Revathy."

"Thanks for understanding, Alice. I came over for advice and after sitting for a while I realized that the environment best for me will be in Kali Key. It will have the most sympathetic pilgrims. I believe RAM Key will become a serious problem for me because that young woman is popular and already has dozens of followers."

"Oh my! The Federation needs to watch RAM!"

Alice may mean the Blues need to watch? An endogenous group issue only days out!

16

BEYOND THE YELLOW FLAG

Melita Rose Tsai, known as a palm-reader and psychic on Nevis, was listed by Pystead's directory as a Clinical Therapist and Personal Counselor for *Key Bury Saint Germaine*, with no mention of her dual personality. She felt ready to assume her listed role by day twenty-four out. The asteroid belt was safely below, and the general quarantine for contagion ended, freeing the pilgrims from medical masks and sanitary sprays. Under those liberating conditions Melita hosted a party with music for her friends. As an interesting site, she chose the vacated corner of an alfalfa farm and ranch. The location retained a pleasant odor because the space had been sealed off from the ranch to quarantine her brother Frank with his twin fiancées and his favorite horse.

Melita invited several computer-selected males—her attempt at matchmaking for Alice's female friends from Nevis. Welcoming each guest, Melita encouraged both men and women to mingle and invite friends and strangers to dance. Melita spoke to her kom and the local public address speakers began playing soft dance music.

Alice whispered to Philip, "You must ask friends to dance, yet not forget me."

"I'm sure they would prefer to chat rather than have their toes stepped on."

Alice led him to the horse barn floor. "Practice with me. You simply must ask our friends and my artist friends to help make Melita's party a success." Alice pushed her eyelids wide and whispered, "Dance with me, Poseidon." After three dances with pointers, she proclaimed Philip ready and sent him off with instructions to hold his partner loosely to make dancing smoother. Then she encouraged mixing by asking a computer-selected male to dance with her.

When Isaac arrived on crutches, Alice greeted him with a warm kiss before introducing him to others. Rhonda was pleasant, yet Alice sensed she was uninterested in Isaac or Melita's selection of eligible males. Samantha and Albert arrived bringing Earl, Rhonda's elderly father. Samantha kept Earl company and did not dance. Rhonda socialized, which came to mean dancing too often with Rao instead of mingling.

Earl's broken wrist was healing nicely and he was otherwise doing well. Philip thought Earl was enchanted with Samantha and pleased that his daughter was enjoying the party. Why not be enchanted? Samantha wore a high neckline pink blouse and white slacks. Her long brown hair with its streaks of pink fell some to her back and some to her front, leading one's eye naturally to the ample curves of her blouse. To complete the most modest attire Philip had ever seen her wear, the white slacks showed off her legs without being tight, unlike the hotpants she was wearing when he first met her on Nevis. He looked twice to enjoy the soft features of her face and was sure she smiled for him. After all, Samantha was his special platonic friend.

Alice noticed that Rhonda asked Philip to dance. Samantha, however, did not dance with anyone, including Philip when he asked, but she did kiss him on the cheek. Alice decided she liked both Rhonda and Samantha.

Philip danced with Lois Hensson and brought her over to meet Earl. Lois introduced Earl to Cavin Allen since both were cooks. Philip, Earl, and Cavin stood together for the one glass of wine served and walked over with a glass for Frank who was tending his horse. The broad, gray stallion had a striking black mane and black tassels at knees and hooves. Frank assured the three men that Rom Baro was gentle and would never push even a child for pulling his tassels, which were better called feathers.

Melita, dazzling in an orange-cream dress above her knees, shook a small hand-held bell. "My brother Frank came aboard under untimely circumstances, for which I believe he has forgiven me. His horse has certainly treated me kindly." Melita raised her glass and proclaimed, "Long live Rom Baro and Pystead's seventeen other horses." She drew cheers, especially from Frank and the twins, Frank's fiancées.

After the dancing music resumed, Melita cut her eyes at Philip, and he realized he'd not asked her to dance. As one of the few fast songs concluded, he hastened over. "Melita, may I have the pleasure of this dance?"

She offered her hand. "You know I adore you."

"My good fortune." He took her in the proscribed formal manner, but she moved closer putting a hand around his neck, whispering, "If Alice complains, tell her this is the way we danced in Romania."

"What do I tell Joan?"

"My alter is unaware and I'll not tell. I will kiss you on the cheek after our dance. The very next slow dance, ask me again."

"I shouldn't monopolize the hostess."

"I'm saving the dance for you and Joan. You may kiss her divinely after the dance, after hands are off."

"I'm happy that our friendships have survived into space."

"The best is yet to come in strange new variations on life. Wait and see."

"Melita, are you aware that Alice has a mermaid persona?"

"Sasha told me. Sheer lace?"

"Cranberry red."

"I envy her. My dual's husband and my duty prevent either of us from being a pretend mermaid. As you know, Melita doesn't date."

"Because of the gift?"

"Yes and no. Our present duality, hence our duties, must not be disturbed. You must do your part and not kiss me on the lips."

"May I love you without kissing you?"

"You may love us both as friends. Now Philip, see that Alice isn't left alone, and please return to dance with Joan."

Philip smiled and turned to see Alice kiss Isaac goodbye and leave him to her three single friends. *She will allow me another dance with Melita if she's so close with her former lover from Nevis.*

Cavin, Frank and the twins tended Rom Baro, showing the horse off to anyone who came over. Samantha sat with Earl. Rhonda chatted with Rao. The computer-selected males danced around, including with Alice. Samantha's Albert asked Alice to dance and she accepted, twice. *My Alice surely plays a mermaid persona when dancing with others, pretending each is the Greek god Poseidon. I hope she isn't Amanda with them—that mermaid should be mine alone!*

Philip rejoined Cavin and Frank in time to hear Frank inquire about a bachelor party. To Philip's surprise, Cavin said it could be done if Earl would do the cooking. The party could be timed to coincide with a galley meal of roast pork and would not use extra provisions or require extra access to ship's stores. Only Earl's barbecue cooking would be needed. The women would not be invited. The men would have what Frank called a dinner feast with dancing girls, but without live music or the spirit of manly drinks. They set the party for day twenty-eight out, four days before the engagement party. Full gravity could be expected as scheduled to facilitate a major period of cooking for one of the occasional and special galley dinners. The three men returned to the group with day twenty-eight firmly in mind.

✻ ✻ ✻

Before Philip reached Alice, she asked Rao to dance. Philip danced with Melita and asked if she were Joan. "Yes, Philip, I am Joan. Let's not tell Prince or Alice! When I married Prince, I told him that on occasion when out as one personality, I would need to switch for a while, but that I would minimize those times. He's not attending today because he doesn't approve of Melita's modestly low neckline. For this dance I am Joan with my hair and my neckline down."

"Joan, on a few occasions I have glimpsed a piece of a puzzle that I have not seen assembled. What is the strange new variation on life already seen by some?"

"Pieces via whom?"

"By Ice, and by you back on Campus with cautions about strange variations on life."

Joan nodded.

Philip persisted. "You once told me that intimate hands-off would last a very long time."

Joan smiled. "Time can pass slowly in some dimensions of life, becoming relatively a very long time."

"And most tellingly, Revathy wearing a sari said I should unwrap her during retirement."

"You know that my Prince is overly possessive?"

"Yes."

"When Prince proposed, he agreed that if Melita didn't date during our working careers, she would be completely independent from Joan during retirement."

"From what you and Alice have told me, I'm surprised he could agree to that."

"Prince loved me enough to allow Melita to be a woman in full during retirement. A time so distant to a young man that the promise must have seemed irrelevant."

Philip was distracted by a thought. *Irrelevant was meaningless as a concession to Joan. How are love and possessiveness entangled? When does a loving possessiveness become stifling—to an extroverted personality?*

Philip shook his head. "Sorry Joan, just momentarily distracted, thinking about love and how it must be relative to the needs of both lovers. As to the puzzle I mentioned, is it assembled in retirement?"

"That's Comte's vision, based on his own very long life and that of his past generations. Comte believes that some platonic friendships should become more intimate friendships since otherwise there could be frustrations. He believes that our closeness aboard ship, even in public spaces, will heighten desires and drive a change of cultural norms."

"Joan, only Melita will be free?"

"Yes, she will want you as a piece of her puzzle."

"You and I are to be hands-off friends?"

"I love Prince enough."

"Something is amiss! While on Campus, Melita told me that you were meant to be my friend, meaning long-term friend."

Joan looked away. "She never told me. Either Prince relents or dies young."

"If Prince relents, would he not want to be free also?"

"That would be fair."

"I would have to free Alice."

"Forgetting me or another woman, Philip, would you love Alice enough to want her to become a woman in full? Do you think Alice can maintain social relations with Isaac without ever desiring him hands-on?"

"Assembling this puzzle is emotionally challenging, perhaps leading more to grief than joy."

"Comte believes a more permissive culture will be necessary for an energized and stable retirement population. As you know, the retired are to contribute as educators, mentors, participants in quality assurance, and for backup duty when needed. By retirement age some will have lost spouses. Already, twenty-nine have come aboard with their spouse staying on Earth at the last minute, Revathy for one. Comte wants each person to be emotionally content and energetic! With empathy for our friends and our spouse, we should mature culturally."

"I must ponder this new potential. I mean that my subconscious process needs time to decide."

"Comte believes that friendship can beget lust, and that lust can beget friendship. The ultimate bond can be the same." Joan winked. "Do you want me hands-on, Philip?"

"My head rejects the possibility, foreclosing such feelings for you."

"If I'm free during retirement, I'll be hurt if you don't. And if I remain true to Prince I want you to have Melita as a friend-plus."

"I wonder if freeing Alice for a known friend would be easier than for an unknown man?"

"Free Alice for lust, Philip! Just as she must free you for lust. In Comte's envisioned culture, orgies and trysts are not sanctioned. Even lust must seek a lasting, platonic relationship."

"I can't imagine Alice participating, although I did see her leave Isaac with a kiss on the lips."

"Your Cobalt Blue fiancée will feel duty and honor bound to support her grandfather's vision! Just as Melita now feels duty and honor bound to remain sexually dormant. I feel certain that a new shipboard culture will develop. The history of humanity is that freedom, resources, technology, and proximity drive cultural change and sexual norms. Some are well on their way on Earth. In Russia and Brazil most adults are promiscuous, and all know it. In Chile the teenagers attend dances and poncear—make-out with everybody. Let's not forget the hippies and their free love in the U.S.'s nineteen-sixties. For Pystead, I anticipate a gradual change spreading from a few progressive social circles."

"Joan, a fourth dance will be too much. Alice is waiting."

"Once hands are off, appearances will be that Melita kisses you sweetly, divinely."

"Alice is my soulmate and first in my heart, yet also I want you in my life."

"That's why I may love you."

⁂ ⁂ ⁂

During the next few days life in space continued with the zero-gravity flips. Both new and experienced crewmembers were occupied taking or teaching classes and adapting to the realities of shipboard life. Hundreds of new crewmembers were already on duty for on-the-job training.

At Philip's departmental reception, Alice inquired about his training. Commander George Snyder explained that Philip could learn his way around on the job, beginning anytime since none in his group were retiring soon. Alice told George that for the present she would keep him busy assisting neighbors and new arrivals. Philip knew she was not exaggerating.

The next day, Alice asked Philip to install sticky pads in their apartment. With a few minutes' practice during the next flip period, both became adept at using their sticky soles during zero gravity to hold to the floor during the rotation, which now lasted only fifteen minutes. Next came Rhonda's apartment as Earl was not up to the task. After installing sticky pads in four of the artist's apartments, and in Revathy's, Alice pronounced him finished with that particular chore, at least until his cousin arrived. Philip replied that he should do her parents' apartment, and received a wide-eyed kiss. *I'm a natural-born spaceman. Amazing for only the fifth generation off a dirt farm.*

Low gravity tolerance affected friendships, just as did preferences for food and entertainment. As families, friends, and neighbors were thrown together, some friends were becoming acquaintances while strangers and acquaintances were becoming friends. *Too, those strange variations on life mentioned by Alice and mermaid Amanda, by Melita, by Joan, by Revathy—have me feeling immersed or emersed in the unknowable. Fortunately, our present lives are unchanged except for musings. Our futures, however, are certainly Hamlet's undiscovered country! And as told by Melita, Alice's subconscious demon of unfulfilled intimate surrenders will require gratification before its demise and her subconscious contentment. O Russel, be strong!*

On the morning of day twenty-eight out, Philip received a message that his package of purple pills from Dreamland Escapades on Earth had been tested and found acceptable. Far from ready for cognitive science experiments, he asked the pharmacy to hold them for a later pickup.

On the evening of day twenty-eight, Philip's male friends arrived and departed with him for his bachelor party, with Frank promising exotic dancing girls. Philip threw Alice a kiss. Everyone knew that Earl was barbequing two pork roasts. Frank promised he would save a taste for the women.

The women were getting together with Revathy at a large galley serving Indian food in *Kali Key*. Afterwards, Prince would play Chopin on the grand piano in his favorite music chamber, Odeum Bechstein. His final piece would be the Polonaise in A-flat, always a favorite. Alice found Collette, Sophie, Kathy, Barbe, Jane, and Rhonda, but not Samantha. Becoming anxious, Alice enlisted the others to help her find Samantha. When passing their pharmacy, Alice stopped for asprin and discovered the pills waiting for Philip. She picked them up.

⚹ ⚹ ⚹

The small dining room for the bachelor party was empty of chairs. Its tables were placed around the side walls, with the food under plastic covers. Tables across the front of the room, set two deep, were topped with a hard mat. Above them, three short ropes hung from the ceiling. Four steps were placed on the right. The meal was a stand-up buffet. Philip found that retrieving a serving from beneath a plastic cover was a bit off-putting, but necessary to protect food in quantity per ship's regulations—which, according to Frank, Melita insisted upon. Eating proved easy given the rigid plates and bite-sized foods. Frank said Earl called the meat pulled pork. The taste reminded Philip of his one meal at Earl's barbecue restaurant in Middle Georgia on his way to Nevis. Lamenting the absence of Earl's Brunswick stew, Philip welcomed the sight of grilled potato wedges. Last, he tasted a cooked apple slice and took a helping of the lightly spiced fruit. He clipped a small cup of iced tea to his buffet plate, ready to party.

Frank brought Philip to the center spot at the front of the room. The small room was not crowded because not all of those invited were attending. Comte was not invited. Joan's husband was giving a piano recital. Samantha's husband was sleeping before working a midnight shift. Isaac did not attend without explanation. Lois' husband, Dusan, and Denise's husband, Alex, both attended. The others were a mixed group of the Brazilians, Hector and Vielou, one of Philip's nearby neighbors, the two males with the Nevis artists Jane and Kathy, and two men Philip did not know—Frank's neighborhood friends.

Frank called to the group, "Salut, and welcome!" The lights

dimmed, except for those at the front tables. Soft, spirited music began. The side door opened and two women sprang through and up, landing on the tabletop with clicks, hops, and jingles. Each grasped an overhead rope to keep her balance. Each wore a colorful party mask, white shoes and a flower-patterned apron held by a string of silver sleigh bells. They were dressed alike in full white skirts to their knees and pouf-sleeved, white blouses. Each wore a colorful, short vest, laced loosely down the front. The vests and aprons matched, except that one dancer's flowers were lavender and the other's purple. The color of their party masks and hair ribbons matched their flowers. Their long brown hair, held by ribbons, fell down their backs. In the next moment Philip recognized them as Frank's twin girlfriends. They danced a quick turn making their sleigh bells jingle. They twirled and did slow, waving shimmies. No hips gyrated and no clothing came off. *Sweetly alluring.* After a brief dance they curtsied low and seemed to fall, but were hopping down one on each side of Philip. They bestowed hugs and kisses before hurrying out the door.

The music turned slower with a heartbeat. Another dancer stepped onto the table. As Philip admired her sexy appearance, he checked to see if she wore tap shoes or bells, and found she was barefooted with sleigh bells around her ankles. She was soon in motion. "Dans din oriental," called Frank.

Frank's neighbor Tudor interpreted for Philip, "Middle-Eastern style dance, maybe a belly dance, can be anything exotic."

This time it meant moderately slow rolling of perfect hips in what might have been a figure eight pattern. The dancer's skirt was lightweight and beige, almost sheer and skintight over her hips before floating loosely to the ankles. She wore a matching halter top that, like her skirt, covered without concealing form or movement of her body. Her stomach pulsed with the rhythm of the music, and her arms picked up the beat sinuously beckoning all to move closer. *Wow, what a tease.* Her next turn revealed leg to high thigh—the skirt being split up each side. She smiled knowingly. She twirled smoothly around, hands on gyrating hips, did a few high kicks and dipped low in front of Philip, throwing him a kiss. He smiled, reacting more to her quivering breasts than the kiss. She grinned, shaking her shoulders for him before smoothly rolling up and turning her back, her body shimmying from shoulders to knees. She did a slow backbend and shook herself to just the right resonance, holding her position while a few men whistled. Before straightening herself, she turned and smiled, then shimmied to the end of the table. She went down the steps leaving all wanting a longer dance.

Tingling from the titillation Philip watched another woman hop onto the table and spin wildly, grabbing two of the ropes to catch herself. She wore a bright pink slip, cut off well above the knees and slit up each leg; her entire bodice was ribbon cut from waist to neckline hem. A fancy pink party mask covered her eyes. Her brown hair was pulled into a bun. She seemed familiar and when Philip spotted a streak of pink in her hair he knew. Samantha was watching him. She curtsied, leaned over and whispered sweetly through glossy pink lips, "When I hop down, I'm all yours. Make good use of your time. I want you to remember me." She began a swaying dance, trying a shimmy that shook only her ribbons. Samantha's second shimmy was revealing and cut short. She made a quick half-turn and with her back to the men sidestepped until she went off the end of the table and out the door. *What happened?*

Heads turned and Philip also looked around, catching a glimpse of Alice in the open doorway.

A young woman entered the room wearing either a flimsy black bikini or fancy lingerie. She wore a black party mask. She moved to the center of the table, leaned over, pulled up her mask and pursed her lips for Philip. The entry door slammed shut with a sharp crack. The girl in black was a practiced dancer. Philip felt compelled to watch for a minute before weaving slowly backwards to approach the rear without upsetting anybody's plate.

⚜ ⚜ ⚜

Across the corridor, Melita, Barbe, and Rhonda were waiting. Melita waved. Philip hurried over not knowing what to think. He blurted out, "Alice was here!"

"Yes, she became adolescent when she found Samantha dancing for you, randomly topless, she said."

"How upset is she?"

Melita stepped close and whispered, "Alice was furious at Samantha's playing a dreamland girl. Her meaning not clear, she was mumbling to herself something about wet dreams. I know she blames Samantha."

"Thanks." Philip started for their apartment, walking slowly, giving both of them some time, hoping Alice would be there. *How could I have known Samantha would dance?*

17

THE DOGHOUSE

Once at their apartment door, Philip pushed the chime before entering. Alice was sitting on the sofa holding Char. She was wearing her white shorts and pullover white blouse. She had tears in her eyes. Philip approached and stopped.

"Don't touch me."

"Alice, I didn't know Samantha would be there."

"I thought she was my good friend. I'm upset with you too." Alice put her hands over her eyes. "Now I'm humiliated for interrupting the party."

"I love you, Alice. Samantha was wearing a party mask and her hair was up. I didn't recognize her soon enough."

"Melita asked me for Frank about dancing girls, and I said okay. When we couldn't find Samantha I just knew she was dancing for you. You could have stopped her. You wanted her!"

"I wanted her as a dancing girl, not because she was Samantha."

Alice looked up, squinting. "Give me some time."

"What do you mean?"

"Please leave the apartment. Pack your small suitcase and give me some time alone. Take your medical mask, your jumpsuit, sticky soles, and your guard pod. Get Frank to put you up. Maybe you can sleep with the horse."

Not knowing what else to do, Philip packed, remembering to take his engagement present, the seven-eleven-bubbles glass ornament he had purchased during his Jupiter exploit to help rescue Rhonda and Earl. He left his guard pod.

As he was leaving, Alice said, "I'm sorry about the horse remark."

At the door he said softly, "I'll wait for you." She lowered her head. Philip opened the door and looked back.

Without looking up, she said, "Please let me be alone! I don't usually cry."

He closed the door gently with tears in his eyes. No thoughts came to mind.

❉   ❉   ❉

Philip wandered slowly along corridors and took a lift down to concourse level. The concourse walkway ran through neighborhoods four and five on each ship and would circle the Wheel when all nine ships were joined together, connecting everybody into one huge ship. He took time to admire the spacious concourse with its eight-meters-high ceiling. As well as the guard station, he could see a food service station and a small park. He thought the concourse was an appropriate luxury feature for humanity's first starship.

At the portal to the next ship, the guards at the station checked Philip's name. When he asked why, a guard explained that one of the ship's eight neighborhoods held personnel who were sick or in extended quarantine. They were checking to be sure nobody had found a way out. The guard assured Philip that he could now walk the concourse without check stops because his passport would clear him automatically at each portal. Philip asked if he could leave his suitcase with them for a while. He could, and thus proceeded more easily and less conspicuously along.

Perhaps the passport is aptly named after all, allowing me to pass portals.

Philip stopped to observe the next concourse portal. The personnel door was open, but a closer look revealed it set within a large round door almost as large as the concourse—a door within a door. *This portal's round door is large enough to transfer foo fighter and cargo Eggs between ships, as is the rim-track circle!* At the security station Philip noticed a small sign with the key's name: SHAN-DONG-NEVIS. A guard said the round cargo door was seven meters in diameter and rolled away to open. As Philip went through the deep portal, he counted the expected six hull-wall sections, three for each ship. In the next ship, his third, he checked the ceiling trim—one silver stripe. Philip passed two couples out for a stroll before he came to another security station, went through another portal, and arrived in a fourth ship having a purple, red, and gray security station labeled RAM. Philip knew this was a non-Federation ship, although the security post apparently used Federation guards because each wore the familiar four chevrons of silver, blue, green, and gold. *Did Alice help with these colors?* He walked on. The next guard station label read E Key, where Philip observed a ceiling trim of three green stripes. Then he entered Blindsight Key with one wide, bright red stripe of ceiling trim.

Isn't this the predominately Russian ship? I should take a look…

another time with Alice. She must be upset with me as well as Samantha to need me out of the apartment. Could Alice have issues beyond my help? Issues entangled in her primary process, consciously unknown to her? O Cosmos, we must truly have a heart with reasons that reason shall never know! Each of us existing in our own mysterious bubble. Is knowing when to hold and when to leave alone an essence of love, respect for another? Even a soulmate is another. One may have without always holding. Surely Alice can need solitude without diminished love for me, nor I for her. I'm not in the doghouse, I'm in my bubble and Alice is in hers. We still have each other through our mysteriously entangled bubbles.

Philip stayed on the main concourse and arrived at the seventh and last key ship of the incomplete Wheel. The orange ceiling trim was an involved row of symbols. Revathy had told him the name was Kali Key and the color saffron. *This ship hosts the Eastern Philosophy Club.* He walked quickly and found the next portal door closed. *Either Marianas or New Ionia will dock here. Bury is gold, Logos is silver, E Key is green. Hence the fourth Federation color is light sky blue.* Philip turned around and headed back. *Haven't seen two dozen people. Strange to have this common space virtually to one's self in decent gravity. Well, the flip comes soon! I'm ready for the barn, certainly not in the mood for a chat with humans.*

He picked up his pace. *Alice will forgive me, for what is not clear! Now, where is that horse from here? And the guard station with my suitcase! One must remember to pick up one's bag when shipping out. He* took a good look at his kom's map and decided to find the farm without looking again. After only two wrong turns, he arrived at a temporary plastic curtainwall separating Frank's horse from a larger farm, allowing access to the horse with a walk-through security scan. The door to the horse shed was closed, but Philip heard voices and knocked.

✌ ✌ ✌

Lala opened the door, and after a moment recognized him. "Come in, Philip." Frank's second girlfriend, Violca, appeared. They were dressed alike in faded blue jeans and gray T-shirts. Each twin held a heavy brush, and Violca also had a white towel. Another voice came from the back and a woman in a jumpsuit appeared. Her light brown hair hung just below her shoulders.

"Hello, Melita. Surely you know that Alice wanted me out of the apartment for the night?"

"We know." Melita turned to Lala and Violca. "Would you both go tell Frank to call me, and please stay in the apartment." The twins departed. "I have a ready chair for you. It reclines and extends into a single-width bed." Melita smiled or perhaps smirked. "As one cannot help noticing, the twins are not the retiring type."

"Melita, I prefer to take my chances with the horse. Alice is distressed that I did not send Samantha away promptly, and I don't want to repeat the offense with more dancing girls."

"I'm sure the problem was Samantha, thought of as a friend and not a topless dancer."

"Half topless for one second. What about our engagement party?"

"Alice…cancelled the party several minutes ago…said she couldn't yet face the men after intruding on their bachelor party. That, Philip, is a consequence of our close quarters for Alice to easily intrude on the party and thereafter not be able to avoid those men without staying in her apartment or taking a distant guest room."

Philip closed his eyes and took a deep breath.

Melita was saying, "Frank, we are going to need that recliner down here with the horse. Yes, you heard me correctly, Philip wants to stay with the horse." Melita smiled faintly. "Frank's okay with your staying in this big horse trailer, as he calls it."

"Will you check on Alice?"

"I've spoken with her already. She's fine with the women. She ate tonight with her artist friends from Nevis. Comte and Lois will visit her tomorrow without Dusan who was at the party."

A large rolling chair appeared with Frank's deep voice behind it. "Where to, sister?"

"Why not make a groom's corner at the head of the horse? Be sure the chair is out of all possible reach. We could flip about to avoid a meteor, or perhaps hit a warp in space."

"A what?" asked Philip. Melita glanced at him so sharply that he dropped the question. "Nothing really."

Frank told Melita, "I liked Connecticut better, and so did my horse."

"We have been over that, Frank. Nothing has changed."

"I'll move my farrier's chest for more clearance."

"I thank you, and if the ship ever rocks about on a quick flip, your horse will thank you."

"Not to mention me!" added Philip.

Melita Rose smiled. "The twins will get you to help with Rom Baro's rubdowns." Then she showed Philip how to operate the recliner and find sheets in its base. Frank showed him the horse's support harness with its three soccer-ball-size lifting pods on each side for control of the horse during low gravity periods, and told him how to remove one section of harness at the time for rubdowns.

Then Frank covered inspection and changing of the horse's two bodily-function bags. Still not done, Philip learned how to hook up the emergency restraint lines with their tension reels.

Training complete, Philip took a good look at the horse and was impressed with the gray beast's broad and muscular chest. "Frank, how much does this horse weigh?"

"Just over seven hundred and seventy kilograms."

"Isn't he tall for a horse?"

"No, but tall for a Vanner at almost fourteen hands. The breed produces strong, gentle horses." Frank pointed to a small refrigerator stocked with snacks for humans and horse. "Keep your palm flat when feeding the horse."

"Pretend the horse is reading your palm," joked Melita. As she was leaving, Melita took Philip's arm and whispered, "You might think this barn to be without adornments, but I suspect the twins will provide some nominal entertainment. We won't tell Alice."

"Fine."

"Easy on the sweets. The horse eats the red and white peppermints, and the girls eat the chocolates. Two a day is all either needs. Fingers are best with the girls, but the flat palm is highly recommended with the horse."

"I've got it."

✳   ✳   ✳

A buzzer sounded. Melita said, "We flip in ten minutes. Move away from Rom Baro and prepare to float. Keep the pack of emergency restraint lines near you. Thus far the medicine has kept Rom Baro's stomach settled, but since he can't talk to reassure us, we give him distance."

"Melita, if we can float through zero here, why all the drills about sitting and strapping in?"

"There are babies, children, the frail, the sick, those with very sensitive stomachs. Floating requires attention and judgment on when to be on the floor and not fall upon return of gravity. The ship's managers agreed that one procedure for all was the best approach. You might like to know there are private float-thru parties, and one adult lounge for floating."

During the flip, Rom Baro floated steady and clear of obstructions and was gently positioned by his lifting pods to be near the floor with legs down for the return of gravity. A buzzer sounded, and Melita told Philip he had one minute to get to the floor, preferably not on his head. *Surely the ranches have simpler snug-up crates than this for other animals during zero gravity? I suppose chickens can flutter to retain orientation in returning gravity? Cross training to support flipping the animals must be an available duty.*

The twins soon entered the barn and removed the two bodily-function bags and the support harness, allowing Rom Baro to sleep lying down if he chose. Two body straps remained in case the restraint lines were needed during an unscheduled flip.

After the last talking creature departed, Philip gave the horse a few pats on the flank and tried out the recliner. The horse appeared to be sleeping on his feet, as Melita had said he might. Philip hooked up restraint lines that would prevent the horse from reaching his recliner. Deciding against reading, he pushed off his shoes. *Yes, Ira, long ago, far away, I had a dream one day, but not about star wars.* He fell asleep under a covering sheet.

18

ENGAGEMENT PRESENTS

In the morning after a late breakfast of fruit and pancakes, Lala and Violca accompanied Philip back to the barn to clean up, feed, and rub down Rom Baro—a name apparently known only to the humans.

Thank goodness their hair ribbons are different colors. Philip asked the twins their last name.

"We write our name Haluska."

"My last name is Russell."

Before all the horse combs and towels were out, Frank joined them and assured Philip that the rubdown would be easy because the horse had not exercised properly and was not sweaty. Frank shook his head in disappointment. "Vanners need their exercise," was his quiet comment as he left the twins and Philip to their work.

The twins began the rubdown with multi-row, hard-rubber combs they used with circular motions. Then they combed the mane, tail, and the short mane at knees and ankles, called feathers by the twins and talaria by Philip. For a second combing Lala handed Philip a comb with fine tines.

After another few minutes of effort, each girl shed her T-shirt and worked in a bra matching the color of her hair ribbon, adding to the barn Melita's foretold adornments. After lunch with Frank in the apartment, the three grooms returned to the barn. They scrubbed the horse with wet, soapy towels for half an hour, then rinsed him with wet towels and wiped him dry. Philip thought that should complete the chore, but the twins brought back the fine-toothed combs. As he pondered how unnecessary the final combing must be, the T-shirts again came off and his efforts seemed less onerous. When Philip let slip a comment about such a long rubdown, Violca told him the job could be done faster, but became hard work without the hose water they had used on Earth.

Finally, as all stood admiring the well-groomed stallion, Lala surprised Philip with a big smooch, saying he made the task easier. With that, Philip remembered the candy treats and retrieved them from the refrigerator. He fed each girl a chocolate cube using the fingers, and then fed the horse a peppermint wheel using the open palm.

⚹ ⚹ ⚹

After lunch Philip found a gym and learned how to use the exercise machines. *Even after exercising and enduring alerts I'll have more discretionary time than I did in Compton. Daily life in California being consumed with one after another personnel issue or error made, equipment malfunction, meaningless paperwork, or fabricated accusation. Plus, the traffic jams and long lines. And public policy not addressing any issue in independent and tangible parameters that one might observe or do something about. No practical approaches; only great quagmires of rhetoric and incompatibilities of mind.*

By the second night of his stay in the barn, Philip and Rom Baro had exhausted the novelty of their companionship. Frank and the twins came by the barn as Philip called it, or the big horse trailer as Frank called it. They fed Rom Baro and strapped on his harness for the upcoming evening flip.

Melita called and asked Philip to join her and Lois in the local galley for a late dessert. He declined because the twins were already pouring orange juice for a post-flip treat. Then his mood sank. "The engagement party is still off?"

"I'm afraid so. Come out with us tomorrow. We want to try the observation lounges."

"Thanks for the invitation but chatting with the horse will be company enough for now. Melita, do you think Frank and the twins could be dissuaded from coming down every few hours?"

"If you will promise to watch Rom Baro closely, they should stay put."

"I can do that. I'll even ask Rom Baro if he has any new aches and pains."

"I'll assure Frank you are an observant person, but he will give you pointers anyway."

"That level of conversation I can handle."

"Should you want meals in, the sandwiches in the refrigerator are for you."

"You're a dear."

"Yes, but no kiss on the cheek until you're back home with Alice."

Soon Frank called and asked Philip to watch for drooling and any sign of restlessness by Rom Baro. Frank said to call if he wanted to move to the apartment. Having no inclination for news or reading, Philip lay back in the chair, enjoying the bliss of a solitude made aware by the occasional hoof stamp or snort of his barn-mate. An hour later Philip dutifully made a close-up eyeball inspection of the beast, only to be rewarded with a swish in the face by Rom Baro's well-combed tail. Philip called Frank with a report, and Frank said calls could stop except for a problem. Frank suggested that wearing a medical mask would improve air quality. The twins would not be back until late morning.

Philip opened the recliner into its single-bed configuration. He decided to sleep in his skivvies and found a lightweight throw blanket, probably Alpaca, as well as a sheet, and pulled both over his legs for the feel of cover. *Fading quickly on a soft pad. Now, Diogenes, this dog feels no further need to try a barrel.*

✼ ✼ ✼

Knocking on the barn door woke Philip before his alarm sounded. Expecting the twins, he got up, draped the sheet over one shoulder, and opened the door. He said after a perplexing moment of standing with mouth open, "Alice!"

She was holding her cat. "May I come in?" Philip stepped backwards. "Is that a yes?"

"Yes, of course yes." Then he raised his voice, "How could you break our engagement?"

"I cancelled the party, Phil, not the engagement."

"Why cancel the party?"

"I couldn't bear to face our male friends so soon after making a fool of myself. Getting mad at Samantha and you was okay, but horning in on the bachelor party was crass."

Philip relaxed. "We humans are complex and inscrutable creatures. I'm not so proud that I didn't think promptly to send her away." Alice remained quiet. "Likewise, for the woman, perhaps thinking is not ideally considered in such circumstances."

"You forgive me?"

"I was never angry with you, just perplexed. I think you were the one hurt, and you need to forgive me."

"I do forgive you. Not for an instant did I doubt you were the only man for me. I cancelled the party, but I have brought your engagement present."

Ah, that twinkle in her eyes!

Alice told Philip she had asked the exotic dancer for pointers. She did her big-eyed pose. "I have come to dance for you. I wore this aqua outfit because I was wearing it when you first asked me to dinner on Nevis."

Philip smiled. "I never thought of long pants as sexy attire until I saw you wearing those."

"Do you still think I'm sexy in it, Phil?"

"The most."

Alice smiled. "Take off your sheet and sit down. Hold our cat. Are we alone?"

"Except for the horse, a male."

"Just right. A dancing girl needs an audience." Alice held out her arms, she swayed and spun and did a high leg kick. She brought her arms in for a series of spins with an occasional swoop. Only after several spins did Philip realized she was unbuttoning her blouse. The blouse didn't hold together on her next spin, and she wasn't wearing a bra. She held her next dip and whispered, "I wanted to wear a lace bra, but I don't have one to match. You'll have to pretend." She stepped backwards doing almost a shimmy and her slacks slipped away. *Matching panties.* She danced forward a step with a low dip and shoulder shakes.

"Wow!"

Alice smiled and spun around, stopping to pick up her slacks. She pulled a small vial from a pocket and held it up with a flourish, dabbing its end on both sides of her neck, and then down her body to the navel. She tossed the vial and commanded, "So toss the cat!" Philip pushed Char Cat off the bed and was surprised at Alice taking a long and awkward leap that landed her beside him.

In the middle of her kiss, she whispered, "The next part of my present is not new, and is mostly up to you, my man in full." For a man being teased, the time between noticing and acting can be prompt under proper circumstances. This was one of those circumstances and soon the engagement was no longer in doubt. After passionate sex the couple spent a half hour cuddling on a single width, fold-out bed, in a horse barn by some accounts and in a large horse trailer by others.

The twins called to say they would be down in thirty minutes. When they entered the barn, they were wearing such loose-fitting blouses that Philip took a second glance to be sure they were the twins. With flourish, he fed Rom Baro a peppermint candy. He searched through the refrigerator a final time, turned to the black cat and said, "Sorry, Char Cat, no catnip. I'll have to make it up to you."

As soon as Lala and Violca left the barn, Philip remembered the present in his suitcase. Alice was watching curiously as he handed her the box. "Sorry it's not nicely wrapped. It's from the Jupiter excursion."

"I've heard rumors about this."

Alice held up the glass curio, apparently counting its interior bubbles. She proclaimed, "It's lucky, it's perfect." Her eyes did their open-wide bobble as she gave the trinket a kiss. They both smiled, their personal bubbles once again merged.

19

WIND AND WATER

Following their exchange of gifts, Alice and Philip pushed back the date of their engagement party. They invited only closest friends. Alice painted small-board scenes framed with a narrow white ribbon as favors for their guests. Once finished with the paintings, she decided to put her bubbles art glass present on their coffee table secured for flips with sticky tape. Philip was pleased, considering its display an unspoken token of affection more intimate than their wedding rings. After all, it represented his risk undertaken to help rescue Rhonda, which Alice thought unnecessary.

For the engagement party, Alice dressed modestly in pastel pink. She was pleasant with Samantha after remarking that she was glad to see her wearing a non-fluttering top and a bra. Melita surprised the guests with wine spritzers. Philip was congratulated, and Alice's diamond engagement ring from far-away Nevis greatly admired. Alice's granddad attended in his famous gem-studded sash. The guests enjoyed Alice's scenes of red poinciana blossoms and the vibrant, wild orchids of Nevis, all with a butterfly. No two paintings were alike, and the butterflies had variants of the Blue-Mati eye on their wings, which nobody mentioned. Alice ended the evening wishing the best for family and friends not yet aboard, evoking a touch of sadness mingled with joy.

✼ ✼ ✼

For Philip and Alice, life reached an easy new normal while the Wheel passed above the asteroid belt, with the orbit of Jupiter another seven days travel. Exercise and training were the activities of the day, reading and petite socials the activities of the evening. The couple visited less with old friends by mutual agreement, affording time for hosting and attending mixers to spark social life aboard ship. The small socials for acquaintances and neighbors were fluid and unpredictable. Friendships were changing, creating new social circles. Philip still pondered the concept of love, deciding that among other feelings love envisioned no end to a relationship. He still wondered about Alice's secret Cobalt-Blue duties although they no longer worried him.

One morning in bed, lying in each other's arms, Alice whispered, "Phil, Samantha and I became friends on Nevis with more in common than you might think. Do you feel that we could be friends again?"

Philip found a ready answer. He raised his left palm to his forehead and said seriously, "I have no intuition for friends or lovers."

"You've been talking to Melita!" Alice leaned back and looked at him intently. "Do you consider Samantha a friend of yours?"

O Cosmos! "Only if she is your friend too."

"That hurt you to say, didn't it?"

"True…but true."

"Phil, kiss me some place soft." He kissed her twice and murmured, "Only you, Alice, only you."

"I want to make peace with Samantha. I'll call and say we want to visit her and Albert." Alice smiled. "Now, Phil, if our probe's quantum bottles prove unreliable and the Wheel proceeds to termination shock, Granddad wants us to marry before getting there. He said to ask Sasha about the timing and please marry sooner rather than later."

"I too vote for sooner."

"I want to paint you in your skivvies, sitting on Frank's horse, holding our black cat. I'll meditate on a few portraits for inspiration. You know expressions are my weakness."

"I think the cat should be floating for those inclined to close observation."

"Of course, Phil, of course something will float. And you may have a word stenciled on your cap."

"Let me guess, that word would be…Alice?"

"You are a clever creature. I want everyone to know where your affections lie. I want all of you, awake and dreaming."

"What do you mean, dreaming?"

"I mean no using those Escapade pills Samantha sent you. No inventing new variations of dreamlife."

"Those pills? I haven't picked them up."

"I picked them up for you. I'm going to make Samantha promise no more pills."

"Alice, those were sent for my cog-sci research by friends in the States, not given by Samantha. They arrived before we left Nevis."

"Oh no! I was furious that she found a way to a dreamtime seduction. Are you sure?"

"Certainly! Friends in Compton, Sandra and Dennis, said they wanted to introduce me to new dimensions of mind and would have pills sent from Cognitive Dimensions."

"I must make peace with her!" Alice gave Philip a quick kiss and rolled out of bed with a palm's up wave. "A healthy creature is up and doing!"

⚹ ⚹ ⚹

Alice arranged a personal visit with Sasha Gutkin, a friend who could advise her on scheduling the wedding. Philip, unlike most new pilgrims, knew of Sasha as the Russian manager and pilot of *Logos Key*. As a recruit, he had been aboard her ship's demonstration flight to Edinburgh. He recalled her first appearance to the recruits before takeoff—tall for a woman, taller than Comte—in a white jumpsuit, speaking with her slightly strident Russian accent in otherwise fluent English. Now, up close and wearing a dress, her appearance captured his attention as feminine and mid-height between him and Alice, about a six-centimeter difference each way. Her most striking feature was her hair, before a golden-blonde bob cut, now probably bleached into a brilliant icy platinum, fluffy wave to her shoulders—much lighter and cooler in color than Alice's vanilla blonde. He wondered what color she would choose if a mermaid.

For her part, Sasha knew about Philip through Alice who described him as her divine fiancé. Sasha recalled Alice's pleasure that Philip had received the most popular votes of any recruit on Nevis, chosen from over seven hundred to be one of a hundred to fly and report to all the recruits on a Pystead ship, Sasha's *Key Logos*. Seeing him in person, Sasha imagined he had received the most votes due to his good looks as well as his outgoing personality. And for her, his not being Russian made him an ideal Poseidon.

The three went for dinner at a galley in *Key Logos* and found a small table for some privacy. Sasha shared information not yet public that *Marianas* and *New Ionia* keys would pass the Wheel about day fifty-five out and would orbit Pluto searching for water-ice before arrival of the Wheel. Sasha was pleased that operations in space had been routine. They joined the buffet line.

Back at their table, Alice announced, "I really like our whole food. The frozen, freeze-dried, and canned foods are good, but I do not enjoy the tube food."

"Yes, but recycling is a must for security until planetary farms are established."

Philip asked, "We recycle all wastes?"

Sasha nodded. "We cannot afford to lose materials, atoms! We are confirming that recycling processes are established on all ships. We are not counting on Mars crops. Philip, be mum!"

He inquired, "Why haven't I noticed recycling for food as a topic in Fednet's directory?"

"Try Amalthea."

"Cosmos, hidden!"

"Surely not the intent." Sasha smiled. "Which reminds me, before I tell you what I know about termination shock, Melita's brother and his horse are scheduled to move near the rim so the horse can exercise on the rim's sports track."

Philip said, "I believe Frank will begin to appreciate shipboard life as soon as his horse can use the track."

"The transfer will happen on Pluto. Even in his present yard, Frank could use a pod as a lunge line to trot the horse for exercise. Melita believes that Frank needs the rim track more than the horse. The transfer parade will give us a unique event for children."

Philip knew he was sidetracking Alice's topic, but asked, "On another subject, Sasha, what of that K.L.J.H. group brought aboard?"

They all took a few more bites before she answered. "They are living together on the rim in a space designed for tennis courts. They take every inconvenience personally, as if they are the only ones affected. They don't believe we are in space. Their computer system has failed, which returns their shoe soles to green—evidently to let Dr. Osgood know if any one of them is no longer under his control and a potential loose cannon. They have no idea how to repair their computer, and neither do we. We have urgent projects and no time for an unneeded and unknown computer system having no technical specifications nor spare parts. We still need brain scans to learn if any one of them is dangerous—for your department, Philip."

Alice exclaimed, "Please, let's not forget my question! Maybe you can marry us, Sasha?"

"I'm honored to be thought of, Alice, but you will be better off with a cleric. I have no inspiring words or poetry for the occasion."

"Please now, tell me about termination shock while my fiancé is still interested."

"From the tale I've heard, I don't think that's a concern. A man who spends the morning with you in a horse barn must be in love." Sasha waited for a reaction, which was more muted than expected.

"I cannot believe you heard that story! What, is it on a Network?"

"No, but gossip is on the rise. Not just among friends. Our

society puts everybody in touch with everybody and stories are told and overheard. The good news is that only people who know you personally know who is being talked about. Wheel-wide, the pilgrims recognize only Comte, Robbie, Lois, Joan, and if a sports enthusiast, Denise. I'd say not one out of a hundred uses the directory to look up the face for a name they have heard, or the name of a face they have seen. Gossip remains anecdotal entertainment without the need for public identification of the characters. The issue of scandal seems left behind."

Philip nodded, pleased. *Could we return to early fifteenth century times before gossip and lies circulated in print? Old fashioned can be best.*

⚹ ⚹ ⚹

"What about termination shock, Sasha? If we go there, I want to be married a few days before, but definitely not after, that place."

Sasha sat up straight. "Has Melita put you up to this?"

"Oh no! It's me and Granddad."

"We do not know precisely where the terminal shock phenomena is located, except that it occurs over a considerable distance throughout space rather than at one specific distance from our Sun. We have instruments to measure the phenomenon for ourselves once we are within the zone. Alice, do you know something I don't know?"

"Oh, no. I thought it would be nice to mark our wedding with a mysterious and unique place in space."

Sasha nodded, but again paused to eat before saying, "Melita Rose is interested in this demarcation zone—for nebulous reasons. Maybe it would be a good omen, or perhaps bad?"

"Suppose, Sasha, we want to be married four days before we get to this location?"

"Alice, we won't know even an hour ahead of time! Also, termination shock is very, very far away. Our deep-space probes are ready for their final test with a signal due from a quantum bottle timed to the moment considering relativity's affect on time. Each probe has seven entangled quantum bottles providing instantaneous transmission of a specific finding, and a bottle for recall to Mars. The Federation Council no longer has need for a ship to go to termination shock, to heliopause, and beyond into deep space. After launching the probes we will return directly to Mars." Alice closed her eyes. "Alice, why not be married on Pluto?"

"I want the ceremony in space."

"Your parents will arrive on Pluto. After completing the Wheel with all nine ships, we will depart Pluto and fly a day or so beyond its orbit to launch our interstellar probes. Then we begin our return to Mars and pass through the orbit of Pluto: a rather definite location in space, yet mysterious because we cannot calculate its long-term orbit! Marrying the third evening after departing Pluto would give you a day of good gravity before the wedding, for preparations and would allow weak stomachs time to recover. Also, we are likely to be Green-Seven after departing Pluto."

"Sasha, would you attend?"

"I expect so. We should be back to routine."

"Oh, please come."

"Is there a seat for Woody?"

"You and Woody are on the list after my parents, Granddad, Melita and Prince, Lois and Dusan, and Philip's cousin, Lauren."

"Try not to place me next to Comte for video, or no one will notice my amber necklace."

"Lois said the same thing. We will buffer him with my mom and Denise who wear little jewelry."

They ate for a time in silence. Before last bites, Sasha mentioned, "My marriage to Woody was performed by a Reform rabbi who believes in both God and evolution and is not offended by gnostics, agnostics, pantheists, atheists, nor wiccans, although he does not marry polytheists, ecstatics, or those with large, visible tattoos. He lives in Marianas Key."

"Sounds good," commented Philip. "What's his name?"

"Josh Issegow."

"Thanks. We'll talk it over. Do you have time for another question?"

"I'm not in a rush, Philip."

"Why are we going beyond Pluto to launch the interstellar probes?"

"You know we are creating artificial gravity by flying either topside forward while accelerating, or bottom-side forward while decelerating in our direction of travel?"

"Yes."

"That orientation presents a large disk for Earthlings to look at. If they have found us, they can probably continue tracking. If Earth is watching, we want them to believe we are leaving the solar system. We will do our best to return unseen to Mars. If our deep space probes prove operational the moderate voices are for going beyond Pluto and rotating to present our sheer to Pluto, which should cause tracking from either Pluto or Earth to lose us."

"Okay. Thanks."

"We have always wanted to experience deep space before making final plans for interstellar travel. The probes are considered satisfactory and save time from taking the first peek ourselves. Our return trip to Mars will be slow and allow time to train for shipboard duties and construction on Mars. We hope to escape detection until several hours before landing. Earth has outposts on both Mars and its moon Phobos, but their monitoring capabilities are limited and at fixed locations because budgets have always been tight."

✻ ✻ ✻

Questions and meal concluded, the three stood. Alice asked Sasha if she had time for "girl talk." She did. "Phil, I need to chat with Sasha about omens and memes. I won't be long. Do you mind giving us some private time?"

Philip received a kiss goodbye and departed. *Is Alice thinking about our wedding, or about strange new variations during retirement that Melita says she will be duty and honor bound to promote?*

Alice voiced her concerns to Sasha. "I'm worried that my recent reaction to Samantha may have been an omen of my inability to properly help lead the transition to a more permissive culture. I feel that among those I know, only Isaac and me, and Samantha and Albert, have experienced anything approaching a permissive retirement culture. Philip is not overly possessive and will socialize with Isaac, but like most of our men was never a womanizer. His friends from California, I believe, are even more inhibited than he is."

"Alice, there is another couple potentially able to transition."

"Oh, who?"

"Someone with amber mermaid's lingerie made like your cranberry red." Alice sat up, her mouth open. Sasha smiled. "Comte took one of his walk-about inspection tours. At the events shop on Campus he spotted a red lace bra with sea-shell cups hanging in the sewing room. He said he hoped the costume wasn't for a college play. The shop manager told him it was part of a mermaid costume for a woman who evidently wanted to spice up her sex life." Alice covered her eyes. "The next week you hosted that private unveiling of your mermaid Amanda painting. Comte soon put two and two together."

After a long moment Alice inquired, "Why did he confide in you?"

"He couldn't bring himself to speak to you about your love life."

"So he spoke to you? He's known Lois and Melita much longer."

"The year before I met Woody, Comte was sleeping with me!"

"Oh, my, oh my!"

"Comte was retired, or should have been! My first husband had been killed over a year before while buying equipment, caught in a terrorist bombing."

"Did Woody know?"

"He knew, but not with whom."

"Then he can transition."

"Perhaps. When he asked me to marry him, I promised to drop my Poseidon within a month."

"True love."

"Yes, I must admit, though, I can't forget Comte completely. I suspect on occasion you may have fond feelings for Isaac."

"Please never mention that possibility to Philip."

"Of course not. Still, Comte's insight is that during our retired years we can care intimately for more than one person. Bear in mind, Alice, if you promote Comte's culture, sooner or later Philip will understand your potential for intimacy with Isaac."

"A good point. I must find a way for Philip to decide if we will participate or not."

Sasha was firm, "In social circles this cultural shift must be promoted and controlled by the women. Melita agrees."

"I agree. Still, even a friends-plus relationship should require some nominal seduction by the man, over time! Don't you think, if we are to have a committed friend-plus? I will promote the transition, but let Philip opt for our participation or not."

"Yes. I'm sorry to have sidetracked your questions. You were the one who asked to talk."

"First, please tell me how Comte came to seduce you?"

"I tried three times before seducing him! Finally, I told him that if friends-plus wasn't meant for us, it wasn't a viable idea! We were good for each other."

"Sasha, beginning in graduate school I chose, vetted, and seduced my men, especially Isaac. Even Philip. He and I are soul-mates and I couldn't risk losing him."

"I'm sure that's not unusual."

"More and more, Sasha, I must feel the loss of having never been truly seduced. That should be an unusual feeling?"

"I can only refer you to Melita Rose."

"I shouldn't. If we participate Joan will surely become a friend-plus with Philip."

"Would you be hurt?"

"I'd rather share him with a friend."

"What of your need to be seduced?"

"I must get over it."

Perhaps in retirement a Poseidon will seduce you?"

"If Philip decides we will participate. I must do nothing that will weaken his love for me. He's my only true love, ever. Perhaps even in retirement I'll not be ready to share him?"

"You really should seek Melita's advice. She would never tell Joan."

"You're right. And I should marry Philip at Pluto's orbit."

"Good gravity for a few days! Drinks at the reception will not require sippy cups. A honeymoon in good gravity." Both women smiled.

⁂

As landing day on the ice planet approached, Alice began reminding new friends and neighbors of the upcoming period of zero gravity. Manager Asif announced that time in orbit was needed to remove their bottom radiation shields before landing on Pluto. Their landing approach would very closely follow the big moon, Charon, which should clear any stray ice and rock. Alice encouraged everyone to watch video of the approach, which she said would show a pale, vermilion-cream tinctured planet of smooth texture, seen against the blackness of space—an intriguing sight. The big moon appearing too near Pluto was Charon. Looking back, the very bright star in the sky would be the Sun.

Almost every announcement reminded the pilgrims that gravity would be very weak on Pluto. Asif urged everyone to wear sticky soles in public spaces. Walking pads for installation in quarters were still available and should be installed to have pleasant days on the planet.

Network video showed the two ships that had conducted the late pickups on Earth, *Marianas* and *New Ionia*, already orbiting Pluto. They looked odd and vulnerable with their partially covering sheets of lead and their glowing red lights atop so many poles.

Earl was right, thought Philip, *we look more like a junkyard than a spaceship. I escaped the doghouse but became a junkyard dog!*

Everybody was excited about the concourse mixer planned for the third evening on Pluto after all nine ships were joined, completing the circle. Communications resumed and Alice spoke with her parents. Philip reached his cousin, Lauren, and his friends from California. Alice used her secret Blue channel to learn for Rhonda that Earl's vegetable seeds had been recovered from Middle Georgia by *Marianas Key*. As a surprise, the artist Colette called with news that her boyfriend, Cole, now her fiancé, was aboard *New Ionia*.

✻　✻　✻

For landfall, as it was called, the Wheel was at a special Red-Two status with each of the eight neighborhoods in each ship sealed, and with the trained crew wearing jumpsuits or Halo suits. Alice opened a group kom channel for her friends and they all waited in their alert chairs to chat. Soon a slight jolt and vibration was felt through the ship's structure, followed in minutes by one and then a second bump to the entire ship. Within minutes Asif announced, "The Tank ship via remote control has separated and will land nearby. Marianas and New Ionia keys have joined the Wheel. Our Wheel is now a complete disk of nine ships for the first time ever. All concourse and rim track portals, magnetic ports, and communications and control contacts are correctly aligned. We must thank the designers, manufacturers, assembly workers, and our inspectors for work perfectly completed."

Asif paused, as if contemplating the magnificence of the Wheel, before saying, "Landfall will be protracted because we must use lasers to profile the rugged terrain of our landing site. The Wheel has three hundred forty-two landing skids that we must extend to correct lengths. The Wheel is designed to sit without undue stress on any structural member as water and materials are added and moved around. I will keep you updated on progress. After landing we will pump all our water to the top hull tanks and remove the topside magnetic shields. We will also check out and integrate the ship's systems. If all goes well, we will have the concourse mixer as scheduled our third evening on Pluto."

The Wheel landed late afternoon ship's time on day sixty-five out of Earth. Minutes later a post by Lois told the pilgrims they had landed on water-ice in an area called the Badlands, and had sufficient energy to melt ice and purify it quickly. Taking water onboard was their only reason to stay on Pluto. They would depart the planet within a few days.

The first morning on Pluto, the concourse's large round cargo doors were opened one-by-one and the wheel declared complete at the all normal and lowest alert level, Green-Seven. At midnight the connecting doors would be closed until the concourse mixer. Thereafter, a palpable sense of relief and relaxation ensued among even the trained crew. Still, no one claimed to feel normal, including Philip.

He no longer worried about gothic minds, ghosts inhabiting binary beings, nor Earthlings. He wondered, *Why am I fretting?*

I'd hate to be so immersed in activities that awareness of the void goes missing. I can say that now that I have a place to belong, even if it is small and marginally prepared to survive. The great void is not about survival, not about sex; it's about existing unhappily among the wonders of the Cosmos…living incompletely without becoming…without having a love of your life. Facing alone the undiscovered country. Perhaps only family and close friends with entangled resonances of mind create a contented heart. Alice is paramount. Only she shares my many dimensions of being, compatible in all dimensions and of one mind in most. True soulmates and lovers! Each an essential part in the other's life, an entangled bond not imagined until you have it—love for your lifetime.

The high-abstracting mind knows not what's what, but what's not. The rational mind knows what's probable. The elect mind knows that it has a heart and seeks to become the authentic best of what it is. Yet, who's to say? Let all say and do in peace with others. The Cosmos shall sort them out; the Cosmos shall have the say! The elect shall have the glory. And let us remember, Amen!

20

UP AND DOING

Although Philip enjoyed speculative thinking as if still a professor, he knew that Alice considered it daydreaming and was right that in their situation the healthy creature should be up and doing. He got busy on his kom. He listed his wedding date as the third evening after departure from Pluto and obtained an after-lunch appointment with the Special Events Consultant. The passenger lists of *Marianas* and *New Ionia* were now posted on Fednet. His friends and his cousin were listed in good health. Philip messaged them that he looked forward to meeting them in *Marianas Key* during the upcoming concourse mixer.

Alice and Philip ate a simple lunch of yogurt and toast in their apartment before Philip set off for his wedding consultation. As he walked, his thoughts wandered as usual. *What a minuscule amount of effort I contributed to getting us here. Why after a few weeks on Nevis did I think I should be shown the secrets of the kingdom for merely hanging around? Because then I wasn't fully real. It was okay to want to know and ask, but not okay to pout when not told. That was my demon from the past. Alice too had her demon. Had or has? O Cosmos, how deep into primary process did they penetrate?*

As Philip shuffled along in virtually nonexistent gravity, he received a call from Comte, who knew that Alice's parents, Jeffrey and Joanne, wanted to toast at the wedding reception. Comte suggested that Philip speak first and then invite others. Nearing his destination, Philip renewed his resolve to ask for a whirlpool tub. *Is that a ridiculous request? How should I know? We need a surprise for the honeymoon!*

Only forty minutes later, on his way back to the apartment Philip congratulated himself on having a reservation for a honeymoon suite with a large hot tub—Pystead had no whirlpool tubs.

Melita called and was happy to hear plans were going well. "I have it on best word, Melita, that you have the gift. Please tell me what is new under the Sun?"

"I can fathom the seas, I can reach the stars, and I know what the bridegroom seeks."

"And?"

"Wait and see, wait and see. Ask again at the first event we share after you are wed. Offer your left palm, but do not ask me to read your palm. Ask what I see for you."

Philip thought that Melita never read the future for friends and asked, "Are we not friends?"

"By the flick of time, we are friends and never lovers. Ask when Alice is present. I will seek to read your stars."

"Thank you. As before on Nevis, I am again troubled about our future for children."

"Until the walking of the horse, friend Philip."

⁂ ⁂ ⁂

Once home, Philip expressed his satisfaction with the events consultant. Alice said she had contacted Rabbi Issegow, who agreed to marry them in a ceremony with only one biblical reference—to Moses. The Rabbi would read a poem of their choosing, and Alice agreed that Philip would step on his champagne flute after toasts. She said although a waste, it was their flute and could provide first shards for recycling glass.

Alice sent Philip to listen to recordings of a quintet recommended by Rabbi Issegow. He listened to three different wedding marches, and then confirmed the group would stay and play a couple of hours of easy dancing music. At the suggestion of Alice via the Rabbi, Philip asked the leader to hold any jokes he might normally make, a condition to which the man was opposed, citing negative public exposure. When Philip promised five bottles of champagne for the group to take home if they played music without comments, the ensemble's leader assured Philip that since it was important to them, he would put the kibosh on jokes.

Alice was certainly right about checking out that ensemble. That bald flugelhorn player is a character. Let's hope thoughts of champagne keep him mellow. This group is musically as good or better than my envisioned string quartet—the piano and flugelhorn add dimensions of sound and I still get two violins and my favorite cello.

⁂ ⁂ ⁂

Alice learned that she would personally need to supervise a Wheel-wide installation of a new security system for the art galleries. Her mother called to tell her that Council had approved the request by Comte and Melita, and that she must assure that its software was programmed by Cobalt Blue personnel and tested in secret to assure it performed according to Comte's specifications.

Eager to begin his own official duties, Philip looked forward to his afternoon appointment with George Snyder, his duty Commander, whom he knew well from his day of assisting the School of Cognitive Science while on Pystead's campus. At their meeting, George introduced Philip to his new colleagues and assigned him a laboratory space and an interview kom. George authorized Philip to interview the K.L.J.H. Organism, but not their leader, Dr. Osgood, who Pystead had living separately from the Organism. Philip was satisfied with only the Organism because it offered the most opportunity for both Pystead's and his personal research needs. In the future Pystead would have difficult decisions to make about the shipboard liberty of each member of the Organism. And the diversity of their human origins was ideal for Philip's personal research of separating innate human instincts from culturally wired behaviors. Philip knew the assignment was not accidental because George knew of and approved of his personal research project.

Finished within an hour, Philip rushed back to the apartment to tell Alice his good news. She was happy for him and said he should relax, have tea, and begin reading about cat and home care. *Well, nobody said being a pilgrim would be all fun. Those K.L.J.H. cyborgs and our late pickups are of such varied origins that comparisons of different innateness should be rewarding. Here we have no politicized funding committee to reject my research proposal. Here the potential for knowledge decides because we are not afraid of what we might find if it's the truth of the matter.*

* * *

Philip and Alice ate a light meal in anticipation of many tasty treats at the mixer. They talked by kom to Alice's parents, to Philip's cousin, and then to his friends from California. By mid-afternoon their circle of new friends again interacted, watching video of the outside work and chatting. The artists agreed their art should be expressive while preserving the objects of their new era. Conversation became unpredictable when Isaac and Brian and the rescued boys, Norman and Bao-Tu, participated, as it did with Frank, Lala, and Violca. Philip's friend, the elusive Arthur Vanderhought, joined them for a few minutes and assured everybody that being a pilgrim would become much like living on Earth after buildout on another planet, although not on Mars.

When Philip closed his eyes, Alice kissed him on the cheek. "We have left Mother Earth never to return. Never to see her again, yet always to long for her in our quiet moments. Forever a loss in the heart. You help compensate for that loss, Phil."

"I feel the same. You are the love of my life, Alice. The only person essential to me." *What makes life here a bit hollow? Absence of the daily hassle? No city skyline? No Sun disk? No pleasant Moon? No vast ocean? Ah ha, no Cosmic Turtle bearing up the Earth on its journey—no planetary security! Unless, of course, Alice is right about One Above who cares being our cosmic security! Dreams that lead to technology are certainly better than dreams that lead to irrational dogma. Even so, why suppose One Above is omnipresent?* Philip inquired, "Alice, does your Blue channel estimate how many days we will stay on frozen Pluto?"

"Five days, with liftoff the morning of the sixth."

"I suppose wedding plans will hold and reset when we depart Pluto?"

"Oh yes."

"How many invitations are open? I must invite Arthur Vanderhought and Lauren, and I'd like to invite Stuart and Irene, and Dennis and Sandra."

"Comte brought half of our champagne aboard. After a gift bottle or so for the individuals and groups involved, we will have enough for fifty flutes." Alice took a breath, "We have twenty-eight acceptances, and I'd like to stop at forty to be sure of both seating and champagne."

They went through the names. All Philip's friends were invited. Alice decided to give champagne to all assisting staff, making the first wedding aboard memorable.

"Alice, what do we wear?"

"I was wondering if you would ask." She began with the dress and suits she would like, borrowed from the Special Events Shop. She suggested Comte for best man. Then she surprised him. "Beginning after the concourse mixer, I'll stay with Revathy. All the women agree that you should not see me until the wedding ceremony. Anyway, I'll be busy overseeing the installation of a new security system for the art galleries." Alice smiled. "I'll ask some of our friends to call on you."

"Please, no! I need the downtime. And what else do I need to know that I haven't asked about?"

"I believe that's all. You can chat with Comte and Melita to work out little details like toasts and handling our suitcases."

✳   ✳   ✳

By early evening of their third full day on Pluto, Lois announced all ships ready for the concourse party, which would begin at seven-forty-five, later than anticipated. Network posts and video revealed that no hazardous or unexpected conditions had been detected on Pluto or Charon, natural or artificial. As a prophylactic measure in a strange land, perhaps with autonomous U.N. rovers about, foo fighters were flying a continuous perimeter watch. *Would be fairer duty for older men who have already done their share of partying,* Philip couldn't help thinking.

21

MAKING PEACE

Philip and Alice both chose to wear khaki slacks for the concourse mixer. Philip opted for his white and blue striped shirt. Alice decided on a blouse new to Philip, a baby-blue pullover with gapping seams sewn together only at points every few centimeters. Philip said she was almost too alluring for the mixer. He suggested she bring the blouse on their honeymoon.

The couple joined the event of walking Frank's horse to the rim zone of *Key Bury*. Melita gave each a golden hat to identify as part of the parade. Melita wore a white feather in her hat, young Norman and two other boys in gold hats preceded Frank, who wore his tan cowboy hat. Frank led Rom Baro in a minimal pod harness girded with a wide surcingle securing backpacks holding restraint lines, bodily-function bags, soap, and towels. Frank looked the part of a leading-man, a movie cowboy in his sage green canvas shirt and blue jeans. Frank's twin girlfriends dressed as rotund clowns followed with large candy canes concealing vacuum cleaners for use should the horse be off schedule. Unneeded for cleanup duty the twins frolicked ahead, now expert at catching the floor's sticky strips, waving to children and urging them to pet the gentle horse. Rom Baro was majestic with his well-groomed mane and feathers. The powerful horse followed Frank's lead, pausing often to let the children pet. The clown suits with their striking pattern of red, yellow, white, and black diamond checks made the parade festive.

Upon arrival at the new horse barn, Frank gave his sister a hug of appreciation. On a close look after Alice's repeated nudging, Philip saw that each twin was wearing a diamond ring. *Much larger diamonds than Alice's.*

⁂

After a quick sticky-walk back to quarters for Alice's gift bottle of white wine, they were off to visit Samantha and Albert. Samantha greeted them in white hotpants and probably the same pink blouse she had worn that night Philip met her on Nevis, now with all buttons fastened. Albert was broad and imposing in his white jumpsuit, like Philip at a centimeter taller. His dark auburn red hair was cut just over his ears. He was striking with a Roman nose and angular features. He explained that his crew was using cavitation technology to purify the melted ice before testing and adding the water to ship's stores—in separate tanks.

Alice held up her bottle of Chardonnay. "I brought wine to celebrate, let's have a glass before Albert needs to leave." Soon all raised their glass of elixir to friendship.

Albert toasted, "To Pystead and Philip, for saving our lives." In a subdued tone he added, "I don't know you well, but I understand that both of you know that Samantha and I had an open marriage when on Kitts-Nevis—only there. Nevertheless, I think it should be known that the marriage is now closed." Alice and Philip sipped their wine in silence.

Samantha finally spoke, "We have been through trying times. I was the cause of those times, although not intentionally. You know, evidently the entire ship knows, that I went to Philip's bachelor party and danced for him in my slip. Samantha cast a wistful glance at Alice. "Only after I learned how much I upset you, Alice, did I realize my mistake."

Alice said softly, "We have gotten past that, Samantha." *You didn't mention your alterations to that slip and lack of a bra! I'll not embarrass the men.*

"I did it because I wanted to be special for Philip, a special, platonic friend."

"I accept that our agreement on that is still good."

Samantha jumped up, bounding almost to the ceiling. On the way down, she hugged Alice around the shoulders. Albert's kom buzzed. "Sorry, I must go. We have water to purify and test before even the park's plants can have it."

Alice stood and stepped over to Albert, cooing, "Since we're going to be good friends, let's start now." She put her hand on his neck and coaxed his head over, kissing him half on the lips for a long moment.

He smiled. "Perhaps I too have a special platonic friend. Delighted to know you both. Please don't break up festivities."

Samantha kissed Albert goodbye. "Be careful."

"I don't go outside the ship." He backed out slowly, sliding his sticky sole to catch a walking strip in the corridor floor.

"Please stay if you can," Samantha urged them. "I have coffee ready to brew if you would like?"

They stayed. Samantha went to the kitchenette. Alice took Phil's hand. "We have a friend in her Phil, I'm happy for both of us."

"You should know that on Nevis when you were still called Ice, Samantha and I saw you and Isaac together at Lamancha House, and she advised me not to give up on you. She told me that if I could fall in love with you at first sight, perhaps I could fall into friendship with her over time."

"I'm glad you told me. Did you notice that I gave Albert quite a kiss for a new friend?"

"I thought so."

"Not because he's handsome—his angular features are not for me. I did it for Samantha. I want to keep our social norm for her and Albert warmer than with our other friends. I don't mind her being special for you."

"You are my only truly special one, Alice."

She did her big-eyed pose.

Philip said sotto voce, "If I'm not going to be jealous of Albert or Isaac, you should not be jealous of Samantha."

Alice said just as softly, "I'm making progress on that."

Samantha was back with coffee and three mugs. All three sat enjoying the coffee and the real, albeit light, gravity of Pluto. Alice asked, "Samantha, didn't you tell me you wrote short stories?"

"Yes, I worked diligently, both on Nevis and in California. We lived in Sunnyvale."

Alice asked, "Are you published?"

"Yes, my novelettes. Anybody can publish, but I did well. I made a living."

"We must read them."

"I'll have them to the library within a few weeks."

"Will you continue to write the same stories?"

"I'm wondering about that. Only time will tell. One is supposed to write for an audience, and I have little idea whom my audience might be." Samantha then said she knew Alice had paintings in the ship's galleries and wanted to see them.

By the time they were ready to leave, Philip was tense, realizing that sooner or later Samantha's erotic stories would become known to Alice. *Should it matter? Well, later must be better than sooner?* At the door, Philip received Samantha's kiss on his lips.

As the couple turned the first corner from the apartment, Alice observed, "She kept her hot social kiss for you. I did right by my friend." They moved slowly using the Pluto shuffle, holding hands, enjoying the charm of lightness of being and light kisses.

Once in the apartment, Philip confirmed an upcoming chamber music concert of Hungarian flute music. Alice nodded. They closed their eyes to rest before the concourse mixer.

22

CONCOURSE MIXER

The pilgrims knew that professional chefs of each ethnic group were aboard and would prepare hors d'oeuvres of their unique cuisines. Each off-duty adult could have nine ounces of wine, at one or more food kiosks of their choice. Duty shifts would rotate every two hours and a crewmember could have three ounces of wine before going on duty. Everybody planned to attend. "This is a mixer," Alice had reminded her artist friends. "Dress to be seen! Split up and mix separately some of the time. Please talk for at least a few minutes to anybody who wants to chat. You could learn something interesting. Rejecting a suitor or simply a sociable person immediately will not make for a successful mixer. In fact, we women need to introduce ourselves to the shy men. Be a hostess! Mix, chat. If you are shy, go in twos. Remember that in our small community somebody you meet or snub today could become part of your daily life tomorrow."

✷　✷　✷

Accustomed to sticky soles, Alice and Philip walked the concourse easily, albeit carefully, with Comte leading, not lingering to read posters or menus. They arrived early for the opening of their concourse portal. When the large, round concourse door rolled away Alice tensed. The other ship's door was already open and several people stepped through quickly, only to jump forward. A guard called out to catch the railing, the three-tiers-high handrails running a few meters beyond the portal. Alice soon called, "Mom! Dad! Over here!" They recognized her voice and hurried to get free of the crowd. Alice caught Philip's hand for introductions. Joanne, Alice's mother, hugged Philip and said she knew all the good things about him except how handsome he was. Her father, Jeffrey, shook hands with a smile and Philip felt welcomed into the family.

Rather than walking more of the concourse, Alice's parents wanted to see her apartment. Comte led them first to their own apartment. En route Philip noticed that Jeffrey resembled Comte, and that Alice had her mother's very blonde hair and big blue eyes. Her parents said their apartment was fine, and hearing Comte's opinion that all apartments were much the same, they settled for a virtual tour of Alice's apartment with video she had taken on her kom. Joanne admired the paintings they had hung, and then urged them to attend the mixer on the concourse and meet Philip's friends, and to stop by afterwards no matter how late.

✷　✷　✷

Once on the concourse, Alice and Philip mixed and chatted with both friends and strangers. Philip spotted Isaac and noticed that he turned away, probably to avoid them.

He told Alice, "Isaac is to your left. If we are going to socialize with him, you should float over and chat."

"If we are all to be friends, you should come too."

"You two should have a few minutes to catch up before I'm part of the story. I'll visit a food kiosk first."

After only one bite-sized pastry, Philip met Melita Rose, who was wearing a light purple, V-neck pantsuit. "Philip, I'm flirting with the men to encourage mingling, but I'm not available, as you know." He smiled. She asked, "Aren't you ever curious about the classic issue with psychics?"

"From all I've heard, I feel sure I should conclude that you're a virgin. Aren't all psychics?"

"Not the men! My celibacy, you may also conclude, is entangled."

"Didn't consider that. My professional interest is more general."

"I am merely a dual personality, both alters are self-controlled, without delusions, without muddled thinking, and without significant crossover. Joan and I maintain continuity of time. Our wrist koms have a special A.I. feature that allows one of us to summon the dormant alter with advice on circumstances once she is conscious."

"I believe science could profit from brain scans."

"I would do them for you, for you personally and in private." Philip was quiet, taking time to sample more food. Melita added, "You would not be asking too much. I offer only for Melita."

"I'm not yet familiar with Pystead's interview protocols."

"Ask when the time is right. Now, Philip, your fiancée is looking around for you."

"Will you visit with us later this evening?"

"Of course, Alice is my best friend…after Prince and Joan."

"Perhaps you can tell me why Alice seems a little insecure?"

"I'm sure she feels secure, but she may have a demon remaining from Earth."

"I may too."

"I want us to talk about those demons, Philip. Let's find time."

"Fine. I'll go now. Alice is waiting, and men are circling for you."

"I will encourage them to chat with someone other than me, a ship's counselor who finds them an interesting Poseidon, yet must remain…floating. You should rescue Alice from her circling bees."

Philip hurried over and took Alice's hand as a bee buzzed away. "Alice, you attract men like a sweet flower attracts bees."

"Phil, this is a mixer! I'm supposed to smile and attract the bees. You were a difficult case, my bee in full, I had to be clever too."

"You are gorgeous in all dimensions."

"You are too sweet. Have you been enjoying the flowers?"

"Merely floating. I did chat with Melita."

"Are you going to introduce me to your newly arrived friends?"

"Of course. Do you think the bees will follow?"

Alice looked around. "Aren't male bees territorial? If we wander off and cross the portal, they won't follow."

"Well, the bees should seek another flower if you kiss me."

The couple crossed through the portal to *Key New Ionia*. They proceeded slowly along as Philip wanted to sample the hors d'oeuvres. Alice asked why he was hungry if he had not been flirting. He said he had talked at length with Melita. Alice said that monopolizing her friend's time was scandalous, but she kissed him on the cheek.

"Alice, I want to walk this side of the concourse because I walked the other way the day you needed to be alone."

"I'd hate for you to miss a cuisine. Let's complete the circle."

"Fine, circles should be unbroken. Was Isaac pleased to see you?"

"Of course. I must admit to kissing him on the lips like Samantha for you."

"A sure sign of friendship. Yet, Melita didn't kiss me!"

"Your's wasn't a new-beginnings chat."

"True." He pointed. "We should try this food."

"Just a few bites because your friends are waiting for us in Marianas Key."

They passed parks and food kiosks. Once through the next portal, Alice recognized the line of sky blue triangles comprising the ceiling trim for the Federation's *Marianas Key*. Philip noticed that the Key's sign read Olam HaBah. Only a few meters past the security check point, people stood around chatting where light fare was served. Philip took a grape leaf filled with rice and lamb. Alice suggested surprising his friends by not using kom-locate.

"I'll watch for them now and eat later."

⚹ ⚹ ⚹

Midway on the concourse Philip spotted Stuart and family and waved.

Irene pulled her two boys away from what looked like potato pancakes. She took a rushed step and found herself in a leap that could have landed badly, although she recovered to give Philip a hug. "Philip Russell, you told Stuart no office on Mars!"

"We're expanding operations. Surely you're good for a little change of scenery?"

"Stuart has enjoyed the little change more than I."

"The reason?"

"Try keeping two young boys in seatbelts, not to mention occupied in a small apartment with no friends. Only their Rube Goldberg eGame, Connect Four in a Row, and Chess have saved us."

"It's good you don't have a dog."

Irene asked, "Are you going to introduce us to this charming woman in blue?"

"Right." Introductions went smoothly, and Alice and Irene chatted easily.

Philip took a moment with the boys and was able to reach a fried potato pancake for himself. He and the boys agreed the pancakes were good.

When Irene took Alice to meet the boys, Stuart told Philip, "We have met decent people. Life should be good if we can stay alive."

"I think our chances must be even with surviving on Earth, especially for those of us who were living on the ocean side of the San Andreas Fault." They laughed. "Here, Stu, the idea of progress is alive and well."

"The people who named our ship are optimistic, but what is different here to warrant such optimism?"

"Stuart, what does your ship's name mean?"

"World to come."

"Ah. To answer your question, here the people are a very select group. The vetting process may not have been perfect, but the objective—my words—has been to form a group of talented, disciplined, catholic-thinking people who can embrace the ideas of progress and live-and-let-live, charity not excluded. Pluralism is embraced. The individual is respected. This group of pilgrims hopes to be a singularity from which a genome of elect humanity might evolve. I believe that sums it up."

Stuart thought for a moment. "People are the key, more important than the formal organization. A decent group requires a preponderance of moral minds regardless of policy and law. A reality demonstrated at highest levels three decades ago." Stuart glanced around. "Thanks so much for getting us out. The news in Compton was all about the many kidnappings by this Pystead Group, including attacks on U.N. jets over the Caribbean Sea and on the U.N.'s Moon Base. In academic circles, however, professors leaving called colleagues to say they had taken a new job with a decent company. We soon knew that the public news was all lies. The U.N. swore to track Pystead to the ends of the solar system the day we were picked up." Stuart looked around, "I should get back to the family."

"It's good to have old friends for company, Stu. Have you seen Dennis and Sandra?"

"They experienced an unfortunate low-gravity event and will be out as soon as they can clean up and change."

"Your cousin?"

"The ship's computer matched your cousin with Robin. Yesterday, each received a visit from your ship's counselor, and they are attending this mixer together. They want to see you later this evening."

After another few minutes, Philip sensed Alice was anxious. "Stuart, I have through happenstance met high officers of the Pystead organization, including my fiancée who oversees the art galleries as a Staff Commander—not in line for a general leadership role. Other officer friends will be at the wedding, but as you may have heard, our culture does not discuss office or duties in casual social circles. Please do not ask about either. And we are all on a first name basis. After the wedding you will meet our close friends a few at the time when shipboard positions and last names can be mentioned. You must keep your knowledge of those relationships strictly between yourself and Irene to avoid such social circles becoming known in public."

"We will be careful at the wedding and thereafter."

"Event space aboard ship is always an issue. We are fortunate as there will be childcare next door during the wedding, so bring the boys."

"Is this good fortune by any chance related to friends in high places?"

"Friends helped without effort on our part, but none of the facilities, cake, or services are unique for us. We will have champagne toasts only because we were engaged on Nevis and Alice brought champagne aboard. I suppose you have discovered the dearth of alcoholic beverages?"

"A small thing to forego for peace of mind. May I propose a toast?"

"You may. I have been advised to let toasts run their course on empty flutes."

"I'll be brief."

The two friends shuffled over to rejoin the family. They all walked to the adjacent key, *Kali*, with its saffron ceiling trim of symbols, one resembling the numeral three with a tail, one of interlocking triangles inside a circle, another a lotus flower. "Nice," proclaimed Philip. The two boys, playfully leaping, discovered more edible delights. Irene said the boys had met a few neighborhood children, and they were invited to a social for families. Alice promised she would invite them for family socials after the wedding, but now she needed to visit her parents who had just arrived. Philip said to tell Dennis and Sandra he'd call. Stuart and family turned back.

⚹ ⚹ ⚹

Philip used kom-locate to find his cousin, Lauren. He and Alice met her and Stuart's cousin, Robin, in *E Key* with its green ceiling trim. Philip and Lauren hardly recognized each other, but he did receive a teary-eyed hug. She was excited to have escaped Earth and her nursing job blighted by Six Sigma quality control protocols. Alice said they would both receive a wedding invitation, and all felt like family before parting.

Philip and Alice walked slowly, pausing at the last food kiosk to munch *Shandong-Nevis's* fusion fare of Chinese and Caribbean spices. Their entrance into *Key Bury* reminded Philip of their wedding. "Alice, when do you leave?"

"I'll pack my suitcase and go after dinner. I'll miss you. It's for the best, the women assure me. You should not wait for Dennis to call. Please call him. Have all the new arrivals over to see the apartment, especially my parents."

✳   ✳   ✳

They reached Alice's parents at ten o'clock. Joanne and Alice shed tears and Jeffery hugged his daughter for at least half a minute. All said they were in good health. Joanne said they were delighted with the apartment. Alice said their apartments were in the same ship's neighborhood on the same deck, and they could easily visit, except during top ship's alert. Joanne gave both Alice and Philip a coffee mug from the last major theme park in Florida, Epcot World, which she called a hologram fantasy world, unlike Pystead's real fantasy world. When Alice explained that she would visit with them without Philip until the wedding, Joanne said that she and Jeffery wanted to see Philip often before the wedding.

Once home, in a strange variation on life, Alice packed quickly and kissed Philip goodbye. She pulled her suitcase down the hall and waved before turning the corner. *My female friends say absence makes the heart grow fonder. Phil has family and friends to visit and to-do items on his wedding list. He will be fine. Soon I shall be fine with a kind and interesting husband to help raise our children.*

23

DEMONS

Philip reached Dennis and Sandra by kom. They were grateful to be out of the university and out of California. Sandra admitted that adjusting to low gravity was challenging, saying they had almost recovered from spills of fingernail polish and orange juice. She agreed that life aboard ship was not nearly normal, yet already better. They wanted to meet for brunch.

He made his list: late breakfast with S & D, pick up suit, call Comte, call Arthur, wrap the small box of art supplies, confirm honeymoon guest room, pack for honeymoon, sign-out for vacation with School of Cog Sci, hear flute concert, set two wake-up alarms, take the wedding ring, take the champagne, take the two dozen glass flutes, think of anything else. He played soft background music and ate two muffins for breakfast. Missing Alice, he began counting the days until the wedding. Depending on time needed to fill the Wheel's water tanks, he faced four to eight days alone.

⁂ ⁂ ⁂

The door chime sounded. Philip opened the door and said as if pre-programmed, "Come in, counselor."

"Counselors do not appear without an invitation." Melita smiled. "Merely a friend." Once seated, she skipped pleasantries. "Demons are difficult because they hide away and appear uncalled to do their mischief." She waited for Philip. He was distracted by his up-close and somehow different perception of her. She seemed warm in personality and color tones, with her pleasant expression, light brown hair, hazel-gray eyes, and muted-red lipstick. "Melita, your overall warm look of today surprises me! I believe your golden-tan dress helps make the difference."

"How so?"

"I picture you in your usual platinum, silverish, or violet colors—cool colors that distract attention from the warmth of your face and voice."

Melita smiled. "I'm pleased to be warm for you. Better for our topic of today. You should know that as a young woman in graduate school, in California, your Alice then called Janice, was lied to by three men who said they loved her. She changed her approach to men and vetted those she thought of as a potentially serious relationship. She selected, vetted, and seduced her men rather than being chosen and seduced by them."

"Ice had my vetting report and said the palm reader approved. Thinking back, I'll say she seduced me by setting the scene, and I helped by wanting her."

"Whatever your experience, her demon was already present and hiding. A few of us believe that her assertive years during graduate school resulted in a psychologically inadequate female development, hence a yearning, a demon!"

"I haven't noticed this demon."

"Neither has Ice, well, now Alice. A few of us have glimpsed it. It hides in what you cognitive scientists call primary process, the subconscious and intuitive mind."

"If so, the demon will not dominate until a moment of decision making."

"I have glimpsed subtle manifestations of her psyche's need. Being unknown and beyond conscious control, the need becomes a demon. A demon to her contentment until satisfied."

"Please name this demon for me."

"I believe Alice needs to normalize her psychological development as a female by surrendering to a male she hasn't formally vetted."

"She needs to be seduced?"

"Yes, and perhaps more than once. Only the demon decides."

"I do want her to go down to her dreams a woman in full."

"Your role is clear!"

"Don't get in the way of her demon!"

"Precisely. Perhaps more easily accomplished than you might expect. Do you know of Comte's proposed culture of increasing intimacy between close friends, special friends, during retirement?"

"I must agree for us to participate?"

"Yes! Not easy to do for most in our present culture. As you might say, for those with present wirings of mind?"

"Strange, unsettling. Yet I do want a contented wife—woman. If I can keep that strange new variation conceptual, image free, perhaps I can free her to participate."

"Once you signal approval of friends-plus, Alice is emotionally changed and her demon may rise, perhaps before the appointed week or month of cultural change."

"For her best chances of a true seduction, I should approve our participation well before the proposed date of change?"

"Yes, my advice is that you express a reserved yet positive potential for acceptance soon after the change is floated."

"How do either of us ultimately ask to be free?"

"I'm working on that. Let's keep in touch on the topic. Bear in mind that Alice will feel honor and duty bound to promote her grandfather's vision. Begin by encouraging her rightful leadership in the transition. Given the demon, if you approve, even philosophically, her primary process will surely favor participation, which to be fair must include you."

"Perhaps Isaac will seduce her?"

"Old loves may rekindle desire, but they do not seduce!" Melita smiled. "We have years, two decades. You and I must assist by allowing proper conditions to manifest. We cannot provide the cure. We can encourage favorable circumstances."

"Alice believes that decent human beings should not be afraid of their natural instincts."

"Then her demon will surely persuade her that a transition is needed, and that humans should acknowledge their innate instincts, their needs. Have you associated the proposed variation with the needs of belonging and friendship? Comte believes that fulfilling those needs in our circumscribed society can energize the retired, thereby producing better mentors, teachers, and reserve crewmembers. Some will have lost spouses and close friends and will need a friend-plus. A lasting, personal relationship may become affectionate, intimate, and Comte believes better sexual than frustrating."

Melita stood. "We need to chat again about Alice, and about your demon."

"You and Joan helped me belong while still on Campus. That somehow suppressed my apprehension about bringing children into a family with Alice's secrets."

"A suppressed demon might rise. I want to help you kill it, friend Philip!" Both smiled as the door closed.

24

A GAP IN SPACETIME

Two days after the concourse mixer, Philip met Dennis and Sandra for breakfast. All were happy together again even though their changed circumstances did not yet feel like full lives. For Philip, in the streamlined white and silver ship, both looked their ages, mid-fifties, which he had not noticed in their university buildings in California. Both had touches of gray in their hair. Sandra showed fine wrinkles on her neck though retaining the cute face that had given her the nickname, Professor Barbie. Dennis with his pleasant smile and slightly concave nose was, of course, known as Prof. Ken. Now, suddenly, their compatible, mid-age cuteness seemed unprepared for strange new variations on life. Philip found himself biting his lip. His friends had certainly led sheltered lives. He asked, "Are you reading Pystead's policy manual? There are surprises throughout."

"Only the introduction," said Sandra. "During the few days before boarding, a Pystead representative briefed us on policy, ship, and staffing basics. We were impressed that Pystead has such an elite and experienced crew, such advanced technology, and nine separate ships. We became convinced that seventeen hundred talented adults could cover all the disciplines with computer assistance and surgical machines as needed. Of course, talking with you, knowing that you accepted Pystead's capabilities, made our decision to join possible."

"The group began in the Czech Republic in nineteen ninety-four. Its first crewmembers were from Europe, chosen for their money or expertise. Recruiting qualified, decent people— not the speed of assembling a crew—was an organizing principle. If you find anything in the policy difficult to understand or imagine, call. Alice has me well versed on policy. If I can't answer a question, she can."

Since Philip still had wedding related chores, Dennis and Sandra said goodbye.

✷ ✷ ✷

Philip was pleased at having accomplished most of his to-do list for the wedding. He had wrapped his small gift for show. It and the wedding ring and carry bag of champagne were at the door, not to be forgotten. He had a toast in mind. Now he needed to call Comte. Following the advice of Alice and his wedding consultant, he asked Comte to be his best man. Comte said he was honored and would like to be early to escort Philip to the chapel. Comte said he would know the date of the third day off Pluto and would call the day before with the time to leave the apartment. Philip was relieved to have a best man who would know schedules and get him to the chapel on time. That night he slept soundly.

His third morning without Alice, Philip ate yogurt at home. For the first time in memory reading did not sustain him. His laboratory equipment was ready but interacting with new colleagues and procedures was too much to bear. Having no assigned schedule, he put off beginning work. He sat in their reclining chair, through habit slipping into thought, or into daydreams as Alice would say. *Resting in the void has its satisfactions. One may overcome stillness by embracing its peace…but not for long! Stillness leads from contemplating our future on Mars to our interstellar voyage. This dimension of serenity isn't for me. One must accept cosmic loneliness; why accept personal aloneness? Being alone without the one you love has little meaning, creates few fond memories. No soulmate the group. Long ago, if reflecting pools and mirrors changed humanity's concept of self, what will images of isolation and vastness change? The cosmos sparkles, visually awe inspiring, yet always the same overall stillness, the same obscuring darkness! Interstellar space travel is made in starlight, yet in the dark!* Philip sat up and looked at their analog clock. *Do I need a tangible image of time? For some things a concept is adequate, even preferable! Was not Pystead's culture in concept less difficult than now in images of reality? Easier to board a magnificent ship than a ship of corridors having low gravity, tanks having too little water, half the crew untrained, an enemy trying to kill you. Too, retirement according to Comte's vision qualifies as troubling. Are Comte and Melita right?*

Philip stared at their large, split-faced, twenty-four-hour analog clock. *Are all things relative? What of married love? It manifests to entangle two lives, slightly differently for any two given lives. The dimensions of mind may be named, the relationship generally defined, but the particulars remain subjective for any given relationship. Is not 'Be-and-Become' a mantra of mine? Wished for myself alone, or as well for Alice? I do want her to be fulfilled, loving me as the soulmate of her life. I must not block her becoming a woman in full. Are imagined images my obstacle to her becoming? Why none from her past? If her past be not an issue, why then her future?*

I need lunch. I need the meme others have already attained. Samantha and Albert's open marriage while in the Caribbean. Melita and Joan being the same person with two personas and only one having a lover. Frank and his twin fiancées—accepted here. Alice shared her lover for two years while on Nevis. Alice, now my fiancée with a mermaid Amanda persona she shares with me. Will she have another mermaid persona to share as a friend-plus? Already I know strange variations! Perhaps the only problem is getting from here to there in the here and now? A catch twenty-three? I need lunch.

⚹   ⚹   ⚹

That evening, which Philip noted as his fourth without Alice, he received a kom message that the hot tub would not be available during his reservation period due to a low dielectric maintenance flag on the pump's motor. After a brief chat with reservations, Philip learned he would have priority during rescheduling. He was disappointed, but glad to know in advance. He accepted another room on the rim near a large galley, a park, an observation lounge, and an art gallery. *Why do I feel strange? Insignificant to the cosmos, I must be significant to Alice. To that end we must reach the stars and continue the lineage of Saint Germaine. For the lineage I must be chosen, so the elect of the elect do bear me! And let me say, Amen.*

Philip attended the flute concert with an audience of almost fifty people. They heard a chamber ensemble with four flutes and two singers. The songs were fast, high register, cavorting melodies,

231

accompanied by rich base runs and clear voices probably in Hungarian. *Exotic, exhilarating, romantic! Songs that move you even in their incomprehensible tongue. Trumps the music of the spheres on a forlorn night on an ice patch, on an orange-marmalade orb having ominous moons and merely an incandescent star for its sun. And with Alice away my heart is sad—without her voice, her smile, her presence. I need the many dimensions of being with my soulmate to fill the void. Surely this flute music is available on a Network. In an observation lounge at noon, like Moonlight on Earth, the music will be enchanting.*

Philip left the concert with thoughts for honeymoon entertainment. *After recommending the Kehchen's Jazz Group from Nevis, I've not been to hear them! Unexpected entertainment, flute music and jazz.*

✳ ✳ ✳

The next morning, restless and hoping to avoid friends, Philip shuffled to a distant neighborhood galley for a hot breakfast. He was careful to avoid corridors that were off limits for him in order not to meet Alice by chance. Afterwards he returned to his hollow quarters, replenished Char Cat's automatic feeder and opened the appliances manual on his kom. After reading several pages, he swapped in favor of an old, hardcopy book. Two pages later he decided against reading and opted for whatever diversions a Network might offer. The latest word on departing Pluto was that the Wheel would fly outward bound for a day or so before turning back to cross through the orbit of Pluto en route to Mars. *Then our wedding. Perhaps cultural change will come naturally over time? Now of no concern! A happy wife and children being my immediate future.*

No delay on Pluto yet—delay, delay. Already I've delayed so much in my life. I lost people for the sake of my education: left childhood friends, aunts and uncles, my cousin. I left school friends twice for career. I spent much of my career trying to relate to colleagues who were secretly contemptuous of me for being a scholar instead of a political activist. Lost my parents. O Cosmos, miserable creatures we are. Cannot protect our children or know their fates, both a blessing and a curse. As a blessing we are largely shielded from the trials and tribulations endured by our individual ancestors; we are largely excluded from the fates of our own descendants. Being, blindly being, in a merely extended moment of time seals humanity in a temporal bubble.

The cosmos entertains all minds and rewards both individual and group success according to its fixed realities. I delayed, but I did leave Compton, did join Pystead, and I did contact my cousin, Lauren. Hopefully, we will be rewarded with an extended moment of liberty in which to live and let live, and to achieve our potential. An enriched variation of previously possible variations on life. Our innate morality should thrive, freed from the lies, illusions, and repressions of Earth's grand deemers! We should become a singularity of humanity kept free by our selection criteria and continual monitoring via functional brain scans!

⚹   ⚹   ⚹

Philip looked around. *I asked friends and family out here and haven't even invited Stuart and Irene, Robin, Lauren, Earl and Rhonda to the apartment.* He called each on kom and invited them over and then to go for lunch. They reacted favorably to the apartment. Irene focused on the paintings, guessing a Miro for the print. She liked the two paintings by Alice, and the one each by Barbe and Sophie. Philip said that Alice rotated the paintings, and they would see something else on their next visit. The boys said their apartment was bigger. Philip pointed out their family was bigger. He found a muffin and cut it in half for them. Lauren said she had an efficiency two decks down and near Robin.

Irene came out of the restroom saying she loved the Vermeer, but wouldn't the living room be a better location? Philip explained that having an exotic painting in the loo should spice up socials. Irene said it would be exotic in the living room, but was erotic in the loo. Close quarters produced changes, Philip opined. Irene ended with the pleasant, "I look forward to socials here."

After each of the adults had visited the loo, they all went for lunch. During lunch, Philip's cousin, Lauren, and Stuart's cousin, Robin, both quietly supported his opinion, saying they liked *Girl with a Pearl Earring* in the loo for a brief erotic encounter. After his friends departed, Philip smiled with relief that Alice had loaned her naked Amanda mermaid painting to the art galleries.

⚹ ⚹ ⚹

Philip's kom buzzed, pulling him out of his thoughts. He recognized Joan's voice. "I didn't want to see you before the wedding, but you should observe a weapons trial happening today. Can you meet me in Hangar C within forty minutes, full jumpsuit?"

"Sure."

"Bring a cooler with your dinner. We're going to a Security Branch outpost on the ice."

Twenty minutes later, Joan led Philip to a foo fighter positioned at a launch tube. He assumed they would wait for a pilot, but she said, "Let's go. Take the far seat."

Joan's the pilot? "Joan, I hope to become an Egg pilot."

"To make Commander, even as Reserved Line or Staff, you must be certified as a foo-fighter pilot."

"Fine with me." *Cosmos, Alice is a fighter pilot. On Nevis, she always flew her Egg on automatic. Not sharing that secret with me.*

"I'll fly manually for you to observe. The center control stick pushes forward to dive, back to climb, sideways to roll. The floor pedals are for yaw, easily changing direction. The speed throttle is here for your left hand. The buttons, levers, and lights take a while to learn and even let you program maneuvers. There is much to flying a cargo Egg, and more to flying a foo fighter if you can actually fight."

Once in the launch tube the Egg was pushed and pulled into position by air pressure—then a thrust hurled them out. They went up with video showing the rugged white expanse of Pluto's surface. Joan soon increased power and pulled her control stick back. Philip sensed a turn and ascent, whether from his inner ear or the video screen he could not tell. Dials moved and digital characters scrolled. One display showed ground speed increasing. A voice told Joan, "On course, Commander. Your E-T-A is three minutes."

"Copy here." Joan looked over at Philip. "I want you to observe the first live-fire test of a new and very secret weapon. We call it the Red Eye of Shiva. Never repeat the name or mention its existence except to me or Alice. Alice has clearance for any information or secret, one of only a few dozen or so, myself not included in that small group. You should tell Alice about the Red Eye.."

"Understood. Why do you not have the highest clearance?"

"I have great power as head of the Security Branch. I have no need to know the capabilities of the key's Security Guards. They report to their Key Manager, or to General Manager Robbie if working together. A check on my power. Should I need to know, Comte, Joanne, Jeffrey, Alice, or Lois would tell me. Others also would tell me.

"Now to our purpose! We have tested the Eye for power and hence safety. Today the test is to begin our experience with acquiring a remote target and cataloging the frequencies of our input energy absorbed by different types of targets. The energy field of the Eye moves in analogous ways to a magnetic field. Bring magnet poles of opposite polarity close together and an attraction field is established between them. Once the magnetic field is established, the materials may be moved relative to each other without severing their linkage, within limits of course. If a magnetic field encounters material between the magnets, then some or all of the magnetic energy will be absorbed. Our Eye's energy field has a complex frequency, and each target material will absorb certain of our input energy's wavelengths, but not others."

"Did this weapon result from a dream?"

"Yes. The properties of magnetic linkage and absorption apply to the field of our Red Eye. Once established between source and target, either can move without breaking the linkage of the field. Since a given target material will absorb only certain frequencies of energy, by monitoring our power supply's complex current waveform with a Fourier Transform we identify the frequency and amplitude of each component waveform absorbed at the passive end of the field, the target in our case."

"How does the Eye's energy field become a weapon?"

"When we increase the input power sufficiently the target will disintegrate—its molecular bonds broken by the quark field. The nature of the field is such that if the mass of the target approaches the mass of the Eye, the entire target will be destroyed along with the Eye."

"Ah!"

"An explosion occurs at the Eye. Its surrounding materials are destroyed by a conventional explosion releasing heat, molten metal, and the overpressure of expanding gas. The enclosure housing an Eye will be destroyed unless very strong."

"Like a physical bolt or explosive shell, each Eye is a weapon for one-time use?"

"Yes, and more dangerous to use because we too must contain an explosion! Also more complex, because the quark's subatomic bonds must be broken before they can be induced to flow. The hot eye metal is exposed to a resonant drive field which compresses the fabric of spacetime enough to allow quarks to flow within the nucleus of atoms, establishing a quark field. If we become able to create quark flow between atoms, we should have an immensely powerful weapon. That capability, however, is beyond practical imagination."

Joan requested permission to land and was assigned Pad 4. "Philip, the throttle lever pulls back to reduce thrust, speed. To open the door, I'll flip open the cover on top of the control stick and push the red button four times. You will get to advanced door operation during training."

✳ ✳ ✳

The terrain now was smooth and white. It simply looked bleak and cold to Philip. The observation bunker and landing pads were low, the color of the icescape, and not easily seen. Having just energized his jumpsuit he was cold walking to the bunker. After a minute or so inside he grew warm enough to enjoy the outdoor view although not understanding what he was seeing.

"Can you identify each of those distant masses, Philip?"

"Some type of metal, then perhaps an electronics frame with computer modules; a block of ice; Cosmos, a dead man?"

"Correct. The dead man was a financial principal. He was picked up by Marianas Key in Central Park, New York after dining with friends. Somebody had poisoned him and his wife. Both died the next day. Their daughter doesn't want their ashes. She hates being aboard and faults her parents for not allowing her to stay on Earth."

Joan motioned to a side viewport and the four domes on the ice outside their bunker. "Those are the Eyes we test today."

The center mass, the Eye, looked the shape of an eyeball, glowing red. It was held atop a tentacle-like support element. "Is it hot?"

"Almost molten metal. The support arm is flexible because position is critical to acquiring a target. We will use the apple-sized Eye to disintegrate part of the body, and the pumpkin-sized Eye on the block of metallic alloy, a type used by the Earthlings for rockets and spaceships."

"Joan, the engineers don't yet know if the field will disintegrate all types of materials?"

"That's correct and the main point of these tests. Our scientists and engineers know how to create the field, but have neither the physics nor mathematics to support design, aiming, or its effect on any type material. They use a containment dome that is transparent to the frequency range of the enclosed Eye. These tests may find that we need additional frequencies for some target materials. The Eye is not yet a fully developed weapon."

Within five minutes the bunker's speakers announced, "We begin with the smallest Eye, for the body. Watch the dome on the right. One of our pods will hold at the dome and the quark field will attach to that pod, which will then fly to the vicinity of the body. When we explode the pod the quark field will seek a new termination. We hope on the body due to the primary frequencies powering the Red Eye. Ready now for the count to zero."

The weapon was energized, glowing more brightly red. The pod at the Eye's dome flew to near the body and the arm supporting the glowing Eye-mass moved slightly. A bell rang and the distant pod exploded. "Let's hope the target is that body and not one of us!" somebody said.

Not funny.

"We are increasing power, watch the red mass." In the next moment the mass flashed in a pulse of colors. A haze exploded outward and the red mass and dome vanished.

Philip looked at the frozen body using binoculars and found a hole in its chest.

Joan stepped over to a control panel and soon returned to tell Philip that the test was successful. "We recorded the frequencies of energy absorbed by the body." She pointed. "The electronics equipment is next."

This next weapon's dome is twice as big.

They tested the Eyes in quick succession. After the last and largest explosion, Philip realized there was now an irregular ridge of ice around the perimeter where the dome had stood. *Ice under the dome melts and is pushed outward as water only to freeze in the next instant.*

Joan again returned from watching the main console. "Ready for lunch, Philip?"

"Yes. Most impressive this Red Eye."

"This weapon bodes well for our stay on Mars. It can instantly penetrate armor that would take minutes for our main lasers to burn through. It has the ability to hit out-of-sight targets. Too, our target leader pods are an extreme challenge to Earth's present defensive technologies. Our next round of tests will determine how close to a target our pod leader must be before its quark field will jump as intended. We hope that by the time Earthlings can detect and destroy a pod it will be within acquisition range."

"The target gone, as if disappearing through a gap in space-time," mused Philip.

MYSTERIOUS BONDS

Philip woke in a daze. *Sparks flow in from the cosmos illuminating unknown dimensions of mind. I am part of Pystead's mysterious becoming! Being alone is one of many trials to come. The memory of my love reaches through this bubble in time. I have things to learn, progress to make, love to share. Though once veiled to me, I see a pole. This bubble may be pierced. It shall not collapse and squeeze me to meaningless babble at a zero point. Up and doing I am a healthy creature—voila!*

He resumed his daily routine of reading, resting, and chatting via kom. Alice's parents were kom linked and told stories about Alice and their own recruiting for Pystead, living with cold weather in Reykjavik, surely colder than would be colony life on Mars. Melita Rose recounted her parents' story about her older brother Frank, born in minus-forty-four-degree weather with wolves howling in the backyard. A high-tech colony on Mars again came out the winner for warmth.

Philip asked Jeffery and Joanne over to see the apartment.

Joanne approved of *Pearl Earring* hung in the loo. Philip took them to two art galleries and pointed out Alice's paintings. He made sure they saw her unsigned mermaid Amanda painting. Philip was relieved when they moved on without asking questions.

The morning of liftoff from Pluto, the fifth day after Alice had departed to stay with Revathy, all pilgrims not on duty were told to remain in quarters. A period of zero gravity would occur that night to allow securing the Tank ship under the Wheel. Passage through the orbit of Pluto remained on schedule as the third evening off Pluto, which would be day seventy-six out of Earth. Two days after liftoff, the flips and good gravity would return.

The wedding is on! Except for eating meals alone in a small galley, except for one dinner with Alice's parents, Philip stayed in the apartment contemplating his wedding toast, reading, tending Char Cat, and avoiding the appliance manuals.

The evening before the wedding, Manager Robbie spoke to the pilgrims for the first time in days. He informed them that for the next few hours they would have a fantastic view of Pluto's dark side disk against the Sun with its thin atmosphere seen as a glowing blue rim. The view would be live on all Networks and recorded for future viewing. If watching from a viewport lounge, Robbie asked everyone to please rotate every few minutes to give others a look. With his wedding the next evening, Philip stayed in for the video view that he felt would be as spectacular as a personal viewing.

After gravity returned, Comte called and asked about Philip's stomach. He was doing well. Comte assured him Alice was fine, as were all those helping with the event. Philip checked status of the hot tub and found it still unavailable.

✄　✄　✄

For the wedding, Philip took a full shower instead of a hygienic towel bath. Awaiting the arrival of Comte, he stood ready in his two-toned gray suit and gray tie. The door chine sounded at seventeen hundred hours. Comte wore light gray slacks and a long-sleeved, pale blue shirt beneath his jeweled sash. He approved of Philip's suit and asked to see the wedding ring. Philip produced the small box from his jacket pocket. Comte looked closely before declaring, "Superb, Philip. The first wedding ring I've seen with such decorative grooves in the band."

"We both liked the design, reminiscent of a peach pit's grooves."

"Her engagement diamond must be an ideal cut?"

"Yes. You have helped immensely with this wedding and do so even now. Would it be improper to toast you for being my best man?"

"Not at all."

"Thank you for everything."

"I am content now that we are out of Earth and I have lived to see my granddaughter marrying a fine young man."

"I will do everything I can to cherish and care for her."

"I wish I could have had more time with you before the wedding, but since we have had three trained Federation crews covering seven ships, I and others have had much to do."

The two men shuffled along for a moment in silence, each adjusting his grip on his carry bag full of champagne. Philip pulled his small suitcase along with his wedding gift tied on top, held by double strands of red ribbon.

"Philip, I have advice for you and Alice."

"Fine."

"We left an Earth having more geniuses than Pystead has pilgrims. And the Earth provides infinitely more resources than do our ships. If any of your descendants—our descendants—ever return, they must be wary of an Earth science potentially advanced beyond Pystead's. The Earth's leaders may be passive-aggressive, and their cultures may be hostile. Do not be lured in by the appearance of little or no progress, of regression, or by small overtures of welcome. With a few key advances we have been able to escape from Earth. With one concealed advance they could lure you to destruction. Even imagination cannot prepare you because you will have no inkling of what you do not know. The unknown must be tested over time before being even tentatively understood. That's why we are taking a look beyond terminal shock with probes."

The two men walked on in silence until Philip replied, "I understand. I worry about the more immediate future, about establishing a culture of self-satisfied and motivated individuals. Also, about hostile U.N. forces saturating our defenses."

"I believe the new crewmembers will meld, and all will develop culturally. Our philosophers and psychologists should help guide the public conscience. Teach philosophy to the children as a form of spirituality and practical wisdom. Philosophy can improve the individual mind, hence over time can improve an entire culture. Teach your contemporaries and their children. Skip one generation of minds and vital circuits are lost, or properly put they are never generated. The mature must teach the immature or history and culture are lost."

"I agree, Comte. And along with that loss goes an understanding of the potentials within humanity."

"So easy it is for too many to admire only raw power and remain savages. Here, with high-abstracting minds, not a problem as in the general populations of Earthlings. Even here, do not take high values for granted. Educate your children to know the range of human potential as manifest historically. Teach them the civilizing values of abstract principles, earned trust, and empathy. Even in a live-and-let-live society do not expect one culture for all. Varied dimensions in a pluralistic culture can form a cohesive group, just as different personalities can form a happy family."

"Yes, the mind may be born with common sense, but can be deluded when submerged in illusions, or when confounded by complexity and mutually exclusive values."

"Substantially withhold one of the five traditional senses from the infant's developing mind, and some lifetime incapacity results. Withhold experiences of some dimension of life from the child's developing mind, and an immature and warped psyche, an incapacity, results. The easiest way to control humanity has been to limit education and truthful reporting, to tell lies twisting reality. Also, without a perception of personal dignity or injustice the mind is callow."

"Comte, in the U.S.A. the U.N. was influential enough to weaken education and honest reporting. Had I not happened upon the Wheaton World Center for Change, I could never have suspected the extent of the U.N.'s reach into U.S. politics. And seems the U.N.'s dark money and dark data are pervasive worldwide! I suspect their influence has denied financial support to decent politicians in all political parties. Why else would educated politicians with families ally themselves with religious fundamentalists and would-be unregulated capitalists, all seeking a return to pre-modern norms?"

"We learned that the K.L.J.H. group was unknown to most top officials in even the major nations. Only through our advanced surveillance capabilities were we able to discover what little we know about them. We investigated and spied on K.L.J.H. while they refused to leave us and dropped their mini spy drones around Campus. Lois has our report, which found considerably less than the full story. You should study the group carefully. Some may be dangerous psychopaths. Their leader, Dr. Osgood, is a dangerous sociopath, a psychological category no longer recognized as such in the U.S.A. They are hidden within a broad group said to have anti-social personality disorders, which is a politicized category used to include decent people deemed politically progressive. By promoting the corruptible and repressing decent people who might be influential, the U.N. is creating world populations that can be pushed into its totalitarian, one-world government. Thereafter, only illusions of group contentment will be found. Music and movies will be strictly controlled. A public individual with an imagination, doubts, questions…will not exist. Each individual will be required to suffer in silence the hardships said borne of wringing a living from nature."

"Yes, Comte, helped along by conspiracy theories against any individual or group seen by the general population to be better than the U.N.'s chosen lot. If your group is too successful, it must be spun as secretive and corrupt to explain why it is not chosen over others. If your organization is known to have countless pedophiles, others must be said even more abusive toward children. If a chosen politician is known to be corrupt, his or her opponent must be investigated for criminal dishonesty. Any alleged false equivalency can be embraced among the undereducated. Pystead's crewmembers know these truths; our children must be taught them in order to understand the potential for evil within the human genome!" Philip glanced at Comte, who nodded.

"Comte, I'm beginning to appreciate why Lois only had one child."

"She's not the only one. My granddaughter, I believe, waited to fall in love until another door had opened."

"I have experienced too much good fortune. I fear my run of luck should turn."

"Your luck to date has no influence on your luck tomorrow. Each of us aboard could claim a run of good luck. Too, imagine the probability of each of us here having had that same good luck. Yet here we are! My advice is to take the good fortune found along one's way and to be cautioned by one's stars."

"I shall take your advice by marrying your wonderful granddaughter."

"She and I are eager for the event."

"May we all reach the stars!"

"My days building this Pystead Singularity will have enduring significance only if our descendants reach the stars. Melita feels the same."

"I feel the same."

Comte smiled. "Philip, almost I forget." He stopped and pulled his gem studded sash up and over his head and twisted it to invert, revealing the blue-on-gold orphrey of its back side. "Study this side with a good glass. There is a message. No hurry." After turning the next corner with his sash restored to its gen-studded side, Comte confided, "After the wedding, Philip, I plan to hang my sash in the nearest antiquarian art gallery. It is for present and future generations, entrusted to the Federation for safekeeping as is. And remember that even in the very distant future, the commander of any visitation to Earth's solar system should wear the sash. You must pass the sash forward through the generations—orally—only to senior Federation Commanders."

"Does Alice know?"

"She knows and others know, but not that I will give the sash after the wedding. Why now, because the need weighs on me! Please do not mention this until after the deed is done."

"I'll wait. Comte, is Jeffrey an only child?"

"Yes, my only child. Alice has video and stories. As for the rumors that you may or may not have heard, they are best left as they are. You should know, however, that only every other generation of the first-born male lives two or three lifetimes, aging no older than mid-forties. A boy of yours is next in line."

"The thought is both reassuring and troubling."

"Care for my granddaughter and your children with all your heart and with all your mind."

"I shall."

"Human cell regeneration fails after some number of renewals, different for each organ. The cells of the heart never renew. I am proof that the number of regenerations can be considerably increased beyond six score. How, I do not know. Everything else that was relevant to my purpose I managed to know about. Be optimistic and be wary. Assume that even Asimov's Mule might become reality."

"I shall pass forward your wishes for the sash and your wariness of Mules."

Comte nodded. "Philip, will you be content to live in only a Federation Key?"

"Sure, unless Alice wants to move."

"Fine. Now, remember for your very closest new friends only, that I am Alpha and you are Omega."

Are not all things revealed in their time? Philip nodded his understanding of not understanding and hoped that Comte would understand.

After another few steps, Comte slowed again. "Another thing."

"Yes?"

"Some of your very close new friends are mysterious, and initiate their gossip, let me call it, with a secret word in its transliteration from Greek."

"Yes?"

"That word is 'hagia,' never written, but if it were, our spelling of h-a-g-i-a, would use an uppercase I. The saying of the word has ritual: only whispered to one person at a time, whispered only once to the same person at any one meeting. If not understood and clarification be needed, preferably the two should part company and come together again in a different place after three days have passed."

"Okay, and as you say, mysterious."

"Your being Omega should not be mentioned unless the diadem is present, and then only when you are addressed."

"Fine."

Comte added, "Do you want to hear my latest gossip?"

"Of course."

"Do you have any to share?"

"No."

Comte frowned. "Initiation, Philip?"

"Oh." Philip leaned over and whispered, "Hagia."

Comte smiled. "It is rumored on good word that you are a mysterious man."

"I do my best to fit in."

"Care for my granddaughter." Comte slowed in his pace. "The number nine and its multiples by a single integer are special. Personally, I have no favorite number that can be numbered—to our knowledge."

Philip was perplexed, as he knew Comte knew him to be. Philip thought of Melita. *The starets has said to wait and see.* "I'm a bit nervous, Comte."

"I'm sure all is well."

✳ ✳ ✳

At the door adjacent to the Barrow Meditation Room, Comte asked for Philip's bag of champagne. "This is chapel's kitchen. I'll be only a minute." Comte returned with one bottle of Ste Wolls, which he handed to Philip. "This is from Rhonda. She baked the wedding cake. She returns her champagne as a wedding present for you and Alice. My advice as best man is to thank her privately and save it for your honeymoon." Philip put the bottle in his suitcase. *Thanks, Rhonda.* "Thanks, Comte, I'll do that."

Since they were early, Philip and Comte lingered, admiring the room. The colors were the customary off-whites and metallic silvers, but the usual streamlined forms were replaced by a floor of medium gray and off-white square tiles run on the diagonal, by walls set with thin and ornate columns creating niches filled with statues and mosaic scenes. The concave ceiling in light blue held in relief a maze of colorful stars, bordered at each wall with a simple, meandering sea-wave trim—a form of Greek-key design in bright blue.

"Comte, I can't imagine a more enchanting space for our wedding."

"I'm pleased. This is one of my favorite spaces. Interesting, beautiful, ornate, yet having plain areas where both the eyes and the mind may rest. Alice saw it yesterday and was delighted." Philip noticed that the center aisle was of good width, ending near the left side of the platform, where the musicians' area began. The seats were white with light gray upholstery, spaced comfortably apart. A round, glass window of deep blues and greens, high in the front wall, drew Philip's attention. Reminiscent, Comte said, of the rose window style of old. On the front platform, to each side of the wide steps sat a display of red and yellow variegated tulips in tall, white and blue vases.

"Quite charming. This must be your doing?"

"I asked Alice to let me select and decorate the chapel. The tulips are silk; the vases are eighteenth century, Delft Blue earthenware. Alice will have a small bouquet of red roses, real, arranged by Lois."

Before they moved, the five musicians arrived. Comte motioned to their seats at floor level, front left where a baby-grand piano sat beside the platform. The musicians were four meters from the first row of seats on the left. Comte and Philip, satisfied with preparations, departed for their anteroom to the right side of the chapel. Within minutes they were joined by Rabbi Issegow wearing a white robe without kippah or breastplate. His role was signified by a white prayer shawl marked with purple and dark blue horizontal stripes near its tasseled ends. He asked if, after the marriage, he could chant a brief prayer in Hebrew. Philip said they would be pleased to have the prayer. The Rabbi said the prayer was derived from Old Testament scripture, but not part of Jewish liturgy. Philip said he liked his religion best in a foreign language. Issegow smiled and asked to see the ring. Philip produced it so promptly that the Rabbi advised him to be slow during the ceremony to allow guests time to appreciate the ritual.

The men sat to await their cue. Philip asked the Rabbi why he had left Earth and Jerusalem.

"Weeks before I became crew, I attended an interfaith convention where convivencia, coexistence, was said in the offing by clerics whose own followers rose to suggest something reminding me of dhimmis status. That night I lay down to sleep, dejected and heavy of heart. I dreamed a strange and happy dream about the stars." He smiled. "As I sought a new country for our residence, Comte appeared and persuaded me that Pystead was the place for me and my family."

Soon came the word. The bride was dressed, holding her bouquet. Comte departed from the anteroom door to the corridor. The Rabbi rose. "Philip, I would like to end the wedding with kein ayin hara."

"What does it mean?"

The Rabbi was solemn. "No evil eye, or beware the evil eye, or knock on wood."

"Fine, even perfect."

"The phrase is slurred with the word 'ayin' elided."

"I'd like you to say it."

25

CEREMONY IN SPACE

Soft strains of Pachelbel's canon sounded in the chapel. In the anteroom, the Rabbi stood. With his white-bound book of poetry, he waved for Philip to follow. Together, they stepped out onto the chapel's platform and stood apart facing each other. The Rabbi motioned with his head, and Philip shifted to allow more space toward the front of the platform for Alice's arrival. Then he remembered to half-face the seats.

He began to scan the guests. On the first row, a woman he didn't know sat beside Comte, and then another woman wearing beige beside Paula, the Manager's wife. In the next row Lois and Dusan sat with Prince beside the empty aisle seat reserved for Melita. Among several people he didn't recognize were the familiar faces of Revathy, Sasha, Woody, and Denise. He completed a quick look around and found his cousin sitting with Stuart's cousin. Alice's artist friends were there, as were his friends from Compton. Rhonda sat beside Rao, with a space on the aisle. The

Brazilians Hector and Andrea waved to him from the rear right. On the last row, Isaac with his leg in a cast just into the aisle, sat with Norman, and Bao-Tu and his mother. Samantha in pink sat with husband Albert, and another man unknown to Philip. The rear door moved and was only half-way open when a grinning Arthur Vanderhought popped through, glanced around, and slid into the aisle seat beside Rhonda. *My sponsor, just in time as in Compton.* On the last row left, Brian sat beside Frank and his twin fiancées. *All here, and my cousin has a friend. I have friends. None of us are socially isolated.* Philip smiled.

The music changed to a perky tune on plucked strings, and Philip took a breath. Both chapel doors opened wide. Melita Rose Tsai stood in the doorway wearing a platinum colored silk dress. She moved rather quickly down the aisle and took her aisle seat. The ensemble began Mendelssohn's wedding march. Half the heads in the room turned as one, slinging out from their midst something like a half-whispered syllable. Alice, escorted by her father and mother began a slow walk down the aisle. Alice wore a soft gray hat with a petite white veil pulled back. She held a small bouquet of red roses by their stems. Her dress was strapless, light gray lace over white for the bodice, and a not so full, pleated, light gray skirt to the floor. Her mother wore a blue-gray dress with a short gray veil covering her face. Slightly nervous, Philip reminded himself not to rush the ring. Alice and her parents approached the steps to the platform and paused. Melita stood, stepped, over and pulled down Alice's short veil, and then lifted Joanne's veil. The three then took their final steps up with Alice standing beside Philip. Comte and Melita followed, moving to the rear behind Jeffrey and Joanne.

Philip glanced at the Rabbi and noticed a fleeting blur against the chapel wall. Then he found it again. *A round pod hanging steady, blending with the background, easily overlooked. Sure, a flying video pod makes sense—like the procryptic surveillance and guard pods we used on Nevis, except this one no larger than a cantaloupe.*

Again the music changed, this time hushed, providing a pleasant ambiance as the wedding party and guests made final adjustments. The Rabbi spoke, his voice mellow. His words were inspirational, spiritual, yet without religion except for one mention of ancient Moses as an instrument of divine deliverance, as was Saint Germaine's role for Pystead.

Finally came the vows. With solemn deliberation Philip and Alice each pledged 'I will.'

On cue, Philip slowly retrieved the ring. He slid it onto Alice's finger. "With this ring I thee wed." He could glimpse very blonde locks and smiling red lips beneath the organza and imagined her big blue eyes.

Soon, slipping a ring onto his finger Alice vowed, "With this ring I thee wed."

Philip experienced an inner peace as the Rabbi made it official, "With witnesses and the authority vested in me by Key Bury Saint Germaine, I pronounce you husband and wife. Philip, you may kiss the bride."

Philip raised the veil and looked into loving eyes. "I love you, Alice." He kissed his bride.

"I love you, Phil. Kiss me again." Philip kissed his bride.

The newlyweds held hands as the Rabbi chanted a prayer in melodious Hebrew. He could not resist saying in English that the prayer was for the Lord's many mansions and for peace and happiness to follow Alice and Philip all the days of their lives. He said that a prayer for happiness was not a prayer for additional days, and the couple should be forgiving of one another and endeavor to enjoy their allotted time to the fullest, not forsaking those in need. The shards found in life, said the Rabbi, must be restored to the cosmic vessel by doing good deeds, so that the cosmos would be repaired for the world to come. He concluded, "May the stars shine for you. May the cosmos enchant you and keep you. May all your pathways lead to peace. And let us say, Amen." The wedding party and guests filled the chapel with a hushed, "Amen."

Philip extended his arm and heard the Rabbi say, "Keinehora." Alice did not take his arm. She turned facing away and with a sure motion raised her bouquet of roses and tossed it high and backwards in the direction of her single girlfriends now standing in front of the seats. Rhonda made the successful catch. Alice took Philip's arm. "Now we may go."

We are married. Alice is mine to have as well as to hold. Thank you Comte and mysterious stars and friends. "Alice, a video pod is on our left." *We have the Blue Mati amulet, and now a spoken charm to ward off that evil eye of malicious envy. The traditional wedding ceremony itself comforting in this strange and undiscovered life. May we be kind and may our ways lead to peace among us.*

"Look left and smile, husband."

27

GEMSTONES

Smiling for a video pod, the newlyweds walked slowly towards their reception next door. Philip asked, "Do you appreciate that the orbit of Pluto is a far more precise location in space than termination shock?"

"Oh, yes, I'm happy." She tugged on his arm and they stopped. "Sasha told me that the orbit of Pluto is not predictable over long periods of time."

"It's inclined to the ecliptic and subject to incalculable gravitational pulls. Let's preserve its present orbit on a plaque, with a small heart to mark where in space we were married."

"I'd like that. Now that we are married, Phil, we should agree to share all secrets of the heart."

"We could, but according to my understanding of the mind, we cannot anticipate our feelings in the future about a secret shared in the present. Our primary process does not decide its reaction until a moment of truth forces an issue."

"Having a rule will eliminate regrets of poor judgment."

"Not necessarily."

"Still, love, let's have a rule: no secrets of the heart from your spouse!"

"If you wish."

"I do. Remember, Phil, I may get mad, but I will never love you less."

"You are the love of my life to share all dimensions of my being. Getting mad, even emotionally hurt, should not end love. Married love should overcome a hurt."

"No matter the strangeness of the future, let's grow old knowing each other in mind as well as body."

He said quietly, "We will truly belong to each other."

"Phil, I want you to be our guide in the strange future. If you are happy, I will be happy."

"Melita advises that we remain open minded."

"She's appointed herself your mentor?"

"I believe so."

✳   ✳   ✳

As the newlyweds stepped into the reception room, the far right corner caught their attention. A lower wall section had been pushed out and up, creating an opening. The musicians were rolling the piano from the chapel into the reception room. Melita waved for Alice. "This is a fine place for the receiving line." Comte, Jeffrey and Joanne, and Philip's cousin, Lauren, joined them. The wedding guests were arriving. Alice stood between her mother and Philip with Comte first, introducing Jeffrey, who introduced Lauren. After a few greetings, Philip realized everybody was kissing Alice with nobody kissing him.

Even Rabbi Issegow kissed the bride. He congratulated Philip and said he would stay only through the toasts, and to remember immediately after the last toast to place his flute carefully on the floor, lying down, not standing, only lying down, and smash it with his foot. Philip thanked him for the reminder. The Rabbi smiled. "Your shoe sole will protect your foot. Drop by to see me after your honeymoon and I'll explain the various symbolic interpretations." The Rabbi produced a large handkerchief. "Drop this cloth to go under and over the flute before smashing. I've arranged a cleanup to follow."

"Thanks."

"Shalom."

The pace through the reception line varied. On one occasion when the line slowed, Philip noticed a small video pod, having a definite camera lens, hovering in front of them. Comte stepped out and moved to Alice. "My life has alternated between long periods of boredom and adventure, spiced by friends and loves. My years with you have been among the best." He kissed her lightly on the cheek. She stepped out to pose with him. Comte moved to each individual and couple in turn, posing for the video pod.

After the reception line, Comte headed for the door. By that time Samantha and Rhonda, both strong on executive skills, were a team. They intercepted Comte, engaging in more chit-chat than Philip could imagine. Comte was smiling. He and the two women were soon posing for the video pods. Frank's twin girlfriends were queued up for their turn, and the five Nevis artists were gathering. By this time, of course, the gem-studded video-op was the focus of activity. The musicians through some mystery of insight managed to play quiet background music.

Suddenly Melita was taking Alice's hand and Lois took Philip's. Comte's inner circle hurried over for their turn beside the gems.

Next, Comte surprised all by crossing the room to pose with Isaac, Norman, Bao-Tu and his mother. Then the quintet leader, the bald flugelhorn player, waved for Comte and he stood for video and a chat with the musicians. The horn player raised his kom and spoke softly, listening. Comte nodded to him and headed for the door. This time Lauren and Robin obtained a photo with Comte, before he hurried to the doorway and waved goodbye as the horn sounded a warm and melodic fanfare—reminding Alice of the Russian Easter Overture. At the doorway, Comte looked for Alice and threw her a slow kiss that all eyes seemed to follow. When eyes again sought Comte, he was no longer there.

✳ ✳ ✳

An unknown male voice spoke. Only the strings were playing and the voice was easily identified as the flugelhorn player. "Ladies and gentlemen, the groom would like to speak, and after toasts we will have dinner and dancing for the evening." Servers were passing out champagne. Philip took a step out from Alice and drew a deep breath. "Thank you all for being here to celebrate with us and add meaning to our wedding. I'm not sure where here is, but it's clear to me that wherever Alice is I want to be. I am grateful to all who made my being here possible, beginning with my sponsor, Arthur Vanderhought, who surely is honorary family. Arthur, please raise a hand." The hand went up without a grin. "Alice and I are fortunate to have so many friends; indeed, we have a rich life. It's as if the stars have aligned for us, and I pray too for each of you and every pilgrim." Philip paused, noticing the ready flutes of escaping bubbles. "With friends and friendly stars, and with my wonderful Alice, surely I live in wonderland. May the stars align for wonderful Alice." Philip raised his flute and all toasted, "May the stars align for wonderful Alice."

Philip took a long sip of the champagne. *Remember the others!* He waved an open hand in the direction of the front door. "Comte Saint Germaine, Alice's grandfather, helped considerably with arrangements for the wedding and was my best man. Alice's mother and father, Joanne and Jeffrey, whom I met on Pluto, accept me as family." He thanked Rhonda for baking the wedding cake and Isaac for the champagne. "Alice and I look forward to our future with each of you." Philip again raised his flute. "Love to family and friends." Amid a flurry of chatter, Philip spoke again, "Alice's parents, Joanne and Jeffrey, long-time crewmembers, would like to say hello. Thereafter, anybody with something nice to say should speak before we cut the cake and begin dining and dancing."

Philip stepped back beside Alice who whispered, "Very nice, husband." The remaining toasts were brief and of good humor. Flutes were empty well before Stuart spoke, saying he and family were fortunate to have Philip and Alice as friends, and since he had always been able to rely on Philip's judgment, he had involved his cousin Robin in the deal, and Pystead probably took him to get Robin as a chemist. His remarks produced smiles and a blush from Robin.

Deciding drama was called for, Philip raised his empty glass flute for all to see before slowly bending to place the handkerchief and flute on the floor. The Rabbi smiled. Philip stomped, feeling under foot an unexpected instant of resistance before the crunching pop. The mind is amazingly quick in some instances, and before the crunching ended Philip was thankful the Rabbi had mentioned his shoe sole and warned him to place the flute with its rigid stem flat. Philip looked up, found himself without an explanation, and said, "No copycats, please!"

✳ ✳ ✳

Melita showed the newlyweds to their table for two. Others looked for their seats by place names. The dinner was served by crewmembers who Alice said were in the hospitality branch, three couples who would each get a bottle of champagne. The beverages for dinner were iced tea and coffee. The entrée was plantain encrusted Chilean seabass. Philip glanced at Alice. She whispered, "Samantha's suggestion, and Isaac's recipe."

The ensemble's leader, the flugelhorn, gave the guests twenty minutes after everyone had been served, then announced that Philip would cut the cake. Duty called and he approached the cake. He decided on rectangular pieces and wondered why he'd received no warning about the task. *I may not be a real-world person yet, but I'm certainly getting practice.* Philip stopped slicing to confirm he would produce fifty pieces, enough to cover drops and seconds for a few. *Another point of feedback for the Special Events Consultant.*

Before eating his own cake, Philip stood with, "Be right back" to Alice. He stepped into the hall where their two suitcases were waiting with his gift for Alice tied on top. Everybody seemed to be looking when he returned with the wrapped package. Alice carefully pulled off the big red bow. As she unwrapped the paper, she was even more careful. "On Earth I saved bows, but not paper. Here we recycle everything."

Alice opened the box and held it up for the video pod, which displayed its picture on high screens for all to see. After a look inside Alice exclaimed, "What a wonderful mix of paints!" The guests heard and clapped.

"Good colors, Alice?" Philip asked in a whisper.

"Oh yes, look, three slightly different pigments for each primary color with lots of lapis lazuli. I will mix my own special colors—artistic fun."

"Alice, this is a representative sample of your present. With the help of the personnel department, I have eight big boxes of paints and art supplies, including canvas."

"Wonderful. Let's keep those a secret. Eventually, I will want to give away partly used tubes, but I don't want artists to come around looking for them."

⚹   ⚹   ⚹

The flugelhorn player soon asked everyone to please clear the center of the room for dancing, and to allow the bride and groom the first dance alone. A few tables were removed as the ensemble began playing one of Alice's favorite songs. Philip took her hand. The song was slow and suited his box step, which morphed into sliding steps of little pattern, which Alice followed when he let her dance out a bit to where he couldn't detect her perfume. *How to tell her the honeymoon venue is postponed?*

Alice danced the second dance with her father. The third she began with Philip and ended with Joan's husband, Prince, who was out in a rare appearance with Joan's alter, Melita. When the dance ended, Alice pulled Philip in the direction of Rao and Isaac who were sitting together with Norman, Bao-Tu and Bao's mother.

"Phil, we need to socialize, and I want to make a point of visiting with Isaac since he can't dance. Would you mind?"

"No. Should I ask Melita to dance?"

"Of course! I'll get Rao to ask Rhonda."

"What if she declines?"

"She won't, I've checked. Phil, about your dance card?"

"Yes?"

"It would be romantic if you were to dance almost every other dance with your bride, and be sure she doesn't spend time alone."

"Of course."

"Before we go on dancing, love, you need to wait for me to slip into something more comfortable."

"I'll try a chat with Isaac and the boys."

✳   ✳   ✳

Alice returned in her alluring, short-sleeved dress of crinkled cranberry lace. Very sheer lace, alluring yet modest with double and triple layers in all the right places because she wore it braless, she had told Philip. *Wow, I want her big-eyed pose in this dress.* Philip waved for the video pod, and when he looked back Alice was holding a yellow-gold tiara having a single large medallion. On second look, he thought the medallion was an abstract eight-lobed flower of blue and gold.

Melita came to the table, and Alice handed her the tiara, which Melita took to Joanne. When her mother put it on all their new women friends stared.

Alice whispered, "Phil, do you like the tiara? Sorry I forgot to show it ahead of time."

"Nice!"

"Mother's diadem."

✳ ✳ ✳

The music was inviting and the small dance floor filled. Philip was pleased to see his friends from the States dancing with Alice's friends as well as with each other. *With so many scientists and engineers aboard, I must not be the only poor dancer.* Philip replayed in his mind that sweetest of all voices, *With this ring, I thee wed.* He looked at his ring, his wife, and his friends. He whispered softly to himself, "Here I truly belong."

According to the flugelhorn, the ensemble's apparent leader, the ensemble played songs popular as long ago as the early twentieth century. The songs were brief, each lasting about three minutes. Philip danced with all the women, including Alice's mother who asked him. Both Melita and Samantha surprised him, Melita with assurances that half his dance with her was with Joan, and that she would put her hair up to see him off as Joan. Samantha did not bestow a kiss but gave his shoulder a finger massage after invoking her special platonic status.

By the time the musicians announced five more songs the newlyweds were sitting together, relaxing. The Rabbi reappeared to sign paper and electronic copies of their wedding certificate, with Melita and Arthur as witnesses. The mysterious thing being that Melita Rose Tsai, hair in a bun, signed as Joanna Roz Dezugi. *Mysterious, my inner circle.* Alice turned to speak to Arthur. Joan caught Philip's arm and swung his back to Alice. She stood on tiptoes and kissed him. *Divine!* Joan stepped away, and Alice was holding up their colorfully decorated paper marriage certificate for all to see.

Philip asked Alice how often she wore the tiara. "I had the safe location and kept it for my mother, but never wore it."

"So, we leave without saying goodbyes?"

"That's right! A man in full can't take time for social graces when his bride is hot and bothered. Look, our friends are waiting to shower us with rice."

"Don't let the shower cool you down."

"Not to worry."

28

SECRET CEREMONY

Alice took the paper marriage certificate and the couple hurried for the door, passing through a few handfuls of showering rice and into the corridor. Their two suitcases were waiting, strapped together with the ribbons to tie on Alice's box of paints. *Have to tell her!* Halfway to the next corridor Philip squeezed her hand. "My charming wife, I am disappointed to tell you that our reservations for a honeymoon surprise were cancelled due to a problem with the venue. We have a room in the rim zone near entertainment and different galley food."

"I'm not disappointed. You are, after all, the main attraction."

"Another day we'll have the small surprise."

"I'll be happy with any surprise that's not a hike on Pluto's ice."

As they approached check-in, Philip whispered, "I can't tell you how much I can't wait to have you all to myself."

She whispered, "Talking will not be necessary…nor sufficient." They kissed before the door was closed. Philip had her cranberry red dress unbuttoned in seconds and caressed her breasts as she undid his shirt and pants. Once both were naked, he hugged her from behind and cupped her breasts for gentle squeezes. She whispered, "Kiss me, Phil." He picked her up and dropped her gently on the bed, promptly kissing her lips and moving slowly to her breasts while her hand pushed into his stomach. The newlyweds continued their play of caresses and sighs until Alice guided him into her warmth for a few passionate minutes. After resting and a glass of wine, Philip explored her hips and soon her neck as she caressed him to bring back her man in full. They made love patiently, savoring every thrust and bump until they hurried for a climax. After a shower of mesmerizing wet and warm caresses, the couple went down to their dreams contented.

Alice woke at nine the next morning and waited without disturbing her husband. He woke a few minutes later and pulled her close. Talking was not necessary. They finally floated out of bed and took a light breakfast of French toast, strawberries, and coffee. Philip wondered, "One of these galleys might serve grits?"

"Near the orbit of Pluto? You should find the pan-browned potatoes and plantains while they last. The plan is to wean us from a steady diet of the good stuff."

"We must hope for productive farming in a bubble on Mars?"

"We'll need to talk about that too—later please"

✼ ✼ ✼

The ship's speakers soon interrupted with five mellow whoops that repeated twice more, signaling an alert level Yellow-Five. The Wheel would provide periods of varying gravity, including some zero gravity during mealtimes with leftovers served in the galleys.

Philip and Alice decided to explore the top deck in *Key Logos* for lunch and look at observation lounges along the way. The cavorting flute music from his recent concert still lingered in mind. They stopped in a small lounge to star gaze. While viewing the bright points in the darkness of space, Philip wondered aloud about the art galleries.

"I had enough time with them," Alice replied. We displayed the Wheel's entire art collection on Fednet and closed the galleries for installation of new and secret automatic door closure and alarm systems. The new security system for the four Federation ships was approved by the Council at the request of Melita and Comte. Its very existence is secret. All the hardware and wiring is concealed and tamperproof."

"Of course."

"Equipment compartments and wiring conduits were already in place as part of original construction."

"Not using all wireless transmission that could be blocked."

Their lunch in *Logos Key* at half gravity was a pleasant surprise of rewarmed spaghetti and tasty meat sauce. Alice pointed out menu variations from *Key Bury*. "I wonder if some of the first cultural tracts will mention food?" mused Philip.

"Comte's believes that different cultures will develop with nine ships and seventy-two neighborhoods. After all, most ships and neighborhoods are of one predominate culture from Earth. Granddad feels our best location will be Key Bury."

"Likewise, he advised me to stay in an original Federation key." Philip suggested they walk the rim track in full gravity and practice hitting tennis balls. Alice agreed to try the game on Mars. She said Commandant of Recreation, Denise Dawsohn, was modeling three adaptations of tennis for Martian gravity. They strolled arm-in-arm, admiring the small parks and checking the menu in each galley. The rim zone's perimeter was less than two-and-a-half kilometers around, and even with stargazing the couple arrived back at their guest room before dinner time.

After a night of gentle lovemaking, they had set an alarm because Philip wanted a hot breakfast. Alice found a cozy café called PJAL, nearby in rim-zone neighborhood eight. After a few steps inside, a robot maître d' raised a hand and asked Alice if she knew the café offered an intimate dining experience. Alice said that would be fine and whispered to Philip, "I need to know what's happening." The couple turned the corner and stopped.

The room was larger than expected, but truly unexpected was the seating—on cushions, eating off low, clear-plastic tables. Before Philip could comment, Alice whispered, "Pajamas! Most are wearing pajamas."

"So P-J in the name means Pajamas…something"

"Adult Lounge, perhaps," added Alice. "We need to talk to some of these people! We can look up the name and evaluations, but we need to get into the heads of these pajama brunchers."

"There are only about two dozen."

"Please try to chat up the sweety in short white pajamas showing her two little bumps—eating alone. I'll try muscleman across the room in the T-shirt and short pajama pants. His biceps are large and defined, must exercise with weights."

"Alice, perhaps this should wait until after our honeymoon?"

"Oh Phil, let's get this done! Take an Irish coffee with a muffin and see if she will chat."

"Please repress mermaid Amanda."

"I certainly will not be Amanda! Be sure you are Philip, not Phil."

"Fine."

✻ ✻ ✻

Twenty minutes later Philip's kom buzzed and Alice said she was ready to leave, but willing to stay if he needed more time. His brunch companion winked at him. "I suppose that vanilla blonde you came in with is ready to go? Are you two swingers?"

"Simply curious. My wife believes the crowding and other realities of shipboard life will lead to cultural changes. What may I tell her about this place from your perspective?"

"Why don't I tell her myself. Invite me over. I'm here to meet men, but not to be picked up for morning dessert."

Philip took his tray, stood, and enjoyed a last glance. She smiled. He punched his wrist kom into at-hand exchange and noticed her last name, Blanchet. "My wife is Alice. We'll get back to you in a few minutes, Yvonne."

Philip dumped his plate and turned for the exit. *Perhaps Alice will know muscleman and introduce the two? Making introductions is the kind of thing established crew should do.*

Alice, however, first wanted to meet Yvonne and went over to invite her for tea at their apartment.

✻ ✻ ✻

After a relaxing day visiting art galleries, Alice and Philip received a kom call from Melita. Since the special part of their honeymoon was postponed, the newlyweds accepted her invitation to dinner with old friends. She asked Alice to bring the purse for her mother. They stopped by their apartment to pick up the purse, with its

271

handle being the large golden arc of the tiara that Alice held for safekeeping.

All were at the dinner table, except Comte who was usually one of the first to arrive. Melita explained that he was visiting his favorite observation lounge and they should begin the meal. Philip took a seat at an end-side position, and Alice took the seat across from him. Melita seated herself at the end with Philip and announced, "I'll call Comte if he isn't here soon for this event."

Is this an event? I suppose it is now! Melita was wearing an orange sheath dress without her platinum accessories. *I suppose she likes a different look every now and then.* A server appeared bearing food and two bottles of white wine. *Only the third time I've experienced table service at Pystead—an event.* They began with salads, eating slowly to wait for Comte. Everyone knew he would drink the wine but eat no salad.

Lois mentioned that Dusan and Woody were attending a piano recital given by Prince. Philip suddenly remembered he was to ask Melita for a psychic reading at their first event after he was wed. Alice was becoming concerned about Comte's absence. Melita disclosed that Comte had said not to worry about him. Then she related that she and Comte had both felt a ripple of dizziness lasting several seconds after drinking champagne at the reception.

Alice was surprised. "Wine never affected Granddad, nor you Melita even after three glasses that one time!"

Philip's thoughts were about the event and his conversation with Comte. *I do have it on unquestionable word that I too am mysterious. So here goes!* He asked, "Melita Rose?"

"Indeed, my friend Philip, indeed I am now Melita Rose."

Stranger and stranger. And strange enough for the others to pause with fork or spoon midway. "Melita, perhaps as a newly-wed I should have a palm reader's look at my stars?" Philip raised his left palm for her.

Alice whispered from across the table, "Phil, Melita never…"

Melita took Philip's upturned palm with a pleasant expression. "I can fathom the seas, I can reach the stars, and I know what my good friend seeks." The other friends in the group were speechless, knowing that Melita never read the stars for a friend. After only a moment's glance at Philip's palm, she leaned her head back and closed her eyes. She stood and faced Philip, leaned forward, and spoke for all to hear, "Your lifeline is the same length as Alice's. She will bear two fine and happy children. Alice will paint you riding Rom Baro and holding her black cat. Your expression will be serene and the scene mysterious—some things will float." Melita stood up straight, her head wobbled as if tipsy. She steadied herself using the chairback.

Philip asked, "Melita, what is new under the Sun?"

Alice gasped. Lois sat with a wide-eyed look.

Melita answered softly and slowly, "Rebirth, rebirth is new under our Sun."

An astonished Lois asked, "Rebirth?"

Melita turned to face her. "For us, peace enough and rebirth of the idea of progress."

"Thank goodness! Finally, finally we have something positive."

Melita smiled, eyes still closed. She shook her head and wiped her forehead with the back of her hand. She grimaced and seemed to stiffen throughout her entire body before sinking into her chair. Her head fell forward.

After a stunned and silent moment, just as Lois was raising

her kom, Melita lifted her head. She opened one eye, then soon the other. "I am Joan." She looked around, then at her wrist kom. "Let's check the observation lounge for Comte."

✳ ✳ ✳

Lois led the way. The door to the lounge, Comte's favorite, was closed. Lois pulled on the door handle. "Please knock," said Alice. Lois gave four sharp knocks. There was no response. She repeated the knocks. Still no response. Alice called, "Come out, Granddad— it's Alice." Still no response. Alice put her hands to her face. Lois pulled the door ajar. The top of Comte's head was visible to one side of a chair. "Granddad?" No answer came.

Philip looked to Joan, who whispered, "It was three days after our passing beyond the orbit of Pluto, Comte and Melita felt a ripple in their spacetime. They thought their boundary was heliopause. Look and see." Philip entered slowly and looked. He reached and touched Comte's hand.

When he looked up, Alice cried a shrill, "Oh no!"

Philip took the golden fleece comforter from the next chair and covered Comte. He came out and put his arm around Alice's shoulder. "Comte's expression is peaceful."

"Oooh, my granddad."

"I'm sure he has passed."

"It's so unfair he will not touch Mars. He devoted his life to us. He was such a fine person." She cried softly into her hands. "Granddad gave us a future of our own dreams. We will remember him." Alice looked up. "Call my parents to come over, please, Lois."

Philip looked around. Sasha was watching her kom and reported that medics were on the way.

Joan spoke to Alice, "Comte often told me how happy he was with his family and friends. How pleased he was with Philip." Joan stepped into the lounge. She returned with the observation that Comte wasn't wearing his sash.

For this I was prepared. No one spoke, so Philip said, "Comte told me that after the wedding he would leave his sash hanging in an antiquarian art gallery for The Federation to inherit and keep intact."

Alice wiped away tears and took Philip's arm. The small group of friends tried to comfort her while waiting for the medics. Sasha went into the lounge and rolled out two chairs that she placed for Alice and Joan, who each sank onto a seat. Lois waved. "Medics, over here."

Two men in jumpsuits entered the lounge. The one with an instrument already in hand soon reappeared in the doorway and told them, "Comte has died."

The two medics waited down the corridor, out of voice range from the bereaved. A couple approached in the hall, and sensing distress passed with silent nods. To Alice the metallic silver and off-whites of the ship suddenly seemed an expanse without form. She stepped into the lounge and looked beneath the golden cloth. *Goodbye Granddad. I loved you. Your line shall not end with me!* After a few moments of silence, Alice rejoined her friends in the corridor, pleading, "Rest in peace, Granddad." Joan closed her eyes. Tears ran onto Sasha's cheeks.

✳ ✳ ✳

Minutes later a stretcher arrived. The group walked Alice and Joan down the corridor. When they paused, Lois asked loud enough for all to hear, "Philip, you had a chat a deux with Comte?"

"During our walk to the wedding."

The group resumed their walk, turned a corner, took an elevator up, and advanced to an art gallery. Through the glass door panels one could see the walls hung with paintings, except to the left rear where hung one narrow golden tapestry set with marvelous gemstones. *Here survives the spirit of my granddad.* For a moment they stood, each in their own thoughts until, "Keinehora." Alice added, "May the idea of progress enchant us all."

Lois used her kom and gave Jeffrey and Joanne their location. Alice wiped away tears. *We need his spirit, his wisdom.* Alice and the others drifted apart, blankly staring at paintings. When her parents entered the gallery, Alice rushed over to hug her father and tell him the sad and unexpected news.

Lois stepped to the doors and pulled shades down over the glass panels. She spoke to the room, "Art Gallery Security, K-B-N-1-D-5-A-G-2, a request via Hermes: lock the doors, dim the lighting, continue alarm monitoring at art locations, stop audio-video monitoring of gallery occupants. Upon departure of present occupants, restore normal gallery lighting and default security conditions. Confirm final status to Hermes."

The friends assembled at Comte's hanging sash. All eyes seemed to be on Philip's shirt. He thought there must be some stain and glanced down. Alice whispered, "Your stick pin." Philip tucked in his chin to see his pin—his cobalt-blue pin! He looked up in surprise and noticed Joan's red pin was now cobalt blue, as was Sasha's normally amber pin, and Lois's normally deep blue.

Lois asked, "You must be Ya, or Zed?"

For this too I am prepared. "Comte preferred Omega."

"I have gossip if you would care to hear."

Mysterious like me. Philip leaned close to Lois and whispered, "Hagia."

"What, Philip?"

"Surely you heard?"

She smiled. "As Lois Beta, let me welcome you to Pystead's League of Saint Germaine, Philip Omega."

Alice Kappa wiped her eyes and took her husband's hand.

Lois spoke to Philip, "Please lift the cordon off the hook." He hesitated. "Have confidence, Philip Omega."

Philip took the two steps to the sash and lifted it. There was no alarm. Joan told him, "Should any person not in this room remove the cordon, the alarm would sound here, at Federation Council, and on our koms. The gallery doors would lock, room and corridor audio-video monitoring would be activated, and ship's guards called. We would act, but not overreact. It would probably be a curious child or an adult who tripped."

⁕　⁕　⁕

Joanne put on a silver headband matching her hair in color. "Alice, the purse, please." Joanne took the gold handle and unzipped the purse. She pulled down the fabric and the circular handle showed as the base of the tiara worn at the reception. When the blue and gold medallion emerged. Joanne held up the tiara. "Alice, the diadem is now for you."

Lois confirmed, "Alice, at the reception, Comte told me that you were his choice to be first among equals. I agreed."

Joan nodded. "Confirmed to me as well, by Comte. I consulted

Melita, who said you were surely chosen by One Above for our world to come."

Alice protested, "I'm not yet thirty-five!"

Sasha urged, "You are mature, informed, and wise. Please, Alice."

Alice leaned over and her mother placed the diadem on her head. Joanne stepped close pressing her headband against Alice's head. She whispered to Alice, "This is the most difficult thing I have ever done." For all to hear she said, "Alice, will you accept the diadem?"

Alice answered in a soft and clear voice, "Without reservation, I choose The League above my life for the sake of our children." Joanne's silver headband glowed with a blue dot, as did the gold headband of the diadem. Lois Beta proclaimed, "The diadem has passed among equals to Alice Kappa, First Among Equals, our Fae."

Joanne wiped tears from her eyes. Alice asked, "Why concerned for me, Mother?"

"One generation may prepare the next, but not act for it. You must continue monitoring for fidelity to Pystead's principles. You are chosen to guide your peers and the rising generation for the sake of Pystead and our children."

Joanne soon pressed her head to Alice's and whispered.

Alice replied, "I will promote a transition."

"Now please, Alice and all, Jeffrey and I will stay in for a while."

Alice turned to Joan. "How is Melita?"

Joan grimaced. "Melita has passed."

Alice hugged her. "An entangled passing of two—a sign may be inferred."

Joan nodded, tears in her eyes. "I shall miss my alter."

"Please steady her, Philip."

He offered his arm.

"Thank you, dear Alice, and Philip."

"Dad, I will call."

"Brief visits will be best."

"Let us bring a hot lunch for several days." Jeffrey nodded. "We will walk you home. Such great and unexpected losses. The spirit and examples of their lives remain with us."

29

INCORRUPTIBLE

Before leaving the art gallery, Lois volunteered to handle Comte's funeral. Alice asked if they could have a double funeral and include Melita.

"Yes, and I agree that would be proper."

"Both were well known to the pilgrims. Can you arrange a procession around the main concourse, displaying Comte's sash and Melita's necklace?"

"Would you like Comte to have a golden urn, and Melita's silver?"

"Oh no, Lois! Comte must have a rather plain sarcophagus with a clear top. He can be placed across from the wall of urns. Melita's urn should be platinum."

"Alice, let's allow some time before deciding on Comte. I will, however, order the sarcophagus."

"Fine, and absolutely no autopsy, embalming, wax or honey glaze, no hermetic sealing of the environment or the like. Long ago, Melita assured me that Comte would preserve without special treatment, and as well as the French saint Catherine Labouré."

Lois took a moment before asking, "Did you know that Melita was once a starets of the Eastern church?"

"Yes. She could have had the gift."

"She herself wondered, until that warning ripple in both her and Comte's spacetime, not experienced by me or her alter, Joan, happening just after Philip crushed his flute at the wedding reception. Alice, leave the details to me. Be a comfort to your parents and Joan, and they to you."

⁂ ⁂ ⁂

A few days later on the main concourse the two funeral displays were set. Comte's display held his gem-studded sash; Melita's her black-flower pendant and a small platinum metal urn. A pod arrived to carry each tray. The relatives and close friends took seats in the tram cars with Jeffrey and Joanne first, followed by Joan and Prince, Alice and Philip, Lois and Dusan, Sasha and Woody, Denise and Alex. Others followed walking.

Alice pulled the tiara from its purse and put it on. She whispered to Philip, "A few friends and others of the crew are here to walk the circle with us. Some will walk along while the procession is in their ship. A few dozen will be Blues—not acknowledged." Alice wiped her eyes.

"Alright." *Spreading the word with Alice instead of Joanne wearing the diadem!*

The procession began with the two displays leading the way under pod power. As they moved along people came for a few steps to offer condolences. While passing through *Blindsight Key*, the predominately Russian ship, the Pathétique Symphony played in the background. After the procession came full circle, back to the familiar gold ceiling trim of *Key Bury*, it turned off the main concourse. Only a few mourners followed.

Down three decks they entered a grape vineyard and took its perimeter walkway until on the far side they were separated from the vineyard by golden columns overgrown with wisteria vines. The outside wall in the typical metallic silvers and whites was made of octagonal niches, some sealed with a plaque. The procession halted near the beginning of the columbarium wall at a man dressed in the off-white island clothing of Nevis.

He spoke to Alice, "Beside Shirley," and gestured to the top row.

In a hushed voice, Alice told Philip, "Comte's friend Jason will say a few words. Then hold my arm and steady me on those steps."

Alice stepped out of the tram car and the others followed. Once assembled, Jason spoke, "Melita's urn will rest beside Shirley's, mother of Comte's only child, Jeffrey. May Melita's spirit of live-and-let-live survive in our hearts, for the sake of our children. We know Melita Rose rests in peace." Jason picked up Melita's black-flower necklace and handed it to Prince.

Alice took the urn and in slow motion kissed it. Philip held her arm as she stepped up and clipped it into place. Jason handed her the covering internment plaque that she clipped on to close the niche. Alice said aloud, "Amen," repeated by the mourners.

As the empty tray departed Alice hugged Joan. Prince placed Melita's necklace around Joan's neck. He said, "I shall miss your alter, as will our friends. We reside in the mysteries of the cosmos thanks to the intuitions of Comte and Melita."

Jason waved for men down the aisle and they brought the sarcophagus. *Dusan, Woody, Alex, Frank, Robbie, and three I don't know.*

Philip bowed his head.

Jason spoke quietly, "Comte has died at a ripe old age, full of days when our group experienced joy and strength. Comte lives in our hearts and lives. Comte's likeness shall come again." Jason paused and looked around. "With the best of our technology we detect no deterioration of Comte's body. We inter him as an immortal." The mourners made way for the sarcophagus covered by a white linen cloth having a center field of gold and purple braid. Jason raised his hand and the bearers stopped across the aisle from Shirley's and Melita's urns. Lois and Denise removed the covering cloth. Comte's body lay dressed in his favorite milk-white clothes from Nevis Island days. He looked as if he could be sleeping. The family members bowed their heads. Jason spoke quietly, "We are here due to Comte's vision and untiring efforts on our behalf. We revere his and Melita's wisdom, courage, work, and their sacrifice. Their spirits sustain us, forever in our hearts. We know that Comte and Melita rest in peace, satisfied with their efforts and with our crew, our pilgrims, our ship, our destination. To their glory and for One Above who cares, our descendants shall become a sub-species of humanity among the stars!"

Alice hugged her father, her mother, and Joan. After a final viewing, they filed into the vineyard. Alice whispered to Philip, "Mom and Dad want to be alone. Sasha wants us for dinner. Dad wants to see us in a couple of days." All began a slow walk back, Alice with her mother and father, Philip with Revathy, and Joan holding Prince's arm.

At her parent's apartment, Alice reminded herself that grieving was an individual matter. She wiped her eyes. Phillip took her hand. Leaving at the doorway, Philip intended to shake Jeffrey's hand, instead they parted with a hug. In the corridor, Philip whispered to Alice, "I'll find Handel's 'Amen' to play for us tonight."

Alice's mourning friends met every other day for three weeks. By then Joan was feeling almost whole as she put it. She returned to duty as an observer, leaving her deputies Andrew and Ethan in charge of the Security Branch. Philip reported to the School of Cognitive Science and began studying the equipment and learning his role in the work.

✴ ✴ ✴

The Wheel proceeded slowly, taking one hundred days for its return from Pluto to Mars, whereas the longer journey from Earth to Pluto had taken only sixty-five days. Time was needed for new crewmembers to be trained in their shipboard duties and for building on Mars. In addition, each new adult was to study job descriptions and list their top choices for cross training in a second shipboard duty. The ship's company would include family members who trained for a part-time or reserved duty.

Life aboard the Wheel was returning to a scheduled workweek with a sense of job and personal security—confidence in the future. An overall sense of well-being seemed to follow the announcement that jumpsuits and canopy beds were finally completed for all pilgrims, including the children. Overlooked by most, old habits were changing to accommodate new circumstances. Alice and her inner circle watched for signs of change, hoping to understand feelings. Although different ships might develop varying cultures, Alice and her inner circle felt duty bound to facilitate the development of a Wheel-wide, unifying sense of identity among all their diverse pilgrims. Their frustration was having no clear ideas for facilitating cultural development aside from plans to encourage Comte's envisioned permissive culture during retirement.

Commandant of both antiquarian and modern art galleries, Alice continued assisting her staff with the antiquarian galleries. Since paintings were rotated biweekly, she was busy. She was unofficially cross-training Philip as art gallery staff. He asked why her art and other contemporary art was held in antiquarian galleries rather than the modern galleries. She explained that contemporary paintings exhibiting traditional techniques or generally having identifiable objects, were not considered modern art by Commander Salcmann. He preferred abstract works such as the plain, all-black canvas with a thin red line down one side, technical works such as color-field paintings, and the paintings of avant-garde movements, Pop Art, and the Harlem Renaissance. Alice sighed. "Salcmann says I'm an old-school painter. When we build larger art galleries on another planet, our older art and his modern art will be in separate rooms. Then we can mix contemporary works in another gallery. My friends are all old-school according to Salcmann, but we have modernists aboard, including digital artists with some truly captivating works."

One of Alice's friends from Nevis, the artist Barbe, was accepted as a reporter and moved to *RAM Key*. Within days of her move, she posted an article on RAMnet about the use and content of art galleries, both real and virtual. The Eastern Philosophy Club resumed meeting, and Revathy asked Philip to attend with her. Alice suppressed her jealousy and encouraged his participation, pondering the future. *The Poseidons should naturally be attracted to the mermaid alters we women can become. Oh my! Comte and Mother supported my becoming leader of this transition! How can I ask Phil to participate and share me? Oh my! I shared Isaac on Nevis, but can I share my husband even in retirement? Will Comte's proposed shift truly benefit our culture and our children? Long-term, even without a major disaster, many will eventually need more affection than our fixed and paired community can provide. Whatever's to come, I shall remain a special woman for Phil.*

Neither Philip's Eastern Philosophy class, nor Comte's envisioned future were Alice's prime concern most mornings when she woke in low gravity with her thirty-third birthday approaching. Having two children before age thirty-seven was set in her heart. She wanted children at least two years apart and couldn't wait two or more years on Mars before good gravity would return aboard ship bound for some exoplanet. Her only consolation being that the Federation Council was aware of the issue and did not want even a two-year period without childbearing. What could they do?

30

HONEYMOON, FINALLY

They were finishing breakfast when Philip learned he could schedule the honeymoon suite. Alice thought she should still be grieving, yet agreed because Philip was excited and a month had passed since the deaths of Comte and Melita. She and Philip sent requests to miss the next week of work because neither had anything urgent. Alice put three bottles of Ste Wolls champagne in the refrigerator, then called her mother, Lois, and Sasha to tell them not to look for her until Sunday week.

Friday afternoon after packing, Alice arranged for a delivery cart to carry their suitcase. The honeymoon suite was cozy, decorated in rose red with flower patterned fabrics. When Alice entered the bathroom, she gasped at the large hot tub dominating the entry room. Her closer look revealed a padded bench across the tub's backside, set several centimeters below a mark for high water.

Skipping dinner out, the couple sat eating sandwiches, listening to the gurgling water fill the tub. Alice said she had a honeymoon surprise of her own and produced a large red pill for Phil to take. She clasped her hands behind her head and did her wide-eyed pose. She received the expected kiss and held the pose for him to unzip her. She dropped her arms to slip off the blouse, glancing at his pants. "I'd like you in first, Phil." Soon naked, he stepped into the tub. "My man in full," she whispered, "I need a long, warm and soapy massage. My first ever."

"Mine too."

Alice arched her back, pushing her eyelids as wide open as possible. He sighed.

"A pose for your eyes only, ever." They smiled together. "I'm feeling quite passive, Phil, but I want you to know me in mind and body more intimately than any other man, ever. We can begin and end with hidden intimacy. Kiss me with an open mouth." *Huum.* "Now give me your tongue."

A beginning. She soon said, "Your turn, be gentle." *Now I'll be passive.* After long moments of sensation with Philip having her tongue, Alice heard him whisper, "I do know you better."

She smiled and laid down on her back. "Have my breasts. Memorize their look, their feel, try them for taste." She closed her eyes. After many and varied sighs, she sat up and whispered, "You should experiment, bounce me!"

He shifted to bounce her and caused his erection to sway up and down.

"You look a little funny swaying about, but I like it. Kiss my stomach, love. I want to lie down and close my eyes. Don't forget to memorize my shape. Oooh, yes. You are just right for my passive mood."

"Alice, would you call the director of a play a passive person?"

"Oh yes. I'm passive and you are active. Are you enjoying your action role?"

"Quite an enjoyable role. I think I'm in love with the director."

"You should get to know her better."

"I know her quite well already."

"Move closer, love, I want to enjoy your shape."

Aaaah.

"I'm still passive, Phil, kiss me again."

He leaned over and kissed her breasts, soon sucking on her nipples.

Alice murmured, "I must be glowing."

"Want champagne?"

"First I want a massage with soapy hands." She breathed deeply, pushing her breasts out and her eyelids wide. "Your eyes only." She held the pose before slowly closing her eyes and sighing until her red lips spread into the sweetest red smile.

My own eyes-only show.

"Oh Phil, I'm too passive to move. Just come on top and let me hold you for a moment." *Huuum, so good.* "Now, Phil, think only of yourself. Be greedy!"

Nice, her passive mood.

"Ooooh Phil, Phil…now love, no pacing for me. I want you to be greedy, all for yourself." She adjusted her hips. "Are you being greedy?"

"I am."

"I'm waiting to help."

Philip let Alice's smile and his rising need drive him. *Sooner than usual…tending toward a conclusion. Aah, ah, ah.* "Alice, three distinct pulses for me. A record I'm sure."

"Only one warm pulse for me. Let's add a final scene. This play is supposed to end with hidden pleasures, you may recall."

Philip rolled over and lay beside her.

Alice rolled over and stepped out of the tub. "I'll get the champagne." Philip followed her out and played the recorded flute music he found so enchanting. High dancing flutes and two soprano voices singing in Hungarian. Soon they were sipping the bubbly elixir while Alice scratched Phil's back with her fingernails. After a while she slipped onto the bench on her stomach. "When you're in the mood, love, I need a soapy massage of my backside. I'll direct the play, of course."

"Let me recover from being greedy."

"I do want you rested."

"A spaceman's work is never done."

"This warm water is fabulous. I knew I was marrying a clever man. Be sure the music repeats. Then why don't you begin by caressing my neck?"

"A lovely neck."

Alice rolled over for another sip of champagne. "After the back-rub, my buttocks need deep muscle massage. Don't forget your lines and let me rest."

Philip remembered his part. As his fingers were tiring Alice cooed, "A little longer would be nice."

"I'm hard already, perhaps we could rearrange scenes?"

"Oh, my! That red pill you took is working. This must be the time-delayed second quarter part. I'm feeling more energetic now. You should lay back and rest."

I get her on top. "Uuum, Alice, you are warm and enveloping."

She smiled. "I want to envelop you slowly for as long as possible on just my right spot. My turn to be greedy."

"No complaints."

"The Wiccans assure me you will have a wonderful coming." Philip relaxed and enjoyed her vibrating rub, more stimulating than other positions. "Phil, you are supposed to have an active role in this scene."

"I thought I was to rest."

"I'm up here bouncing for you, and you close your eyes and rest your hands?"

She's right.

"That's better, now I feel loved. Intercourse can too easily avoid togetherness!"

"I'm feeling better too."

"I hope I'm not moving too slowly?"

"Your warm rub massages my head, more stimulating than usual."

"We can add hidden techniques in a final scene."

"One honeymoon may not be enough."

"You must bring me here often. Oh my—no talking!" Alice increased her speed, and Philip began thrusts to go deeper. A few adjustments of hips later, Alice closed her eyes with a soft, "So good, Oooh my!" *Now you will slip away.*

They cuddled, caressing each other. Philip whispered, "Don't' you think I could get a reputation reserving the hot tub too often?"

"I think you could attract too many friends-plus in a future variation on retirement. Oh, Phil, you do know that I must promote Comte's proposed retirement culture?"

"Promote warming personal affections and intimacy?"

"Yes. I have been chosen by the League of Blues. You must decide participation for us in a couple of decades. Let's not be concerned now."

We might avoid concerns at the conscious level…our primary processes will continue their subconscious meanders along with our natural instincts and demons. Thanks to insight from Melita, I believe my primary process accepts that Alice will need to be seduced. "Love, your slow envelopment was perfect. Let's repeat that scene."

Alice said sweetly, "You lasted so long, so powerful I felt your pulse. You could rinse us and bestow erotic kisses for me if you're in the mood. Memorize all of me." Phil splashed her and kissed. "Phil, love, I've never had such pampering. Oooh." *We women shall have norms! A friend-plus is not due hidden intimacies or soapy massages. A mermaid may not give her Poseidon more than the first quarter of a red pill. The wife must remain special.*

Alice moaned and sat up, breathing heavily. "A perfect honeymoon."

"For me too. I'll refill the flutes."

"We can repeat the play twice more. We have two more bottles of champagne."

"Practice makes perfect."

"Each time, Phil, you must explore me in more detail until I'm every centimeter yours. A first for me that I want for the love of my life."

"Certainly a first for me."

If we participate, Samantha will want him. Her bigger boobs as variety will be an occasional spice in his life. Still, I cannot ask for Isaac. When, if, the time comes…Phil can no more ask for Samantha or Joan than I can ask for Isaac or Albert, or who knows who two decades hence! Oh my, oh my, Rhonda will be a friend-plus and a decade younger than me with her incredible figure. Still, Phil will know me more intimately and last longer.

Alice led the second performance of their play to be more intimate than the first. *We women are chosen to promote cultural changes. Comte and Melita were never wrong! Friends-plus deserves a try! My divine Phil, I'd exist in a void without you, I know you would be there without me. We have lost our Earth, we must not lose each other preparing for an undiscovered future.*

Alice finished her champagne. "Phil, just now I am concerned about my Cobalt-Blue role as First Among Equals, as Fae. Now that we may talk about all things, you must not avoid a topic that troubles you. Promise?"

"We promised no secrets of the heart and that should cover everything. And you promised your love always, even should I need forgiveness."

"I can love only you."

"You are the love of my life, Alice, only you share all my dimensions of being. Only you are essential."

"My intimate lover and soulmate, you are the only person I must not lose. The only man ever who will know every centimeter of me. The only man I have posed for, ever."

The honeymoon suit was theirs for eight nights, Friday evening through Saturday week morning in Earth days. The last night they used the hot tub for the third time and drank their last bottle of champagne. Saturday morning, they were out by the appointed ten a.m. and decided to go home but not call friends and family until Sunday.

Alice couldn't help thinking, *Two decades along when we retire, hot tubs will be more available. Retirement norms will be easier kept by not allowing hot tubs or showers together for friends-plus.*

SLOW RETURN

Fifty days after departing Pluto, with fifty days remaining before the Wheel would reach Mars, the return trip seemed slow to most everyone since the entire trip from Earth to Pluto had taken only sixty-five days. The hours passed faster for the officers responsible for training new crewmembers for shipboard duties and buildout on Mars. The training was as never ending as the current four flips per day of the Wheel, one at two a.m. while sleeping under nets for the daytime shifts, which included Alice and Philip. Commandant Lois on the public address often reminded the pilgrims of three years of farming on Mars before leaving for an exoplanet. Only Federation Commanders and the Blues knew that new crops were desirable for variety but not required for an interstellar journey.

Alice, now First Among Equals for the Blues, had standing to be heard by the Federation Council as a voice for the crew, or a counselor with sources. Few of the Council's members knew how Fae was chosen, or that Pystead's League of Saint Germaine existed. They respected Comte and Lois's endorsements of Fae's standing to be heard as prescribed in Federation policy.

Philip's training was minimal since he needed only on-the-job orientation for his cognitive-science duties, and he had already decided to cross-train for Reserved Line. For colony buildout he requested a job suiting his aptitude, yet to be determined. In the meanwhile, Alice kept him occupied helping with the art galleries. Also, physical exercise took their time, as urged for those eight years and older. Muscles built during one's youth also built the heart and led to living longer in good health. Muscle tone kept when aging led to more enjoyable older years. Exercise was a new shipboard norm, and couples double dated to jog the rim track.

For buildout on Mars, the administrative algorithm selected Rhonda to operate a regolith-block making machine. Her pride was hurt, thinking the job had been offered because she was a country girl. When Alice also volunteered to bake regolith, Rhonda felt better. Alice was as pleased with the job as any.

✳ ✳ ✳

As Fae, Alice worried. Both Lois and Sasha felt that Comte's cultural shift would take years. Based on her few chats with Philip's friends from California, Alice agreed. Feeling the loss of Melita's insight, she tried to compensate by keeping in mind the human dimensions of primary and secondary processes that the cognitive scientists cited as the whole mind. Primary process being that ever-changing, inscrutable, intuitive dimension of mind built on inherent human instincts. To change the mind, Philip had said, was a two-part process of discrediting counterproductive memes and replacing them with memes consistent with reality and progress.

The mind of conscious thought, secondary process, would naturally inform the subconscious process, but the mind of intuitive proclivities must agree—without a fully knowable result.

Alice recalled a conversation on Nevis when her friend Samantha had explained that swingers were a subspecies of humanity. *Yes, we must face it that occasional friend-plus sex in retirement is petite swinging! O Comte, Mother, why was I chosen? I shared a lover when we never intended to marry. How many retired wives will want to be shared? How many husbands will accept it? Oh my! Mother and Father could never lead this transition for our generation. The League chose me to lead given my understanding husband and my flexible schedule of noncritical duties. Perhaps my sharing Isaac while on Nevis was a plus. Surely most of us have a different mindset than that of our Earthling's cultures? We have accepted the probability of troubling issues. We are not the faint-hearted. For the sake of our children we must succeed very long term. Comte and Melita were never wrong. Never!*

Philip was out and Alice reclined with her eyes shut. *This is how he contemplates issues. What present meme should be changed first, removed? Since physical intimacy should be preceded by true friendship and affection, we must foster friendships with the opposite sex! Is Philip already close to anyone? Joan may be closest. Revathy, after they have attended that Eastern Philosophy Club together for a while. By retirement both Samantha and Rhonda will be close, surely. Is my relationship with my ex-lover close? Well, yes, I would not need Philip's permission to have lunch with Isaac, or dinner. We are known to be close friends.*

Phil asked my permission to attend that club with Revathy. A friendship dependent on a third party is not close! I approved our friendship with Samantha. I discourage our friendship with Rhonda. Oh my! Envy of her figure is interfering. Sven dumped me for a woman striking like Rhonda. Still, Sven never thought of being in love, just playing around. I dumped my share of suitors, but for their personality or behavior and not for a reason I knew of before accepting the date.

I must talk to someone. Sasha is better because Joan is too detached from cultural issues. Before that I need ideas if I'm to be a leader. Alice closed her eyes. *I promised to share the feelings of my heart with Phil. I'm not even sure of those feelings. How would I feel if he told me we should participate in Comte's plan because he wanted Rhonda in retirement? How do we share such a secret of the heart? Am I in danger of losing my soulmate?*

Alice escaped her daydreams by reading a kom message from Barbe in *RAM Key.* An unhappy young woman just twenty-two years-old had established a coven of the Old Religion, the Wiccans, but without an apprentice period with the reining High Priestess. The original High Priestess wanted to forbid the newcomer from calling herself a High Priestess. Barbe, a reporter for *RAM Key,* wanted to know Pystead's policy on the matter. The next day, before Alice had answered, Barbe wrote her that B.B.H.'s coven had been secretly in existence since Pluto. That the young woman, Barbara Bains Hunter, had been class president in high school and was adept at building a following. Alice consulted Lois on the issue and both agreed that for unofficial positions and titles, Pystead played no role. Alice advised Barbe that the original Priestess could post a complaint on the key's Network, but *RAM Key* could not force Barbara to drop the title. *Who's to say how learned or experienced a priestess must be? Who's to say a heresy should be banned?*

✶　✶　✶

Well over half-way to Mars, Alice received a personal message from General Manager Robbie acknowledging that she had succeeded as Fae should she need to bring a matter before the Federation Council. She replied with thanks and that she would not ask to be heard for other than an important issue on which she had something to add.

Alice knew that her mother had addressed the Council only twice. Alice shut her eyes, sad with unhappy memories. Decades ago, Joanne had moved to Nevis pretending to be a single woman, an English teacher, to try and understand how Pystead Group might be accepted if building a campus on the island. Within weeks, and unexpected, U.N. officers were asking her for dates. Joanne felt she could not refuse all and remain considered merely a single teacher. Alice wiped away a tear. Her mother had made out with two of them before being passed to a roughneck, Captain Telaobade, who was insistent on their second date. Joanne decided that consent was better than dubious consent or rape. She said he was worth it because on their next date she had been able to bug his office on Nevis. She left Nevis after their fourth date. The bug worked for months until removed with a change of furniture. And Joanne wasn't the only one to endure repulsive intimacy for Pystead's future! Just before Pystead left Nevis, Melita Rose let the same man, now an Admiral, strip and grope her in her palm reader's tent for the opportunity to obtain a secret, high-tech brain scan of him. Alice sighed. She foresaw no such repulsive sacrifice in her future. Worse would be losing her closeness with Philip. She clenched her teeth. *The League before my life, for the sake of the children.*

⚹　⚹　⚹

Another week structured by flips of the ship and crew training passed as the new normal. Alice, however, did not feel normal. Mentoring their new friends and neighbors crowded out much of the socializing she had enjoyed for years. Too, the duty to promote a cultural transition weighed on her heart and mind.

One morning, Lois called for Philip to please stay with his kom. That afternoon he received a call from Joan. She said he was released from full-time duties at the School of Cognitive Science. She sent him instructions for the next day. Philip told Alice who was not appropriately curious. *She already knows! Knows what?*

When Philip entered the room specified by Joan, he was shown to an Egg simulator, computer driven, set on short, crossed tracks atop an extendable crane arm, and held on a swivel joint inside a gimbal ring. *Six complete degrees of freedom.*

A man approached. "I'm Roger Yates, Philip, your instructor for pilot training."

"I had no idea why I was here."

"Joan has you scheduled for the fighter pilot rating in eighteen months."

"I thought she would put me on a slow training schedule?"

"Eighteen months is typical to combat squadron participation. Before that, seven months for foo fighter basics with the first five months for Egg pilot's wings. Twelve months to fighter pilot rating. You are already qualified in half-Halo jumpsuits, and full-Halo suits are similar. Joan said you may train at a slower pace if other duties or personal needs interfere."

"Fine. I do want to fly the Egg."

"I'll download an instruction manual to your kom. There will be a quiz on the first chapter when you're ready."

⁂ ⁂ ⁂

One evening Rhonda asked to visit. She arrived in tears, again upset about operating a regolith kiln on Mars. Alice assured her the job was a form of cooking, of following a recipe for dirt and a bonding agent and then mixing, shaping, and baking the blocks to perfection. "If I learned to operate food processing equipment on Earth, you can learn to cook regolith on Mars."

"What eats this cooking, Alice?"

"Little by little, cosmic rays eat it. The blocks will be used as radiation shields under our pressure tight farming dome."

"Will I like this kitchen?"

"Oh yes, and it's close to the ship, within ten minutes walking distance although rides will be provided."

"I still think it's because I came from farm country."

"Remember our encounter with the police in Florida?" quipped Philip. "Maybe aptitude assessment concluded you could use a pistol if attacked by little green men."

"Not funny, California boy!"

"Sorry."

"She's right, Phil."

"Very sorry."

Rhonda took Philip's hand. "I have a wonderful new life because of you. I want you to be part of it. Please don't make me worry."

Alice looked away to hide her hurt. *This woman, Rao's steady, already has a friend-plus in mind, and in the moment she has him in hand. Neither one suspects I'm unhappy. I can't share this secret of my heart without infringing Philip's rightful friendship as a Poseidon. What have I done?*

The next day, with Philip out of the apartment and the bubbles art glass sphere from Philip's rescue of Rhonda and Earl in Florida reminding her of Philip's fondness for Rhonda, Alice took the small sphere off the coffee table and secured it in a cabinet drawer. A few days later, on a day like any day, Philip answered a kom call, and Alice heard him say hello to Revathy and thought nothing of it. The Eastern Philosophy Club was to meet that evening. He told Revathy, "I'll check." He called softly, "Alice, am I free to go early? Revathy wants company for dinner before the meeting."

Alice's answer was on the tip of her tongue, *Ask her over.* Then she thought, *They have only a third-party relationship and need my approval of their outings. According to my own ideas, I should have no direct role in their friendship.* Alice said boldly, "Phil, we have no plans. I'm not sick. You don't have to ask my permission."

He accepted. "She wants to eat Indian in Kali Key."

"If you like the food I'd like us to try it." *Oh my! I'm promoting dates with Revathy, who retires in eleven or so years and is single, unmarried. Philip must wait almost two decades to retire. Much too long for Revathy to wait for a friend-plus! Others are retiring now, and more every year. We must only begin platonic dating for the older generation. What will my mother say? Chats with Sasha and Samantha should also help.*

✻ ✻ ✻

Alice reminded herself that she and Phil had promised mutual forgiveness and never to love each other less. She explained the visit to Philip. "Sasha has invited us over for an intimate chat."

"Aren't those chats for you alone?"

"You and I are sharing secrets of the heart. Sasha said you should come. We want to discuss strange new variations on life and need a male's perspective."

"I'm told I've led a sheltered life. Surely my perspective is of little value?"

"You are representative of a high percentage of the men."

O Cosmos. "Alice, I agreed to share secrets of the heart, but not with Sasha."

"You may share with me later."

Sasha had baked bite-sized, cheese-and-artichoke squares using the last of her ingredients. From her large purse, Alice produced a bottle of Albariño wine. After a few bites and sips, Sasha began, "Alice, you do recall there is one woman aboard with amber mermaid's lingerie made like your red?"

Alice purposefully took a moment before saying, "You said you were an amber mermaid sleeping with Comte?"

Cosmos! Philip was shocked.

"My doing. We were good for each other before I met Woody. Alice, soon after Comte's discovery of your mermaid fetish, he asked the Council to procure large amounts of shear and semi-shear silk lace, dye pods of many colors, seven hundred small voice modulators, eight hundred honey-blonde costume wigs, considerable amounts of lightweight, aqua-colored canvas, and long tinsel streamers. The vote was unanimous with smirks, but no questions asked. Typical for any low budget request by Comte. Comte asked me, Melita, Lois, Denise, and your mother to advise Fae of the resources when the time came. We believe the time to know is now."

Sasha turned to Philip. "The older generation has suffered

losses from natural causes as well as two industrial accidents. We lost a few to crime like my precious first husband. Over the years, a few dozen women and a dozen men have been left without a spouse, and in a small society with few eligible men or women. Most never again had an affectionate or even platonic friend of the opposite sex. They suffered with no remedy. Remember, Alice, the childless woman who committed suicide?"

"Yes, heartbreaking. That cast a pall over prospects for long-term happiness in our small group."

"Pystead sponsored mixers, but too many of our men are intro-verted, technical types. Too many at the time were young men not interested in dating a woman even a few years older. A similar situation can recur."

Alice nodded.

Sasha smiled for Philip. "I will dance with you in the basic box Alice has told me about, Philip."

"Perhaps, Sasha, we should all have dancing lessons?"

"Yes, all from the same teachers for compatibility of style." Sasha had a second thought, "All Comte said to me of his vision was that he had provided materials for an extension of mermaid personas as a transition toward a less inhibited retirement culture."

"Any hint on use of the streamers?" asked Alice.

"No. Only that a high school or college sculpture class could make decorative, papier-mâché facemasks for mermaids."

Alice took another artichoke square. "Incredibly good, I hope we grow artichokes on Mars."

"So glad you like the recipe."

Philip ventured, "Comte's materials surely intended a large costume party...or many small parties."

Sasha added, "I'm sure we have materials for enough costumes to promote mermaid personas to the entire Wheel's adult population." She asked, "Philip, have you heard more than the basic concept about Comte's proposed retirement culture?"

"Unofficially, that it's about increasing intimacy between close friends during retirement."

"Yes, and Comte's proposed culture, like all cultures, will manifest with variations, perhaps some outright rejections. That's not a problem. That the general culture becomes permissive enough to allow intimacy among caring friends is the need. A new culture that overcomes the lack of eligible friends and lovers inherent in our present small and fixed population."

Alice took Philip's hand. "Phil, I must promote the culture, not necessarily participate."

Sasha added, "That's a point to emphasize within any trial group. Future participation is the choice of each couple and their private decision. At socials nobody will go around inquiring. Some socials, however, must transition with an alluring costume worn by participating mermaids."

"Fine," said Philip. "And our social circle will go first to give the increasing intimacy a try?"

Sasha nodded. "Except Joan. Prince is quite inhibited and possessive, yet has redeeming qualities according to Joan. She will participate in our group discussions, but not as a home or public mermaid."

Alice nodded. "I don't think mermaids being revealing at home or risqué at parties will lead to a cultural transition any more than party dresses led to friends-plus for my parents' generation. When the time comes, mermaids must flirt and encourage a transition to platonic dating. Dances can provide events for easy mingling."

"Alice, you will have me, Lois, Denise, and Revathy to help. If we wear ritual facemasks, we can look alike and flirt as cultural avatars. We can hint for dates with friends and invite the shy ones out."

Philip asked, "Alice, can't you get at least seven or eight women if this is to expand to the entire Wheel? You may as well go with a top number for effective oversight and build a large, branching vine of active mermaids."

Sasha asked, "What about Lalah?"

"I haven't thought of her, probably because Philip doesn't know her. Philip, although from Iran, Lalah insists she is Persian!"

"Fine."

Why have I excluded the ribbon-cut-dancer and the sweet peach? Alice said, "I'll ask Samantha and Rhonda, that would give us eight."

"My ex-colleague from California, Sandra, might participate."

"What of the others? Your cousin?"

"Please wait for some experience before approaching them."

Alice said, "Sasha, do you have time to talk about initial approaches?"

She nodded.

"I have an idea besides mermaids at home and public mermaids at parties. Revathy asked Philip to have dinner with her before a philosophy club meeting. That gave me an idea. We should promote platonic dating among friends. Philip enjoys the Eastern Philosophy Club and wants to play tennis more than I do. He should be encouraged to have female as well as male friends in such activities."

"I like that. What do you think, Philip?"

"The idea is okay, but unless spouses are to keep up with the other's schedule, one person could have two places to be with somebody left alone. Perhaps sometimes threesomes?"

"No, Phil," Alice said quickly, "group dating will not transition. Platonic interests would be established but without slowly increasing affections."

"That does sound right. If I don't need to ask before making a date with Revathy, what about other friends and acquaintances?"

Alice hesitated. "That's ideal, but I'm not quite ready. Let's test our feelings within our inner social circle and refine the approach with norms before including others."

"Alice, I can teach beginning tennis to Philip during full gravity periods. That would explore scheduling issues since those times are often not known in advance. Denise could help teach on Mars after she finds an adaptation to low gravity."

"A good beginning. Philip would attend more musical events if he had a friend, because mostly I like to stay in and paint. Phil, what about Samantha and Rhonda?"

"I don't know beyond cooking with Rhonda and chatting about short stories with Samantha."

If he asks either to a concert, she will like music! "You should invite them to chamber music concerts."

Sasha observed, "We need a general norm, Alice."

"Which is?"

"Philip, and you, and me, and each of us in our social circle, must be free to ask another out. Each of us must do so because it's up to us to introduce platonic dating! To be purely platonic, our initial invitations should arise from a conversation of the moment. That would even create the scheduling problems mentioned by

Philip. I think as an early transitional norm the spouse must be the one disappointed."

"I agree for our social circle. Also, Sasha, let's start a club called Mermaids for all who will be an erotic Mermaid for their husband or lover at home, a risqué Mermaid in public, and who will allow platonic dating. After experience with our feelings and issues, we women will naturally generate dating norms. From there we can expand the club meetings to group receptions for the men. We'll call each man 'Poseidon.' They can call us by our public Mermaid's name. We will create a public costume that's risqué like a party dress. If we dress alike in public, wear wigs and decorative masks, using the voice modulators most of us will not be identifiable except to our closest friends."

Sasha said, "We have a way to go with the men. They like a bachelor party, but not with their woman dancing! I don't wear a two-piece when swimming and neither do you. Our little group must learn to live as permissively as we are imagining before extending our ideas to others! Simple platonic dating and risqué party dress will test everybody's feelings. We must proceed cautiously. For a cause endorsed by Comte and Melita, everyone will try for the sake of our group's future."

"Oh yes." *I will push myself to include already risqué Samantha and modestly stunning Rhonda.*

"Sasha, before we finish, let me confirm the new norms. If I am asked out, or ask anyone out, I need not first check with Alice when there's no apparent conflict?"

Alice answered, "Correct, as soon as we identify the couples willing to participate. Revathy, of course, is participating as is Sasha."

"If I attend Eastern Philosophy every month, and tennis perhaps once a week, how many more dates would I have time for? Besides, we have two decades until retirement. How many years are we to date without increasing intimacy? I'd say we are beginning the transition too early! What about the generation retiring now? Alice, your parents, Lois and Dusan, Robbie and Debrah, Denise and Alex? The many others I don't know."

"That's right," agreed Alice, "our role is ship wide and for two generations. Our generation of women has been chosen to lead even the older generation of my parents. We need a public club to lead an immediate transition for the older generation. Feedback from them will help guide our generation."

Sasha said, "Two decades of friendship dating will be too long as Philip suspects. But waiting two decades for tennis lessons is also too long! So, Philip, I will date you for tennis lessons with the norm being nothing more affectionate than a social kiss."

"Great."

Alice added, "I'll begin recruiting for home and public escapades, including among the retiring generation. For our generation, I like Sasha's norm for friendship dates. Phil, if you play tennis every week, then not more than one other date every month, and all from among recruited club Mermaids."

Sasha said, "Alice, you could ask Woody and Isaac out, for example."

"Yes. Do you agree, Philip?"

"Fine."

Alice stood. "The artichoke bites were incredibly good, Sasha. I'm going to say artichokes should be grown on Mars."

Saying goodbye, Sasha kissed Philip on the cheek.

"Perfect, Sasha." Alice looked at Philip. "Now stop smiling and walk me home."

Sasha said curtly, "I'll introduce Woody to platonic dating. I hope, Alice, you will take him to the art galleries, which he would not appreciate on his own. It must be a date!"

Alice got the message. "I'm sorry, Phil, you may continue smiling until we are around the corner."

"Perfect, Alice. Dating is no fun without something to smile about."

Within days Alice had ten full members for the club, to be simply called Mermaids. Each had on order a home costume of her chosen color and a large golden comb. Joan was an honorary member with only a golden comb, for a total of eleven members. None were yet from the older generation, although Alice's mother promised to join and bring along several of her friends.

Philip asked that Alice's club name not be Amanda, and her color not be red. She agreed. She felt that Philip's tennis lessons and philosophy club were bona fide platonic interests. But what of her relationship with Isaac now that she no longer needed his help with Co-op paintings or socializing on Nevis? Were dining and dancing legitimate platonic interests for non-professional dancers and diners? And merely a kiss on the cheek for an ex-lover? Alice closed her eyes, distraught. *Is a future culture of friends-plus intimacy merely a dating game that begins now with platonic interests? Will we merely pretend some platonic interest is the key to a friendship? What would be more energizing than dining and dancing, looking forward to sex in a hot tub? Is Comte's envisioned culture merely one of swinging with strict norms? If I date Isaac and Phil dates his girlfriend or wife, would dating at different times and places avoid swinging? Oh my, Sasha wants me to date her husband. Comte's envisioned culture requires a bona fide friendship, caring for a friend, a petite form of love before intimacy. If swinging, however, only sexual desire is needed. For a friend-plus only a caring friendship may lead to physical intimacy. That's bonding, not swinging! I like Woody as a social friend, just not attracted to him for long-tern platonic interests, nor conversational intimacy. Our dating will not transition. What of Sasha and Philip? Oh my! Others too I can already name! This floated cultural variation is becoming a matter of when rather than if.*

⁂ ⁂ ⁂

Thirty days out from Mars, Lois announced that colony building skills were sufficient for further development on the job. With extra time available the Mermaids Club began planning their introductory party, which could not be held until after buildout on Mars. They decided on risqué halter tops to be worn at their public parties. The first event would be a mixer to introduce themselves as a club to their men. They would promote dancing lessons and thereafter have a party. The Mermaids felt their social circles would gel for both generations with dating norms. Alice felt both generations would gain the emotional experience needed for expansion to other social circles such as her artist friends, Lalah's friends from theatre, Lois's friends in administration, and Denise's in recreation.

Alice did not want to date Woody but knew she would offend Sasha if she didn't. And whom would she enjoy dating in addition to Isaac? Rao, her bodyguard from Nevis was an interesting man in more ways than one and would have free time when Rhonda was out with Philip. *Perhaps somebody will ask me for painting lessons? What fun would that be unless he was trying to seduce me? Oh my, is that a secret of my heart? Phil was right. Our generation is two decades from needing a transition. We must not begin platonic dating for our generation! I can't stop Phil's tennis lessons and philosophy club! Will they become a problem?*

✳ ✳ ✳

Twenty days travel out from Mars, Alice received a visit from her friend Barbe who lived in RAM Key. As a news reporter for RAM, Barbe received tips on everything that anybody thought amiss. She was concerned about gossip on RAM concerning her casual friend, Revathy, who had confided to a neighbor that she had lived a past life in French Catalonia. A young woman named Barbara Bains Hunter was using the example of Revathy believing in a past life as evidence that subcontinent Indians and Asians should be scanned and those found irrational removed from critical positions because they were a threat to future planning.

Alice raised her voice, "Barbe, I have known Revathy for years. Her belief in a past life in no way interferes with her rational thought on practical issues. She once told me she was afraid of being shunned or sent for therapy and would move to Kali Key."

"She is planning to move. That will not end problems in RAM Key! Barbara, known as B.B.H. who started a coven of the Old Religion when on Pluto, now has a following of young people who agitate for doubled brain scans of anybody not wanting an immediate return to Earth. Your friend Rao told me that RAM Key was monitoring outgoing and incoming kom messages. He suspects that routine brain-scans have been suspended for some. Those of us who support the Federation are concerned about this movement of impressionable young adults led by High Priestess B.B.H. Our

RAM news Network is filled with misinformation about life on Earth, and the lack of opportunities, parties, and entertainment aboard this tiny ship that pretends to offer a better way of life. Only power-crazed people would give up so much on Earth just to be leaders here, according to B.B.H."

"Barbe, stay in your apartment as much as possible. I'll send you a kom query about a visit and ask about active visual artists in RAM. You should reply and everything will seem ordinary to anybody monitoring koms."

After conferring with Joan and Lois, Alice visited Barbe and gave her a plug-in flash-cube drive that would allow her secure and untraceable tunneling access in and out of RAM's kom Network. Alice asked Barbe to continue with chatty personal messages to her and Isaac, but no longer contact Rao by kom. He would teach her how to embed coded messages in her chat. And avoid being seen with Rao except where a romantic interest could be inferred, say, in his apartment for about an hour during each visit.

Within days after Alice's visit, Barbe used her new tunneling drive to messaged Alice that the unhappy Barbara Hunter was calling for an increased wine ration. Barbe said that B.B.H. was also promoting an immediate return to Earth for RAM Key as self-determination allowed by Pystead's policy.

Lois knew the young woman's case. Barbara and her parents were picked up by *Marianas Key* after a dinner with friends. Both parents died suddenly the next day because they had been poisoned at dinner. Barbara blamed her parents for not telling her where she was going and for joining Pystead only because they were power hungry. She couldn't believe they were one of many voices at Pystead. She hated her sudden plunge into poverty and the lack of rich suitors and high-society parties. She wanted to return to Earth and claim the mansion and endowment that were in her name. Lois was alarmed at that latest revelation and felt that Barbara would not have known any Pystead policy, especially about the right to self-determination. Lois assumed that Barbara's charisma empowered the movement and Dr. Osgood provided its options.

✳   ✳   ✳

Fifteen days out from Mars, Alice Saint Germaine, wearing a wig and introduced as Fae, addressed the Federation Council. Manager Markwaters asked her the sources of her information. She named Barbe, a Network reporter in *RAM*, and Rao, a Federation Security Branch officer posted in *RAM*, both friends. Fae asked that all contact go through her ostensibly as friendly chat, because *RAM* was monitoring outgoing and incoming kom calls, and her friends' safety was believed in jeopardy. Fae reported that Rao had observed undue changes to schedules for brain scans and violations of Pystead's questioning protocols. Her final revelation that many in *RAM Key* were proposing an immediate return to Earth left Council members with open mouths, wide eyes, or slumping shoulders. Pystead's officers had not imagined any ship leaving the group so soon. And even a few engineers returning via Earth's Mars Station would create a security problem.

The Council put *Key RAM* off limits to crewmembers with critical skills. Joan expected that such personnel would not be allowed to leave the ship if *RAM* voted to return to Earth. The two ships adjacent to *RAM* were informed. Both added security guards at their concourse and rim track portals to *RAM*.

Using the Blue's tunneling drive, Alice messaged the few Blues in *RAM* to secretly track locations of trained personnel because quarters were being reassigned without changing addresses in the ship's directory. She messaged Barbe, including a hidden message that Barbe need not make contact again unless she learned of potential or actual harm to personnel, or of an impending action that she felt must be known or stopped.

Alice asked Lois and Joan over to discuss the situation. On the issue of Barbe all agreed they had a new Cobalt Blue who must be protected, and that Alice would brief Rao in code via Barbe. Joan said she would plan for the worst: an armed assault on *RAM*. She asked Alice's opinion.

"Pystead's contingency plans do not include such a prompt return to Earth by any ship. You and Lois must plan to save personnel and our secrets in the password protected and hidden files of the engineers. *RAM* could discover the specifications etched into library and engineering department walls under the wall-mounted plaques. Because the font is too small for reading without magnification, those files will take time to video. We cannot expect peace on or off Mars if our technology falls so soon into Earth's hands! We must save our search files for a new planet. We don't want the U.N. having a short list of places we may be! I will address the Council again if we get new information."

Lois said bitterly, "We have not brought our children out here to die at the hands of Earthlings using our secret technology! We must prevent them smuggling our secrets by transmission or via a memory cube returning to Earth with someone like B.B.H. or Osgood."

Joan assured the others, "We can secure our secrets and personnel by force if necessary. B.B.H. must have some loyal security personnel, in which case there would be casualties. In addition to stopping data transmissions and checking personal computers, we must search for chip implants. We must scan those with great memories, including performers like singers and actors. Too, engineers and techs cannot be allowed to return so soon."

Alice wondered, "If B.B.H. waits to arrange a return through the U.N.'s Mars station, that would give her reliable assistance and us more time, wouldn't it?"

Joan spoke as she stood. "We have a problem. Dr. Osgood knows quite a lot about Pystead. He will assume that our technical files are stored in different type media and places. The Mars Station supply ships would return *RAM's* leaders in exchange for our secrets. And would probably kill them after interrogation."

Lois and Alice nodded. Joan said, "Earth getting our specifications would be worse for us than their getting a ship. Reverse engineering of the unknown is a slow process."

"We must rescue our loyal crewmembers and their share of the food and other supplies aboard *RAM*, before any are interrogated," added Lois. "We can search anybody wishing to return via Mars Station, although I doubt the U.N. wants them without our secrets."

Alice exclaimed, "If the U.N. had B.B.H.'s psychological profile on Earth, perhaps their artificial intelligence decided to kill her parents and create a potential problem for us? A.I. could have concluded that with Dr. Osgood aboard the two would cooperate!"

"Joan said, "A possibility. Having Dr. Osgood in *RAM* almost assures the two are cooperating."

Escaping the Earthlings had now acquired unexpected dimensions of risk, especially given Pystead's morality of minimizing harm done to others. And knowing of the cruelty inflicted by the

U.N.'s forces on Earth, the three Blues parted as worried as they had ever been. Pystead would prevail, but at what cost?

✴ ✴ ✴

At eight days out from Mars, Joan, Commander of the Security Branch, announced to all adults that Pystead's probes had found a nuclear bomb orbiting Mars. It was surely meant for anybody landing on Mars without a permit from the United Nations. Joan informed all but *RAM Key* that the bomb would be destroyed when the Wheel was three days from landing. She did not reveal that it would be destroyed using a new weapon dubbed the Red Eye of Shiva. She reminded that the possibility of orbiting bombs had been considered likely, and any satellite orbiting Mars, Phobos, or Deimos would be investigated.

Although Alice knew finding a bomb was expected, even planned for, she was disturbed at its being true. Philip wondered aloud if Pystead would be able to provide even a temporary haven for the pilgrims. Alice's personal concern focused on the safety issue possibly pushing Phil to postpone having children until they were well underway to another planet. By then she could be too old for more than one child. She and her inner circle of Blues knew that having a boy to follow as the next Saint Germaine was highly desirable. Alice hoped for a mysterious dream from One Above that would portend the birth of a future Saint Germaine.

Philip couldn't help pondering the problem of *RAM Key*. He asked Alice, "What chance of flying would RAM have if Joan were to destroy their flight deck's viewport window and its pressure-tight hull covers? And then a few control panels!" *She knows so much. Will she find fault with that approach?*

316

"Phil, a ship or the entire Wheel can be flown from any one engine room, and from one large refuge station in each ship."

Will RAM Key's pilots in training already know that's possible?

✻　✻　✻

Alice answered their apartment's kom the next evening and was speechless when Joan asked to speak to Philip. *No hello for me. No mention of training for Philip. Oh my. Could she be calling for a date? No! Prince is agreeable if she talks to the Mermaids and combs her hair with a golden comb, but not for a single date.*

After taking the kom, Philip looked in Alice's direction, seemed to change his mind and said, "Yes, I can make it. Goodbye."

"Going out?"

"I'm invited to a briefing on a new and secret development. Why don't you come along? Is there anything too secret for you to know?

"No."

"Please get ready. We should leave in fifteen minutes—Joan said briefing room K-B-N-2-D-7-P-R-0-4."

"An adjacent neighborhood, deck seven. We'll need a map for room location—a Presentation Room."

✻　✻　✻

Joan introduced the topic: gravity mats. Long considered feasible because their ship's aether-energy engines had slightly changed local ship's gravity depending upon their orientation to the Earth. Joan introduced their speaker, Arthur Vanderhought.

Alice beamed. *Philip's friend and sponsor! Why did I think Joan could be calling for a date? I'm not a natural to lead this cultural shift, although I must! If Philip could transition from sheltered professor to taking physical risks in my real-world, I should be able to transition from a traditional wife to taking emotional risks as a club Mermaid. Or not? I'm sure my divine husband would say the change must be more than rational—for success my subconscious mind must dream of pleasant things. As must his! I'm already dealing with a probable future variation in life. Not to mention remaining healthy in the low gravity of Mars soon to come.*

When Alice began listening, Arthur was saying, "Our engines can absorb aether energy from any direction to function. But to create local gravity the absorbed energy must be from a monodirectional flow. The absorption per se exerts a force on the mass—hence produces local gravity! We have encountered varying aether energy densities in our journey thus far, and will again as we traverse interstellar space. Gravity mats will be produced in layers for full gravity aboard ship and with a layer that can be removed for full Earth gravity while on Mars.

"We have three conjectures about how to achieve a strong directional flow into a relatively small mass, such as floormat. Most promising is to immerse the mass in a ship's resonant-drive field and maintain electromagnetic resonance until the mass absorbs a unidirectional flow of aether energy. This will be our first manufacturing attempt since a similar technique led to our trident sword, which attracts a spherical flow, yet maintains an internal aether density three times the normal on Earth. That high density is capable of breaking through weaker spacetime aether densities. The trident can cut through any mass sustained by a less dense spacetime—a vorpal sword. Well, that's our best explanation of what's happening! We hope to create a lasting directional flow into a mat and anybody standing on it. We may need a continuous electrical input to maintain the monodirectional flow of aether energy. The big unknown at this point is whether the manufacturing process will be linear, and hence how much mass and time will be required to make a mat producing a given local gravity. Also, if a power supply is needed, materials to manufacture portable battery powered units will not be available on Mars. The engineers prefer not to add wiring from the ship's power supply across walls and decks to gravity mats."

Joan returned to say that women wanting children within the year would not be able to wait for gravity mats. To provide full gravity for childbearing and rearing, *Key Bury* would fly around Mars at some distance with four flips per day to generate full gravity at safe speeds. It would be a secret that gravity mats were being produced during the flight, lasting perhaps twenty-four months. Joan said if the mats could be produced, the breakthrough would make living in space almost like living on Earth. She warned that *RAM Key* must not be told about the mats. "We," said Joan, "must retain our technological superiority because we cannot hand the Earthlings the means to follow us out of the solar system."

✸ ✸ ✸

Mars was six days travel away when *RAM Key* formally requested to be assigned the cave location on Mars. Two Pystead ships had enlarged a cave to serve as a hangar during their trip to Mars made three years earlier. *RAM Key's* personnel had researched files and planned ahead because the topic was not on the Council's schedule until just before landing. Selection of landing sites was envisioned as a pseudo-random assignment matching each of the five ships having inexperienced crews with one of the four Federation ships for assistance and training. After considering the issue, Joan was in favor of assigning the cave to RAM, thereby having them out of sight and easy to contain without access to further training and status updates.

Philip, officially training for Reserved Line, took Alice to the flight deck to watch Pystead attack the bomb orbiting Mars. A surveillance pod was positioned at each of three Red Eye weapons flying a short distance from the Wheel. The Eyes were energized, glowing red, with each quark field attached to the pod flying with it. The Red Eyes were launched to find and fly near the orbiting bomb. Mars Station's radar would not detect the pods approaching the bomb because they were small and smooth, returning no radar signal that could be detected on Mars. At four days out, the three pods began orbiting with the bomb as it crossed to the side of Mars visible to the Wheel. The leader pod targeting for the smallest Red Eye remained near the bomb and the other two retreated to provide video. The computer took over and exploded the leader pod just after its orbit hid it from the following Red Eye and the approaching Wheel ship. Its quark field jumped to the bomb. Video switched to a split screen showing the bomb and the glowing Red Eye weapon. Power increased and the Eye exploded in a blue flash and some of the orbiting bomb vanished. A cheer went up. The two remote surveillance pods climbed into geosynchronous orbits to observe the U.N.'s Mars station. Regardless of how damaged the bomb might be, it was now physically asymmetrical and certainly not capable of a targeted reentry to Mars. Joan hoped Mars Station was not aware of the damage. To be safe, however, as they landed she would send a small pod designed to physically attach to the bomb so that any reentry could be controlled by Pystead.

Pystead's chances for living safely on Mars were greatly enhanced because of the Red Eye weapon. Still, Alice remembered Philip's reluctance on Nevis to having children in what he believed unsafe living conditions. She asked Joan to personally confirm to Philip that Pystead had sufficient materials to produce both gravity mats and Red Eyes in abundance.

The Mermaids Club met, and Alice told the Mermaids that she had made a mistake in timing for both generations. Final organization, social norms, and costumes would need to wait until completion of buildout on Mars and the return of a normal shipboard life. Then, they should include members of the generation about to retire. They could assist the older generation's transition, which should prove a valuable experience for their own transition two decades later. The Mermaids departed, pleased with the delayed cultural transition.

32

KEY RAM'S GAMBIT

Day two out with no apparent response to Pystead's attack on Mars Station's orbiting bomb, Pystead began preparations for landing. Joan launched autonomous and piloted foo fighters to patrol their landing zone and return video to be compared with video taken three years earlier. Robbie published approach and landing protocols. No obstacles to a smooth landing were foreseen, but each ship would be sealed to neighborhood and deck levels. Same as the next to highest alert level, a Red-Two, Alice told Philip. They put on their full jumpsuits as Alice said all established crew would do.

Alice, Philip and their friends were ready to land, yet apprehensive. Theirs the feelings of the entire crew, they assumed. *This is Poseidon's bittersweet nirvana*, mused Philip, *this is as good as it's going to get on Mars with the ever-present burden of being prepared to fight or flee at a moment's notice.*

The Federation Council assigned *RAM Key* the cave per their request. The other eight keys would reside in hollows or behind ridges, veiled from a direct surface view in the direction of Mars Station, itself located on the opposite side of a hilly ridge.

✳ ✳ ✳

Twelve hours out, the nine ships separated and approached Mars at a constant speed, flying circular edge forward to create their smallest radar and optical returns. The ships landed in daylight, such as it was, about three kilometers apart on an irregular, circular perimeter about eight kilometers across. With *RAM Key* isolated, the remaining eight ships formed four sectors, each having a Federation ship of fully trained crew. Within minutes, the Federation ships deployed Red Eye weapons and covered them with ground-red canvas. Joan stationed autonomous foo fighters outside the Federation ships as a rapid response force. With no provocations from Mars Station, not even drones overhead, normal activity resumed aboard the ships for all but the defensive duty crews.

Nightfall was peaceful with favorite meals served in the galleys. Alice was positive as she made her plans. "Tomorrow, love, please help us open the art galleries."

Philip smiled. "We made it to Mars. Now we must prove worthy of the countless hardships endured and sacrifices made to get us here, Comte and Melita notable among them. As well, Alice, as the sacrifices made by your mother and father, and yourself. So many of you enduring circumscribed lives for decades. Our established crewmembers are entitled to be known as the elect, and we pilgrims as judged by Comte are certainly a singularity of humanity."

"Phil, within two years, once departing Mars with good gravity aboard ship, we pilgrims will have an environment suitable for procreation."

"I too want children for us."

My soulmate knows my heart. The lineage of Saint Germaine shall continue as wished for by my granddad and my parents. Hallelujah.

33

BUILDOUT BLUES

Key RAM personnel unloaded their earthwork equipment and began leveling the floor of their cave. They asked questions of the Federation's experts but would not accept outside crew inside the cave. They heightened the cave's entrance at center to clear the high peak of the ship, which they moved completely inside. Though concerned for the trained Federation crewmembers aboard *Key RAM*, Joan was pleased to see its flight deck slip from view. The next day, crew from Joan's Security Branch placed optical, infrared, and vibration monitoring stations around the red mound, dubbed Cave Hill. Joan agreed that *RAM's* dose of radiation would be less than others, but she did not believe that was their reason for choosing the cave. She doubted *RAM's* officers had thought through the reason. She was concerned about their refusal to allow outside crew inside the cave, as if afraid of surveillance devices. *Key RAM* became a high security risk in the Federation's opinion.

Key Bury unloaded its earthwork equipment for use by others.

Bury was chosen by the Federation Council to fly around Mars for the full gravity essential to conception and childbearing. Couples thirty-two years of age or older, with or without children, from all ships, were invited to participate in the procreation flight that could last as long as two Earth years. *RAM Key* declined to participate and ended daily communications with the Federation. Joan's Security Branch began active preparations for a rescue on *RAM*. *Key Logos* would lead any action taken against *Key RAM* while *Key Bury* was away.

A second essential purpose of the procreation flight was known only among the four Federation ships. Recycling crews took metals and plastics in secret from the Tank ship to be used in manufacturing gravity mats on *Key Bury* while flying around Mars.

Morale aboard *Key Bury* was high. Couples would, however, delay conception for at least thirty days. Everyone knew that men returning from the microgravity of one of Earth's space stations produced more than the usual percentage of male babies. Waiting would preserve the normal birth ratio of genders. Alice knew that ship's manager, Asif, was also waiting for a report that gravity mats could be made before prospective parents were told that good gravity would be available on Mars for child development. Meanwhile, the children aboard played with renewed enthusiasm in the good gravity. Parents kept play periods short with no contact because the children's bones and muscles had weakened while living in less than forty percent of Earth's gravity on Mars.

With each flip, the ship took a ninety-degree turn to remain near Mars. The first side of the flight outran Mars in its orbit enough to flip and turn, decelerating while crossing in front of the oncoming planet. Then after a flip and turn, they accelerated again to keep up with the planet. Alice teased Philip that *Key Bury* could do the box step as well as he could. Philip now looked forward to Alice having two-and-a-half years between the children they both wanted.

During their third week of the box-step flight, Alice received a call from Joan. *RAM* had ended all contact with the Federation except to allow individuals brief visits to friends on *RAM*. Joan assumed the visits were to appear reasonable and delay intervention by the Federation. Alice and her inner circle foresaw a crisis in the making. The doctors had set two years in Martian gravity as the maximum for children before irrecoverable developmental damage. They were monitoring glucose levels for increased insulin resistance, and calcium in their urine for bone loss. Other developmental problems were difficult to measure or even identify. Alice called Lois who said that aboard the seven ships outside on Mars, no women were pregnant. Lois assumed that Federation women on Key Bury knew to avoid pregnancy. Still, all the pilgrims, including adults, needed good gravity as soon as possible, definitely by twenty-four months.

✳   ✳   ✳

With nothing yet to be done about *RAM Key*, Alice focused on Philip, and with a return to chamber music, dining, and dancing lessons her romantic mood returned. They were sociable when out, but never planned an outing with others, which seemed the norm for those aboard. Then success of the procreation flight was assured with the announcement that enough gravity mats were being produced for all aboard to have full gravity apartments, children's schools, and playgrounds upon return to Mars.

After a month of trying to conceive, Philip wondered if there could be a physical problem. He noticed that his art glass gift to Alice was no longer displayed on their coffee table. He wondered if all was well with the relationship. Alice began checking her temperature. She was anxious to have her first child while young enough to have the second before turning thirty-seven years old, which increased chances for complications. The first night of a slight dip in her temperature signaled Philip's first command performance. She woke him six hours later for increased probability. Again, before lunch she called upon him for the final opportunity during her ovulation cycle. Afterwards he held her gently, hoping not to have triplets.

Once pregnant, Alice felt an inner well-being, charmed by the miracle of bearing a new life into the cosmos. Her joy touched Philip, and her positive medical reports and surprisingly little anxiety comforted him. The fetus was male, and Philip prayed to the Cosmos that he would be an adequate father for the next Saint Germaine. His burden was lightened upon realizing that the men of their inner circle would also become role models as the child grew. Their son would have advantages relative to most children remaining on Earth. Some would say privileges, yet a quality of life bestowed by generations of innovation, work, and sacrifice by family and friends was the product of evolutionary design, deemed a privilege only by those less fortunate. Philip felt an inner peace knowing that his children would live beyond the grasp of those who would usurp their inheritance. *Yes, if you build it, they will come, and they will try to take it away from you. There will always be a need for Saint Germiane!* Philip whispered to himself, "Amen."

✳   ✳   ✳

After thirteen months of flight, *Key Bury* returned to Mars with secret gravity mats, twenty-three babies, and five pregnant women. Alice and Philip returned with a healthy baby boy named Dario S Germaine Russell. Dario weighed almost nine pounds at birth. He had his great grandfather's large head, a few of his father's ash-blond locks, and his mother's blue eyes—already he looked the part of a future Saint Germaine.

Within a week, without mention, crews had installed gravity mats where most needed in all ships except *RAM*, which continued to refuse participation with the group. Given the return of continuous gravity in their apartment, Philip hoped their bubbles art glass would be removed from safe keeping and returned to the coffee table. Although hurt by its removal, he didn't want to ask for it, and after a few days consigned it to becoming a surprise event when Alice next thought about it.

In the eight outfitted ships, the concept of secret gravity mats became popular, and Manager Robbie requested that if they must be mentioned to refer to them as segramats. Within thirty days the mats were taken for granted. The Council called for another ship to fly the box for procreation. The trip, of course, was primarily intended to manufacture gravity mats and red eye weapons. With only a half dozen couples intent on procreation, *E Key* departed with its secret stock of metals and plastics. Each couple was given a high precision thermometer. The flight was announced to last no longer than twenty Earth months. Gravity mats would be available for all upon return, whether or not they had a newborn child.

* * *

Lois, Commandant of Administration, wanted the work crews outside on Mars to feel safe with their children well cared for. She released Alice from her assigned duty of regolith making and asked her to monitor outside crews with frequent kom calls while they were working away from the ship, and to provide childcare for several of their children. After all, Alice had cross-trained as a nurse.

Philip took her regolith baking job, happy to leave a tunneling machine crew even though the one tunnel would be cut-and-cover construction. Too, as he and Alice knew, the tunnel was merely for show, to convince Mars Station that Pystead would continue growing crops for another two years or more. A greenhouse pressure dome, a half cylinder shape made of red metallic glass had been built while *Key Bury* circled Mars. The first regolith blocks were placed above the crops like a ceiling, shielding gardeners and crops from the strong cosmic radiation striking Mars.

At the end of his third week of kiln work, Philip regaled Alice with regolith baking stories and his high rate of meeting specifications for the orders. He had endured a fierce dust storm, unable to open his control-room door for lunch or dinner because the fine dust would have filled the room and pushed through unseen voids between instruments and the mounting panel to clog the interior of instruments and controls—a design oversight. Alice asked if he would rather change diapers all day long. He decided that taking a cooler with an emergency meal would be the preferable option.

Philip and Rhonda came to appreciate their job: nearby, low hazard, in a radiation shielded cabin without constant noise, vibration, or messy diapers. The two met for a hot lunch and commiserated about how long it would take for life in space to become as easy as that depicted in the movies. Rhonda told Philip that after Pystead departed Mars she would marry Rao and wanted to continue seeing her California boy. "Eventually, Philip, I will be Mermaid Peachie. I'll have a twist of fuzzy pink and cream-yellow for my intimate colors."

"Nice." *Whatever fuzzy pink might be.* He asked if she would consider them dating according to the Mermaids' plans now on hold.

Rhonda said she'd tell him once out of the dining room. She did so with a kiss. "Being a public Mermaid will be a challenge for me. I've always dressed modestly. The club has chosen a sleeveless, crop-top, fuchsia halter and diaphanous pantyhose decorated with a fuchsia fish-scale pattern of several shades of pink, blending with ever more green toned scales into a half-green tail that turns out in a flipper over each foot. The costume isn't revealing, but it's definitely sexy."

"I know Alice and others believe that risqué costumes will force each of us to experience and accept the personal emotions needed for a transition."

"You will have to accept Alice showing skin."

"Yes, her being a Mermaid will challenge me."

"It should. Back in Middle Georgia we said a woman dressed modestly wanted to be courted. Dressed risqué she wanted to be seduced, and in revealing attire she wants to be propositioned."

"Sounds right to me!" *Good for Alice according to the late Melita's intuition.* "According to Mermaids' plans for the future, Rhonda, isn't a Poseidon supposed to court his platonic-friend and eventually seduce her?"

Rhonda smiled. "Sounds right to me."

✄   ✄   ✄

Several days later, Manager Robbie announced to all except *RAM Key* that the gardeners had harvested their last greenhouse crops. A second greenhouse would not be built. Their supply of extra regolith block would be used to build defensive redoubts for faux laser cannons. Prospects for a variety of food on another planet seemed easily doable to the pilgrims, raising spirits. Not mentioned by Robbie, planned amenities had been sacrificed to have metals and plastics for segramats and red-eye weapons. Not mentioned by Joan, the possibility that if an Earth ship or fleet attacked Pystead it would become a source of materials for salvage.

Mars Station soon increased drone flights to observe the work, and Pystead's Council felt the Earthlings had no idea of their impending departure from Mars.

Then Robbie ended buildout on Mars. The fine dust and extreme cold on Mars had been more troublesome than anticipated. The good news was that no one and no equipment had been harmed beyond repair. The bad news was that the hardships of being a pilgrim were stressful. Even the elect had to remind themselves that they were safe on Mars and their diligence would accrue for the benefit of their children if not for themselves.

After twenty-two Earth months on Mars, Robbie declared a week-long vacation. Alice's inner circle of friends met for dinner. All were satisfied with Pystead's accomplishments and looked forward to a future with musical concerts and stage plays, plus having enough segramats for Earth-style court games. Philip opined they were living the non-professional lives that would soon have been their fate on Earth, except now with the potential for a new life of the authentic self. Alice agreed and thought that all pilgrims living through the same fire would help foster a future group identity.

Philip nodded with the others. *Alice is not Fae merely by luck of lineage, she's a new renaissance human! She deserves to go down to her dreams a woman in full. The goal is clear, even if my role be veiled, except to be resolute.*

⚹ ⚹ ⚹

RAM Key became a critical topic among Federation's officers, with concern for its pilgrims' health reaching crisis proportions. Adults and children could not be left on *RAM* or any other ship another few months without lasting medical consequences. The Federation Council concluded that *RAM Key* would not want to leave Mars with the Wheel, and that longtime crewmembers aboard RAM would not be allowed to leave because their skills were needed. A vote was taken. The Council called for an immediate rescue on *RAM*.

Alice, as Fae, spoke to Council for her second time and supported a rescue of the pilgrims aboard *RAM*. Those wanting to return to Earth could do so if accepted for return via a U.N. supply ship from Mars Station. Fae told the Council that many quarters on *RAM* had been reassigned and new locations not posted. Her friends were tracking as much as possible and could provide some addresses before a rescue. Fae said that her friends could also give an opinion of the best duty shift for an assault. Manager Robbie thanked her for the brief and said Council would meet with Joan and specialists to decide a course of action.

⁂

Alice and friends were buoyed by prospects of an imminent rescue on *RAM* and preservation of friends and high secrets. Philip began considering assault options and best uses for their Red Eyes, even though he would not participate in planning the assault.

Two days later Joan announced that Mars Station had begun sending surveillance drones over their location day and night. Pystead told Mars Station that if the dones were not stopped, Pystead would begin low-altitude patrols on their side of the separating hills. Mars Station did not reply and foo fighter patrols began. Joan used their initial distraction to plant small surveillance pods around the station's perimeter. She also had long-look radar stations installed on the two moons, Phobos and Deimos, for an all-hours warning of approaching ships.

Days later Joan's surveillance stations around Cave Hill reported unexplained vibrations, and the next week a sighting. Joan called Alice, "You should know that Mars Station personnel and equipment are being allowed into Key RAM, using a small tunnel that opens on the back side of Cave Hill. The exchanges take place at night with Mars Station using a ground shuttle without lights or radar. They follow a periodic homing beacon from Cave Hill. We must assume they are readying the ship for a return to Earth and searching for our technical specifications. They surely will take *RAM's* administrative computer system off-line to avoid the possibility of our backdoor monitoring. The Mars Station personnel aboard will need time to gain confidence in operating the ship's engine-drive and navigation systems."

"Are you saying that our Blue information system will be

taken off-line with the administrative computer?"

"Yes! We must learn as much as possible about their plans. If we cannot get a surveillance rod in, we will need to capture a shuttle and scan its crew."

"Do not use Philip for that operation!"

"We have tactical-ops. Philip is not involved, not yet fighter pilot rated, and never will be tactical-ops. All is top secret. We expect complete success and believe we will rescue every person wanting to continue with the Federation. What do you think of telling Mars Station that if they want to return any persons to Earth, they must do so on their next supply ship because all who remain aboard Key RAM will soon be taken on a gravity flight for their health?"

Alice agreed and shared the news with Philip. He relaxed, but Alice felt that a rescue on *RAM* would be necessary. Why would the U.N. give up the ship before finding its secrets?

⚹   ⚹   ⚹

Alice and her close circle of in-home mermaids kept a formal club in mind and met twice before finalizing the design of their risqué public costume. Each mermaid was scheduled for measurements. They decided to introduce the club to their men after the problem with *RAM Key* had been resolved. They favored an elaborate grotto-themed event, using decorative masks, the wigs and voice modulators provided by Comte. The public Mermaids would look alike, except that Lalah, Revathy, and Barbe could be identified by skin tone, and Rhonda by her height. Except, Alice reminded, at first events with the older generation participating, even those four could not be positively identified! The Mermaids agreed to continue their in-home mermaid personas and not begin platonic dating. Alice agreed, except that Philip could continue his tennis lessons and attend the Eastern Philosophy Club.

✳ ✳ ✳

Joan and her deputies were satisfied with the defensive capabilities of the colony and for their ship's safety when departing Mars. *E Key*, still flying around Mars would coordinate to fly with the other ships seeking a final departure from the Earthlings. Using their surveillance pods that were virtually invisible to Mars Base's optical and radar trackers, Pystead continuously monitored the station's communications with Earth and found no messages suggesting any planned attack on Pystead. Philip and Alice, privy to defensive capabilities, felt secure. They would have been happy pilgrims except for the problem of *Key RAM*.

Joan knew *RAM* held experienced crew against their will. Rao had returned to shipboard life in *RAM* without any security related duty, and again had his personal kom. He had sent a coded message that two engineers were missing from engine-drive crews, and none of their colleagues or friends knew where they were posted or living, and could not reach either by kom. Suddenly, messages from Rao and Barbe no longer contained embedded reports, suggesting their fear of sending a report. Joan had gotten a surveillance rod into the cave with a group of Mars Station personnel, but the rod could not get out, and Rao could not safely transmit its findings even if he had the rod, which he should. A rescue on *RAM* was indicated, and soon! Joan knew what needed to be done first and consulted with Fae for her perspective before speaking with Robbie and Lois.

34

TAC-OPS

Both commanders knew the circumstances, the options, and the risks. Before seizing *RAM Key*, Joan needed the files from her unrecovered surveillance rod. Information on the influence of Mars Station personnel aboard *RAM* could be critical to minimizing casualties and preserving Pystead's secrets. Too, both Alice and Joan feared that if RAM Key could not find Pystead's technical specifications nor return the ship to Earth, Mars Station personnel would use the ship to cause as much damage as possible. Possibly poison stores of food and water. Possibly plant explosives aboard to detonate upon some preset condition. Possibly exit the cave and attack Pystead's ships. Simply destroying computers and control consoles could be easily done as a last resort before losing the ship. Keeping *RAM Key* on Mars would give the Earthlings more time to capture it. At least the engine rooms were safe from last minute destruction because their walls and doors were made of triple space density construction like Poseidon's trident.

Alice and Joan believed the Federation guard Rao was likely under arrest in quarters, if so he would surely have the surveillance rod that was programmed to return to him if it failed to escape from the ship. Joan's anguish was that Alice, Fae, was the only person who could retrieve the lost rod.

Joan knew that Alice must be at her best to focus without distraction during the rescue attempt, her solemn duty as Fae, the only Cobalt Blue who could act alone with all of the Blue's resources. *RAM Key* was still maintaining appearances, allowing brief visits to friends, and Alice had visited Barbe before. Joan knew that Philip must be left out of the plan. Fortunately, his solo certification flight for the basic fighter pilot rating was due. He would patrol on Mars Station's side of the ridge and mock attacks on him would occur on his return flight. He would not know that while in Mars Station's space he had backup waiting seconds away. He would not know that Alice would be on *Key RAM*.

Philip received his order to report to the foo fighter pilot's ready room in Deployment Hangar 1 in *Key Bury*. A Halo suit was waiting for him. *My solo-rating flight? With no communications allowed from this room, Joan doesn't want me telling Alice.*

✼ ✼ ✼

Commander Joan whispered to herself, "For the sake of the children," and handed Fae four small packets of three pills each. "A backup pack for each of you. Barbe doesn't need them. The pale pill acts in thirty minutes. Remember, one blue pill only is the antidote. Two blues after a pale speed death to immediate." Joan hugged Alice. "We need you, Fae. Your frozen eggs are our last resort for another child. Scrub the rescue if not doable as planned."

Alice was driven in full jumpsuit to the visitor's airlock of *Key RAM* wearing underneath a half-Halo pantsuit, a protection unknown to *RAM*'s new crew and hence to any personnel from Mars Station. She carried her tiara purse and wore a wrist kom. When the outer hull door to *Key RAM* closed behind her, she was alone, but known to *RAM*'s guards from previous visits. After hanging up her jumpsuit she stood for facial recognition. When asked her name, Alice realized that Pystead's administrative computer was surely off-line as Joan had anticipated. She smiled and gave a name not on the manifest, "Alice Russell."

A guard grabbed her purse and she let go before being jerked. *Oh no!* He handed off the purse and told her to sit down. *They could be monitoring my heartrate or micro facial twitches.* She breathed through her nose and felt that her conditioning was holding her calm. *These guards are young men in jumpsuits and not wearing gloves or helmets—not at high alert.* Alice reflected on *RAM*'s alert level. *Getting into Halo suits can take ten minutes, to twenty for any who aren't experienced or fitted for boot and glove sizes. If this rescue is to end well, we must get out quickly or get lucky.*

Five minutes later a guard returned and demanded, "What's the crown for?"

"For my friend to wear at her engagement party." Alice felt her voice was steady enough not to raise an audio flag.

"Who do you want to visit?"

"Barbe Frett."

The guard returned in a couple of minutes. "She lives in Neighborhood Five, Residential Corridor Three, off Main Corridor Two. Give me your kom! Use this one with a current map." He handed back the tiara. "You have forty minutes."

"I should be back sooner if she isn't too far away."

"A three minute walk."

"Great. Thanks." *Less than five minutes from Barbe's to a hull door. Time enough to look for the rod and Rao.*

✻ ✻ ✻

On Main Corridor Two, not its Pystead name, Alice recognized it as a radial to the peak end of the ship. She looked for a secret Blue refuge station, and lingered until nobody was in view. *Must take the chance that the corridor monitors are off since our computer is down.* She held her breath and removed the tiara from her purse. While pretending to clean the tiara's medallion, she used it to scan the ceiling trim where the corridor's audio-video monitors were located. She found no infrared signal for 'On.' She pushed on the tiara's medallion in just the right places with the correct four timed pulses. The refuge stations's doorway slipped, she pushed the door just right and was in. No corridor alarm sounded. A check inside showed another Blue cache on Barbe's residential corridor. She took only two wrist koms for Blues and two procryptic surveillance rods looking like short pieces of pipe. On second look she found a utility belt that fit under her specially made pantsuit. She took the around-corners spy tube, found the corridor clear, and stepped out quickly as the secret door sealed behind her. *Central monitoring is down. Local Blue systems are up. Now to find Rao, who should have the surveillance rod.*

Around the next corner Alice came to the intersection of Barbe's corridor. A guard stood there leaning against the wall. Alice took a deep breath. *Is he here to stop me or to report on my progress? Or what? Rao and others are quartered in unknown locations!* Alice zipped down her blouse to be revealing and proceeded. *Don't want him looking too closely at my hips.* The guard waved her over.

"Yes?"

"Name?"

"Alice Russell, to visit Barbe Frett."

"Show me the crown!"

Alice leaned over, unzipped her purse, and pulled out the tiara. She held it with the medallion just below her breasts.

"You may pass. You have thirty-five minutes remaining."

Alice smiled and passed through the intersection. *Why guard dozens of apartments when you can control the intersections to all of them? Without corridor monitors yet on their new computer system, local guards are necessary. If I'm lucky many under house arrest are on this very corridor!* Once the guard was out of sight, Alice released her rods and instructed one of them to search for Rao's Blue identification chip, probably in a secret wall slot across the corridor from his quarters.

Within seconds she had the answer. Rao was a few apartments farther from the intersection than Barbe. Alice's knock on his door was coded. He answered promptly. "Rao, I'm going to get Blue toys. Can you be ready to go half-Halo in a minute?"

"Monitoring must be off?"

"Yes."

Rao stepped across the hall and reached his identification chip. "Don't want *RAM* learning a few of us have these!"

Rao's the only man aboard any ship tall enough to reach those wall slots in his shoes. Saves us time. "Do you have the surveillance rod?"

"Yes."

Alice handed him two of the pill packs and reminded him of the timing.

Just steps down the hall Alice found the Blue's local cache and in less than a minute had a bullets pistol, a Greek-fire pistol, two hull antenna interface units, a procryptic Halo cloak, and six smoke bombs. She took a Blue's kom for Rao. The smoke bombs she put in her purse. She wore the tiara with an added chin strap to be able to run. Before leaving the cache she used its hull antenna interface port to tell Joan she could be at Hull Door Eight in six minutes or less if no resistance were encountered. She received the green light reply.

✳   ✳   ✳

This visit is now a rescue operation! RAM will not know that, but they will go to high alert in four minutes when Federation troops sieze control of their cave floor.

Rao took the bullets pistol and kom. He swallowed a pale pill and concealed a blue pill between his teeth and cheek. He set his kom's vibration alarm for twenty-five minutes. Each secured their backup pill pack in a pocket. Alice nodded.

Rao said, "Let's put the rod's files on our koms for backup." The transfers were done quickly.

Barbe was surprised and overjoyed to see Alice. She wanted to escape with them. Alice gave her the purse with smoke bombs and a lesson on use. "These could be vital to our getting out, Barbe. Hold the purse tight and be attentive to me because you may need to use them more than once!"

Rao went first holding up the procryptic cloak in front of the three in single file. Alice had twenty minutes of her pill time

342

remaining. The guard at the intersection was facing their way but relaxing more than watching. Alice sent a rod with instructions to hit him in the head with a preprogrammed knockout blow. He fell without a scream, and the three ran. Alice soon took them off the main corridor to move parallel to the outer hull. "Rao, we're going to Hull Door Eight. Find our next turn while I post surveillance rods ahead and behind us."

Approaching an intersection Rao found the way. "The first left beyond this next intersection leads to Hull Door Eight."

Alice checked her kom and sent one rod to look for guards at the intersection and down the next left. As they approached the intersection, running footsteps were heard from the right. "They're looking for me! Pystead's troops have taken control of the cave floor. Barbe?"

"Yes."

"Throw a smoke bomb into the intersection. Hold tight the purse and we all run and turn left into this first corridor. After we turn, toss another bomb back into the intersection. Hold tight the purse. Stay beside the far wall in single file. Rao cloak us. Rao, shoot any guard emerging from the smoke in the head. They're in jumpsuits without helmets."

The three turned the corner in smoke and hugged the wall on their knees. Alice used her kom and called her rods to lead and follow her in any corridor she was in. The footsteps of the approaching guards thundered into the intersection. Alice's heart raced. Without hesitation the guards turned the corner. Alice stood. "Up, up! We're clear for the moment. Let's make it close to the hull before we cut through to our exit corridor. Let's hope those guards hold at the intersection."

The rod following Alice showed guards behind them on her kom screen. "Barbe, one smoke bomb behind us now! Rao, give me the cloak and you go first. Rao, stop us at Door Three for our cut-through apartment."

"Aye for Door Three."

"How do we get through?" asked Barbe.

"Backdoor!"

A few red laser blasts cut through the smoke down the middle of the corridor. Alice screamed even though not hit. Rao shot twice and a thud was heard. They moved. Rao stopped "Here's Door Three."

Alice punched the number into her kom and pressed a lobe of her tiara's medallion. Rao opened the door. They found the apartment unoccupied. Alice handed Rao the around-corner spy tube. She sent her two rods to look both ways in the hull-door access corridor, then pulled back the apartment's entry wing wall and held her head close to it. She pushed to slide a panel and plugged her hull antenna unit into the port. Rao was back. "Full Halo guard at the hull door."

Alice said to her transmitter, "Joan, full Halo guard at Number Eight door. I can get him on oxygen. We need the code to open both hull doors together."

After what seemed like minutes, Alice received: 7750867462 and typed it into her kom. She checked her screen. "Our rod shows three jumpsuits without helmets holding at the intersection. The Halo guard at the inner hull door seems alert, but probably doesn't know to look for slight ripples in his field of vision." She handed her programmed kom to Rao. "Push the execute tab when I get back inside and give the word."

Rao handed Alice the procryptic cloak.

"Rao, send Joan the files while I'm out. You'll know what to do if I don't get back." She handed Rao both hull antenna interface devices.

Alice opened the backdoor. *For the sake of our children.* She held the cloak in front and approached the hull door and the powerful Halo guard. When the guard finally moved to draw his laser pistol, she shot Greek Fire onto his helmet. The flames blinded his vision, and he reached to close his helmet's ports and go on oxygen. Alice spun around with her cloak flying and ran to reenter the apartment. A step away she was hit in the shoulder. She fell against the door with a scream, "Barbe!" Barbe pulled her in and slammed the door.

"Now Rao, now!"

They heard the woosh of corridor air escaping into Mar's relative vacuum. Her rod's video showed the Halo guard go out headfirst on his back. The jumpsuits up the corridor were slammed to the floor gasping for breath. The outer hull door closed.

"Rao, give me an interface unit. Barbe, smoke bomb to the right!" In the smoke all three ran for the hull door. For extra protection, Alice shot Greek-fire behind them. "This airlock will be a tight fit, Barbe up front with me." Alice closed the inner door and pressed her antenna interface unit into the hull-door port. "Joan, we're all three in at fourteen-point-seven." Alice got a green light and a blinking yellow.

Then Rao's voice, "Alice! The inner door is heating, probably laser pistols."

"Say when if we must go."

Rao said, "Your shoulder took a laser hit. Open your mouth for this pain pill."

Alice swallowed the pill and handed back the cloak. "Shield yourself. Let's not go before full pressure if possible. We don't want even a mild case of the bends." *No three laser pistols are going to crack that inner hull door soon enough.*

Ten seconds later the outer hull door slid open and they almost fell into the rescue pod. "Any problems?" asked Joan's voice.

Alice was breathing deeply, and Barbe shouted, "I don't think so! We're all three in."

✼ ✼ ✼

On the Mars Station side of the separating ridge, Philip began his low altitude observation patrol, relaxing since he would not have to fight mock attackers until returning from patrol. The pilot leaving patrol told him to watch the dozen containers just unloaded from the station's supply ship from Earth. Two minutes later personnel in spacesuits exited Mars Station and walked to the containers. Philp zoomed his video in for a close look. Each person opened the end of a container and pulled out an open-frame personnel shuttle of the type typical for Mars Station. Except? Philip sent video to Joan with the query, "One new tube mounted each side of these shuttles! No laser generators seen. Could they be rockets?"

Philip moved his foo fighter closer and suddenly remembered that during his help rescuing Rhonda and Earl back on Earth, his foo fighter pilot had spun their fighter and escaped severe damage when hit by heavy machine gun fire. *If they plan to shoot at our ships or greenhouse, they will shoot at me!* Philip began rolling his Egg craft and set his lasers for auto response to an attack. Seconds later he was hit with a laser burst that burned a line across his rotating hull, dissipating the heat by not being focused on one spot. His lasers auto returned fire and the attack ended. *Have to love a fixed target.*

Joan 's voice called, "Surely rockets to hit our greenhouse dome. I've sounded refuge stations for the dome. Philip, stay below the hilltop!"

"Roger that. The supply ship fired on me. I had my lasers set for auto return and hit the source. I'll go after the rocket shuttles."

Then he heard Alice's voice in the background, "He's not trained. Recall him now!"

The answer, not from Joan, was, "Recall has already failed."

"It's never failed. Joan, you trained him Blue?"

"His right for the sake of our children."

Philip muted Joan's audio to concentrate and didn't hear her order, "Have the forward fighters and refuge pods hold at hill's edge for immediate assist. Operation Take Down, hit that supply ship!"

⚹ ⚹ ⚹

Seconds later nine of the shuttles were rising. Philp fed his video to Joan and set his fire control to target the shuttles in order from highest in altitude to lowest, and to hit a front corner propulsion rocket. One shuttle was near the hill-top and Philip fired a long laser burst and abruptly changed course. The shuttle rolled and dropped. Before it hit the hill, the pilot jumped and fell in what seemed like slow motion until Philip remembered Mar's low gravity. He was already upon another shuttle and skimmed it, letting the back half of his egg-shaped craft push it into a spin. The shuttle crashed so he did the same for the next one. With six to go he hit the highest with a laser and spun out another two to avoid more laser bursts that would be tracked and his trajectory calculated. He changed course for the last three and fired on the highest as it crested the hill. Now near the top himself, he dived to stay below the hilltop and avoid his own side's lasers. The two surviving shuttles topped the ridge. One fired its rockets as both were hit by Pystead's main cannons. Philp unmuted his audio.

Joan commanded, "Philip, a squadron has arrived. You are relieved. Come home. Land in Cargo Bay Two."

"Roger." He watched his video while departing slowly and saw Pystead's fighters fire rockets at the supply ship that had lasered him. The hits exploded on two support fins of the ship, and it tipped over and fell. *Our Valkyrie has acquired materials for salvage!*

Alice's voice asked, "Is the Egg pressurized?"

"Yes, I rolled it."

"You aren't hurt?"

"Not in the slightest, although I'm sure the Egg is no longer completely procryptic."

Joan took over. "Can you find Cargo Bay Two?"

"I see five flashing green lights."

"That's us. A temporary parking pad is on your right."

"I've trained for that landing."

"Your steady blue light will signal full atmosphere in the cargo bay."

"I'll await my exit for steady blue."

✶　✶　✶

Two minutes after landing they all had a steady blue light. Philip opened the door to his Egg. Alice ran from the control room to greet him. He took her hands. "I expected to see you in an Egg hangar, Alice, not in a cargo bay." He glanced over to the control room. "With Rao and Barbe!"

"I expected to see a routine certification flight, quite without a bumper-car rumble!"

"How did those two get out of RAM?"

"Only Fae could do it. We have the files from Joan's surveillance rod." Alice frowned. "Both of us went out of our way for the children. Let's settle down and raise Dario. As soon as he becomes a toddler, we should expose him to the arts, beginning with the paintings and art glass in our apartment. I want to use our bubbles ball to teach him to be curious and observant, to count, subtract and add."

Alice returned the tiara to her purse. Joan came over. "Are you in pain, Alice?"

"A light burn, Rao gave me a pain pill. A laser pistol hit on my right shoulder. The half-Halo pantsuit saved me. I'll say not even a first-degree burn."

"Need a medic for a possible second-degree burn," Joan called to her kom. She waved to Alice. "You and I must speak to Rao in the control room." Once in, Joan said, "Both of you deserve a citation on your record." She asked, "Alice, Rao, did you take an antidote pill?"

Alice nodded. "I swallowed my blue pill while in the refuge pod."

"Rao?"

He fished the blue pill out of his cheek with his tongue and swallowed it.

Both handed their extra pills to Joan.

Alice took a deep breath. At least that's over!"

Joan nodded. "Comte and Melita supported a perfect Fae! They were never wrong! And you found the perfect husband. Pystead found a perfect guard. Debriefings can wait."

Alice joined Philip and they headed to the Ready Room.

"Bittersweet, as usual," commented Philip.

"We should conclude, Phil, that in our strange new variations on life Poseidon's nirvana is a fine outcome."

⚔   ⚔   ⚔

Joan took a kom call and hurried over to Alice and Philip. "RAM Key has energized their propulsion drives and is inching out of the cave with landing skids still down. I'd say with unpracticed pilots. Let's get to the flight deck. The medics will meet us there."

Joan called on speakers, "Sound Orange-Three on all ships and at the Greenhouse. Deploy troops and execute Ops Eye Opener. RAM Key must not fly if we have to destroy all eight space drives!"

The three hurried to the flight deck. Through the portal they could see the flight deck of *RAM Key* outside the cave, creeping forward. In the next moment three pods arrived near its view-port window. The nearest pod leader exploded, and the window dissolved with an outflow of white mist as moisture from the flight deck's escaping air froze. The mist was cut short as the outer and inner hull covers slammed shut. A second pod exploded and the outer hull cover vanished.

Joan explained, "We are using very large Red Eyes to clear the entire opening for troops. We hope to control the ship without a fight beyond the flight deck."

They all watched as the third pod exploded and the inner cover vanished with another rush of mist out the opening. A surveillance pod went in, followed in seconds by a Halo guard with a dozen more in line, including pilots.

✻ ✻ ✻

Alice told Joan, "I must talk to this woman B.B.H. as soon as possible!"

Joan ordered, "Ops Eye Opener, find Barbara Bains Hunter, about twenty-two years old, known as B.B.H., possibly dressed as a Wican High Priestess. Scan her for weapons, protect her, have female guards bring her to Key Bury's flight deck—no shackles. High priority!"

Alice met the shaking young woman at the entrance to the flight deck. She was a beauty, dressed in an expensive, chartreuse pantsuit. "Don't be afraid, Barbara. I am Commander Alice Saint Germaine, here with good advice!"

Barbara nodded.

"We at Pystead believe in self-determination and in protecting our children. In your case, these objectives may be mutually exclusive. Do I have your full attention, Barbara?"

"Yes."

"Without knowing your reasons, or how many followers you have, if nobody has been physically harmed by your authority, I'll make you a deal. Do you have enough influence to have valid brain scans performed on Dr. Osgood and the Mars Station personnel aboard RAM Key?"

"Yes, with our guards in control."

"Fine. I'll give you a portable computer. Have the scans done and ask what fate these people think awaits you if you return to Earth. Say you want a copy of the scan files for safe keeping. Then follow my instructions and check the results against what you have been told. You should have a few friends scanned as your control group. Tell them to lie about their name, desire to return to Earth, or anything you will know is false. Understand?"

"Yes. What's the deal?"

"I'm sure you will learn that your wealth on Earth has been seized by the U.N. and will not be returned. Your fate will be working a very dead-end, low paying job to stay alive, or you could be put in an officer's harem. Give them trouble and you'd be shot. Pretty girls are a kicu a dozen!"

"I heard no such things while on Earth."

"You were superrich and sheltered from the poor, the oppressed, and the abused. Why do you think your parents were so desperate to get out?"

"Power hungry!"

"They were merely one among equals here. This ship cost many times more than any one person could contribute! Your parents could have lived out their lives in at least the high middle class on Earth. They knew that your generation would be even more repressed. They got out for you, Barbara!"

"They should have told me!"

"You were not mature enough, nor informed enough, to make the decision. That's just the way of human development. My offer, Barbara, is this: Have the scans done; check them carefully; let me know if you and your friends want to return via a Mars Station supply ship, or remain with Pystead as one among equals.

"Aboard the Wheel you would have your own apartment. There are many single men aboard, all educated and handsome enough. There will be parties after leaving Mars. You will have a first-class education and career of your choice. But be warned, the return offer by Earth may not last long. Let me know your decision within a couple of days."

Barbara nodded.

"Please give me a verbal answer."

"I accept the computer and the choice that is mine."

"Fine. Remember, this is more time sensitive than was running for class president in high school. Unfortunately, in this contest there is punishment for the wrong outcome! Let me know if you encounter any resistance. Send me a message on something trivial every six hours, day and night. If you miss a message or say something serious, I'll intervene. You and your friends will be safe because Pystead's guards are in control of the ship."

"Thanks, Commander."

"My name is Alice Saint Germaine, Call me Alice. I live in this key, Bury Saint Germaine."

"A Germaine, you must be important?"

"Yes. I have the duty to help protect our children. Barbara, if you know, I'd like to know how Mars Station personnel got aboard and how many were they?"

"Dr. Osgood developed a following and had a tunnel dug using many of his own group of deviants. He let armed men in, surprised our few guards, and took control of the ship. My close friends and I found out during the middle of a coven meeting. The Mars men told me I could return to Earth on a supply ship. That's all I know."

"How many came aboard?"

"Not more than twenty. They locked up our few active-duty guards and even knew how to find and lock the weapons cabinets. Most were armed officers who ordered around several of their younger technicians."

"Thanks! Remember the deal, Barbara?"

"Yes."

35

POSEIDON'S NIRVANA

Alice called her mother to say they would soon be home. When the couple entered the apartment, Joanne asked Philip, "Did you pass?"

Alice answered, "He passed with top marks. He's the only Ensign who's foo fighter pilot rated. He'll attend squadron and top-gun schools on our colony planet."

"Congratulations, Philip, on your performance and on choosing a wonderful mobile for Dario's room! My precious grandson is fascinated by its colorful, moving geometric shapes."

"Thanks for taking care of him."

"If you two are returning to duties tomorrow, Jeffrey will come over with me. Like Philip, he wants to sing to Dario. Your father is listening to Twinkle, Twinkle, Little Star and Brahms' Lullaby. Little Star has five verses, and the lullaby eight. Also, he's creating his own lyrics for Dario."

Alice said they would return to duty within a few days.

"Let us take care of Dario, often."

✼　✼　✼

Still groggy, Philip opened his eyes. *This place is weird…strange, almost seems underwater, yet does feel like a kindly niche of the cosmos.* The bedroom door was open, the side panels on their canopy bed were pulled back, the faint smell of coffee reassured him that some normality survived in his new world. He heard a cabinet door shut softly in the kitchen. *Alice is first awake as usual. Dario should still be asleep.*

Philip was soon up and surprised to find Alice in her mermaid's attire—her cranberry-red, sheer-lace lingerie. She smiled, and he kissed her good morning. "I feel almost normal, Amanda, and much as I'm fond of you, I need to be with Alice this morning."

"Don't let the bacon burn, Poseidon." Mermaid Amanda swam away. Alice soon appeared in a golden dress.

"Alice, does being a pilgrim on Mars seem as strange to you as it does to me?"

"More a burden. On Earth I had no comparable responsibilities weighing on me. My fiancé wasn't a fighter pilot, and I wasn't Fae."

"I must admit that the aroma of breakfast settles me."

"It should my man in full, that with your new-found kissing friends, Joan, Sasha, Samantha, not to mention Revathy simmering."

"I have adapted to the real world." *Not to mention Rhonda.*

"As a Poseidon not being Russian, you are superbly suited for Sasha. She assures me she will have you playing tennis within a few months."

"You too, Alice, said you'd learn to play."

Alice almost smiled. "Now, Phil, apprehensions about life and love are frequent with us upon awaking. Remember that a platonic friendship need not transition to friends-plus in retirement. My dating Woody certainly will not." She gave Phil a quick kiss and returned to the hot plate of hash browns. "Why not start a bagel, buttered. Let's begin again with comfort food. I'll do eggs. We'll eat healthier tomorrow."

"Sasha should last long enough to get me to a decent beginner's game."

"Let's eat before it's time for me to feed Dario."

Philip recalled Melita's warning that Alice would need to promote Comte's retirement culture, and that he should support her as the means toward exorcising her demon. "Alice, I want you to be a leader in the cultural transition as is your right. I want you to be a woman in full because I want a totally contented wife." After another sip of coffee, he asked, "Don't we have a party to host for your inner circle of club-Mermaid couples?"

"Once we are transitioning for our age group, two decades hence! Our club's schedules have become realistic. The immediate issue will be helping my parent's generation. They and others retire soon with more each year thereafter. Our generation will help with the Mermaids most involved. Our husbands can keep the children while we're out schmoozing with the mature men." She smiled. "Introducing them to the club and platonic-friends culture."

"Definitely, changed circumstances should bring cultural change, as throughout human history. Still, in this strange new niche of spacetime we must mind the unexplored country."

"I feel that strangeness mostly when you are away, Phil."

"Then I must not be away often!"

"Perfect."

After they tidied up from breakfast, Alice announced, "Lois

and Joan each called earlier this morning. Lois feels that we are truly an elect group, already maturing as a singularity of humanity. Joan said we will leave Mars as soon as we scan all the Mars Station crew aboard RAM, and check RAM Key and its computer systems for tampering. Commander Snyder has already found two Mars-Station technicians with atypical thought processes similar to those of mini-stroke victims."

"Once at work I'll learn the details. I'd say those two had cyberknife surgery to excise specific memories. George will consider that. The problem being that we probably cannot learn anything from them! Meaning there was some sabotage aboard RAM."

"Yes. Perhaps the water, even time-delayed bombs hidden most anywhere. Anything to later unsettle as many as possible in hope of RAM Key returning to Mars or Earth."

"Could take several weeks, but George and Joan will secure RAM Key. Thereafter we are much better prepared to defend against the U.N. than I could have imagined on Earth. And we will have a new stock of materials from that U.N. supply ship we are salvaging."

"Robbie is not punishing the coerced personnel the U.N. sent up here. His deal is take Dr. Orlando Osgood and you can keep the spacesuits, oxygen, medical supplies, food, and water."

"Perhaps most of the single scientists will defect to us since we are salvaging with compassion for Mars Station personnel?"

❦ ❦ ❦

The morning before Philip was to leave for the cognitive science department, Alice took his hand. "We are sharing feelings of the heart, are we not?"

"True. I am, I believe, Alice, beyond being shocked by any glimpsed variation on life. As you have said, we must move beyond being shocked by our own humanity. Our free and circumscribed community should naturally develop cultural changes."

"Yes, Phil, we must begin again and hope for an undiscovered life that is nurturing."

"We have chosen wisely for the sake of all the children, and for our Dario. We are very well defended and live in full gravity. I am loved and content in our strange new world."

Alice whispered, "Phil, I have felt ripples of the undiscovered life in my personal spacetime. One day I will live there in any variation and grow old with you."

"Perfect. Before then we have children to raise."

Alice went to a drawer and brought out the seven-eleven glass curio that Philip had given her after his Florida rumble helping rescue Rhonda and Earl. "Phil, this is our very own good luck keepsake. Let's display it on the coffee table using sticky pads to keep it safe from Dario in just several more months."

"Now I know you love me."

Alice smiled, and as she pushed her eyes open wide for Phil her primary process spoke. *For the sake of all our children, the League before my life.*

ABOUT THE AUTHOR

For the technical background of this story, Pryor drew on his experiences as an electrical engineer and as an officer and classroom instructor at the USAF's Aerospace Research Pilot School. His world view has been influ-  enced by a diverse set of experiences and friends. To inform his natural curiosity, Pryor has traveled, read, and taken continuing education courses ranging from child development to cultural, historical, and scientific topics. Pryor has lived and worked in Georgia, Virginia, California, Mississippi, Texas, Florida, and Maryland; he currently lives with his wife in Baltimore County, Maryland.

9 798987 325735